# PLAYING

## With Fire

E.A. Copen

COPYRIGHT
Playing with Fire

A Judah Black novel

ISBN: 978-1977907790



Cover Art by Ravenborn

Published in the United States of America.

# DEDICATION

For Liz. Always keep believing..

# ACKNOWLEDGMENTS

Thank you to R.R. Virdi, D.R. Perry, Amy Valleaux, for their constant encouragement and advice. Additional thanks to my cover artist, Ravenborn, and editor, J.D. Cunegan, as well as my beta readers, Ann Shannon and Ivy Hope. I never could have finished this book without them.

I also need to thank my fan club and review team who worked tirelessly to pick me up when I was down.

And of course I need to thank my husband and children for leaving me alone long enough to write and edit each and every day. Sorry for all the take out.

As always, any and all errors that remain are mine.

# Chapter One

The fireball missed me by an inch.

My bare feet slid over cool, slick tile as I dodged right and snarled. I raised my arm in a protective gesture, gathering my willpower and projecting it forward in a concave shield of spinning black and orange kinetic energy the size of a dinner plate. It was the best block I'd managed all day and it still wasn't enough to stop the second fireball. It sailed through the air and slammed into my pathetic shield, the force of the impact shoving me back. I pushed everything I had into the shield, grunting with effort as sweat stung my eyes and slid down my back. I slid one foot back, intending to bear down and push against the force of the spell.

And, of course, I lost my footing.

With all the grace of Wile E. Coyote, I fell forward, feet scrambling against damp tile in true cartoon fashion. My chin slammed into the floor along with my chest and the rest of my front. But especially my chest, which was surprising considering how unendowed I was for a thirty-something woman.

A hard smack to the boobs for me is a lot like getting kicked in the balls if I were a guy. At least, I think so. I couldn't tell you for sure, as I've never had balls to kick. It feels like a getting hit with...well, a floor. The whole floor. If it were made of angry hornets.

Stars danced in my vision as the shadow of my attacker closed, gripping his weapon in his hand. I tried to push myself up on my elbows, but didn't get that far before he placed a foot on my back.

"Aye, lass, ya call that a shield?" He leaned into the leg he held on my back. "I seen pixies put up a better defense."

I pushed up against his foot with a grunt. The move surprised him enough that he lost his balance for a moment, throwing all his weight on the foot he still had on the floor. I reached out and grabbed him by the ankle, yanking it out from under him. He fell to the floor with a loud, "Oomf!" The carved, wooden staff that served as his focus clattered next to him and then rolled away.

With a frustrated growl, I sprang up, jumped on top of him and threw a punch at his throat. If I'd wanted to, I could have focused the strike with enough force to collapse his windpipe and kill him. Lucky for Creven, we were only sparring. I pulled the punch at the last second, leaving my fist to rest against his throat, my chest heaving and damp from effort.

Creven's indigo eyes flickered and a sly grin spread across his face, the tips of his pointed ears turning a purplish shade of crimson. "Why, Judah, if ya wanted me on me back, all ya had to do was ask."

I rolled my eyes and stood. "Pervert."

"Cheater," he answered.

"It's not my fault you made the mistake of closing the distance before the finishing blow."

I backed away and Creven did an acrobatic flip to stand. Damn him. Even in defeat, he was better than me. "Marcus hired me to teach you magick, lass, not karate."

Every Thursday night for the last nine months, I'd showed up at the gym Shauna co-owned just after close to spar with Creven. Creven was an elf and easily one of the most powerful practitioners I'd ever met. About a year ago, he'd helped me take down an ice giant. While we didn't make short work of him and a lot of people got hurt along the way, he'd been essential to making it work. His specialty was defensive magick, which he was slowly teaching me.

I wasn't particularly good at defensive magick. The fact that I managed it at all was impressive. Mostly, my abilities focused around manipulating auras. Still, if I was going to fight a Faerie King named in the old Irish legends, I'd need every edge I could get when my year and a day was up.

Of course, he hadn't actually said he'd fight me. He just promised to make my life hell. Given that Seamus was a fae necromancer, he might just decide to summon spirits to haunt every cup of coffee I drank, the monster.

"I don't technically know any karate," I told Creven. "They teach aikido and krav maga at the academy."

"Love it when you speak Greek at me." Creven winked and pulled a towel down from where it hung on the retractable bleachers. He toweled sweat off his pale face.

The gym was a world-class affair, complete with two floors, an Olympic style swimming pool, two boxing rings, a whole lot of exercise machinery, and the basketball court we stood in. I was a little surprised the first time Shauna showed us into the gym and flipped on the lights, telling us not to wreck the place. That's why Creven and I had spent the first two sessions warding the place against the ill effects of things like fireballs.

I walked back to where I'd dropped my gym bag under one of the basketball hoops and chugged a bottle of water. The gym was air conditioned, but only during business hours, which meant it was a sauna when we were in there working. Creven barely seemed to notice most days, while I looked like my back and armpits had stood in a rainstorm.

"Come on, then," Creven urged. "You up for another round? My turn to land on top."

"Watch it, elf," snarled a deep voice from the doorway.

I hadn't heard the doors open, but then I didn't always hear Sal when he came in. He could be shockingly silent when he wanted, one of the gifts of being an alpha werewolf, I suppose.

Sal was tall, well muscled, his skin just on the brown side of bronze from all the time he was spending outdoors recently. Half Shoshone Indian, he had a love affair with the sun that I was intensely jealous of, since I couldn't soak up any color but red. And I could afford to be a little jealous of anyone he was spending more time with than me, even if it was a celestial body. The only body he was supposed to be paying any attention to was mine. Not that I'm a jealous woman. I just don't like to share.

My fiercest competition for Sal's affections let go of his hand and toddled forward full speed with a toothy grin, her curly pigtails waving behind her. "Ju!" Mia screeched her version of my name. Halfway across the gym, her right leg turned inward and she fell, throwing her chubby hands forward to catch herself.

She never touched the ground. Creven stretched out his hand and sent a small wave of energy at her. Mia landed on a cushion of air several inches off the ground. Without his focus, it was more difficult than normal to achieve, but Creven managed it with nothing more than a small grunt of effort. "Now, now. What's this? A new challenger?"

Mia blinked. When she realized she wasn't going to fall, she decided Creven should turn her into an airplane and fly her around, putting her arms forward and stiffening her legs into a Superman pose. All the while, his fingers wove through the air as fluid as if he were directing a choir.

Creven put her down. "I'll do ya one better if ya fetch me staff."

Mia screeched, wiggled free and went after it, bringing it back. As soon as it was in his hands, Creven spun it once and touched the knobby end to Mia's nose. Mia giggled wildly as she floated a few inches up off the floor, safely inside a protective bubble.

I watched Sal's face carefully as he strode across the gym toward me. The first time Creven had done that, I thought Sal was going to have a heart attack. Today, he didn't look the least bit concerned. He stopped next to me, leaned down and planted a gentle kiss on my lips and then turned to snort at Creven. "You sure you don't want me to send Shauna to keep an eye on him?"

"Relax," I said, touching his arm. "You know Creven. He doesn't mean anything by it. Flirting is as natural to him as breathing."

"Well, I'd appreciate it if he'd tone it down some before someone gets the wrong idea." Sal said it loud enough that Creven was sure to hear, but the elf didn't turn away from the ball of ice he was forming between his fingers.

"Nobody here but us." I stood on my tip toes, which put me just tall enough to kiss him because of how he was slouching. "Besides, I know who I'm going home with."

"I still don't like the idea of you training with him. He's sworn to Kim Kelley. Isn't there someone else you could train with? Someone from BSI?"

I grunted at that and turned back to my gym bag, shoving my water bottle back inside. BSI, the Bureau of Supernatural Investigations and my employer, was one arm of the United States Government. Sal and I lived constantly in the agency's shadow on the Paint Rock Supernatural Reservation in Concho County, Texas. I wasn't supposed to be fraternizing with my constituents because that created a conflict of interest, but I also should have registered my fourteen-year-old son, Hunter, with them. He was a werewolf and a member of Sal's pack, but he was my son. If BSI knew, they would separate us. It was thanks to Marcus Kelley, local vampire philanthropist, that Hunter had stayed off the radar. He had a lot of friends in high places.

"I've already had all the training I'm going to get from BSI," I said. "And I don't trust them. As soon as they catch wind of Seamus, they'll cut him a deal. They'll play into his plans and put my back against the wall. If you want me to call BSI, you might as well ask me to cut my arms off."

My phone chirped in my duffel bag and I glowered at the sound of a text coming in. It was probably Hunter asking us to bring home pizza again, which was the last thing I wanted to do.

Puberty had hit him hard over the last few months. For human boys, that means cracking voices, pimples and weird body hair. Werewolf puberty is ten times worse. Teenage moodiness was nothing new, but Hunter's mood shifted with the moon, alternating between fits of intense apathy and dangerous anger. He could also eat his weight in pizza and not gain an ounce. Sal said it was something to do with high metabolism, high body temperature...something like that. It was expensive, that much I knew.

I fished the phone out of the bottom of the bag, put in the lock code and frowned when I realized it wasn't Hunter texting me. It was Sheriff Tindall.

Need you here ASAP. Possible arson. Suspect resisting arrest. Violently.

He sent a second text with longitude and latitude numbers. When I put them into my map app, it showed the middle of a field off State Route 765, roughly halfway between Eden and San Angelo.

I frowned at the end of his first text. He wouldn't call me to come out to just any old arson where a suspect was resisting arrest. Tindall had to be dealing with something supernatural.

"Duty calls?" said Sal, looking over my shoulder.

"Sheriff needs a consult out near Eola." I dropped the phone back into my bag along with my clean clothes and zipped it up. I'd planned on taking a shower in the locker room but that wasn't going to happen. Given the number of grammatical errors in Tindall's text, he'd sent it in a hurry. I needed to get there yesterday.

I picked up my bag and tried to remain casual, since I didn't want Sal to worry. "I'll meet you at the car."

On Thursdays, Sal and I drive separately. The truck was too small to fit me, Mia's car seat, and Hunter, and my car is a 1968 Firebird, a sleek and sexy black, two-door coupe with no back seat. Well, it was sleek and sexy black in the seventies. Now, I'd had to replace so many parts that it was a Franken-car. The doors were red, the antenna bent, the interior a faded gray.

In the last few months, Valentino Garcia, my mechanic and Sal's second in the pack, had replaced enough parts that I basically had a new car, save for the exterior. He'd offered me a paint job to cover the mismatched parts, but I declined. The sad truth was that the Firebird wasn't a family car and I was looking to sell her to buy something bigger. I loved my car, but hauling two kids around demanded something bigger, a family car. I say car because Hell will freeze over before I buy a minivan.

Sal refused to let me go around after dark alone. Between the Vanguards of Humanity, vampires and faerie necromancers, I'd made enough enemies that he was worried. I'd told him repeatedly that I could look after myself, but Sal saw himself as my protector, and it was easier just to indulge his protective instincts than fight about it. I was sure that, even with him as back-up, I wouldn't stand a chance against anyone that wanted to kill me. Still, it was nice to know back-up was always right there with me.

Sal came out of the gym and buckled Mia into her car seat while she babbled. Then, he leaned against the door while Mia babbled behind him. He'd parked right beside me.

"You shouldn't come with me," I said as I threw my bag behind my seat. "Tindall implied it'd be trouble and it's past Mia's bedtime."

"He wouldn't call you if it wasn't trouble," Sal answered. "Besides, what bedtime?" he snorted. "You know as well as I do what Mia thinks of bedtime." He pushed my door closed after I climbed into the drivers' seat and leaned in the open window. "I'll follow you out to Eola and let Tindall take over. Hopefully, she falls asleep on the drive home."

"Put on one of Hunter's CDs. She'll go right to sleep."

Sal wrinkled his nose. "No thanks. I like my eardrums." He kissed me on top of the head.

I turned over the engine and let it purr a minute, waiting for him to get into his truck before I revved it once, threw her into reverse and pushed the gas to the floor and left him in the dust.

Speeding is dangerous and stupid, and I don't do it often except to get away from Sal's escorts. I didn't want them following me out to the crime scene, as that was no place for kids. Besides, half of the police force under Tindall already saw me as weak and incapable. If I showed up with my boyfriend as a chaperone, that would just re-enforce those whispers.

Just because I'm a woman doesn't mean I can't kick their asses. It did mean I had to work extra hard at projecting an image of strength and professionalism. It's stupid and wrong, but that was the way of the world, especially for women in law enforcement.

I pushed the car up to fifty in a thirty-five before sliding onto the exit ramp out of Eden toward San Angelo. There weren't any headlights behind me, so I assumed Sal got the message and set my attention to driving through the desert in the dark.

The coordinates Tindall had sent me were way out in the middle of nowhere. The land between Paint Rock and San Angelo was mostly ranching land and almost all of it was for sale. Has been ever since I moved out there. I didn't have much occasion to drive out to Eola, which was an unincorporated community that had been dying in Eden's urban chokehold over the last decade. What struck me most about the area was the absolute darkness. You don't get that in cities. The glow of San Angelo lit up the sky in the distance but, between me and the city, there was nothing but utter darkness.

Except for the flashing lights of emergency vehicles and the hungry, orange light of a dilapidated ranch house in flames.

I saw it from the state route, even though it was down another side road and a long driveway. Not many trees in central Texas to obscure the view, especially out there. As I got closer, I counted two fire engines, three police cruisers and two squads.

The problem was evident the minute I parked behind Tindall's Cadillac and climbed out. The police cruisers had torn through the field to park in a semi-circle a hundred yards back from the fire, lights flashing. Cops squatted behind the safety of their bullet-resistant doors, guns pointed forward. A silhouette staggered back and forth in front of the fire, swinging what looked like a sword back and forth.

I pushed the door closed and jogged closer, pausing when a hair-raising howl pierced the night. A werewolf hunting howl. I broke into a run, closing on the line of police cruisers just in time to see a skinny, black werewolf leap through the air. The swordsman, whose face I still couldn't make out because it was caked in ash and mud, caught the bite with a forearm and kicked the werewolf away.

"Black," Tindall said and trotted around the back of the nearest cruiser to crouch next to me. "Thank God you're here. This whole thing is nuts. These two were going at it when we pulled in. I didn't know if he was one of yours or a stray, and nobody here has any clue who has what to do with the fire. I'd shoot the suspect down, but last time we tried, he sent a fireball at us. I figured we'd wait until we heard from you. Your jurisdiction, seeing as magick's involved."

I held up a hand. By one of mine, what Tindall really meant was one of Sal's, but there wasn't time to split hairs. Whoever the swordsman was, he knew his way around the single-handed blade well enough that the only thing keeping him from cleaving the werewolf in two was the werewolf's superior speed. Not that the sword would have done much damage to a werewolf unless it was made of silver. Short of cutting off his head, the swordsman didn't have much of a chance with that blade.

I stood clear of the cruiser door. "It's Ed," I said and then shook my head. Impossible. Of all the werewolves in Sal's pack, Ed was the last one I would have expected to take on such a capable enemy.

"Petersen?" Tindall questioned and stole another glance out at the fight.

Ed crouched and lunged at the swordsman again but, this time, the swordsman flung his free hand forward. Magick buzzed through the air, strong enough that it threatened to suck the air from my lungs. Liquid fire erupted from the swordsman's fingers against a battle cry in Latin. That was all I needed to be sure of who it was Ed was fighting and to know that he was in way over his head.

I pushed around the cruiser door and rushed from safety and into the fray just as Ed barely avoided getting singed by rolling to the side. Tindall called after me, but his voice was muted and quickly forgotten as I closed the distance. I called to Ed and slid to a stop that would have made my middle school softball coach proud. My hand slid into a patch of fur just behind Ed's ears and squeezed in a reassuring gesture. He lifted his head, pink tongue panting and whined. A large section of the fur on his nose had burned away, replaced by red, raw skin and blisters. I couldn't focus on how badly he was hurt. There was still an enemy on the field.

I turned my attention forward, clenching my jaw and staring down the swordsman. "Father Reed, what the hell is going on?"

The priest lowered his head, his eyes reflecting the raging fire beside him. For a minute, I thought maybe he'd put his sword down and talk to me, but I had misunderstood the look of intent.

"Succendo!" He flicked his wrist and sent a wall of flame five feet high straight at me.

# Chapter Two

I put up one of my shields, this one even stronger than the last. Stronger meant smaller, though, and I was only able to protect an area three feet high and two feet wide. Instead of the normal five-foot concave area that covered my entire body, this shield would only cover me if I stayed low to the ground, and it would only save Ed from the blast if I pressed in tight against him. I only barely had enough time to get into position to ensure that neither of us got burned.

Reed's fire spell hit with enough force to push me back. I ground a knee into the earth, trying to slow my backward slide and leaving overturned ground behind. Ed crawled back with me to stay behind the shield. The wall of fire broke over top of us, scorching the air so that it hurt to breathe. Grass on either side of us turned to ash. The shield flickered and, as soon as the blast of flame subsided, dissipated into nothingness. I was tapped already, but Reed was far from it.

Fire was the priest's element. I'd seen him stand in an incinerator while it was on and redirect the flame to escape untouched. Back then, he'd been on my side. Until the moment he threw his latest ball of fire at me, I'd assumed the two of us were still at least on speaking terms. The enraged look on his face made it clear now that he didn't want to talk.

Magick no longer being an option, at least so far as I was concerned, I needed to come up with a back-up plan, preferably one that didn't end up with anyone dead. I hadn't come with my gun, and Reed was an expert swordsman, so getting close and tackling wasn't an option, not unless I could somehow do it before he cut off my head. The only way that would happen was if I had help. I glanced down at Ed and hoped he understood what I had. "Don't kill him," I whispered, knowing his werewolf ears would pick it up.

Reed raised his sword and moved to close the distance, his eyes still distant and angry. Ed staggered to stand on all fours and growled, showing sharp, white teeth.

But it wasn't Ed that sprang out of the darkness aimed at Reed's throat. A big, gray werewolf with chevrons of black fur on his neck and chest leapt away from the line of police cars, snarling.

Sal. Reed spun just in time and swung his sword. It struck Sal just behind the shoulder and slid away red. The momentum of the strike sent Sal sideways, but he landed on his feet. Blood dripped from where the sword had caught him. Sal bared his teeth, crouched low for another go, and snarled again.

Ed zipped away from my side to snap at Reed's ankle on the other side. Reed swung his sword, but Ed scampered out of reach. His left and right exits blocked, and his back to the burning barn, Reed considered the line of police cars in front of him. If he charged them, the officers would fire. The only reason they hadn't yet was because they still thought we had it handled.

I glanced over at the police and saw that one of them had made his way atop the squad car in the center, a sniper rifle perched on the flashing lights. He peered through the sight, finger on the trigger. With a word, he'd fire and put a well-placed bullet in the center of Reed's head. Rampaging madman or not, I didn't want this to end in any more blood.

My feet pounded across the scorched ground and I did my best to place myself between Reed and the police sniper. "There's nowhere to go, Reed." I spread my arms wide to block their aim better. "Why don't you put the sword down and talk to us? There's no need for this."

Reed ground his teeth. "I...can't. *He* won't let me!"

Sal and Ed prowled closer, moving into attack position to take him down if he didn't comply. I stayed where I was. If the sniper hadn't fired yet, it was only because he didn't have a clear shot. Moving an inch either way might change that. "At least tell me what happened here."

Something changed in Reed's face. The rage died away a moment and he blinked. His eyes wobbled back and forth and he scanned the area as if he were seeing it for the first time. Surprise rolled over his expression, and then fear. It lasted just a moment before it was gone and the anger was back in control.

I risked a half step forward. "Tell me what I can do to help you, Reed."

"Stay away from me, Judah. I don't want to have to kill you."

I flinched when Reed raised a hand and flicked a spell off to his side. It wasn't fire he sent out, however. It was a swirling vortex of white flame that split open the night with a steaming hiss. He sprinted the short distance to where he'd placed his Way, stopped to give me one last, serious look, and then stepped into the ring of fire. Sal leapt after him, but the Way closed before he could follow Reed through.

Sal landed, swayed and then stumbled slightly before Ed leapt forward to support him. I approached with caution. Werewolves could be funny about humans when they were hurt but, apparently, Sal didn't mind me coming close enough to check it out. I knelt in the grass and ran my hand over some of the blood-matted fur. He flinched away and growled. I couldn't tell how deep the cut was, but he wasn't putting any weight on that leg and it wasn't closed yet, which meant it had gone deep. "You stupid idiot," I muttered, pressing my face into Sal's side. "He could've killed you."

Behind us, Tindall ordered the fire trucks forward and they roared to life, charging through the field around us. The firefighters hustled to pull down their hoses and douse the fire while Tindall and a few other officers closed on our position. Sal gave another growl, this one a low, warning tone. He'd tolerate the firemen being so close, mostly because they weren't paying him any attention, but Tindall and the other officers were armed. That made them potential threats, and Sal did not want anything threatening to see him injured and bleeding.

I stood and gestured for them to stop before jogging to meet them a good five yards back. "What the hell was all that?" Tindall put his hands on his hips.

I stopped in front of them so that if any of the other officers decided to move forward, I could stop them. "I'm not sure yet. Was Reed like this when you got here? What happened?"

One of the officers, a heavy-set guy, shifted forward, straining his neck to get a better look at the pair of werewolves behind me. I cleared my throat and drew his gaze before shaking my head. He dropped his eyes to the ground.

Tindall shrugged. "Your guess is as good as mine at this point. Wait a second. Did you say Reed? As in the priest, Gideon Reed?"

I nodded slowly. "That was definitely him, but he really wasn't himself." I turned to look at the place where he'd stepped through the Way. "Something was wrong with him. If I could have gotten a look at his aura, I would have a better idea of what we're dealing with. The way he acted, it didn't seem like he was in control of what was happening."

"Like maybe he was possessed?" the heavy-set cop suggested.

It was possible, I supposed, but Reed would be the last person I would suspect of possession. The guy had Faith with a capital F and practically lived in his church. If there was a holy warrior anywhere in Concho County, it was him.

"Maybe," I said, "but there's no way I could know without getting a better look at him from a non-threatening angle. You said Ed was here when you got here?"

Tindall gestured behind me. "Yeah, the werewolf and the priest were going at it when we arrived. A passerby saw the flames from the highway and called it in. No idea what happened before we got here, though."

"Who set fire to the barn?"

"Burning when we got here," Tindall answered with a grunt. He tugged his cigarettes from his shirt pocket and smacked the pack against the meat of his palm a few times. "I'm going to assume that was Reed, too. Information is scarce right now unless you can get the werewolf to talk. How bad is the other one hurt?"

"The other one is Sal." Sal would have been irritated that Tindall, who had lived in Paint Rock for going on nine years, couldn't tell him apart from the lowest-ranking member of the pack. "And he's a werewolf so he'll heal, but he'll be grumpy until he does so it's best if your men keep their distance. Werewolves don't like guns."

Tindall stuck a cigarette in his mouth and lit it, blowing the smoke away from me. "Do you think you could get Ed to shift back so we can talk to him?"

"Depends. It's not really up to me. He might be of a mind to stay in wolf form to protect his alpha at this stage, but I can try."

"Well, at the very least, you'll want to get them out of the way while these guys fight the fire."

"That I can probably do." I nodded and uncrossed my arms. "You boys stay back and don't approach until I've given the all clear."

I walked back to where Sal and Ed waited. Sal sat very still, but upright and sure to keep his head above Ed's. He looked stiff, and favored the injured side, but someone who didn't know him very well wouldn't have noticed anything at all was wrong. Sal would keep it that way as long as he could and project the image of power and control over the situation. The look he wore on his wolfish face straddled the line between alert and irritated.

Meanwhile, Ed paced in a wide circle that stretched between where his alpha sat and where Reed had disappeared, his nose to the ground and tail low, but not tucked. When I came close, Ed casually picked up his pace as he circled, making sure that he crossed in front of me before I reached Sal. He stopped an arm's length away, stretched, yawned and sat between Sal and I. Protective mode it was, then.

I scratched Ed behind the ears and squatted to get a better look at the burn on his nose. It was red and raw, but healing. There were other patches of singed fur all the way down his back, but he looked unharmed. "Ed, I'm going to need you to shift back if you can. The police want a statement and it seems you know more about what happened here than the rest of us."

Ed's tongue, which had been hanging out, rolled back into his mouth. He perked his ears, glanced back at Sal and let out a slight whine.

"Sal is going to heal. He'll heal better if we can get him out of here and away from all these people where he can focus on that instead of trying to be stoic and badass." My comment drew a huff from Sal and the werewolf straightened his back, bristling. I ignored him. "Besides, the two of you are sitting right where the officers need to be to begin their investigation. You're in the way of progress here, boys."

At that news, Sal stood. Ed trotted back to stand shoulder to shoulder with him, gently supporting him from the injured side. Sal's limp was barely noticeable as the two of them walked back toward the line of police cars. Tindall and the officers waiting with him stepped aside to allow the pair to pass. The werewolves didn't stop walking until they were far removed from the crime scene and safely hidden beside the second ambulance.

I put a reassuring hand on Tindall's shoulder as I passed, following the wolves. "Leave your men and come help me get this statement, will you?" I didn't need his help, but I did want a witness. Given my unusual relationship with the werewolf pack and my involvement with the incident, I wanted to head off any potential conflicts of interest before they ever got started.

When we made it to the squad, Ed had already begun his change. The soft, pained whines and cracking of bone coming from beside the squad gave him away. Sal growled at our approach and Tindall froze, his hand straying toward his gun.

"Easy," I said and grabbed Tindall's wrist. "That wasn't an aggressive growl. Just one to let you know how grumpy and alert he is."

Tindall relaxed, but frowned. "I don't know how you can tell the difference, Black. I've been working with supernaturals for years. To me, a growl is a growl."

"Comes from spending so much time with them. You pick up a little body language here and there."

"He's not going to change back, too?" Tindall cast Sal another wary glance as the werewolf shifted his weight away from the injured side. Either he was in too much pain to continue hiding it, or he didn't consider Tindall a threat.

"Sal will heal faster this way." I turned to Sal and tried to ignore the loud, wet ripping sounds of Ed's change. "Sal, where's Mia?"

Sal jerked his head to the side. I followed the motion and leaned to get a better look. His truck was parked a short distance away, right next to a motorcycle I recognized. It was Bran's Harley and Bran leaned against it with Mia in his arms. When I thought of what a mean, outlaw biker might look like before I'd met the Tomahawk Kings, Bran is the image I would have called up. Bran was a huge, hairy guy of Japanese and Russian heritage. He had a green Mohawk, wore plenty of studded leather and never went anywhere unarmed. He was also the most pleasant member of the Kings, despite being their sergeant at arms. As odd as it might have looked to everyone else to see a big, katana carrying biker cuddling a sleeping toddler, to me it looked natural now.

I gave Bran a wave that he returned, and then turned my attention back to Sal. "Will you let me see?"

Sal huffed as if to say, "It's not that bad." Translation? It hurts like hell but I don't want to seem like a wimp in front of another man. Typical.

I came closer and knelt, looking at the cut on his shoulder. Now that I had enough light to see, the cut looked worse. It wasn't just a simple slice. The blade must have been hot when it sliced into Sal, because the edges of the wound were dark. Black fur surrounded the wound and blood still oozed from the hole. He flinched slightly when I touched it, and I could see the white of bone. "It should have healed more than this," I said and looked Sal in the eyes. "Silver?"

He snorted and shook his head.

"If not silver, then maybe it's spelled."

"It smells fae to me."

I looked beyond Sal to Ed who lay curled up on the ground with his back to me. Tindall pulled open the squad doors, dug around until he found a blanket and handed it to me. I stepped around Sal and placed it on the ground within Ed's reach. Most werewolves didn't much care about being naked in front of people but, given the crowd and the news vans that had started pulling in, I figured Ed would want to cover up. He sat up stiffly and grabbed the blanket, pulling it over him without unfolding it.

"Fae?" I tried to call up a mental image of Reed's sword. The one he had tonight looked just like his normal weapon of choice. Ed had been in that incinerator with me when Reed deflected all that fire and he'd seen Reed use that sword several other times as well. "Has it always smelled fae to you?"

Ed shook his head, his shaggy, brown hair bouncing back and forth. "I don't get to smell his sword that often, to tell the truth. Usually, when that thing comes out, my ass is in the fire already and he's saving my bacon, not burning to a crisp." He rubbed the healing sore on his nose and winced.

I waved a hand over the wound again, this time concentrating on the flow of energy around it. There was magick there, alright, but it felt residual. That meant it was on the blade itself and not on Sal. That was good. With a little healing magick, Sal could pull simple spellwork like that apart. Unfortunately, he couldn't do much while he was still a wolf and shifting might make the wound worse.

"Will he heal?" Tindall pointed at Sal.

Ed closed his eyes and leaned back against the squad's wheel. "You said you had questions."

"Yeah. What the hell happened, Ed? Why were you even out here?"

"Mara." Ed's voice was a strained whisper.

I looked up at the barn fire. Even with all that water pouring down on it, the fire was still raging. It dawned on me why Ed might be out this far, alone, so late at night, without telling anyone where he was going. A terrible, sick and sinking feeling settled over me. "Oh my God," I said, fighting panic in my voice. "Was Mara in there?"

# Chapter Three

Ed shifted the blanket across his lap and reached up to scratch his face. He winced when he accidentally rubbed the scab off the end of his nose.

The red and blue emergency lights reflected over the side of his face, betraying healing bruises. "No," he said at length. "I'm not sure where Mara is right now."

He chose his words carefully so that it wasn't a lie. Werewolves and lots of other supernaturals can sense when someone is lying. I'm not one of them, but Ed had grown up in werewolf packs. He knew how to lie without lying.

"Tell us what happened, son," Tindall said, putting his hands on his hips.

Ed looked at Sal. "Someone should stop the bleeding." He nodded to his alpha's wound.

I climbed up into the open squad and rooted around a few places for sterile gauze, antiseptic and medical tape. While I was looking, the EMT popped around the side of the ambulance free of werewolves and asked if I needed a hand. I leaned back out the door. "Will you let him help?"

Sal's answer was a huff and roll of his eyes as if to say, "I'm a werewolf, not a monster."

"You should be okay to try and patch him up," I told the EMT. "But don't bother with stitches. They'll just tear out when he shifts back. Just get the bleeding to stop." I hopped back out of the squad while the EMT gathered his supplies. "Okay, Ed, tell us what you were doing out here."

Ed chewed on his lower lip.

I turned my head to Tindall and the EMT. "Give us a minute and some privacy, would you?"

Tindall nodded. Ed scrambled to tuck the blanket around him toga style. We still weren't out of Sal's hearing, but human ears wouldn't have been able to pick up anything we said. I stepped forward to grab Ed by the arm and lead him off a few paces. Ed jerked his arm away and snarled at me, the unfamiliar sound freezing me in place. Sal, Valentino, and Nina had all growled at me at one time or another but to have Ed do it felt unnatural.

Ed turned on me. His upper lip twitched as if he wanted to curl it back and show his teeth but he didn't. "I'm not the same person I was two years ago, Judah. Don't think you can scare me into telling you anything."

"That was never my intention, Ed, and you know it. Come on. I thought you knew me better than that."

He turned away and stared at the burning building in silence.

I sighed and forced my shoulders to relax before I uncrossed my arms. "I know that, if Mara was in trouble, you probably wouldn't tell Agent Judah Black anything, Ed. I know you're pissed at me for how the situation was handled at Aisling."

"You let Mara get *tortured*. By a vampire. You traded her like currency."

I winced.

"You killed her parents in front of her," Ed continued. "I know they were bad people and that they were hurting her, but imagine what that was like for her. You killed her parents and then tried to be her parents. She felt like your prisoner."

He wasn't wrong. I hadn't seen it at the time because I thought I was saving Mara. Instead, I smothered her and pushed her further down a path that took her dark places. She was Ed's first real love. I had hurt her and, by extension, him.

"I can't change what happened," I said. "I would if I could, but I can't. The past sucks. Mara's especially. I won't sit here and fight to justify all the decisions I made but, yeah, some of them were bad. For that, I'm sorry."

Ed lifted his chin. "Sorry doesn't take away the scars. Sorry doesn't take away the night terrors and heartache. It doesn't fix Mara."

"No," I said gently. "It doesn't."

The firefighters shouted directions back and forth and the fire blazed, but we stood in strained silence.

"I know you wouldn't tell Agent Black about Mara, but would you tell a friend who shed blood with you? For you? Someone who just wants to know she's safe and loved."

Ed's throat worked. The wind shifted and blew smoke and ash toward us. I blamed that for the tears Ed wiped away. "I couldn't stop her in time."

I raised a hand. "Hold up. Let's start from the beginning, okay?"

Ed nodded and swallowed. "Mara was never really missing. I've known where she was this whole time. Actually, I've been helping her stay under the radar."

He turned to gauge my reaction. I wasn't surprised to hear that Ed had been helping her, only that she had stayed so close to home and been so successful. The whole county was looking for Mara and I sent her picture nationwide. I had been outsmarted by two kids who weren't old enough to drink.

I must not have looked too surprised, either, because Ed lifted his chin and continued, bolder. "We'd been seeing each other weeknights. The place we meet changes, but it's on a rotating schedule. I knew something was wrong, that something had changed, but she wouldn't tell me what it was. Over time, she got more and more distant. I thought she just needed space. Then, last week she..." He choked and put a hand over his mouth. It was several minutes before he could compose himself. "She said we couldn't see each other any more."

"Oh, Ed. Breakups are always tough." I reached forward to put a reassuring hand on his shoulder, but he jerked away.

"It wasn't a breakup! I mean, not a normal one. It was that stupid cult, that boy she was hanging out with, Warren Demetrius."

I held up my hands. "Slow down, Ed. What cult?"

He huffed out a deep breath and tilted his head to the side, thinking hard. "Do you know anything about the Tribulation Adventists?"

I knew enough to be worried the minute he brought them up. The Tribulation Adventist Church was a Christian fundamentalist group, an offshoot of Pentecostals, I think. They sprang up right in the middle of the Revelation and were one of the first groups to openly embrace supernaturals. That might sound good but I promise you, it isn't. The church was exclusively supernatural and preached a doctrine straight out of the book of Revelations. According to them, we were living in the end times for humanity, soon to be replaced by a chosen, superior race of supernaturals. They weren't openly anti-normative human, but BSI had kept tabs on when and where the church operated and how as well as they could. When the government flags a fundamentalist religious group for surveillance, nothing good is happening.

"Yeah," I said. "Sorta. I mean, I only know the basic info BSI sends out in their e-mails. Why?"

"Well, Mara started hanging out with one of them. A guy

named Warren. His dad is the leader of the group here in Concho County. About nine months ago, they purchased a parcel of land not far from here and started to build." Ed made a sour face. "Then, out of the blue, Mara says she can't see me anymore. She's going to be with Warren now in his dad's little cult. Thing is, I'm not convinced he isn't manipulating her somehow, maybe with magick."

That didn't sound like the Mara I knew. She might have been desperate to find somewhere to belong, but she wasn't stupid and she wasn't mentally weak. If the church tried to pressure her, she'd never cave. She wasn't the type to do well in a cult. She liked her independence too much. Ed was right. It didn't seem like something she'd do of her own free will, but I hadn't seen Mara in almost a year.

"She was hiding out in a women's shelter," Ed continued. "Moved around a lot to keep from being noticed. She wasn't interested in the cult at first, but the more she hung out with Warren, the more she talked about it. I think she might have gotten involved with rem. I know the Tribulation Adventists use it."

Rem. Holy hell, this was bad news. Rem was the street name for a drug that was a cross between magickal speed, LSD and heroin. It's little sister, Pixie, had started showing up on the streets of Eden a few months back and Tindall was having a hell of a time combating it. Made from some plant that had been imported from Faerie, the name of which I couldn't pronounce, rem had two uses for magickal practitioners. First, it was, well, magickal speed. It would keep you going for crazy amounts of time without sleep or rest. That made it popular with stressed-out teens and college kids. The second use was a massive ability boost. I could spark a tiny flame in between my fingers with a snap. With a hefty dose of rem, I could probably call up fire hot enough to burn bone to ash.

"I tried to check in on her. Then she stopped answering her cell. She didn't answer her e-mail or text. I spent the last two days trying to get in contact with her before I resorted to...other things."

"Other things?"

Ed nodded.

When he didn't elaborate, I pressed, "What kinds of *other things*?"

"Magick." He wiggled his fingers in the air, forgetting he was holding up the blanket. As soon as it started to slide, he grabbed for it and tucked it better.

I waited for him to smile, laugh or otherwise make a gesture that said he was joking. Time stretched on into more uncomfortable silence before he stuck out his hand, palm up. "Give me your cell."

"Why?"

"Do you want to know how I tracked Mara here or not?"

I glanced back over at the ambulance. The EMT was wrapping some gauze around Sal and Tindall was pretending not to be interested in our conversation. "Okay, Ed. You've got my attention."

I tugged my cell phone from my pocket and slapped it into Ed's hand. He immediately squatted down to draw a circle in the dirt with his finger. A few inches inside the big circle, he drew a smaller one and then started connecting the two with several lines. It only took me a few seconds to recognize the simple circle. It was the one everyone started with.

Circles aren't inherently magick, not until you add something to make them so. Usually, that's a drop of blood, spit, or some other bodily fluid, depending on the purpose of the circle. With that and focused will, just about anyone with a hint of magickal talent could perform simple spells inside the circle. Inside a powered circle, energy is amplified and, since the circle acts as a barrier, the energy stays inside, trapped and feeding off whatever's inside as a fuel source. Fire and water were standard offerings, though you could use almost anything. Whatever you put in that center circle as a fuel source, however, changed the nature of the spell so you had to be careful. Putting anything living inside that center circle to be consumed was not something a person with good intentions would do.

Once he was finished drawing the connecting lines, Ed placed my cell phone in the center circle. He fiddled with a few buttons to find my GPS program and then put it back down. He plucked a few hairs out of his head and tossed them into the inner circle under the cell phone before he closed the circle with a little spit. A small static charge zipped around the outer circle and then funneled to the inner circle. There weren't any magick words for Ed's spell, but he did spend a few minutes sitting there with his eyes closed and kneeling at the edge of the circle, long enough that the backlight on my phone turned off. I was just about to interrupt him when the light turned back on and my phone made a sound I'd never heard it make before. The GPS program queued up with a message that said it was searching. The map zoomed in, first on Texas, then Concho County, then on the nearby county road.

I flinched when the phone made a loud hissing sound and a small puff of smoke flew out of the charging port. A breath later, fire jumped out of the screen. I flinched back at the sudden pop while Ed broke the outer and then inner circle.

"Fuck!" He swung the blanket at the fire.

I put a hand on him and pulled him away before he set the blanket and himself on fire. It was better to just let the phone burn and bill BSI for a replacement. I was still too busy processing what I'd just seen.

Theoretically, it made sense. He'd satisfied all the ingredients for a simple tracking spell, except that normally people used paper maps. That he'd been able to manipulate something as complicated as my cell phone's GPS using such a simple spell, that was the part I couldn't figure out. Anyone could do simple magick. Ed was the only one I'd seen use an electronic screen as the output.

I closed my eyes and called up my auric sight. Ed had never been much to look at as far as power went. Like most werewolves, his aura had always been streaked with a touch of magick, but werewolf magick drew on pack bonds so it was difficult to tell how much of that was his and how much of it belonged to the pack as a whole.

When I looked at Ed in that empty field next to the burning building, however, it was alive with colors that hadn't been there before. Rich hues of electric blue and neon red streaked and swam like particles in a collider. The colors swirled and crashed into each other, flickering briefly out of existence before coming alive again a few centimeters away in brilliant flashes. They moved in pre-set lines and patterns, as if his circulatory system were a circuit board. Beautiful, but odd.

"Ed, how are you doing that?"

A proud smile flashed over Ed's face, but it soon faded and his shoulders slumped. "Mara. She was teaching me."

"Dammit, Ed, magick isn't a game."

"I know that," Ed snapped. "I'm a fucking werewolf. I know a thing or two. I read the papers and browse the internet. Mara's a spirit sensitive. She can let ghosts possess her. We weren't helpless children. Everything was fine until..." He cast a wary glance back at the fire.

I placed my hand on his shoulder and squeezed. "It's okay, Ed. You said you tracked Mara here. Then what happened?"

He blinked several times and turned back to me slowly. "Moving as a wolf is faster so I got here on all fours. I could smell her. There were others, too, at least three counting Reed, but I didn't know he was around. I didn't recognize his scent right away. I did hear voices on the other side of the door. Mara's voice and another man. She sounded hurt. I didn't even think about it. I charged the door. That was a mistake." Ed looked back over at the barn. "There was this old dude inside with Mara and Reed. He was bald and had crazy green eyes. As soon as I came through the door and they determined I was a threat, the old dude shouted something in another language—not sure what—and Reed went berserk on me. Threw fire everywhere. That's how the fire started."

"You said there were three other people besides Mara and Reed. That makes five people total," I said, counting on my fingers. "So far, you've only named Mara, Reed, and the bald, green-eyed guy. Who were the other two people you scented?"

Ed shrugged. "Beats me. Might've been fae, but there was so much magick in the air, and I was kinda upset, thinking my girlfriend...ex-girlfriend was in trouble, so I didn't pay much attention." Ed gave a pained expression when he called Mara his ex-girlfriend.

I narrowed my eyes, glaring at the dying embers of the fire. The firemen had almost conquered it now, and the barn was a smoldering pile of ash. It was still too hot for them to go in and search for bodies, and the water would have destroyed any residual magickal energies, effectively making the crime scene useless to me.

"The old man and Mara?" I asked. "What happened to them?"

Ed shook his head. "Gone. Reed kicked me aside, opened them a Way and they hopped right through."

So, whoever baldie was, it looked like Reed had allied himself with him. Now, *that* was odd. In all the time I'd known Gideon Reed, I hadn't ever seen him make friends. Something about the way Reed had acted during the fight didn't sit right with me, either.

"Do you think Mara's okay?" He fidgeted with two fingers and stared at the ground.

"I think you and I are going to have a very long chat when

things have calmed down." The dull thud of uneven paws on ground made me turn my head. Sal limped out toward where we stood. "But I think I'll give your alpha the privilege of ripping you a new asshole first about keeping secrets and getting involved. You and me, we're going to talk about this magick." I pointed at him sternly and then turned my back to walk away.

Sal gave me a tired look as he limped past but I didn't stop for him. I needed to talk to Tindall. I walked closer to the crime scene and stopped beside Tindall and a fireman whose helmet announced was the fire marshal. Tindall greeted me with a bob of his head. "Find out anything useful?"

"You having a problem with rem in Eden?"

"Fuck." Tindall scratched at his chin. "Drugs are always a problem. You get one off the street, the pushers have got another, stronger, more deadly one lined up. Yeah, I know a few corners where it's a problem, but nobody's dying from rem and funding is limited. I'd rather get the heroin pushers since I have to choose. Best I can do until legislature catches up and pick up the overdoses and harass the dealers. Why? What's that got to do with the fire?"

"Word on the street is your victims might have been involved with the Tribulation Adventists and maybe the rem trade."

"Fuck," Tindall breathed and scratched at his chin. "Don't suppose you got stuff to back that up?"

"Not yet, I don't. And the fire probably destroyed anything inside the building." I shook my head, trying to think through the smoke and noise. I dismissed the reference with a wave. "We need to find out who this property belonged to and go knock on their door."

The fire marshal, a muscular and mustached guy nodded. "I can answer that. Flagged in the system when I put the address in to find the place. This whole parcel belongs to that group of weirdo new-age people with the compound over that-a-way." He pointed southwest. "System said they still owed on a fine for a permit violation."

"Tell me you don't mean the Tribulation Adventists? That'd be too easy."

The fire marshal nodded. "That does sound right, yeah."

I tipped my head to the side. "You feel like throwing a few badges my way to go ruffle some feathers over at the compound?"

"Careful, Black," he said with a grunt. "I don't need a Waco incident on my badge."

"I won't go busting down doors without a warrant," I promised. "I just need a few grunts with badges. Enough to let the head honcho know I'm onto their rem operation. Maybe he knows something about all this."

Tindall did a half turn, put two fingers in his mouth and let out an ear-piercing whistle that drew everyone's attention. "Espinoza!" He made a big gesture with his arm. "Get over here!"

A Latino cop in a beat uniform jogged up and I was suddenly reminded of my weakness for a man in uniform. Lieutenant Espinoza was the kind of cop they put on calendars: broad shouldered, ruggedly handsome, medium height with well-kept dark hair and flattering facial scruff. He was fit enough to grace the cover of a men's health magazine without being too buff to be on *Entertainment Weekly* as heartthrob of the week in some cop drama. I'm not kidding. Espinoza was *pretty*. With a name like Otilio Espinoza, how could he not be? That name begged to be said aloud. Go ahead. Try it. See if you don't melt. I almost did when he smiled at me and extended a hand.

"Agent Black, meet Lieutenant Otilio Espinoza, head of my newly-formed special response team," Tindall said.

"It's good to finally meet you, Agent Black," Espinoza said in a formal tone and squeezed my limp fingers.

"Lieutenant." I finally shook the stars out of my eyes and squeezed back.

A sultry smirk crossed Espinoza's face and a small shock of magick power traveled down his fingers and into mine. Surprised, I jerked my hand away. "You're—"

"Gifted? I know." He offered me a wink.

Not sure how to respond, I turned to Tindall. "What's the special response team for?"

"For you." Espinoza answered in Tindall's place. "Or, more specifically, the squad was put together to be your back-up on the force. My men are volunteer only, Agent Black, so no one's on your team that doesn't want to be. And I fully vetted each of them with thorough background checks." He dropped his voice an octave to keep from being overheard outside our circle. It made the skin on my arms prickle. "No Vanguards of Humanity on my team. You can trust every one of us to have your back."

"He's ideal for your situation," Tindall informed me, "if all you want to do is talk."

"In addition to being the sexiest cop on payroll, I happen to be a practitioner," Espinoza said. "Not on your level, of course, but I do have a little talent you might find useful."

Tindall patted Espinoza on the back. "If you want info, he's your man."

I finally convinced myself to look away from Espinoza's face. "Alright, Espinoza, you know anything about rem?"

Espinoza nodded. "I've got the most experience dealing with it on the force, ma'am, which still isn't much." He flushed and shifted his weight.

"You okay, lieutenant?"

"I'm fine. Just..."

Espinoza jerked forward when Tindall slapped him on the back. "Espinoza's your biggest fan."

I blinked. Fan? I had *fans*? This was news to me.

"It's true," Espinoza admitted with a sheepish grin. "I've been following your work for some time, Agent Black. Judah the Giant Slayer. That was damned impressive."

I huffed. "You didn't see how close it was to turning out the other way," I said and nodded toward one of the squad cars. "We'll make a better showing if we go in with the lights on."

"I'll drive," Espinoza offered and swaggered off.

I sighed and gave Tindall a long look. "Don't worry," he said, scratching the scruff on his chin. "Espinoza's a good guy. Just be careful."

"Why?" I scoffed. "What's he going to do? Sexy me to death?"

"Maybe. He has that effect. Lot of women really like to talk to him. Not sure if that's part of his so-called talent, or something else." He looked over at the cruiser where Espinoza was leaning on the hood in a lazy pose. "But he's also got a reputation."

"What kind of reputation?"

"The kind that usually gets people in trouble." Tindall sighed and rubbed the bridge of his nose. "Really, he's probably too good for this job. One of the best cops on the force. Problem is with people that think they can save the world, they tend to get hurt. He's got what I'd call a Superman complex. Man of steel for sure, but the kind who might be a little too eager to apply truth and justice when he ought to look the other way." He patted my back. "But you've got magick. You'll be fine."

"May God have mercy on my poor, little soul," I droned and waved to Tindall as I walked over to the cruiser.

Espinoza opened the passenger side door of the cruiser for me and tipped his hat. "You know where the compound is, Agent Black?"

"That-a-way." I mimicked the fire marshal and then added, "Better call dispatch and get an address."

"You don't have some kind of magick spell to find the bad guy, huh?"

Espinoza said it in jest, but it made me think of Ed's spell. It might have seemed like harmless magick to him, but all his dabbling had changed his aura around and I didn't know yet if that was a bad or good thing. Ed was young and untrained learning magick from someone else who was young and untrained. That by itself was a bad thing. Or maybe, just maybe, it would be the edge I'd need to get a leg up on Seamus when he made his appearance.

# Chapter Four

"Okay," I said after we'd pulled away from the scene, lights on and sirens blaring. "I've got to know. If you've got magick, what are you doing working from EPD instead of BSI?"

Espinoza chuckled. "I'm not *that* talented. Besides, I've never had any interest in working for the government. The fact that I became a cop at all is a surprise. But *mi mamá* didn't raise a criminal. I grew up on Superman and Batman comics. Being a cop is my form of hero worship, I suppose."

I gave him a sideways glance and tilted my head to the side. "You're into comic books?"

He chuckled. "Yeah, but don't call me a comic book geek. I'm the thing most of them wish they could be," he said in a cock-sure tone.

I turned my attention out the window to the landscape passing by. It wasn't a far drive to the compound. There was nothing but empty desert between the barn and there, that and empty road. We barely had time for conversation before it loomed up in front of us.

The compound was a hodge-podge of simple buildings connected and built onto each other. Some sections were three stories high. Others were only two. I counted four sections in the dark and one more under construction. The compound sat on three acres of land, some of which had been converted into greenhouses. I made a note of that. We couldn't search them without a warrant, which I wouldn't be getting. There was still no evidence to back up Ed's claim that they were growing rem. I needed more than unreliable testimony to get a warrant.

As the car came down the long driveway in front of the compound, a small light came on in front of a covered entryway and faces pressed against the windows. One by one, shades and blinds closed. The compound was probably going into lockdown with our arrival. I wondered if I'd brought enough back-up.

We parked in front of the covered entry but Espinoza left the siren running an extra second or two before shutting it off. He didn't bother to kill the lights. I'd told him that we wanted to be seen. If people were being held in the house against their will, I hoped they'd make some noise so we could come in. If not, it would communicate that we were there and meant business.

We got out of the car. I pulled my badge from my pocket. As soon as I started for the front door, it opened and a man stepped out. He was tall, thin, and bald with an angular jaw. I would have placed his age somewhere between forty and forty-five and described his complexion as milky. He was dressed in gray pajama pants, a white t-shirt and a thin, blue bathrobe. Dark rings under his green eyes and the coffee cup in his hand told me he'd been awake when we pulled in. Worry lines creased in his forehead while sweat formed on mine. This had to be the guy Ed had seen.

One of my primary abilities allows me to see people's auras. Red, blue, purple and green are all common colors. Each one has its own meaning...sort of. It's more complicated than red means angry and blue means sad. The location of the colors has its own meaning along with how large the aura is.

Gold was not a common color and I'd seen it exactly one time before, once when I peeked at Father Reed's aura. This guy's aura made Father Reed's look like muddy water. It was the brightest, most glowing gold I'd ever seen streaked with light blue and black. Holy hell, this guy had some serious mojo.

"Officers," he said in the form of a greeting. "Is this about the fire?"

We stopped in front of him. "You've been watching?" I asked.

"One of my people called it in. We saw the blaze a while ago." His jade eyes darted from me over to Espinoza. "Can I assume it's a total loss?"

I decided to ignore his question and his attempt at leading the conversation. "I'm Special Agent Judah Black, BSI, and this is Lieutenant Espinoza, SRT. And you are?"

His eyes narrowed. "What's this about?"

"I've received an anonymous complaint that a young woman is being held here against her will," I said, tucking my badge away. "If you'd consent to a search of the premises, we could get this all cleared up, no problem."

The man's smile was strained. "I'm afraid I can't allow that. This is a sacred place. My people are peaceful. I assure that no one is being held here against their will. My flock is free to leave at their pleasure. Perhaps if you'd give me the name, *I* can clear it up."

I almost told him it was Mara but stopped when Espinoza put a hand on my arm and gave me a subtle shake of his head. Of course. What was I thinking? If I told him about Mara, he could still deny us entry and punish her for causing trouble. The best way to protect Mara was to distance myself from her.

"Someone has also claimed you've been growing some plants of questionable origin," Espinoza said and jabbed a thumb toward the greenhouses. "What do you grow in your greenhouses? Maybe you wouldn't mind giving me a tour?"

The man avoided the question entirely. He sighed and his shoulders slumped. "The old house was to be our next project. It was here when we began work on the property and we hadn't yet had time to clean it out and renovate it. My people have not been inside or near that house in months. If there was anything growing in it, we were not the caretakers."

"You see anyone hanging around on your property?" Espinoza asked. "Maybe out by the old house? Strange cars? Prowlers? Anything like that?"

"Nothing of the sort," the bald man said and waved his hand.

"I didn't catch your name."

His glare at me intensified. "I am Reverend Hector Demetrius."

I tilted my head to the side. "Are you registered with BSI, Hector?"

Hector pressed his lips into a thin line. "If you're not here simply to inform me about the damage to our property, perhaps I should speak with a lawyer before answering any more of your questions."

"Sure thing." Espinoza pointed a thumb back at the squad car. "If you want to come down to the station and wait on your legal counsel, I'd be happy to take you. It'd save you the cab faire, seeing as how you don't have any cars parked out here."

"We have transportation." Hector sighed. "Officers, it's very late. If you have questions, I can meet you at the station tomorrow. Would that suffice?"

"Better to get it out of the way tonight," I said. "No telling what could happen overnight. There are all kinds of monsters out there." I tried to keep the acrid tone out of my voice but it crept in anyway. I didn't appreciate the way he was stonewalling us.

"Unless I'm under arrest, I won't be going with you tonight. I need to be here with my people."

I stepped out of line and put a hand on the man's shoulder. "Someone else can keep the vigil until you get back. Looks like you've got plenty of people." I started to pull him back toward the cruiser.

The door opened again. "Judah?"

I turned to see Mara step out of the compound, only it wasn't the Mara I knew. She'd lost a lot of weight, giving her face a more angular look. The pink and blue coloring in her hair had faded, replaced by her natural, dirty blonde. Instead of a tank top, jeans and plenty of jewelry, Mara now wore a plain dress of slate blue. She stepped outside barefoot. "What are you doing here?"

Another popped out of the darkness behind her, this one a boy about her age. He wore pajama pants and a white tank top. "Tamara," the young man hissed.

"It's fine," Mara said, raising a hand. "I know her." I swallowed as she stepped closer and asked, "Is something wrong?"

"Mara, I..." But I trailed off, unsure of what to say. "Is everything okay? With you, I mean. It's good to see you."

I expected her to lash out with an insult. The Mara that I knew would at least dismiss me with sarcasm. This Mara, however, stood poised and calm with a blank smile. "Yes, I'm happy here, and I'm glad to see you're still alive."

"You're not still mad at me, Mara?"

Mara looked at Hector, her grin wider, but strained. "The reverend has helped me to let go of my past. I'm at peace now. With everything."

The young man stepped out onto the porch beside Mara, his eyes steely. "What are you doing here? What do you want?"

"Warren," a middle-aged woman hissed from the doorway. So, this boy was the infamous Warren Demetrius who'd convinced Mara to join his dad's cult.

I only caught a glance of the woman in the doorway, but she was wearing dark fabric, a head covering and had a rather plain face. Mara looked well-fed, though, and I didn't see any bruises or signs she was in distress, leaving me no just cause to intervene.

"Child, obey your mother," Hector said and nodded. "These people won't harm me."

"But they're the enemy," said Warren and he cast a hateful look at me. "You can't trust them to keep their word."

I let go of Hector's arm as he turned to address his son. "And what does Jesus say we should do to our enemies?"

Warren didn't answer, but Mara came to stand beside him, taking his hand. It was she who answered, "Love them."

"Very good." He turned back to me.

The woman I'd seen in the doorway stepped out to usher Warren and Mara back inside. "Nice kid," Espinoza commented to the woman. "Yours?"

Hector stood stiffly. "You will address *me*. Everyone here is *mine*. These people are under my protection, officers. They huddle here away from a world that has rejected them and so they reject it in return. If you insist on bringing me to the station now, you will have to carry me away from them in chains." He extended his wrists to us. "If you arrest me, I will not resist. However, I will not be taken away from my flock under false pretenses. Either arrest me or leave."

Espinoza and I exchanged glances.

"We're not here to arrest you," I said and he lowered his hands. "We're just here to try and get information."

"Yes," he sighed, impatiently. "Information I have promised to provide tomorrow. We can go in circles all night, Agent Black, and neither of us will get any closer to getting what we want. Now, you can either accept my assurances until I've had time to confer with my lawyer, and believe that I will come willingly to the station to meet you tomorrow morning for an interview, or you can arrest me. Anything else is a violation of my constitutional rights."

"Tell you what." Espinoza pulled a business card out of his uniform, blew on it and held it out to the woman. "We'll spend the night looking into things so we can have plenty of questions ready for tomorrow. If you think of anything else in the meantime or see anyone prowling around, you call the number on the card."

The woman reached out and clutched the card with a thumb and forefinger, but Hector snatched it away before she could take it. "Thank you," he said curtly. "Now, please leave."

~

"That could have gone better," I said, sliding into the back seat.

"It went better than expected," Espinoza said. "I got her to touch the card. Hopefully, that counts for something. I would have preferred her to hold it."

I leaned against the metal grate that separated the front seat from the back. I'd meant meeting Mara again. Ed was going to flip his lid when he got the news that I couldn't do anything about her. Mara seemed to be there of her own free will, and she'd seemed... maybe not happy, but better. I closed my eyes and let out a deep breath, willing my mind to refocus on the task at hand.

"You spelled the card?"

"Of course I did," Espinoza said, smiling. "Hector has some powerful magick. Did you see it, Agent Black?"

I nodded. "No idea what kind, but he's sure got something big and scary. He's probably registered with BSI but I seriously doubt Hector Demetrius is his real name. If I were going to start a cult, I'd use a pseudonym. I'll see if I can track down who he is."

I paused and then added, "What will the card do?"

"Everyone who handles it is now eyes and ears for a limited time so long as I hold the card's twin." He produced another from his uniform pocket and waved it. "I don't make them in stacks. Just two at a time. Anyway, if you want to listen in, we can do it anytime. At least until Hector figures out the card is spelled."

"Make it so," I said.

Espinoza flashed me a roguish grin. Then, he lifted his copy of the business card and flicked it once. It made a sound somewhere between a tuning fork and radio static for a minute and then we heard voices.

"...I'm sorry," the woman was saying. "I shouldn't have interrupted."

"They were only here to unsettle us," Hector said. "They have no evidence or they would have arrested me."

"The police are about to be the least of our problems." That was a third voice. Was it...Warren? "What do we do?"

"We continue on as if nothing has changed because nothing has changed."

"We should break off contact," Warren said.

"When we're so close to a breakthrough? We are not about to walk away because of a nosy werewolf and two overzealous police officers."

"Are you really going to the police station tomorrow, Hector? They'll just twist your words. They are the enemy for a reason."

"We must be in the world, Amanda. Not of it. I will oblige them as far as I'm required, but no one else is to speak with the police." There was a short pause before he repeated. "No one, Amanda. And that means you, too, Warren."

"I've said my part," Warren said.

"What about the lieutenant's card?" Amanda asked.

"I'll burn it," Hector offered. "Go and tell everyone else to go back to bed."

A moment later, Hector made good on his word. The connection cut out and the dull glow coming from the business card faded.

"Well, at least he's coming to the station tomorrow," Espinoza said, raising his eyebrows.

"But we're no closer to finding out why Reed attacked Ed." I sighed.

Espinoza started the police cruiser, adjusted his mirror to look back at me and said, "Hey, Agent Black. Did I see a for-sale sign in your car window?"

~

Espinoza and I talked about cars all the way back to the crime scene. Apparently, he was a collector of the classics and was interested in purchasing my car. We'd just started haggling on the price when we pulled in.

Tindall stood with Ed near the squad. Bran waited nearby as well, Mia still sleeping in his arms. I got out and Ed immediately started across the grass to meet me. "Any luck?"

I shook my head. "Nothing you'll like," I told Ed. "As far as I can tell, Mara's there of her own free will. Without a warrant, there's no way I can get into that compound to investigate. Everything I have that might get me a warrant is sketchy and limited to your testimony. I need more."

Ed dropped his head, sulking in silence.

We stopped just short of the squad. "What's going on here?" I asked.

"Sal. He changed a short while ago after Bran said something to him."

"Dammit, he shouldn't change yet. Not until he's healed."

"That's the thing," Ed said as we picked up the pace toward the squad. "He's not healing."

I looked down at my watch. We'd arrived at the scene somewhere close to ten and it was inching toward midnight. Even with a cut that deep, he should have been completely recovered by now. Whatever magick that had been worked on the blade of Reed's sword, I hoped it wasn't going to lead to any further damage.

We reached the squad and I leaned in for a look. Sal was back in human form, lying on the gurney holding a wad of gauze against his ribs just under his arm. The EMT pulled the gauze away and blood rushed out of a wide, gaping hole that was definitely bigger.

"No dice, wolfman," said the EMT. "We can't wait for your friend to come patch you up. Have to transport you out to the hospital."

Sal ground his teeth together. "I said no."

"Doctor Ramis is on his way," Tindall said.

"He's losing a lot of blood and the longer we wait, the worse the damage could be." The EMT looked at me as if I could tell him what to do. "I'm not even sure how he's still conscious. His body must be working overtime to keep him awake."

"He's drawing heavily on the pack bonds," Ed explained with a frown. "But it's not an endless well. Right now, that's pretty shallow." He turned to me, his face pained.

I nodded. "Sal, you need to go. Let them do triage at least and put a bandage on. I'll call Doc and send him to the hospital."

Sal didn't look happy but, once he tried to move and fell back, woozy, he decided a band aid wouldn't hurt. The EMT nodded his thanks, closed up the squad and they sped off, lights and sirens blaring.

I turned to Tindall as soon as I could hear myself think again. "Did Espinoza bring you up to speed?"

"Close enough. Hector Demetrius, huh? He's going to stonewall you so I hope you've got a lead." Tindall started back across the field toward the parked cars and I followed.

"I've got nothing," I said. "The best I can hope for is to find something useful at Reed's house tomorrow. It should be easy enough to get a warrant to search there. We can't go into that compound without ironclad evidence, Tindall. They're going to hide behind their status as a protected religious group."

I noticed Ed trailing behind with Bran and Mia and paused. Tindall and Espinoza stopped with me. "Go on ahead, you two," I said to the cops. "I'll catch up."

Tindall eyed Bran and frowned, but walked off with Espinoza, making for where his car was parked.

"What's going on?" I asked Bran as he came closer. I held out my arms and he passed Mia to me. "Is it club business?"

Sal hadn't been very active inside the Kings since bringing home Mia. He'd given up his officer position as road captain, passing the duty to a guy named Phil. He still went to their meetings once a week and their social functions, but that was it. I couldn't see why anyone would call him from the club unless it was an emergency.

"I couldn't help but overhear your problem," Bran said. "Legally, you're back is to the wall. The club may be able to help. We can go places you can't, find out information you'd have to get a warrant for. If you want us to get the girl out, all you have to say is the word."

I stopped walking and turned to face Bran. Bran stopped with me. He meant well, but I couldn't take him up on his offer. I'd made it a point to distance myself as much as possible from the Kings lately, hoping that, eventually, Sal would get completely out.

"Thanks, Bran, but I'd rather handle this the legal way unless I have no other options."

He nodded. "I understand. We will be here if you change your mind." Bran inclined his head and the three of us started walking again. "I will load my bike into the back of Sal's truck and drive it back to your place. If you'd like, I can also take Mia home and put her to bed. I'll stay with the children until you return."

"You're not going to the hospital?"

Bran shook his head. "I avoid going there in my club colors, especially when there will be a heavy police presence. Whenever I can avoid it, I prefer for my personal life and professional life not to clash. Besides, I have an early shift tomorrow and could use at least a little sleep."

By day, Bran was a prison guard. I'd never seen him in that role, which I suppose meant he considered me a friend on the club side more than the law enforcement side. "I guess that works. Did Sal leave you his keys?"

He lifted his fingers and the truck keys dangled. "What about you?" Bran jerked his chin toward Ed. "What are you going to do?"

Ed looked at me and then quickly dropped his eyes to the ground. "I think I'll stick with Judah if she's going out to the hospital."

We walked back to the cars and I buckled Mia safely into her car seat in the truck. She woke up for a minute, yawned, asked for something to drink, and fell back asleep before Bran got into the front seat. "Make sure you relieve me by five thirty," Bran said, adjusting the mirrors. "I am up for a perfect attendance award at work."

I promised him I would, kissed Mia on the head one more time, and shut the door.

"You're getting pretty buddy-buddy with the Kings." I turned around. Tindall stood behind me, arms crossed and a deep frown on his face. "After everything that happened last year?"

"The shooting wasn't their fault, Tindall."

"No, but you know the Kings are in bed with Marcus Kelley."

"So are you," I snapped back before I could stop myself.

Tindall's shoulders heaved with a sigh. "I don't have a choice and I ain't doing anything illegal, Black. So far, the Kings have done a good job staying off my radar, but it's only a matter of time before that changes."

I wrinkled my nose and shook my head. "Things have settled down. The Vanguard have been quiet. This is the first major case to break in nine months. I'd call that a good thing."

"The quiet's what I'm worried about." Tindall lit another cigarette and took a long drag. His eyes traveled over the open field and settled on the smoldering remains of the house. "It's not a good quiet, Black. It feels like the last deep breath in before you drown or the moment when you can see the car's going to crash, but it's too late to stop it. Last time I felt this way was in the days leading up to the Revelation Riots. Something big is coming. I just wish I knew what direction it was coming from."

Tindall was right. I'd felt it, too. Even though I enjoyed the quiet, something about it felt wrong. Most of my focus had been on my family and preparing for whatever it was Seamus was going to throw at me, so I hadn't had much time to worry about it. But it was there, lurking under the surface. You could see it in people's faces, the fear, worry and paranoia that everyone felt but no one spoke about. It had been that way ever since the shooting downtown.

"You're a bunch of pessimists," Ed said and both of us looked at him. He'd opened the trunk of my car and pulled on the spare pair of sweats I kept back there. They were too big, even with the drawstring pulled tight. "You killed a giant and gave a faerie king the middle finger. I find your lack of faith disturbing."

I raised an eyebrow. "You realize you're quoting the bad guy, right?"

Ed raised a finger and wagged it. "Was he? Technically, he was the ultimate hero of the story."

"Right. I'm really interested to hear you explain that one." I waved to Tindall and walked around to the driver's side. "Go home and get some sleep, Sheriff. I'll call you if anything weird happens."

# Chapter Five

The drive to the hospital wasn't as tense as I expected. Ed put the window down and the whoosh of wind at highway speeds filled the car until we took the exit near the hospital. At thirty-five miles per hour in the middle of the night, the only sound was the distant wail of a siren as another squad headed out.

Ed rolled his window up while we sat at a red light, waiting to pull into the hospital. "Am I going to be in trouble?"

"What would you be in trouble for, Ed?"

"The magick. I know I'm not supposed to use it. I'm not registered as a practitioner."

I drummed my fingers on the steering wheel. Ed was a friend, and I didn't generally turn in friends, but if he continued to use his magick during the investigation, I'd have no choice. "It's dangerous, what you're doing." He began a protest, but I cut him off with a wave of my hand. "I know you know that. I just wanted you to know that *I* knew. Reporting what you can do isn't my first choice. It's not even a close second, Ed. If I have to, though, I'll do what needs to be done."

"What needs to be done," Ed repeated and shook his head. "I was afraid you'd say that."

"I didn't mean it that way. I'll go as far as needed to save a friend, but there are lines even I won't cross. Torture is one of them." I stole a glance sideways at Ed, whose face was serious. "It was never my intention that any of that happen to Mara. She made decisions and kept me out. I understand why she did. I understand why the two of you have spent the last nine months moving around in secret, but that has to end if we're going to continue to work together. No more secrets, Ed. No more lies."

The light changed and still we sat, staring each other down. Ed took longer than I expected to drop his gaze, ending the power struggle. "Yeah, I want things to go back the way they were. I miss playing fetch."

I smiled and pressed my foot onto the gas as the light turned yellow. "Once we close this case, I'll get you one of those squeaky geese to fetch. Promise."

"So, um, if I had questions about magick..."

"I thought Mara was teaching you?"

Ed shrugged. "Mara's in a different league. Different abilities. She got me through the basics, but you saw. I'm still no good."

"That comes with practice," I said as I drove around the drop off toward the parking lot. "And focus."

"You don't use a focus."

I shrugged. "I don't use a lot of magick that can be focused."

There was one spell, one that I still didn't know much about. Fire and shadow, Chanter had called it, which seemed descriptive enough. Calling up the black fire was dangerous. The last time I had to use it, the spell felt sentient. Hungry. That had scared me away from calling it up again unless I had no other choice. That didn't mean I had the best control over it. Sometimes, that magick had a mind of its own that made it rise to the surface almost unbidden. Ever since I'd started sparring weekly with Creven, it had been less of a problem. If I didn't feel it lurking there, underneath the surface every time my emotions ran high, I would have said I had it under complete control. Maybe a good focus object would help.

"I could use a wand," Ed said, excitement in his voice. "How awesome would that be? It's like built in cosplay. I already have my Hufflepuff scarf and everything. I wonder if I could get some yew. That'd be freaking sweet."

"This is Texas," I reminded Ed as I pulled into one of the few empty parking spaces.

"If you can find wendigos and ice giants, I can find some yew. It's called Amazon Prime, Judah. You should join this decade and try it. Two words, Judah. Two-day shipping."

"That's three words."

Ed held up two fingers. "Two. It's hyphenated."

Inside, we inquired at the information desk about Sal. I expected them to be reluctant to tell us but the nurse at triage looked relieved. "Oh, Lord if you ain't a sight for sore eyes, honey."

"Has he been a problem?"

I knew Sal didn't like hospitals or enclosed spaces, but I didn't expect for him to throw a fit or anything. That wasn't like him.

The nurse shook her head. "It's the little guy who came in shortly after. Shooed everyone out and ordered a few of the nurses around like he owns the place."

"Little guy? Glasses? About so high?" I held my hand out flat just a few inches above my head.

"He looked a little taller with the afro, but yeah."

She meant Doctor Ramis, the clinician Tindall had called in from Paint Rock. Doc wasn't employed by the hospital, and tended to be high strung, but he was the best of the best when it came to supernatural medicine. He was also the only doctor Sal would ever trust.

I thanked the nurse and stepped toward the entrance to the emergency department.

"He's in room five," she called after me.

Ed fell in line right behind me when we pushed through the double doors. Several doctors cast curious glances in our direction until I asked for directions to room five. Then, they seemed to get it and did all they could to get out of our way.

The door to room five was open, but only by a crack. I pushed it open the rest of the way against a loud hiss of pain from Sal. He lay on a hospital bed with a pile of bloody dressings beside him. Doc Ramis had the nozzle of a bottle pressed into the wound, presumably a saline solution to clean it out. The water washed out a deep pink and splashed into a plastic tub under Sal's arm.

"Complain all you want," Doc said, his forehead wrinkling in concentration. "It could have been a lot worse if these second-rate hacks would have gotten ahold of you. They'd have used silver to stitch you up."

Sal grimaced again and turned away.

"What's the prognosis, Doc?" I asked from the doorway.

"It doesn't look like the blade was coated in a physical substance, meaning whatever's keeping him from healing falls on the magick side of things." He withdrew the saline bottle and opened another package of sterile gauze, pressing it against the wound. "Hold this."

"Unfortunately, I don't know the first thing about what Reed does with his sword to keep it battle ready," I said, trying not to notice how pale Sal was. "Will he heal now?"

Doc's hair wobbled as he shook his head. "I doubt it. At least, not at an accelerated rate. I'm going to stitch it back together and check on it tomorrow when you two bring Mia in for her check-up. See what eight hours of rest can do." He raised his eyes to Sal's face and then added firmly, "And I mean rest, Sal. No heavy lifting, no shifting, nothing. These are regular stitches I'm putting in you and if you tear them, the damage is only going to get worse."

Sal shook his head. "I'm not going to sit on my ass for a day, Doc. I can't. I got Mia to think of."

"Unless you want Mia to find her daddy bleeding to death, you'll listen to me." Sal growled at Doc, who leaned back and sighed. "It's for your own good. Now, I need you to hold very still."

Ed slid past me and knelt at the end of the bed with his back to the wall. Plastic rustled as Doc fought to open more containers containing sterile forceps and other equipment I didn't know the name for. As soon as he brought out the needle with attached thread, my stomach turned. I suddenly wished I'd gone home with Mia.

Doc bent over Sal, his body blocking my view of his work. Sal sucked in a deep breath and ground his teeth. His fingers tightened on the edges of the bed. Beside me, Ed made a small sound and leaned forward. I didn't have to look at anyone's aura to know it was because Sal was drawing strength from the pack bonds. Ed, being in closest proximity, would have felt the brunt of it, but everyone in the pack likely knew something was wrong. I was surprised I hadn't gotten a phone call yet. Then I remembered Ed had destroyed my phone. If anyone had tried to call, they were probably in a panic. No one outside of Ed knew that Sal was safe and alive.

"I should call someone," I said out loud. "The pack needs to know that you're okay." I took a half step toward the door, but hesitated when I realized I didn't know who to call. It should be Sal's second, but whether that was Shauna or Valentino wasn't immediately clear to me. I knew Sal trusted Shauna more, especially since Valentino had challenged him for the position of alpha, but I didn't know if she was officially his second. If I called the wrong one, there was sure to be hurt feelings somewhere. Werewolves with bruised egos tended to lash out violently.

Sal must have sensed my uncertainty. "Call Shauna."

I nodded and stepped out of the room. Relief washed over me as soon as I was back in the hall and the tension shifted. My head felt clearer with the change of venue, but I still needed coffee if I was going to make it through the night. Rubbing the sleep from my eyes, I shuffled back out to the waiting room and to an alcove on the far side lined with vending machines and payphones. Graffiti marked the wall next to the phones, which probably didn't see much use in an age dominated by cell phones.

My first stop was at the coffee vending machine where I collected a cup of filmy looking, weak black coffee. To replace the dinner I'd missed, I grabbed a package of fish-shaped cheese crackers out of the machine next to it and then dropped my remaining quarters in the nearest payphone. I didn't know every pack member's phone number by heart, but I did know Shauna's because it was also Daphne and Ed's. I grimaced at the sticky feeling of the number keys on the payphone as I typed her number in.

Shauna picked up on the second ring. "Who is this?"

"Nice to hear from you too," I answered.

"Judah? Where's Sal? What's happening?"

"He's going to be fine." That was the most important part, so I made sure I got it out first. "He's at the hospital in Eden. Doctor Ramis and Ed are with him. He just needs a little patching up and—"

She cut me off. "Was it silver?"

"No, but I think there was magick involved. He got a good slice from Father Reed's sword."

I explained vaguely what had happened, doing my best to relay the information in a neutral tone. Werewolves hate talking on the phone or via the internet because they find it difficult to judge emotion and intent. At a distance, they relied heavily on voice inflection and intonation to provide clues. Basically, the phone robbed Shauna of her heightened senses and so I was afraid she'd misread my explanation and blame me.

When I was done, Shauna asked in a terse tone, "Do you need me to come down there?"

"Ed is here," I repeated. "And they're releasing him anytime now. There's no reason for anybody to do anything. I just wanted to make sure everyone knew we were okay."

There was a muffled sound, as if someone in another room had shouted something. Shauna sighed. "Daphne wants to know if Ed is okay."

I glanced around and then leaned further into the phone. "Physically, he's fine. But emotionally he's pretty torn up about Mara breaking up with him." I debated asking her if she knew Ed had been toying around with magick, but decided against it. Until I knew more, I didn't want wild rumors to spread.

"First ones are always tough," Shauna commented. "If it were me, I'd just go out, kill a few goats and be done with it. Ed probably just needs to drown himself in video games for a while in his nerd cave. He'll be fine." She hesitated. "Why did you call me and not Valentino?"

"Sal told me to call you."

The other end was silent for a long time.

"Shauna?"

"I'm here," she said, her voice strained. "I'll fill in Valentino and the rest. You make sure he gets back in one piece." She hung up without saying goodbye.

~

A short while later, I collected Sal from Doc after promising to do my best to get him to behave again. Sal insisted he walk on his own, despite Doc's worries over his dizziness. Ed came around to stand on Sal's right while I flanked him on the left all the way out to the parking lot. Rather than leave Sal standing there with only Ed to support him while he swayed on his feet, I paid the valet five bucks to go and retrieve my car.

While we stood, waiting under the buzzing entrance sign, Ed asked, "So, what's your next move?"

"First, I buy a new cell phone." I gave him a scolding look and then finished with a smile. "And look into finding someone to help you out."

Ed drew his eyebrows together. "I mean Mara. Do you really think she's there by choice?"

I shrugged. "She seemed better, Ed. Better than I'd seen her in a long time. I was right there. She could've left if she wanted."

"Maybe she couldn't talk freely or they're blackmailing her to stay. She might have to stay or else they'll hunt her down."

"Find Reed," Sal said. He shifted backward and I thought he was falling, but he stopped when his back hit the wall and grunted. "Find him and get some answers. He and Mara are connected somehow, and Reed was not himself. It was like he was under a compulsion."

"Maybe Mara is too," Ed said, hope surging in his voice. "Judah, you have to acknowledge she'd never join a cult by choice."

"Your focus has to be on finding Reed," Sal continued.

"Without him, there are no answers and you can't help Mara."

I shook my head and helped Sal away from the wall so we could inch toward the parking lot. "To do a proper tracking spell, I need biological material and to get that, I need to get into Reed's house unless he just happened to have some lying around the church. That's not going to happen without a warrant. Given that he's now a suspect, I should be able to secure one, but not until tomorrow morning."

Ed turned to face me. "What about the rem? You said the compound had greenhouses, right? That's probable cause."

"Not until I can corroborate your testimony. No offense, Ed, but you're not the most reliable witness. I need to do this the right way. We're not vigilantes."

Ed narrowed his eyes at me. Or, maybe it was against the headlights of my car as it drove up.

The valet got out and opened the passenger door and Sal sat down, wincing. He didn't like it much, but I had to help him buckle in so that he didn't twist in his seat. It was as I was fumbling with the buckle that I realized I had a problem. My car only had two seats and Ed still needed to get home.

I turned back to offer to call a cab for Ed but he was already storming away, head down, hands in his pockets. "Ed," I called and took a few steps down the sidewalk after him. "Where are you going?"

"To see about that yew," he called back and waved as he rounded the corner. He didn't sound like he was going to go get into trouble. Maybe that's why I worried.

"Should I stop him?" I asked Sal through the open door.

Sal shifted in his seat and closed his eyes. "If it were you behind enemy lines, do you think I'd go home and wait until tomorrow?"

"Shit."

I rushed around to the driver's side, got in and tore out of the emergency room lot. I brought the car around the corner of the building and slowed. It had only been a few minutes, so he couldn't have gotten far.

About five yards down the sidewalk, I spotted something and stopped the car to get out and confirm that it was, indeed, Ed's discarded pair of sweatpants. I squinted against the darkness, searching the hospital grounds for any sign of him and came up empty. Ed was in the wind.

# Chapter Six

There was nothing I could do to find him in the dark. Sal might have been able to help if he wasn't injured and on pain meds, but the best thing for him would be to take him home. I was too tired to drop him off and go driving around the desert in search of a werewolf. Time in the ER had eaten away the night and, by the time I made it back to the reservation, it was almost morning, closing in on the time I'd promised to relieve Bran.

I paused at the border crossing and glanced up at the razor wire-topped towers of concrete, waiting for someone to come down and raise the mechanical arm so I could drive through. It used to be, there were only two night watchmen on the walls but, ever since the drive-by nine months ago, the feds had stepped up their presence in the area. I counted two armed guards and one new camera as I waited.

After a long moment, the guard leaned out from his post and waved at me. The mechanical arm lifted and I drove through. Dark windows, dead, empty yards and deep shadows met me on the reservation. The rez had no real sense of organization with doublewides and cottages sitting right next to each other. Half of the trailers weren't even facing the same direction, the dirt paths and many of the roads put in as afterthoughts. Some folks had tried to brighten the place with rock gardens or painted fences, but the red, Texas dust had rolled over the town in the drought and turned everything a copper shade of brown. Gnats swirled in the sickly yellow light of the reservation's lone streetlight.

I rolled down the window and turned up the radio as Queen asked the important questions on my radio. *Is this the real life? Is this just fantasy?* Man, they were deep. Freddy Mercury was just hitting the high notes of the song when I pulled over alongside a weather-beaten white mailbox to retrieve my mail.

Technically, I lived in the house next door to Sal. Mine was one of the few houses on the reservation with an actual foundation, even if it was mostly made of chipboard and plaster. Last year, some vandals broke in and wrecked the place. The pack had pitched in to help me get it cleaned up.

I never really went back after that, partly because I'd already moved in with Sal. Considering he'd suddenly had to take on raising a daughter he only recently found out he had, it worked out. The man needed all the help he could get and Hunter needed close guidance from a male role model. I maintained a skeleton presence at my house, just in case things didn't work out, but I only went inside once or twice a week when I needed quiet to work.

With four of us in a three-bedroom trailer, space was tight but comfortable. We almost felt like a family. A weird family sewn together from all kinds of different scraps of lives, but a family nonetheless. After sorting through the mail, I drove over and parked beside instead of behind Sal's truck so that Bran could get his bike out and shut off my car.

Sal had dozed off, but woke as soon as the engine died. I reached over and hit the release for his seatbelt before he could fumble with it. He was tired and sore enough he didn't protest, not even when I helped him out of the car and up the stairs.

I expected Bran would still be snoozing on the sofa when we came through the door, but he wasn't. He stood in the kitchen, staring into the glow of the microwave while a breakfast burrito spun inside. I wouldn't have called the green uniform on him flattering, or maybe it was just how exhausted he looked. I scrutinized him for a second and realized that the green hair was gone, too. "What happened to your green hair?"

"A little Just for Men goes a long way, Mrs. BSI," he answered and patted the coffee pot. "Refilled it to be ready when you are, though you look like you could use some rest."

"I just need a power nap." I waved at him as Sal and I slid through the kitchen toward his bedroom. "This guy needs to take it easy, though. Doc's orders."

After dropping Sal off in the bed, I came back out to thank Bran and asked him if Mia went down okay.

"She is a good girl," Bran said. "Slept all the way home and barely woke when I moved her into her crib." He scratched at his chin. "Are you in the market for a toddler bed instead of that crib? I know where you can get one."

I shook my head. "We're afraid she'll fall."

"She falls a lot, Mia?"

I shrugged. "Kids are clumsy."

"I see you are worried."

"Of course I'm worried," I said, sinking into the sofa. Bran sat in the chair opposite me, the breakfast burrito steaming in his hand. "She's eighteen months now. She should be saying more words. She should be walking better. I keep worrying... maybe this is because of what happened. The ghost sickness."

"You cured her of the ghost sickness."

"I did," I said, nodding. "But no one knew how much damage it really did or what the long-term effects of that cure might be on her. What if I didn't act fast enough? What if I did this to her?"

Bran smiled and reached out to place a hand on my leg. "To be forgiven, we must first let go of our own guilt. You can't continue to live in the past, not when the present needs you so dearly." He stood and squeezed my shoulder. "Now, I will take my leave and let you get your rest. If the idiot in there doesn't listen to you, tell him he will have to answer to me when I get off work." He placed his hat on his head and headed out the door.

As soon as the door shut behind him, I leaned back and spread out over the sofa, practically melting into it. I don't think two minutes passed before I was drifting off. My head fell forward and I jerked awake, but something wasn't right. In fact, a lot wasn't right.

Sal's living room was gone, replaced by a dark cavern with deep shadows. Watery light filtered through massive green crystals. The sheer walls of the cavern stretched up a hundred feet into darkness, emeralds and diamonds glittering in them. I sat on a precipice of crystal that sloped down behind me. In front of me, a gap separated me from a mossy knoll upon which sat a throne of polished, white bone.

A man sat in the throne, a man I hadn't expected to see for another three months. Seamus. His sword was drawn, the blade resting against the ground and his hands gripping the pommel. The mullet of silver hair on his head coiled down over his shoulder. "For in that sleep of death what dreams may come when we have shuffled off this mortal coil must give us pause." He raised his golden eyes to behold me and I suddenly felt naked under his gaze. "Your Shakespeare wrote that. I often ponder your people's reverence to someone of so little consequence."

I pushed up off the crystal to stand and fought not to lose my balance. A tumble over the side would send me careening to my death and still leave Seamus' hands clean. He'd promised not to kill me for a year and a day, but the fall would technically be my fault if it happened, absolving him of any guilt.

"You said a year and a day." I pointed at him.

"Relax, Judah Black. I'm not here to do battle with you."

I lowered my arm but didn't relax. "What is this place? Am I asleep?"

"Sleep has long been the domain of the fae." Seamus stood and brought his sword with him as he paced. A deep purple cape fluttered behind him. "It is easy enough for us to manipulate. In a sense, yes, your body is asleep, but your mind is here and I assure you that *here* is as real as that trailer where your body lies unprotected." He smirked at me and it made my muscles tense.

I tried not to show how much the whole situation unnerved me by gesturing at him. "Not a Shakespeare fan?"

"Shakespeare's works are part of the reason my operations have been increasingly more difficult since the debut of that ridiculous play featuring a character by my brother's name. Oberon is hardly the character Shakespeare would have you humans believe. And yet he is remembered, made more powerful for that memory, and I have become all but forgotten."

"I knew who you were." I didn't mention that the only reason I knew anything about Finvarra was because I'd studied Gaelic languages in college as a linguistics major. You can hardly study a language and a culture without learning some of the old myths.

"Soon, everyone will know Finvarra." He paced back to his throne, sighed and sat down, lying the sword on the ground beside him. "But I didn't call you here for that. You and I have a truce for some time yet. However, I am open to a... renegotiation of our earlier contract."

"You're all about making deals, aren't you, Seamus?" I counted on my fingers. "First Crux, then Marcus, me, now someone else. What is it? BOGO on bad deals week at the fae necromancer emporium?"

Seamus ignored my quip and brushed something invisible from his sleeve. "You are acquainted with one Gideon Reed?"

I tilted my head to the side. What could he possibly want with Reed? "I know the name."

"Don't play games with me, Judah Black. You have seen him this very night."

I took a step forward. A tiny stone tumbled forward and rolled off the edge of the crystal into blackness. I didn't hear it hit the bottom. "What do you know about Reed? Where is he?"

Seamus regarded me with a bored look. "Your dedication to those who hate you is applaudable. Naive, but applaudable. Such loyalty is rare indeed."

"What about Mara?" I pressed. "Is she involved?

Seamus drew his lips into a thin line and narrowed his eyes. "I cannot say anything definitive about her."

"Can't or won't?"

"Can't," he answered quickly. "Not without breaking my word, which I will not do."

So, he *did* know something, but there was nothing I could do to get him to spill it. Even if I could have crossed the chasm between us, the only thing that might hurt Seamus would be iron. I couldn't match him spell for spell. If I so much as tried to whisper a spell, I'd be dead before I got through the first five syllables. Maybe I could back him into a corner and trick him into telling me what he knew. "What do you have on Reed?"

Seamus made a fist and struck the arm of his throne. I flinched at the sound of bone cracking. "Nothing, unfortunately, but I have a use for something he has in his possession. If you were to bring it to me, I could be persuaded to call off my vendetta with you."

I cracked a smile. "Do you think I'm stupid, Seamus? I'm not making any deals with you, especially with such loose language and not in writing. I know what happened to the last guy who made a deal with you."

"Crux Continelli is currently learning the consequences of insulting me and mine." He closed his hand around a skull at the end of the chair arm and squeezed. The bone groaned and then exploded into dust and shards no bigger than an eraser.

I fought a shiver. Whatever Seamus was doing to Crux, I didn't want to know. "You said you want something Reed has. What is it?"

Seamus sat up straighter and adjusted the upturned collar of his shirt. "Have you heard of the sword known as Claíomh Solais?"

I thought for a moment. The phrase sounded familiar, but it took me a moment to connect the dots. "The sword of light?"

"One of the four treasures of my people, scattered about the mortal realm by Oberon so that no one man may possess them." He folded his hands. "I believe that Gideon Reed is in possession of none other than this treasure."

I shook my head. What were the chances of that? Actually,

with everything that had happened since I'd come to Paint Rock, the idea of the local pyromancer priest being in possession of a legendary fae blade shouldn't have been that much of a stretch. But this Oberon guy had scattered the four treasures for a reason. I'd made the mistake once before of stepping in Faerie politics and it didn't end well for almost everyone involved. If I jumped in deeper, it would be even worse.

The question was, did I have a choice? I couldn't fight Seamus and win, not even with three more months of daily practice. He'd had a millennia to get good at magick. He'd kill me.

I crossed my arms. "If you want it so bad, why don't you just take it yourself?"

Seamus was silent.

"You can't, can you?"

"The sword has a long history of choosing its master." He sighed. "It chooses only those whose intentions are pure. I mean to wage war on my brother. I make no excuses. My quest is for vengeance. Innocents will die. It would not come to me. You, however, it may just judge you worthy."

I shook my head. Even if it saved my life, I couldn't hand something that powerful over to Seamus, knowing he meant to kill innocent people with it. "No way. I'd rather fight you myself. Find someone else to do your dirty work."

Seamus sighed again, his shoulder slumping. He didn't look disappointed so much as irritated. "Very well." He stood and turned his back to me.

"Hey, wait. I've still got questions. How is Mara involved? Is she safe? What are you going to do? Dammit, Seamus, answer me!"

But he didn't. He descended stairs behind his throne and disappeared into the blackness below.

# Chapter Seven

I woke up with a start and a gasp, bolting forward and almost throwing myself off the sofa and into my fourteen-year-old son, Hunter. He held out his arms as if to catch me and stepped back. "You okay, mom?"

I checked my head and blinked. A dream? Dreams didn't normally make that much sense. Mostly, mine were filled with dark, disjointed images and voices. No, it had to have been real. But what did it mean? "Fine." My voice came out hoarse and strained. I turned my head and saw light outside the window. "Shit, what time is it?"

It was early August, so school hadn't started back up yet. The lazy dog days of summer were dwindling, but dawn still came early. The brightness could mean it was six or noon and I'd have no way of telling. Hunter often slept until noon unless I woke him, so I assumed it was later rather than earlier.

Before he even answered me, I was off the sofa and scrambling to turn on the coffee. A whimper down the hall alerted me to yet another problem. If I'd slept in, Mia's diaper was going to be a nightmare and there would probably be extra laundry. I pressed the button on the brewer and dashed down the hall to check on Mia. She stood in her crib, grabbing the bars and bouncing up and down on the mattress in a very full diaper. It had yet to leak through to the sheet and blankets, though, so I'd lucked out. I grabbed her and put her on her back on the changing table.

"It's only eight," Hunter announced from the doorway. "Your stupid phone alarm was going off every few minutes and woke me up."

"What phone alarm?" I said, gathering supplies. "My phone went on the fritz last night so it wasn't mine." Mia cried while I changed her as usual, which made it difficult to think. It dawned on me as I closed up Mia's diaper. "It must've been Sal's phone. Mia's supposed to have a doctor's appointment this morning. Shit!"

I dragged myself down the hall, placed Mia in her high chair and dumped some cereal in front of her. When I went to pour the coffee, I spilled some of it on the counter when I turned, burning myself. Of course, when you burn yourself, you flinch and spill more. The boiling hot coffee scalded the pinky on my right hand

and I wound up dropping the whole cup into the sink with a curse. The burn wasn't too bad, and I didn't have time to worry about it. I still had to get Sal up. Doc had said he wanted to see him in the morning, too.

The door to the bedroom creaked when I pushed it open. Sal was still face down in bed where I'd left him, snoozing. Waking a sleeping werewolf, especially an injured one, was more an art than a science. Sometimes, it was better to get a long pole and poke them from across the room. Other times, I was better off setting the alarm for a few minutes in the future and walking away. Sal didn't like to be woken up either way. Sudden, loud noises automatically put him on the defensive and he'd thrash or strike out at anything unfortunate enough to be in close proximity. He'd broken more than one of my cell phones because it rang when he was asleep.

I walked around to the other side of the bed, my side, and slid in next to him. The movement of the mattress stirred him a little, but he didn't fully wake, so I put my arm over his back and kissed the top of his ear. His response was a small groan. "Morning, Tanto."

He lifted his head and tried to roll over, stopping halfway through the motion to clutch his side where the bandage was. "Ugh, how many horses ran me over, Kimosabe?"

"Try sliced open with a magic sword." I tugged his shirt up to look at the blood-soaked bandage. It would need a change. "The Lone Ranger never had to deal with this kind of crazy shit," I said, gently touching the edges of the bandage.

He pushed my hand away. "Help me up. I need a piss and a shower. I smell like day-old bloody gym socks."

"I'm not sure you should get that wet." I stood and went to the other side of the bed to help Sal up. "It still looks pretty bad."

"I'm not going anywhere smelling like this. I'll keep it dry." He grunted when I pulled him up and helped him steady himself. "How long do I have before Mia's appointment?"

"About a half hour. You want me to help you?"

Sal shook his head. He probably needed my help, but his pride was shouting louder than his pain. "Just get the kids ready, will you?"

I smiled and stood on my tiptoes to kiss his chin. "Already on it," I told him and left him at the bathroom door.

Hunter was chewing on cold pizza at the kitchen table, staring distantly. I ruffled his hair as I walked by and he jerked away. "What are your plans today, Hunter?"

He shrugged one shoulder. "Hang out, I guess."

"With who?" I stopped in the living room to do a drive-by pick up, tossing a few toys into Mia's diaper bag.

"People. Whoever."

I slung the bag over my shoulder. "And do what?"

"Stuff."

"What kind of stuff, Hunter?"

He rolled his eyes. "We're going to sit around and drink beers and smoke weed. What is this, Mom? An interrogation? God, do you need to know everything?"

I did my best to keep a neutral expression on my face, even though he probably sensed my surprise at his reaction. Teenage mood swings were one of the hardest parts about being a mom. Hunter's had gotten a lot worse lately. Maybe if I gave him the space and freedom he seemed to crave, things would get better. They'd go back the way they used to be. I missed those days, when he and I could get through a whole conversation without it erupting into accusations and arguments.

"Just be home for dinner, okay, Hunter? And call Sal if you're going to be late."

He rolled his eyes again and pushed up from the table. "Whatever," he growled at me on his way past. A minute later, the door to his room slammed shut and the sound of his Xbox booting up carried through the house.

I sighed and went to get Mia down from the high chair. She toddled after me down the hall as I went to put a few more diapers and wipes in her bag. After I dressed her, we went back down the hall, my hand in hers and she sat on the living room floor, playing while I went in to change. By the time I came back out of the bedroom, Sal had finished with his shower and stood in the bathroom door in his sweatpants, fiddling with a new bandage. The cut was in an awkward position that he couldn't quite reach.

"Here," I said, reaching out to help. "Let me."

"Thanks." He ground it out as if thanking me were as painful as the cut.

I smoothed my hands gently over the medical tape and applied another layer.

"So," Sal said in a tentative tone, "Reed's the bad guy this time around, huh?"

"If I'm right, being controlled by the bad guy somehow. I don't know how involved he is." I grabbed a black t-shirt from the pile of laundry waiting to be put away in the hall and handed it to him.

Sal pulled it on, barely showing any pain as his movements strained the stitches. "And Ed and Mara never stopped seeing each other. That means he lied to me."

"Can he do that?"

"He's not supposed to be able to," Sal growled. "And I'm going to get to the bottom of it."

"Later," I said and went out to fetch his shoes and a pair of socks. I tossed them at him and he caught them. Finally, he winced and grabbed at the wound. "Right now, I'm taking you and Mia to Doc's for your check-ups before I run to work."

~

"Open your mouth and say ahh!"

Doc leaned in close to Mia, who sat on my lap in his office on one of those paper-covered beds. The leather on the corners of the bed was cracked and some of the stuffing showed through. Other cracks and scratches had been covered in duct tape. The sink in the corner of the room was a plastic shop sink. He didn't wear a white doctor's coat, but instead a short-sleeved plaid button-down and a yellow bow tie with pink brains on it. Other than that, the room held all the trimmings of a typical pediatrician's office from posters illustrating the importance of vaccines to a station with superhero stickers.

Mia opened her mouth and stuck out her tongue, mimicking the noise. Doc Ramis shined a light down her throat. "Great. Now, Mia, I need you stand up. We're going to go in to the hall and go for a little walk."

I looked over at her father who stood in silence, leaning his back against the wall, expecting him to go with her. Sal moved to go, but Doc gave a quick shake of his head, the message clear. He wanted to see what she'd do when we weren't watching.

I helped Mia to the floor and she took Doc's outstretched hand. The two of them walked into the hall, leaving the door open behind them.

"What if she falls?" Sal asked, his voice strained. "She's not used to walking on the type of carpet he has in the hall. Maybe we should have taken her shoes off. She does better without shoes."

I sighed and turned to stare through the open door. "What you really want to know is what if there is something wrong with her."

"If there is, I'll rip Doctor Han's spine out," Sal said, followed by a growl.

The feeling was mutual, but killing Doctor Han wouldn't solve anything. We didn't know what, if anything, Marcus' personal physician had done to Mia while she was in Marcus' custody, but Sal blamed both Han and Marcus for Mia's delays. It could have just as easily been her mother, Zoe, but I didn't dare open that can of worms. Sal wasn't fond of his now-deceased ex-wife, but I wasn't going to play the jealous girlfriend and use Zoe as the convenient scapegoat. Zoe might have been a monster in the literal sense, but she cared about her daughter.

"No, you won't," I said, my voice barely above a whisper. "You'll take care of Mia. Han is hiding behind Marcus Kelley, which makes him untouchable so long as you're one of the Kings. Something tells me you don't want to be on their bad side, Sal. Or Marcus'."

"There has to be something we can do."

I pressed a finger to my lips. "Let's wait to hear a diagnosis before we go looking for a cure."

A long moment passed before Doc brought Mia back into the room. He stopped to offer her a sticker from the kiosk before Sal picked her up so he could look her over. She didn't resist, too busy folding her sticker over and over. "What's wrong with her?" Sal insisted.

"Nothing's *wrong*," Doc said, his voice hesitant. "She's in good health overall, but I'm sure you're aware she's missed some milestones over the last year. The poor coordination is your main concern, right?"

I nodded. "Does she need special shoes? Physical therapy?"

Doc crossed his arms. "I think what you're looking at is only one piece of the puzzle. Normally with a kid that's missed so many milestones, I'd recommend a developmental specialist or a pediatrician that's more familiar with this sort of thing." Doc shrugged. "A child psychologist, maybe."

Sal reached out and grabbed Doc by the arm. Doc let out a loud yip and his eyes widened as Sal ground out, "Just say it already!"

"Sal," I said in a warning tone, "let go of the doctor."

He didn't like it, but he let Doc Ramis go just the same.

Doc grabbed at his chest and staggered back a step before reaching up to adjust his glasses which had fallen askew on his face. "First of all, like I've been telling you all along, I'm not a specialist and a specialist might have something different to say. All I can tell you is what I know in a general medical sense, but keep in mind I'm not qualified to give a full diagnosis. My background is in internal medicine, not developmental delays in kids."

"Out with it, Doc," I said before Sal could bark the same thing.

He looked from Sal's face to mine before continuing. "I can't find anything wrong with her physically. Out in the hall just now, she walked just fine. She plays just fine with Leo according to you two, and while she's a little behind verbally, it's not enough to raise a lot of red flags yet. Socially, she makes eye contact and responds to her name." He sighed and pushed his glasses up his pointed nose. "I think Mia's condition is psychological. She has been through a lot."

Sal wrinkled his nose. "What are you saying? She's depressed or something?"

"Post-traumatic stress disorder wouldn't be a stretch, and that's just for starters." He grabbed a prescription pad from a drawer and started scribbling on it. "I'm going to refer you to a child psychologist I know. She's very good, very affordable. Discreet, too."

Sal clutched Mia tighter to his shoulder. "I don't need your shrink, Doc."

"I know what you're thinking," Doc said, tearing the top paper from the pad. "You're thinking that Daphne Petersen can handle this. Well, you're wrong. I know Ms. Petersen's got a degree in counseling, but her area of specialty is addiction, not child psych. Trust me when I say you need a specialist. Someone impartial would be even better." He held the paper out to Sal. "Mia needs to talk about what happened. Honestly, you all do. But, since I know you won't listen..."

Sal leaned forward and showed his teeth. "Listen carefully, doc, 'cause I'm only going to say this one more time. Mia. Doesn't. Need. A shrink. If you're going to dismiss everything as mental, fine. Just do it. But I'm not going to let some asshole fuck up my kid's brain and pump her full of drugs! Now, if you don't have anything else to say, we're done here." He turned and pushed past me and out the door.

I turned to Doc, searching for the right way to apologize. Sal just wanted what was best for Mia. Modern medicine hadn't exactly done her any favors yet, and Sal was extremely distrustful of doctors as a whole, especially since Mia's incident. He was just being overprotective. Again. Forming that into words to explain to a professional like Doc, though, felt impossible.

My mouth fell open and I stuttered through the beginnings of several explanations before Doc raised both palms in a gesture to stop me.

"It's okay, Judah. I understand. He's not the first overprotective parent I've run into." Doc offered a tired smile and held the paper out to me. "But maybe if you could talk to him, get him to see how much it could help Mia. You of all people should know how important mental health is with werewolves. I don't want Mia to be another statistic."

I took the paper from between Doc's fingers and felt my face redden. "I'm sorry he's so difficult."

Doc shrugged. "He can't be anything other than what he is. Which reminds me... How is he? He didn't give me time to look at his shoulder. Is it healing okay?"

"Slow, but it's not swelling or changing colors, so I don't think it's infected. Have you ever seen a blade that isn't silver cut someone like that?"

"No," he answered, shaking his head. "And if it was silver, there'd be some necrosis in the tissue. That cut into him as if he were a regular guy instead of an alpha werewolf. I figured if anyone knew anything about it, it'd be you."

"Sorry, Doc. I'm as lost as the rest of you when it comes to this case." I waved the prescription paper. "Thanks for the referral." I turned my back and walked to the door.

"Judah, wait."

I paused with my hand on the door and turned back, waiting for Doc to add something else, maybe hand me another prescription for antibiotics for Sal, just in case. Instead he stepped up to me and gripped my shoulder. "Mia's not the only one who's been through some traumatic experiences lately. How are you, really?"

My eyebrows shot up and I fought the urge to laugh. My boyfriend had taken a sword to the ribs, Mia probably had some serious mental damage from everything she'd been through, and he wanted to know how *I* was doing? Me, who had taken down giants and wendigos, who had faced vampires and demons head-on? I'd seen more terrifying monsters than he'd probably seen corpses and lived to tell about it. I couldn't tell Doc that, though. He meant well. Doc was one of the good guys.

"I'm fine, Doc," I said with a tight smile.

"Fine isn't the same as good. Losing Chanter was hard on everyone, but you were there."

"I'm a cop. I get shot at a lot, Doc. Buried a lot of friends, too." My throat felt a little tight with that last sentence, but it was true. Forming connections at the academy was frowned on, and I've never been what you'd call a model government employee, so I'd never lost friends in BSI. But there were others who wore the badge, innocents. Alex. I swallowed the invisible cotton stuck in my throat.

"I had an uncle who was a cop," Doc said. "Worked vice. Some of the things he saw... Well, he worked himself through three wives before he married his whiskey and put a bullet in his head. I know all about cop therapy, Judah. Burying yourself in your work so you don't have to face that empty feeling of loss." His fingers squeezed on my shoulder.

I shrugged his hand away. "Look, Doc, I appreciate your concern, but I really am fine. I'd love to stand here with you all day and chat about my feelings, but I'm late for work. Thanks again for the referral."

He nodded once. "Of course. Anytime you need me, Judah, just call."

I shoved the script into my pocket without folding it. The paper wrinkled and crumpled there, which was probably all the use it was going to get. No amount of talking would ever change Sal's mind. He wasn't about to take Mia to a shrink. Maybe if Daphne encouraged him to, but I doubted it. The Silvermoons liked to handle things inside the pack. Taking her to a stranger would mean admitting weakness, defeat. Injury. Predators don't do that, not unless there was no other choice. At the very least, maybe I could get her to talk to Daphne. Sal trusted her.

I met Sal in the parking lot leaning against his truck with his back to the door. A long trail of smoke drifted up to dissipate several feet above his head.

"I thought you said you were going to quit smoking."

He flinched as I spoke. He must have been deep in thought if he didn't hear me approaching.

Sal pulled the cigarette out of his mouth and stared at the smoldering end of it. "Yeah, I should, especially after..." He trailed off.

Chanter. The unspoken name hung between us, heavy like six feet of dirt. Neither of us had spoken it since that day. We buried his name with him. That was their tradition, to not speak of the dead. Sal believed they couldn't rest as long as the living kept bringing them up. I'd never told him how Chanter had helped me the day I saved Mia. If not for him, I would have never survived the spell. Even in death, Chanter had given everything to protect me, something I'd never felt like I deserved.

Sal put the cigarette back in his mouth, took one last, long drag and then dropped it to the ground to crush it with his shoe. "You know, I can't help but wonder how things would be different if he was here. He would've loved being a grandfather. Mia would have been his world." His fingers jerked up to crush against his palm until the knuckles turned white.

I slipped my arm around his and leaned into him. He released the fist. "I'm sure he'd be proud of you and never say it. You two'd be bickering about everything, just like you always did, but deep down, he'd be proud. He always was."

"It doesn't feel the same since he's been gone. Nothing does."

Not knowing what to say, I just stood there. The silence felt hollow. Something chewed at my gut and a new heaviness settled in my chest. In the distance, a car backfired. I felt Sal's arm jerk at the sound as he jumped at it.

He cleared his throat. "You think I should take her to Doc's shrink, don't you?"

"I think Doc knows what he's talking about. I also think you shouldn't throw away an idea just because it's different. But you're her father. You know best."

He tilted his head, resting his cheek on the top of my head. "If it were Hunter, what would you do?"

I'd taken Hunter to counseling before, after he'd been kidnapped by a wendigo. Mostly, that resulted in an hour of him sitting across from the shrink, shrugging his shoulders and crossing his arms. He didn't want to talk and I couldn't make him. After a while, getting stuck with the ninety-dollar-an-hour fee once a week just got to be a waste of money, so we stopped going. It never helped him.

The last shrink I'd seen was the one BSI sent me to in Cincinnati. She told me I should spend less time at work and more time focusing on myself. Yoga, she told me, would help calm my body and mind. I never followed through. The only reason I even went was so that BSI would clear me for duty.

I sighed. "It'd be easier if it were Hunter. He's older. I know he wouldn't cooperate. It might help Mia. One or two appointments can't hurt, can it?"

"I suppose not," Sal said and turned to kiss the top of my head. He tugged open the passenger side door of the truck and held it. "Come on. I'll give you a lift to work."

I slid in next to Mia, who offered me part of a mushy graham cracker she'd found in her car seat. She stuck it in her mouth when I declined.

I suppose if I'd been a perfect stepmom, I would have taken it away from her and wiped her face and fingers with some designer baby wipes. In real life, though, you choose your battles. A mushy graham cracker wasn't going to kill her, and I'd never sprung for designer wipes. That's life as a parent. You always start out with the best intentions, but exhaustion and expenses often dictate more decisions than you care to admit. Real life parenting is dirty, messy business with lots of gray.

Sal climbed in behind the wheel and shook out another cigarette. He put it in his mouth and tugged the lighter from his pocket. I cleared my throat, drawing his attention, and pointed my chin at Mia.

"Right," he grunted and plucked the cigarette from between his lips to tuck it behind his ear.

I frowned. I hadn't seen him smoke two cigarettes in a row for a long time. The stress of everything was getting to him. He needed an outlet, a life away from me and the kids. He needed friends, something the Kings had provided for him before Mia came along. I didn't want him to hang with them any more than he had to, but he needed somewhere to be without the expectation of responsibility. He needed space. I couldn't give him that, not with this case landing on my lap. There wasn't much of anything I could do but be there.

I reached across the seat and put my hand on his. "Thank you."

"For what?" He asked leaning back in his seat, staring straight ahead. "I screw up everything I do."

"You didn't screw me up. You saved me, in more ways than one." I offered a smile that he didn't return.

Sal blew a breath out through his nose and started the truck. "You're late for work," he said.

I withdrew my hand. Dammit, why couldn't I find the words to make everything better?

~

Mia's appointment had been before hours. It was early when Sal dropped me off, so the station wasn't alive yet. It was mostly cops from the redeye shift, dragging themselves to coffee pots or filing their last reports while waiting for the morning shift came in. I got a few nods of acknowledgement but not much else on my way to my office on the second floor.

My office had either been a very large broom closet or a punishment at some point. Nobody gives a cop a corner office that tiny as a reward. I had enough space to hold my six filing cabinets and my desk only if I stacked the cabinets. There was a window, though, and that was the room's only selling point. In the colder months, it was freezing and Hell was probably cooler in the summer. The wi-fi was spotty and I'd shooed away more than one mouse who decided to make my bottom drawer home. But it was my office, dammit, and the door should not have been standing open at nine o'clock on a Friday morning.

I stopped just short of the door at the sound of papers shuffling inside. A filing cabinet drawer rumbled closed. Whoever was in there wasn't trying to be covert.

The door creaked when I pushed it open wider. My intruder was a man of six-foot-three with a crooked nose and wavy, chin-length hair. He'd stripped off his long, leather duster and hung it on the back of my chair. A wide-brimmed leather hat sat amongst the unsorted mail on my desk. A black leather vest, black pants and black boots rounded out the nice goth look that went with his pale skin. He held one of my files, flipping through it with a very unimpressed look on his face.

His gray eyes danced with a smile that his face didn't betray when he flicked them up at me. "*Dobroe utro*, Agent Black. You are late."

# Chapter Eight

"Abe," I said, pushing the door open the rest of the way. "What are you doing here? And why are you in my files?"

He closed the folder and gestured at me with it. "Your office is a mess, Judah. How do you find anything in here?"

I dropped my purse on the floor behind the door and kicked a cardboard box full of more files further into the darkest corner of my office. I was pretty sure there was a colony of man-eating spiders back there. "Mess? It's pronounced organized chaos."

"Do you even have a filing system?"

"Yeah, it's called Windows and control F." I grabbed the file folder out of his hands and dropped it in the closest drawer. "Most of these are just paper back-up copies of stuff I've already digitized." I put my hands on my hips. "So why are you here?"

Special Agent Abraham Viktor Helsinki was one of BSI's top agents and a liaison between the agency and several foreign vampire clans. We'd worked together on only one occasion, though I'd consulted him over the phone several times since then. I didn't usually get along with my co-workers inside the agency, especially letter of the law guys like Abe, but the half-vampire had his own unique charm that made him hard not to like. Since he was technically my superior, I was obligated not to trust him.

As far as I knew, Abe only worked high-profile cases, and I didn't have any of those on my desk that he might be interested in. An abandoned, burning house might have been big news locally, but it probably didn't even make the statewide papers, let alone national news.

Abe's face sobered. He placed his hands on either side of him, gripping the desk as if he were supporting himself. "I am here for two reasons. After several incidents across the country, BSI has opened an investigation into the Vanguards of Humanity."

I raised an eyebrow. "A formal investigation?"

"The brass currently feels that the group here in Concho County does not represent the organization as a whole. This investigation does not have wide support within the upper echelons of government."

One of the lower drawers in my filing cabinet was sticking out, so I kicked it closed. "In other words, the only reason an investigation is happening at all is to placate a minority and nothing's likely to come of it."

"Just so." Abe inclined his head. "Unless someone were to find irrefutable evidence that could not be buried. BSI has sent me without specific instruction. It was heavily implied, however, that burying any evidence I found would be a wise career move."

Dammit. That was even worse. I liked Abe and could trust him to a degree, but he walked on the right side of the line. If BSI had sent him down for a cover-up, he might just do it. Or, maybe he wouldn't. Not following those unspoken instructions would be career suicide. Who knew what BSI would do if their poster boy gave the board of directors the finger?

And then it hit me. If he was planning on a cover-up, I would be the last person he would tell. "You're not going to do it?"

Abe shrugged. "We shall see what evidence I can find. I believe this is a test of loyalty from the new director. He does not trust me. Perhaps he is right not to." He offered a tight-lipped smile that made me feel a little better.

I walked around my desk to sit. The desk wobbled when Abe pushed off it to stand and face me. I pressed the power button on my laptop and waited for it to boot up. "You said you were here for two reasons?"

"Yes," Abe said and then put his hands behind his back so that he was standing in a parade rest. "I am here to evaluate your performance in the field."

My fingers froze as they walked across my keyboard and my heart picked up speed. An evaluation? That could be good or bad news. Considering my history with BSI, it was probably bad. After a bad review, they could can me, and nobody seemed to know what happened to agents if they were removed from their post. All my research said they disappeared and something told me it wasn't because the government was sending them to Tahiti.

I swallowed the lump of nervousness in my throat. "You don't say?"

"They were going to send Gerry but, since I had to come anyway, I volunteered. I told the brass you and I have rapport." His smile widened and he spread his fingers over the surface of my desk. "Do not worry, Judah. Unlike Gerry, I happen to like you. Just do not give me any reason not to and this will be easy for both of us."

I cleared my throat. "Well, then, you might as well make yourself useful while you're here and help me with my caseload. Will you hand me that red folder over there?" I pointed to a pile of folders sitting on a shelf.

"This one?"

"No, other red folder. On the right in the basket on my door. Yeah, that one. Thanks, Abe."

"Abraham or Agent Helsinki, if you please."

My response was an absent affirmative noise. I was too busy flipping through the file, looking for a name among the dossiers there. I flipped one of the pages over and scanned the back before I found what I was looking for on the next page. Hector Demetrius' name was halfway down the page. It sat alongside the other fifty names of new occupants in Concho County that I still hadn't got out to visit as of last week. I was supposed to check in with every name on the list and see if they needed anything. Unfortunately, there were so many new BSI registered residents in Concho County every month that I was hopelessly behind.

I pulled the page out and held it out to Abe. "Hector Demetrius," I said. "Registered practitioner. Nothing impressive. Looks like he barely registered on the XYZ scale."

XYZ was short for the Yates-Zimmerman scale. Whenever the bureau printed results of the XYZ, they printed out a line and stuck a big, red X at the corresponding point. Hence, XYZ. The further along the line the X, the more dangerous BSI considered the practitioner to be.

Abe frowned. "If he is so unremarkable, then why are you pointing him out?"

"He's part of a case I'm working. You did hear about the fire out by Eola?"

He nodded once. "The arson case, yes. I heard about it on the radio. He is one of your suspects?"

I opened my middle desk drawer, pulled out a clean file folder and stuck the page inside after circling his name. "No. The primary suspect in the case is Father Gideon Reed. You met him last time you were in town. Unfortunately, I have no idea where he is. I'm waiting on a warrant to go through so we can search Reed's house. It should be here any minute, actually."

"And this Hector Demetrius has what to do with our case then?"

“He and his group own the property where the barn caught fire. He was evasive and even insulting when we tried to question him last night and I have eyewitness testimony that says there was rem being grown in there. When we drove out to the main building, I saw more greenhouses. I think this guy is in on the rem trade.” I pulled a thicker file folder from the corner of my desk and flipped it open. Stapled to the inside was Mara’s picture. After looking at it a moment, I spun the whole folder around for Abe to see. “And Mara is involved.”

Abe drew his hand over his chin with a gloved hand. “You have a thing for hopeless causes, do you not, Judah? Yet you cannot find time to organize your office.”

“Mara was never hopeless, just a little lost.” I jabbed a finger at her picture. “She’s been avoiding me. I don’t know her status, state of mind or anything. I spoke to her at the compound, and she seemed okay, but according to my witness, she may have been taken against her will. I think Hector is hiding Reed or they’re working together. He’s sure as hell not himself. I need to bring them both in.”

There was a knock at the door and Quincy Adams, Tindall’s old partner, stuck his head in. The precinct hadn’t yet given him a replacement, so he was doing the detective thing solo. He’d lost enough weight that it showed in his cheeks and his face had a permanently frazzled look in it. He held up a handful of papers. “Were you waiting on some warrants? They just got faxed over.” His eyes traveled to Abe and then widened. “Sorry, darlin’. Didn’t know you were in a meetin’.”

Abe held out his hand and Quincy deposited the papers with a mumble of thanks before he slinked away. I stood, expecting Abe to hand the warrants over, but he decided to flip through them first. “‘All available members of SRT are prepared to assist with the execution of the warrant at your command,’” he read. “What is SRT?”

“You still driving that ugly truck, Abe?”

He sighed. “It’s Abraham and yes.”

“Get your coat. I’ll brief you on the way.”

~

I gave Abe the short version of everything and brought him up to speed on the way across town after calling Espinoza. Most of SRT was already on the rez when I called and they were just waiting for my signal. The two missing members, Espinoza said, were questioning someone else on an unrelated case. The whole team was in position by the time I arrived at the church.

Paint Rock's only church was a small, white and steepled building. Reed rented a power washer from someplace in Eden once a month to keep the dust from settling into the siding and re-painted it once every few months. He spent hours every week pulling weeds and placing rocks strategically around the property so that it stayed attractive. He loved his church, but he loved the people in Paint Rock even more. He made it a point to visit the sick and troubled, even those who didn't attend church. That was the kind of person Reed was. I still couldn't believe he'd attacked me and Ed like that. The whole thing felt off.

Reed lived in a tiny, white two-bedroom house behind the church surrounded by an iron fence. Stepping stones traced a path from the back door of the church all the way up to a gate. Red-tipped Yucca plants brushed against the fence in the light wind, creating the illusion of whispering as I walked toward the house.

The black van that SRT had arrived in sat behind the church and, when Abe and I came into view, the double doors in the back opened. Four officers in modified SWAT gear emerged. Black, Kevlar body armor rustled and I paused, worried, when I saw they were armed with M4s.

Espinoza got out of the front of the van and walked toward us. He wasn't wearing all the same tactical gear, but he did have the vest on over his uniform.

"Reed lives alone with his cat," I said to Espinoza. "I hardly think his cat warrants military grade weapons response, Espinoza."

He gestured to the four men who had already assumed defensive positions at the gate. "Old Boy Scout motto. Always be prepared. You don't know what's hiding behind that door, Black. Wards, werewolves, shapeshifters, giants..." He shrugged.

Abe bobbed his head in agreement. "She does tend to draw the attention of trouble."

"Good to know." Espinoza thrust out a hand at Abe. "Lieutenant Espinoza of the Concho County Special Response Team."

"Special Agent Abraham Helsinki," Abe answered as the two traded grips.

Espinoza nodded. "My guys are carrying basic protective wards on their equipment but, given that you two are more equipped to deal with any magical protections that might be in place, you two can take point and we'll cover your six."

"Good enough for me," I said as we started toward the fence gate.

"What exactly are we looking for?" Abe asked.

"Anything that tells us about Reed's state of mind, evidence he was involved with rem, or that he knew Hector Demetrius. Espinoza, did Hector happen to show up?"

"No, but there is someone at the station you'll want to talk to."

"Who?"

Espinoza paused at the gate and stopped to address me, hooking his fingers in his belt. "Remember that unrelated case I mentioned when you called about the warrant? Might not be so unrelated after all. Trespassing and harassment complaints got filed this morning by some girl out at the compound. Guy we arrested for trespassing happens to be your witness, Black. The kid who was fighting Reed last night."

I closed my hands into fists. "Ed. I'm going to wring his neck if he compromised this investigation. Are they pressing charges?"

"Don't know yet. It was all pending when I left." Espinoza shook his head and then gestured to the gate. "This is as far as me and my guys go until you've checked for magickal booby traps."

Abe slid in front of me. "Allow me." Abe placed a hand on the gate handle and raised an eyebrow at me.

I was more than a little irritated at being shoved aside. He knew I was just as capable as him at disabling any defenses that were on the property.

"Wards are my specialty," Abe said with a smug grin.

He unhooked the gate and the SRT officers standing nearby stiffened. "Iron disrupts the flow of magick," Abe explained with all the patience of an intro level professor. "The iron fence forms a complete circle around the property. Unless it is broken, even the most skilled practitioner would not be able to see what magicks wait on the other side."

The smile that Abe flashed me made me feel stupid for ever thinking he would discount me as an agent. He knew better. The two of us had already fought side-by-side before. By taking command of the operation, he hoped to teach SRT a few things before they got in over their heads. It hadn't been about me and my abilities at all. I rolled my shoulders and pretended not to notice.

Abe swung open the gate and extended both hands into the space the fence gate had once occupied, his thumb and two fingers extended. "The walkway and front yard are laced with an early warning detection system. There is something stronger attached to the deadbolt ahead and laid over the windows, but I cannot determine its purpose at this distance." He lowered his hands. "The house is safe to approach, but do not touch the doors or windows until I have finished."

He took off through the gate and up the walkway, his long strides leaving the rest of us scrambling to catch up. I almost had to run to arrive on Reed's porch in the same breath as Abe. He stood in front of the door, fingers extended in the same position he'd used a moment ago, eyes closed. "Your priest has a knack for fire spells." A smile touched Abe's voice, though it didn't show on his face. "Opening the door uninvited would be very bad for anyone's health."

I extended a hand toward the window in front of me and sent a quick pulse of magick into the air, feeling for Reed's wards. True to Abe's word, there was something there, something with enough power to knock me on my ass, but I couldn't tell what kind of ward it was or what it might do once triggered. I withdrew my hand. "Can you undo it?"

"Not if you wish it to remain a secret. The moment I do, he and anyone else who is watching this location through magickal means will be aware that his protections are down."

Abe gave me a wary look. He hadn't said it aloud, but he was worried someone else might be watching and waiting for a chance to come in and search the place. We might be doing their dirty work for them, breaking down the wards. Once we left the scene, anything we didn't take with us in an evidence box would be free for the taking.

I nodded once. "Break it down."

He closed his eyes again. The air on the porch took on a heavier quality, making it more difficult to breathe and magick hummed briefly against the door. Then there was a loud pop, a spark of light, and the door popped open of its own accord.

Abe was the first one through the door. He took two steps and then fell forward, flailing like a cartoon character. Reed's skinny, white cat scrambled out of the way, narrowly avoiding Abe falling on him. Abe crashed to the floor with a resounding thud. The cat flicked his tail and jumped up onto Abe's back where he proceeded to sit and lick his paw without so much as acknowledging the rest of us. I stifled a chuckle while Abe had a few choice words in Russian for the cat, who scampered off when Abe pushed himself up off the floor. Abe turned to sneer back at the doorway while several of the SRT guys snickered at him. "You should have warned me about the familiar, Judah."

I stepped into the narrow hallway and sidestepped Abe. "Pretty sure he's just a cat and not a familiar. Come on. We'll take the room at the end of the hall. The rest of you, fan out."

Abe stood, dusted himself off and muttered something about cats never being just cats.

The room at the end of the hall was Reed's living room. I'd only been in Reed's house a few times before, but I thought he was an immaculate housekeeper based on how he kept the rest of the place. The living room reflected that. His coffee table held neat stacks of newspapers and a notebook with a pen resting against the pages. An old, rotary-style phone sat next to the notebook. Behind the coffee table was a well-loved sofa with a Navajo blanket thrown on the back. His Bible sat open on the cushions beside where he would have been sitting if he were writing in the notebook.

Abe went to check out the sofa and the items on it while I walked the perimeter of the room. Reed's walls were mostly bare. There wasn't a photograph to be found anywhere in the room and no knick-knacks. That made the few items on display even more noticeable. I stopped in front of an oil painting depicting a dark-skinned man in a striped tunic holding an infant. The artist had captured Joseph's fatherly smile as he looked down at his crying son. It was an odd choice of moments to capture, the Son of God crying helpless just like any other child and his father attempting to calm him with a calloused hand on the babe's chest.

"Looks like a diary."

I glanced at the notebook. "More like a devotional journal. Looks like he stopped mid-sentence, too." I shrugged. "Not a smoking gun, but might be useful. I'd bag it."

I turned back to the wall and walked along it until I came to a bookshelf. It held exactly what you'd expect to find in a priest's bookshelf. Devotionals, various editions of the Bible, theological guides, concordances, atlases, and histories lined the shelves. The third shelf was only half full, the books stopping abruptly halfway across the shelf against a kneeling angel bookend.

The living room began to feel crowded as more SRT officers flooded in, so I walked back along the wall to where another narrow hallway waited. An agent stood at the mouth of the hall at a parade rest, having searched the rooms down the hall and found them clear. I nodded to him and stepped past to search the first door on the left.

It looked like a bedroom. Reed's neat freak streak disappeared. The room was a mess. Blankets had been torn from the bed, dresser drawers pulled out and turned over. Reed was a neat freak, and every man's bedroom is his sanctuary. If it was a mess in there, it was because someone else had made it that way. The place was tossed, but not destroyed. Someone else had been searching for something, someone who could get past Reed's wards.

I stepped in cautiously, sweeping my eyes back and forth and drawing my gun. I kept the barrel pointed at the floor. SRT had declared the house clear, but they could have missed something or someone, especially if they weren't looking for signs of magick.

"Who were you and what were you looking for?" I muttered. "And the better question is, did you find it?"

I spun at a sudden sound, leveling my gun at the closet. A dark shape shifted on the other side. "Come out with your hands on the back of your head!" I shouted. "I know you're in there."

"Take it easy, love" said a familiar voice. The white slatted doors of the closet slid aside and Creven stepped out with his hands in the air. "And don't alert your vampire friend that I'm here." He pressed one finger to his lips.

I cast a look behind me at the open door, dropped my gun and stepped over to close it. "What the hell, Creven? This is an active investigation and my suspect's home. You can't just break in here and contaminate any evidence! What are you doing here?"

Creven slowly lowered his hands. "Orders from above," he reported. "It's unrelated to your investigation."

"I find that hard to believe," I said, dropping my gun back into its holster. "You just happen to be tossing the home of my suspect? Orders from who? And what are you looking for?"

Creven pressed his lips together. "Those answers are more complicated than you realize, lass."

"Creven, so help me—"

I stopped when the elf's head shot up, eyes glued to the door. A heartbeat later, muffled screams sounded on the other side of the door followed by rapid gunfire that lasted only a few seconds before going eerily silent. I looked to Creven for an explanation, but he shook his head. This wasn't him or whoever had hired him. Neither of us spoke. We passed about five seconds in silence before we noticed the smoke coming from cracks around the door.

# Chapter Nine

Where there's smoke, there's fire. In this case, it must have been on the other side of the door, meaning Espinoza, Abe and members of SRT were either trapped in it, had retreated to a safe distance, or they were dead. The gunfire and its abrupt end suggested the latter. With the smoke pouring in and the temperature steadily rising, Creven and I were about to meet the same fate if we didn't act quickly.

I grabbed the blanket off the bed and stuffed it firm against the bottom of the hidden door. My knuckle brushed the doorknob and I came away with several blisters. The fire had to be right outside the door for it to be that hot.

"Can you get the door open?" Creven asked as I stumbled back away from the door, cradling my burned hand. He stood with the back of his hand against his mouth, ducking just beneath the growing ceiling of smoke.

I shook my head. "It's already too hot. Nobody's getting that open without severe burns and even if we did, we'd be walking into fire."

"What about a window?" Creven turned and ran to the window, pulling it open.

Something warm brushed against my leg. I shouted and almost jumped out of my skin before I realized it was Reed's cat. Had he followed us in? No, I would have seen him. How the heck did he get in? He meowed at me and paced to the window. The cat stopped, turned back to look at me, flicked his tail once, and then jumped out the window.

I turned to look longingly at the door. We could get out, but we might not be able to get back in to help Abe and the others. What if they were trapped or injured?

"You're thinkin' of rescuing them, aren't you?" Creven said from halfway out the window.

"Can you make enough water to flood out the fire?"

He sighed, looked out the window. "My focus is outside. I'll be useless without it, lass. Come on, let's go. Maybe they all got out?"

I stepped back up to the door. The smoke pouring through it was more intense now, burning my eyes and scorching my lungs. Even with my shirt over my mouth and nose, I couldn't get within a few feet of the door. Creven was right. Without focusing his magick through his staff, his magick could go haywire and make things worse. If we hurried, we might still be able to come in the front. Maybe the fire hadn't spread that far.

I turned and ran to the window, feeling blindly for the far wall. Creven grabbed my hand and pulled me through.

We landed on a slight hill at the back end of Reed's house. The air above me was painfully hot on the back of my neck. I could hear fire crackling and see glowing debris and smoke floating in the air. I tumbled down the slight slope before standing on wobbly legs to look up at the house.

It was engulfed in flames that shot ten feet into the air. The sirens and horns of a firetruck drowned out everything but the loud crackling of the fire, but they didn't have any water going down on the blaze, at least not that I could see. I jogged back up the hill alongside Creven and came around the side of the house to the sound of shouting voices. Two members of SRT stood there and turned their weapons on me when we came up on them unexpectedly.

I threw my arms up in a surrender gesture. "Easy, boys."

They lowered their guns, but eyed Creven with suspicion.

"This is my friend," I explained. "What happened? Is anyone still inside?"

"Fire came out of nowhere," the one on the right reported. "I thought I saw someone walking through the fire and let off a few rounds, but it got too hot too fast. The lieutenant and your partner stayed behind to try and get to you. We tried to go back for them but we can't get through the front door." He turned away.

"Stay here and secure the scene," I said, nodding. "We'll handle it."

"Aye," Creven added. "Just let me fetch my staff. I'll be right back."

We broke into a run back to the front of the house. Before I saw it from the front, I was certain that I could create a small bubble of air around myself or use my shield to get through the fire and get the three men trapped inside. When we came around the front, however, I had to reassess my chances of success. The fire had raged out of control. Huge arms of it flashed across the doorway which stood behind a wall of heat that stretched to where we stood. The wood groaned against the weight of itself. Inside, we could hear beams cracking and falling. Even in full protective gear, the firefighters had decided it was safer to stand back rather than attempt a rescue.

My tiny little shield wasn't going to be enough.

A new commotion made me turn around. Creven was trying to push his way past the line of other spectators who had gathered and the firefighters were pushing him back. "Let him through!" I shouted. The police stepped aside and Creven rushed to my side.

"Stick close," he said, shifting his staff. "If Luck is with us, we should be able to manage a rescue without becomin' a barbeque ourselves." He didn't say anything else, just turned his staff sideways and marched toward the burning building. The bright blue hue of a semi-circular shield enveloped us on three sides.

I kept as close as I could. The porch creaked as we stepped up onto it. Fire leapt up off the railing dangerously close to my unprotected arm and I jerked back. Creven steadied me with a hand. "Don't fear it, love. It's not a normal fire. This fire is something else." He ducked through the front door with his staff still out in front of him. I followed.

The inner hallway was an oven of distorted wood. The fire licked at the walls here and there, but hadn't yet taken hold in the center of the house. Heat and smoke were their own problems, though. It made the air almost unbreathable. Every gasp felt like swallowing glowing, hot ash.

"Where?" Creven shouted over the sound of breaking glass and roaring fire.

"Straight ahead." I hoped Espinoza and Abe were in the living room. Anywhere else, and we'd lose valuable time searching for them. Creven broke into a run and I worked to keep up with him.

The living room was in a full blaze, with fire leaping from the sofa to the chairs and the wall. The bookcase was a charred, black inferno. I scanned the room, frantic to find Espinoza and Abe. "There!" I shouted and pointed to two still bodies curled up under the broken coffee table. "Let's get them out, Creven!"

"Let's do something to make the room a little more bearable first. Hold your breath, love!" Creven spun his staff once and then slammed the end of it into the floor. The floorboards splintered and water sprang up out of the hole he'd made with all the force of a geyser. Hundreds of gallons of water flooded into the room all at once and slammed into the fire where it went out with a hiss.

I scrambled forward to pull bits of wood and glass off Espinoza and Abe. With a little magick, I found the strength to hoist them both up with a grunt before the flood swallowed them. Creven waded through the water to come and help me fight my way to the window on the far side of the room. He shattered the glass with his staff and rolled the bulbous end around the edge, knocking out the rest of the glass before helping me hoist Abe through the window to the firefighters on the other side.

We picked up Espinoza and had him halfway through when a blast of fresh fire struck the wall beside me. I let go of Espinoza to dodge aside and he fell out the window, hopefully not breaking his neck when he hit the ground. I tried to grab the wall, but slipped on the torrent of water still rushing into the room and went down on my back just in time to see Reed close on Creven. Creven brought up his arm, ready to call his protective shield, but he wasn't fast enough. The sword bit into the meat of Creven's forearm and came away bloody. Creven stumbled back, his shield flickering into place as he hit the ground on his back. The water all around him ran red.

"I told you to stay away from me," Reed said, turning his attention to me. He raised the sword again. I scrambled away from him toward the hallway, but couldn't beat his advance. In just a few strides, Reed stood over me, the sword pointed at my throat. "Now I don't have a choice." He gripped the sword with both hands and drove it down at the center of my neck.

I rolled out of the way just in time. Reed pulled the sword free of the warped wood and hacked at me. Without a weapon, all I could do was try to stay out of the way. I rolled and slid out of the way, all the while doing my best to scoot out of his range. As he swung at me and I repeatedly moved out of the way, I lost track of where I was in the room and let him back me into a corner. Reed closed on me and readied a killing blow.

Just as he raised his sword, there was a loud whirring sound followed by a *thunk*. Reed staggered on his feet, grabbed at the back of his head, and turned to snarl at Creven who stood on the other side of the room, poised as if he's just thrown a javelin instead of his staff.

"Pick on someone yer own weight class, padre," the elf said and smirked.

A loud hiss carried through the room followed by a rattle and a snake reared up out of the water. It struck at Reed who swung his sword, but the snake was too fast. It bit deep into Reed's arm.

He jerked the snake out of his arm and threw it at Creven. When the elf caught it, the snake stiffened and transformed back into his enchanted staff. Reed charged at him with the sword. Creven blocked his advance with the staff.

I jerked my gun up from the holster and aimed it at Reed's back. I should have pulled the trigger. Every muscle in my body screamed for me to squeeze it, defend Creven by shooting Reed. Three shots. Stop the suspect with deadly force. Save your friend, your partner. No man left behind.

But Reed was my friend, too. He didn't deserve to die. Something else was going on. Killing him was wrong. My hands shook.

Creven fell on his rear. Reed brought the sword down and it sliced through the wood with ease. With his back against the wall, there was nowhere else for Creven to go. I saw the realization in his face as he looked at me in a panic. I had to make a decision. Shoot Reed and save Creven, or let Reed kill Creven and hope that I could save Reed.

I closed my eyes, let my breath out and pulled the trigger.

The gunshot rang in my ears. I stood frozen, too afraid to look at the aftermath for a moment, but self-preservation took over. If I had missed, Reed could still come for me. My eyes snapped open. Reed lay in a puddle, wheezing and gasping, his eyes wide. Creven had jumped up and backed away, only the top part of his staff still in his hand. He pointed the knobby end of it at Reed with a shaky hand.

Reed made a deep, rasping, sucking sound and touched a spreading dark stain on his white collar. "Ju...dah..." he gasped and then fell over.

# Chapter Ten

The gun fell from my hands and into the spreading water with a dull plunk. Water sloshed up around my shin as I closed on Reed, my legs moving of their own accord. "Medic!" I shouted as I fell to my knees beside him. "We need help in here!"

The fire was still raging down the hall and wherever the water hadn't touched. A portion of the ceiling on the other side of the room collapsed. I put my hands up and ducked my head on instinct.

Creven scrambled to his feet and swayed before tugging on my shirt, trying to pull me up. I ignored his insistent tugging and pressed my fingers to Reed's neck. There was a lot of blood, but he still had a pulse. "Help me!" I shouted to Creven and put my arms under Reed's, pulling him up.

He was heavy, too heavy for me to move on my own under normal circumstances. If not for the icy feeling of adrenaline still pumping through me, I'd never have been able to get him anywhere. I grunted and managed to drag him a few feet. Creven cradled his bleeding arm and fumbled with Reed's legs using the other. Somehow, the two of us managed to get enough of him out the window that the guys on the other side could take over.

Creven and I both half-climbed, half-tripped out the same window and I lay there on the damp grass, staring up at the clear blue sky streaked with gray smoke. Firefighters in full gear hovered in my vision and lowered an uncomfortable piece of plastic over my mouth and nose. Somewhere in the distant, thinking part of my brain, I registered it as oxygen. The fog over my brain lessened and the full force of all the magick I'd used to hoist three men through a window and fight Reed hit. Every muscle in my body felt like someone had tenderized me with a sledgehammer. The effort of drawing in breath almost felt like too much.

With a small force of will, I turned my head sideways. Half the side yard was a black, simmering wasteland. The firefighters were scrambling to put out the last bits of flame with their hoses. Creven had put pressure on the gash in his arm, but it didn't look like it had slowed the bleeding much. Blood still poured out from between his fingers. The EMT peeled Creven's fingers away and even more blood came out. He turned, shouted a series of orders for supplies at someone and then turned back to Creven.

With the charred grass, the smoldering remains of the house, the squad of police, firefighters and EMTs crowding in around the house, it didn't look like the house had just caught fire. It looked like a war zone.

A dull thud on the other side of me made me turn my head back the other way. Abe knelt next to me and put a hand on my shoulder. He gave me a nod of thanks. "Are you hurt?"

I tried to tell him it was just me, overextending my magickal muscles so to speak, but it came out as a garbled, "Hrumphel."

"I have seen bomb blasts close up," Abe said. "Some of them have been less destructive. You did the right thing, shooting Father Reed."

My hand flopped up to grip the oxygen mask over my face and move it aside. "How bad is he?"

As if in answer, a squad gave a loud sound of its horn and its siren cut through the cacophony of sound. Abe glanced up. "On his way to the hospital, which is where you should go as well."

I pawed at the strap that kept the oxygen mask on me and fumbled to pull it off. Abe reached down to help. "Can't. Hospital won't help. Too much magick too fast. Just need rest. Be fine soon."

Abe sighed, raised one knee out of the mud and leaned on it. "I did not suspect you would listen to reason. Well, if you are going to lie there and refuse treatment like the stubborn woman you are, you might as well tell me about Creven. What is he doing here?"

"Helping." My throat felt raw, my head floating. I couldn't tell him Creven had broken into the place to look for something, mostly because I didn't know what it was he'd wanted. The elf might still have it on him, and I couldn't let Creven get arrested, not while he was still my teacher.

Abe shook his head at my non-answer and gripped me by the forearms. "Come on, then. Let us get you up and on your feet where you belong."

He stood, pulling me along with him. The world turned into a tilt-a-wheel and my stomach lurched into my throat. My legs shook with the effort of keeping me upright. Abe gave me just enough support to stand without holding me up until I finally steadied myself.

"A moment of your time, lass?"

Creven's voice beside me grabbed my attention and held it.

They'd loaded him onto a wheeled gurney in a sitting position and had heavy, bloodstained gauze pads taped over his arm. Beads of sweat dotted his pale forehead. He glanced to Abe and added, "Alone."

"I'll be fine," I told Abe. "Go check on Espinoza, will you? He's human. He won't recover as quick as you did."

Abe frowned, but let me go without any verbal protest.

I gripped the railing of the gurney. "I need answers, Creven. I'm going to have to explain what you were doing in there."

He shifted his injured arm and grimaced. "In me trousers, lass. Make sure no one sees."

My eyebrow shot up. "You want me to do what now?"

"The pocket, Judah. Now's not the time for flirtin'."

"What'll I find there if I go digging?"

Creven swallowed. "Answers, probably to questions you never thought you needed to ask."

"This had better not be some kind of trick." I sighed, lifted my right arm and reached across for his pocket.

Creven grabbed my wrist with his one good arm. A grave shadow crossed his face as he warned, "Make sure no one else in BSI knows. Not even your new partner. Promise me. Swear it."

I swallowed the scratchy, steel wool feeling in my throat. Such promises carried a lot of weight, especially when they were made with a fae. Creven had never used my word against me like most fae. The seriousness with which he spoke set off alarm bells in my head.

"I swear it, Creven. I won't show Abe or anyone else in BSI."

He nodded, his face relaxing, and took his hand from around my wrist.

Fishing around in someone else's pockets is always awkward. Creven was no exception. Considering how short I was, I had to lean across him to do it. Holding myself up while leaning forward proved to be difficult. Luckily, whatever he had hidden there wasn't anything small. My fingers closed on something metallic and thin. It snagged on the inside of his pocket as I slid it out, but came free with a little wiggling.

The thing I held in my hands was only slightly bigger than a deck of playing cards. It was a metal case with a white label bearing all kinds of technical specs I didn't understand. I did recognize it, however, from when I'd had to replace one in my laptop a few years back.

"A hard drive?" I asked, searching Creven's face for answers. "Reed's? Creven, who asked you to get this?"

He gave a little shake of his head. "Quick, get it out of sight, Judah. Remember your promise."

The EMTs, who had been standing nervously a few feet away, finally had enough standing around and came to collect Creven. I hurriedly jammed the hard drive into my jeans, hoping my clothes weren't damp enough to damage it.

"There's one more thing you should know," Creven said, leaning forward to catch my eye.

"Sir, please try not to talk," one of the paramedics said, strapping him in.

"What is it, Creven?"

He winced as the paramedics tightened the straps. "It's Seamus. He's here."

"He swore not to harm me for a year and a day."

"Aye, he did, but that won't stop him from using an agent to do it on his behalf. This could just as well be him as anyone else."

"That's enough," The EMTs lifted the rails on the gurney and rushed him toward the waiting squad.

"What did the elf want?"

My head snapped back to see Abe standing beside me, his head tilted to the side quizzically. "Nothing," I answered, clearing my throat. "Nothing too serious, anyway. Just wanted to make sure he wasn't in trouble. He did kind of intrude on a police investigation, Abe."

Abe gave me a sideways look, his face blank. I couldn't tell whether or not he bought it. Could half-vampires hear lies in your heartbeat like vampires or smell them like werewolves? Shit, I wished I'd thought of that before I opened my big mouth. I cleared my throat again.

Abe held a bottle of water out to me. I took it, unscrewed the cap and dumped half of it in my mouth. The other half went to washing soot and blood from my hands. "Well, you are standing on your own," Abe said. "I am surprised at how quickly you have managed to recover. Good, for a human."

I tipped the water bottle up and swallowed the last of the water. "How's Espinoza?"

Espinoza, who sat on the grass a short distance away, coughed, drawing my attention. He looked terrible, his face covered in streaks of black and gray. He held an empty water bottle in his hand that he laid on the grass in front of him. "Is this Seamus someone I should know about?"

"I don't think so." I shifted my right hand away from my pocket, hoping he hadn't watched my exchange with Creven. "I'm going to need to talk to Ed as soon as possible."

Both men frowned at my change of subject. "Ed Petersen. How is he connected to this case?" Abe asked.

"He's Mara's boyfriend, and he's not buying that Mara joined the Adventists voluntarily. I can't say I blame him. She's never struck me as a girl to fall in with a cult. Something else is going on here. Reed wasn't himself, either. Too many people are acting contrary to their personalities, Abe. We need to get to the bottom of this."

Abe raised his head to look at Espinoza. "Will you live?"

"Smoke inhalation's a bitch," Espinoza answered. "But I'll be good. Let me catch my breath and deal with this shit before I start digging up what I can through informants, see if anyone's seen anything. In the meantime, Judah, you'd better go down to the station in Eden and bail out your werewolf friend. You can expedite his release by claiming he's a key witness. Can't promise those trespassing and harassment charges will go away, though. I'll call you when I know more, I guess."

"Call me? Call me how? My phone died last night."

Espinoza pulled a cell phone from his pocket and tossed it to me. "Take it. It's a burner. You ought to invest in a couple dozen of those."

I thanked him and dropped the phone in my other pocket.

"Would you like me to give you a ride?" Abe offered.

Under normal circumstances, I would have accepted. The weight of the stolen hard drive in my pocket, however, reminded me that my bailing out Ed would serve a dual purpose. If anyone could find out what was on that hard drive and why Creven might have been sent to steal it, it would be Ed. But I wasn't in any condition to drive the twenty miles to Eden from Paint Rock, either.

Espinoza seemed to sense my hesitance and dug in his pocket, pulled out a set of keys and tossed them to me. "She's parked around the corner from the church. Consider it a test drive. If you like her better than your Firebird, we'll talk about a trade."

"Thanks again, Espinoza." I waved to Abe and let the keys dangle from my fingers. "Can you finish up here while I go deal with this other mess?"

Abe pursed his lips. "You are certain you are fine to drive? A moment ago, you could barely stand."

"I'm fine." Another lie. Maybe Abe wouldn't pick up on that one either. My heart rate could be elevated for any number of reasons. I'd just shot a man and jumped out of a burning building, after all. I still ached all over, and I wouldn't be able to tap into my magick for a while unless I wanted to completely lose my ability to walk or move, but I wasn't going to die. I suppose there was a grain of truth in my lie. I was more fine than Reed, anyway.

The image of him bleeding out in the back of a squad on his way to the hospital hit me. Gideon Reed had been my friend, even if we hadn't always gotten along, and I knew deep down that he was innocent. Someone or something else was making him attack people. No matter how many times Abe assured me shooting him was the right thing to do, it still felt wrong. You don't shoot your friends.

I closed my hand around the bright red key fob and turned my back to Abe and Espinoza to walk away. My feet felt like they had lead weights attached, and my hip hurt something awful, but I fought the limp. Abe's eyes made the back of my neck itch until I slipped around the corner and stopped to press my back against the wall of another building. The air I'd been holding in my lungs escaped in a slow breath. My shoulders relaxed as the pounding in my chest faded to a gentle flutter. I slipped my fingers into my pocket to feel the hard drive sitting there.

*Answers to questions I never thought to ask.* What the hell did that mean? Why would Creven want me to keep it from BSI specifically? Did Reed have dirt on BSI? That didn't make sense. Reed was a priest. It wasn't like he kept confessions on his hard drive. Whatever it was, it had to be something big. Creven wouldn't have gone after it if it wasn't.

Aside from being my magick tutor, Creven also worked as Kim Kelley's bodyguard, which linked him to the vampire, Marcus Kelley. I'd long suspected Marcus was up to something. The guy was the CEO of a multi-billion dollar pharmaceutical company that had employed a wendigo named LeDuc, plus whatever the hell

Doctor Han was. His company, Fitz Pharmaceuticals, had an exclusive government contract to provide testing materials for supernaturals. It was Fitz's equipment every school, employer, and agency in the country used to identify supernaturals. Even BSI used them.

*Could that be the link?* I wondered, gliding my thumb over the cool surface of the hard drive. *Maybe what I've got here isn't about BSI at all, but dirt on Marcus Kelley.* He wouldn't want BSI to have that and he just might send Creven to get it. But then why hand it over to me? That didn't fit. Besides, why would Reed be looking into Marcus? He worked for Marcus as far as I could tell. Half of Concho County worked for him.

I needed to know what was on that hard drive and the only person who could help me was sitting in a holding cell at Eden PD.

I pushed off the wall with a grimace and stumbled down the sidewalk, mashing my thumb on the lock button of the key fob. A car up the block chirped and I stopped in my tracks at the sight of what he considered a trade for my beat up, mismatched old Firebird. Espinoza drove what looked like a brand new, jet black Dodge Charger SRT Hellcat with tinted windows. I hit the button again, just to make sure. The headlights lit up and it gave a quick beep. There was no mistaking it. This was the car he'd loaned me.

I stole a glance over my shoulder, wondering if he'd hit his head on the way out of the building after all. But hey, I wasn't allowed to look a gift car in the grill. I unlocked it, pulled open the door and peered in on black leather interior with red accents. When I sank into the seat and it contoured to my aching rear, I thought I'd fallen in love and things couldn't get any better. Then, I put the key in the ignition and started her up. She *purred*. There was no other word for it.

The CD turned over and ACDC's Thunderstruck kicked on. I stared at the bars jumping up and down on the screen set beside the dash. "God, Espinoza. Where have you been all my life?"

I pressed down the parking break and shifted the wheel. "Well, let's see what this baby can do," I said and gave the car a little gas.

# Chapter Eleven

I got from Paint Rock to the police station exit in Eden in twelve minutes flat. Two minutes of that were spent sitting at the border crossing on the way out of Paint Rock while they checked my ID and ran my tags. Guess I must've been driving it like I stole it or something. It was easy to do in a car like that where eighty felt more like forty. Driving down the street to the station at twenty-five felt like torture.

The parking lot beside the station was mostly full, but Espinoza had a pass sitting in his dash with the number thirteen on it, so I pulled into the lot anyway. Each space was numbered and, like I thought, space number thirteen was empty. I carefully pulled into it, flanked on either side by dusty trucks.

The hospital cast its shadow directly over the main branch of the Eden police department. The police headquarters were significantly smaller than the hospital, but that didn't make it a less impressive piece of modern architecture. It had gotten a facelift in the last few years. The whole front was made of reflective glass, which made it look like there were two flags out front, whipping in the wind. Two stories tall, the building stretched back, made of red bricks placed in diamond patterns around white. A polished wall of steel gray held the inscribed names of the men and women who lost their lives in the line of duty. It was mostly full.

I walked past it to one of three sets of glass double doors. The station lobby had a gray floor of polished granite and a glass ceiling up on the second floor. Stairs stacked on either side of a big desk in the middle of the room leading to a narrow catwalk filled with doors of wood and frosted glass. A detailed painting of a police shield decorated the floor between the front doors and the information desk along with the words: *tendit in ardua virtis*. Virtue strives for what is difficult.

I walked up to the desk and leaned on it, producing my badge. The young man at the desk wore a clean, pressed uniform. Probably fresh meat from the academy. That's what they do with the new guys, stick them on desk duty until they've earned a few stripes. "Can you point me to your holding cells?"

The young cop picked up the phone and put it to his ear after pressing a button. "If you have an appointment, you can wait over there." he said, gesturing with his chin toward a seating area off to the right. "I'll call someone down to escort you."

I frowned and shoved my badge against his nose. "I don't need an escort. Your guys are holding a material witness in one of my cases on a trespassing charge. I need him released *yesterday*."

Finally, he looked up at me, his features blanching. "Oh," he squeaked out and slowly lowered the phone, "you're a fed."

I clipped my badge back on my belt. "Ed Petersen with an E. Where is he?"

"Let me pull that up for you." The greenhorn's fingers walked across a keyboard at breakneck pace. "He's in interrogation two pending formal charges." His eyes flicked back up to me, his cheeks reddening. "Would you, ah, like me to take you?"

"Just point me in the general direction."

He turned and pointed to an open area behind him where stairs descended into the belly of the station. "Fourth room on the right at the bottom of the stairs. You can't miss it. Big sign on the door."

"Thanks." Whoever said I wasn't polite when it counted?

I pushed off the desk and walked around it to the stairs. No one stopped me. You can walk almost anywhere without being stopped as long as you look like you're supposed to be there. Of course, if anyone had stopped me, all I had to do was give them the same speech I'd just given the green kid at the desk.

I must have looked the sight, though, because several people near the stairs nearly crashed into each other when one of them stopped walking to stare at me. My clothes were wet and my face streaked with ash. There were blood spatters on my arm. I noticed them as I approached the stairs and tried to pull my sleeve down to cover it.

"What's the matter? Never seen a plainclothes cop before?" I snapped at the woman who'd stopped to stare at me.

Her face flushed and she turned her perfectly contoured face away before her heels clicked off noisily. And that was why I didn't have many co-workers as friends.

Narrow hallways and low ceilings created a more cramped atmosphere below. Doors lined either side of the hall, clearly marked with signs. The first one on the right was an observation room. I glanced in through the cracked door at the dark room where two cops stood, arms crossed, watching a rookie try to intimidate a suspect into giving up information. One of the cops saw me looking in and reached over to close the door with a scowl.

The next room was interrogation one, so I skipped it and opened the third door on the right to the darkened observation room for interrogation two. Someone from SRT was in there, a heavyset guy with a goatee. He stood, leaning against the back wall, typing into his cell phone. When I pushed the door open, he glanced up.

"Agent Black," he said with a nod and wiggled the cell phone back and forth. "Espinoza said to expect you. My name's Olson."

We traded grips and I glanced to my left where a large observation window took up most of the wall. The interrogation room on the other side of the glass was a simple one. A plain table, plain chairs, camera, trash can. Ed sat in the chair farthest from the window, his arms crossed and thumbs tucked in his underarms. His gaze was fixed on the floor between his knees while his legs bounced up and down in a hyperactive pace. He was wearing a pair of olive jogging pants and a mismatched, pink tank top.

"Did he give anyone any trouble?"

Olson shrugged. "No. Complied with every order given, but hasn't said much of anything. Hasn't even asked for a lawyer or if he's being charged."

I looked back at Olson. "Did anyone call his alpha?"

"That'd be protocol, but Espinoza said there were special circumstances. Said we were to wait for you to handle it."

That was a good thing. Sal wasn't exactly happy with Ed right now after finding out that Ed had lied to him. If Sal knew Ed had gotten arrested, he'd give Ed an ass chewing he'd never forget. He might even do more than that. Ed was playing a dangerous game, running off and getting into trouble without the pack there to back him up. He'd get himself kicked out if he wasn't more careful. I was sure Ed knew it, too. Maybe he didn't care. Mara would be worth it to him. He would have crawled into an active volcano for her.

"That was the right call," I told Olson and sighed, putting my hands on my hips. "Are they pressing charges?"

"They're running out of time to if they want to. We can only hold him for twenty-four hours and he's been on ice since six this morning. I haven't heard one way or the other. Either way, federal jurisdiction would trump that. You want us to spring him, Agent, he's yours."

"Hold off on that. I'd like to talk to him first." I waved to him and stepped back out with him on my heels.

Olson slid a keycard through a magnetic reader and the little light turned from red to green. The door slid aside and he gestured into the room.

Ed's head snapped up and he went stone still, eyes wide. Fear colored his face for a moment before he quickly turned his head away. "You here to yell at me? Or am I finally getting booked?"

"That depends on you." The door slid closed behind me and I crossed my arms. "Why don't you tell me what happened, Ed?"

He kept his arms crossed and shrugged.

"We can still do this the hard way. Process you. Keep you in a holding cell. Get you a public defender and let the courts have a crack at teaching you a lesson."

Ed lowered his head and slumped his shoulders. "It'd probably be better than whatever Sal's going to do to me."

I stepped forward and put a hand on his shoulder. "You know better than that. He's worried about you, Ed. So am I. Everyone is. It isn't like you to get into this much trouble."

Ed let out a bitter laugh. "If you're saying that, then you really don't know anything about me. Everyone thinks I'm harmless. Geeky little Ed who fixes computers. I might not be big and scary, but don't assume I'm harmless."

"I know you're not a troublemaker, not like Sal and Valentino."

Ed pressed his lips into a thin line hard enough that the skin around his mouth paled a shade. "I don't want to go to jail," he said in a quiet voice. "But I know Mara wouldn't join a group like that. I know it like I know a bard needs charisma points, Judah, like a ceiling is up and the floor is down. It just doesn't make sense. She *can't* be there by choice. She... She..." He sniffled and lowered his head, putting a hand over his eyes.

I knew what he was trying to say, and there weren't words for that kind of loss. He loved her, and she'd just left, not for someone else or a reason that made sense to him. Mara left him because she wanted to find a missing piece of herself. Maybe she thought the Tribulation Adventists could help her find it. Maybe she was up to something else. I couldn't know. But if it didn't make sense to me, I couldn't imagine how confused Ed must be. There wasn't anything I could do to make him better, but I could tell him he wasn't as alone as he felt.

I leaned over and put my arms around his shaking shoulders, giving him a tight squeeze. "I know. I know it hurts, Ed. I know how shitty you feel right now and how all you want to do is get back what you lost. And maybe you're right. Mara might not be there of her own free will, but you have to know that charging into private property and harassing people there isn't going to win her back."

"I know," he choked out and sniffled some more. I pulled my arms away. "I know you've got a case and that I got in the way. I just don't want to sit on the sidelines this time. I can't stand to be so..."

"Helpless?"

He raised his bloodshot eyes to meet mine and sniffled again. "That."

"Well, you're not helpless. Not completely. I have something I need your help with."

His throat bobbed. "Will it help Mara?"

"I don't know. I do know it has something to do with Gideon Reed and that you're the only person in the whole county who can help me with it." I leaned in closer to whisper. "And it'll have to be off the record. BSI can't know about it. I've got a hard drive I need you to crack."

Ed blinked and licked his dry lips. "Really?"

"Would I lie to you? You'd know."

Ed stole a glance at the two-way mirror on the other side of the room. "So, about the charges..."

"No charges are being filed," I said with a faint smile. "And Sal doesn't even have to know if you don't want him to. This can be our secret."

His eyes met mine again and his face went blank. "You mean that? I thought...I thought you two didn't keep secrets from each other?"

"Well, Ed, let me let you in on a secret. Everyone's got secrets. No matter how close two people are, there are just things they don't tell each other. It's important to have secrets, places in your head you know are yours. You understand?"

"I think so." He nodded and rubbed his palms on his jeans. "How about we bust out of here, then? I'm dying for a cheeseburger and a soda."

I smiled and clapped Ed on the shoulder as he rose. "We'll hit a drive-thru on the way out of town," I promised him. "But first, I need to swing by the hospital."

Ed shrugged away from my hand on his shoulder. "Sal's not still there, is he?"

"No." I put an arm around Ed and led him to the door. "I'll explain on the way."

~

The hospital was close enough that we could walk. By not taking the car, I avoided paying for parking, too, which I was convinced was one of the hospital's largest forms of income.

We came out the police station into the late afternoon sun, the scent of cooking asphalt, and car exhaust. Bass from a passing car mixed with the distant wail of a car alarm and the muffled chatter of people on the street. Ed stepped up beside me, hands in his pockets. He stared at a crack in the sidewalk and kicked at it. "I'm sorry to be so much trouble."

"You're not trouble, Ed. You're a friend. That said, if you keep getting yourself into trouble with the law, I can't keep bailing you out. Next time I tell you to leave it to the cops, please do. Or at least don't get yourself caught if you're going to take matters into your own hands."

I turned and started down the street. It wasn't crowded, but it wasn't empty, either. The early shift at the hospital hadn't let out yet, and the restaurants up and down the short strip hadn't yet gotten their dinner rush. Two uniforms, beat cops coming back from the coffee shop judging by the iced coffees sweating in their hands, halted when they saw me and gave me a once over, stopping when they saw the bloodstains. I waved to them as we passed. "Fellas. How's the coffee?"

They didn't answer me, but I heard one of them say to the other once we'd passed, "You know who that was?"

"No," said the other. "Should I?"

"She's the fed."

"You mean that werewolf's bitch?"

The back of my neck itched as they stared me down.

Ed leaned forward, watching my face. "Why don't you tell them to shut it?"

"Why? What good's it going to do, Ed? You can't change people. I can argue with them all day about me, my reputation, anything, but it won't change a thing. End of the day, what I do has to speak louder than what I say. They're not my enemies."

"But what if they're members of the vanguard? The way they're glaring at you..." He turned to cast a glare of his own behind him, one that could have made toddlers cry and dogs bark. Ed's eyes took on a slightly lighter shade of honey brown.

I put a hand on his arm. "It's wasted effort to stop and argue with those who choose to be ignorant. What they think of me doesn't change the fact that I've got a job to do. I'm here to help people, not to make friends or win any popularity contests."

Ed planted his feet, turned ninety degrees and gestured down the sidewalk toward the cops who still stood, staring at me. "Yeah, but they—"

"Trust me, Ed, I'd love to break their smug little jaws." I turned and glared back at them, making sure to say it loud enough that they could hear me. "But we don't need to stoop to their level. We can be better. Maybe not perfect, but as long as we're a little better every day, someday maybe that ignorance will disappear."

Ed nodded, shot one more angry look behind him, and we started back down the street. "So, you said you'd fill me in. Who's at the hospital?"

"Gideon Reed. I shot him."

Ed stopped again, this time with a dumbfounded look on his face.

My statement clearly warranted further explanation, so I gave him a quick rundown. When I got to the end, I stopped and pulled the hard drive out of my pocket. "This is what Creven was after. Now, I don't know who hired him, or what's on it, but he said it contains answers to questions I never thought to ask."

Ed plucked the hard drive from between my fingers and turned it over in his hands. "Creven works for Kim Kelley."

"Yep." I waited for him to work through what I had.

"Kim is Marcus' daughter. Marcus is Fitz's CEO and Fitz supplies supernatural testing materials to BSI..." He lifted his head and stared off into the distance, eyes fixated on the Fitz logo on top of the tower across from the hospital. His head snapped back to me, his eyes wide. "This has to be something big."

"Can you find out what it is? Off the record. Wherever you plug that thing in, it's got to be somewhere BSI can't know about."

Ed nodded once. "I can do that."

I pushed the hand containing the hard drive down. "In the meantime, don't let anyone know you have it."

"I can do that, too."

I waited for him to put the hard drive in his pocket before we started down the street again.

~

Hospital air smells like formaldehyde and disinfectant. It's painfully dry. After spending only a few minutes on the other side of the double doors of the emergency department, the lining of my nose and mouth were on fire. The heavy chemical clean scent in the air was like acid.

The lady at the desk, a nurse with a dimple in her chin, shook her head as she typed something into her computer a third time. "I'm sorry, Officer. There's no one here matching that description."

"They took him from the scene in a squad. He has to be here. Try again."

"I've already looked three times—"

I slammed my hand down on the desk, making her jump. "I said try again! Where else would he be if he's not here? That squad wouldn't take him anywhere but here!" I pinched the bridge of my nose and let out a sigh. Maybe if I tried the description again. "The patient is male, mid to late forties with auburn hair. Gunshot wound to the upper chest."

"Is there a problem here?"

I looked up and met eyes with a hospital security officer, his hand resting on the weapon in his belt. I pushed away from the desk and was just about to explain the situation to him again when I caught sight of the breaking news on the television screen. It showed a scene on Highway 83 north of Paint Rock near an old, closed-down gas station known locally as Four Corners Concho. The abandoned building was ablaze with helicopters swirling overhead. But that wasn't the interesting part. An ambulance sat overturned in front of the building. One of the rear doors sat, charred black, propped up against a telephone pole several yards away.

I stepped past the security officer for a closer look at the letters crawling across the bottom of the screen. Crash at Four Corners claims two lives.

I exchanged glances with Ed before turning back to the lady at the desk. “I think I found your missing squad.”

# Chapter Twelve

Twenty minutes later, I pulled my borrowed Hellcat up in front of a road block a quarter mile down the road from the Four Crossings Concho building. Ahead, a helicopter circled, but this one wasn't white like the local news chopper. It had a sleek, black design and missile launchers mounted to the side. Those were serious guns for a random crash at an abandoned gas station. The men at the checkpoint were carrying heavy hardware, too. Military grade M4s and tactical armor with no identifying logo. They definitely hadn't been there when I saw the news broadcast a short while ago. How the hell had they gotten there so fast and, more importantly, who the hell were they?

"Ed, whatever you do, don't say a word." I glanced at him from the corner of my eye. He sat still as stone, clearly on full alert.

I rolled down my window as one of the men stepped past the temporary cement blocks that had been placed across the road, his rifle in his hand and pointed at the ground. He spoke before I could. "This road is closed. You can use 380 to connect to 381 if you want to go north."

"I'm with the government," I said and raised my fingers from the steering wheel. He tensed. "I'm going to grab my badge from my hip." His fingers shifted on the gun as I moved to unclip my badge from my belt. "See?" I said, showing it to him. "BSI. Special Agent Judah Black. The patient in that squad up there is a suspect in my investigation."

"Hold please." He straightened, grabbed the radio attached at his shoulder and spoke into it in a muffled tone. I couldn't quite make out what he was saying because he stepped back from the car, careful never to let me out of his sight.

Whoever these guys were, they were highly trained. Military, maybe? The Blackhawk hovering above the scene seemed to suggest that, but there weren't any military bases nearby for them to have mobilized from. Closest thing was the border patrol, and these guys were not border patrol.

The goon with the gun stepped back up to my car. "Sorry, ma'am, I can't let you through. You're not authorized to be in this area. I'll have to ask you to turn around. If you want to go north—"

"Not authorized? What the hell do you mean, 'not authorized'?

I'm the lead detective on this case and I know the patient in the back of that squad is a practitioner. You tell me what trumps BSI jurisdiction."

"You need to turn around and vacate the area."

"No," I snapped and grabbed my door handle. "I want to speak to whoever's in charge."

His gun snapped up, pointed at me. "Do not exit the vehicle!"

"Get your commanding officer down here right now!" I opened the door and put one foot on the ground.

An unseen force jerked me out of my seat and pinned me to the ground. Before I could process that I'd been slammed face-first to the side of the road, there were four guns pointed at me, little red dots dancing all over my skin. Whatever had jerked me out of the car held me down, the weight increasing.

"Okay," I ground out. "Okay, my bad."

"Judah?" Several dull thumps followed as someone pushed their way through the crowd of paramilitary assholes pointing their guns at me.

I moved my head ever so slightly so that I could look up. A tall, lanky figure stood over me, the wide brim of his hat blocking out the late afternoon sun. "Abe?"

He made a gesture with his hand and all four guns backed off me. His shoe scuffed over the ground, removing a fresh ring of white paint that I hadn't seen. A ward. Of course. That's what had knocked me face-first to the ground. It would have triggered on contact. When Abe broke it, the pressure released and I wheezed out a breath. Abe reached down and helped pull me to my knees. "What are you doing here, Judah?"

"Same thing as you, probably. Trying to figure out what the hell happened. Why was Reed's squad heading away from the Eden hospital?" I looked up at him. "That is what you're doing here, right Abe?"

Abe stared blankly at me before turning to look at Ed. "There is nothing here that concerns your investigation."

"Nothing here?" My fingers clenched into fists as they rested on my thighs and I squared my jaw. "Where the hell is Gideon Reed, then?"

"Not here." Abe put his hands on his skinny waist. "And you cannot be here either. The fire, it is dangerous. There are petrol pumps and perhaps some residual flammable material in the underground tanks. The situation is unstable and could blow at any time. It is best if you are away from here."

"You don't need unmarked military goons and a checkpoint to secure a potential gas leak and fire hazard."

Abe was silent. The only sound was the constant whirring thump of the chopper a quarter mile from us.

"Gideon Reed attacked the drivers of the ambulance and escaped on foot," Abe said after a long minute.

"Impossible," I said, rising to my feet.

The four guns shifted, ready to fire on me if needed.

Abe gestured for them to stand down and they obeyed. Was he in charge here? What the hell?

"I put a bullet in his clavicle, Abe. I'm surprised he survived long enough to get this far. There's no way he got up and overpowered two EMTs, not with the bullet in his shoulder."

"I suspect Gideon Reed may not be entirely human. He likely possesses some ability to heal rapidly. Nevertheless, what I tell you is what happened and he is no longer here. If you wish to capture him, you will turn around and go back the way you came."

A gust of wind swept over the ground where we stood, threatening to blow Abe's hat from his head. He didn't make a move to secure it, despite the way it tilted. The wind threw dust in my face, but I blinked it away to continue staring Abe down.

Abe reached forward and put a hand on my shoulder. "Go home, Judah. I will take care of things here and get you up to speed tomorrow, *da*?" He patted me on the shoulder and strode off, gesturing for the military goons to follow.

I turned and watched him slide behind the barrier and begin the trek to the crime scene. Meanwhile, goons one through four took up their positions at the barrier, giving me the stink eye. There were things I could do to get past them, magick things. I wasn't great at offensive magick, but I might be able to gather enough strength to punch their lights out. If I hadn't used everything I had earlier in the day to survive a fire, that is, and if there were only two of them. Four was a lot more than two, and I had a passenger in the car carrying what Creven had called answers.

"Looks like those are the only answers I'm going to get," I mumbled and sank back into the car. I shut the door behind me and sat behind the wheel a moment, my hands shaking too bad to drive.

"You ever see the episode of *X-Files* where Scully and Mulder find out the FBI is up to some next level alien shit, hiding their DNA in an old coal mining complex in West Virginia?" I heard Ed's seatbelt click into place. "You know this is starting to feel a lot like that, right?"

"There's no such things as aliens, Ed." I put the car in reverse and backed her into the next lane to turn around.

"So, what now? Reed's in the wind. You've got no evidence, no way to find him, and no idea what you're up against. We're back where we started."

I nodded to the hard drive resting on his hip. "Not quite. Let's plug that baby in and see what she's got. Maybe we'll finally get some answers."

All the way back to Paint Rock, the scene played over again and again in my head. I couldn't make sense of it. Abe outranked me in the BSI hierarchy, but he'd never pulled rank. Mostly, he let me take the lead on the few cases we'd worked together. I knew he hadn't been telling me everything but this... This hadn't even registered as a possibility. Abe was supposed to be a liaison between BSI and high-profile vampires in Europe, not working with some off-the-books spec ops group to conceal car crashes. It felt like I was standing at the mouth of a gaping tunnel that led into the Wonderland of government conspiracy theories.

I pulled up to the trailer where Ed, his sister, Daphne, and Daphne's girlfriend, Shauna, lived. It was a well-kept singlewide trailer with stepping stones and a gray, plastic mailbox.

"This could take a while," Ed said. "And it's kind of late. Sal will be wondering where you are pretty soon." He pointed to the clock on the dash, which read five twenty before turning in his seat to face me. "What if I find something on this hard drive I shouldn't?"

"You mean like proof of the existence of aliens?" I asked, my tone try.

Ed's face remained as stone. "I can't help but see breadcrumbs. LeDuc worked for Marcus Kelley. Remember him? The guy who broke both my legs and ate Hunter's finger?"

I shuddered at the memory. Being trapped in LeDuc's lair still gave me nightmares. "I remember."

"And I know there was an attempt on Marcus Kelley's life and that this Seamus guy who's supposed to come after you was somehow behind it. Mia got caught in the crosshairs. It's how Sal found out about her. You said you thought someone was controlling Reed." Ed took a deep breath. "What if that someone is connected to Creven and whatever we're going to find on this hard drive? What if BSI wanted to silence them before this—" He raised the hard drive from his pocket and waved it. "—went public. Only now, silencing Reed isn't enough. He recorded something or has some records here." Ed cradled the hard drive in his hands and looked down at it. "What if knowing the answers gets me killed?"

I put my hand on his shoulder and gave it a squeeze. "If you don't want to do it, I won't make you. I'm not going to lie. It's a possibility that just having that hard drive is dangerous. That's why you can't let anyone know you have it, especially not Abe."

Ed's jaw muscles flexed. "You know I have it."

It suddenly dawned on me the point he was trying to make. It wasn't a question about the danger. Ed had already faced down experiences worse than most people could imagine and lived to tell about it. He wanted to know what I'd do. If he was right and the hard drive did contain something BSI wanted buried, I'd have to make a choice. Do my job and destroy the evidence, whatever it was, or let the truth get out. Freedom of information, or protect my job and my family.

"And I wouldn't be asking you to look at it if I was just going to turn it over or destroy it blindly, Ed. I need to know what's there before we can start making decisions." I withdrew my hand from his shoulder. "Either way, I'll protect you from any fallout. I won't let anything happen to you, Ed, even if it turns out there is something big on there. As far as we know, it could be a porn stash."

Ed's eyes widened and he whispered, "Are priests allowed to do that?"

I rolled my eyes. "Get out of the car, Ed. And call me when you know what we're dealing with."

Ed complied and shut the door before bounding up the stairs to the trailer. I waited until I knew he was inside and in relative safety before pulling out of his driveway.

I was halfway across the rez, on my way home, when the burner in my pocket began to ring. I fished it out and glanced down at the number on the screen. Someone had programmed that one in, since the caller ID showed the EPD building instead of a number. "Black," I said in the form of an answer as I pressed the phone to my ear.

"How do you like the ride?" Espinoza asked.

I smiled to myself. "You're a crazy person if you want to trade this for a beat-up old Firebird, Espinoza."

"It's sentimental value, mostly. I hate that Hellcat. Too many bad memories. An ex bought it for me, you know? Anyway, you following this shit north of Paint Rock?"

For a second, I thought about telling him I could neither confirm nor deny anything. After all, from Espinoza's point of view, I was part of what was keeping him and his men out of the crime scene. I could just as easily dismiss the conversation and hide behind my status as a fed. Any information I gave him was really just a courtesy. I didn't have to tell him anything.

And on the off chance that he was somehow a BSI plant to keep an eye on me...

I shook my head. Ed's crazy conspiracy theory was already getting the best of me. "Yeah. They set up a road block and turned the scene into an Area Fifty One knockoff. I couldn't get through and the answers I got were bullshit."

Espinoza sighed on the other end. "Well, I've got half my crew pulling a double to try and dig up something on Reed's background before Paint Rock. All anyone would tell me is that Reed was up, on the run, and to be considered armed and dangerous. We're working to try and find him. In the meantime, I figured you'd want to know Hector finally showed up."

I nearly wrecked the car doing a U-turn in the middle of the street. "Make sure he stays put until I can get there in..." I glanced down at the clock. "Might be able to do it in ten minutes."

Espinoza chuckled. "I think that car's getting to your head. Don't hurry. I'll make sure to let him sweat."

"Just one more question, Espinoza. Have you called Abe?"

There was a moment of hesitation. "Should I not?"

"Abe's got his hands full with something else. I'll bring him up to speed the next time I see him. See you in ten." I hung up before Espinoza could ask any more questions and pressed the gas to the floor.

# Chapter Thirteen

The Eden police station was even busier than it had been when I'd come in earlier. A small crowd of people gathered around the information desk, swarming the rookie cop. The phone in front of him rang incessantly. He'd pulled his tie loose and tipped his hat back. His cheeks were red, and it wasn't just because it had warmed up inside.

Espinoza stepped away from where he was chatting with another cop to greet me. "Eleven minutes, Black. I was starting to get worried."

"I hit a red light," I explained. "How's Hector?"

"You're not going to like it," he said, gesturing forward. "Bastard lawyered up before he even got here. The lawyer arrived a few minutes ago."

Espinoza led me back downstairs to the fourth room on the right. It wasn't the interrogation room. Rather, it was the viewing room beside it, a plain, narrow room lit only by the low light filtering in through the two-way mirror that allowed us to see next door where Hector waited.

But Hector wasn't alone. Sitting in the chair beside him was a man in a navy suit. White-haired and sporting glasses, the briefcase and tie screamed lawyer. Hector himself sat with his hands on the table, staring down his knuckles while the lawyer leaned in close to whisper to him.

"Shit," I grumbled, crossing my arms.

Espinoza shrugged. "It's nothing we can't handle. I think it says a lot, though. Innocent people don't bring lawyers to pre-arranged chats."

"Unless he is afraid his civil liberties might be violated." I sighed and turned my head to see Espinoza giving me a look that said he wanted to hear more. "What are you looking at me for?" I snapped. "He's not sitting in there because of his religion. He's in there because he knows something and won't spill it. Besides, he's not even under arrest yet."

"Yet being the important part of that sentence. So, how do you want to play this?"

We'd let Hector stew long enough. It was time to get some answers, but that lawyer was going to block any real progress with loopholes and doublespeak. "Espinoza, do me a favor. Go and get us some coffees while I get him warmed up."

"Coffee?" He crossed his arms.

"Trust me. It'll help with the lawyer."

His irritated frown turned into a knowing smirk. "I think I know where you're going with this. Two cups, right?"

"Two cups and a stack of napkins."

Espinoza made for the stairs while I opened the door to the interrogation room and stepped in.

Whatever Hector and his lawyer had been discussing before I entered, the conversation halted abruptly. The lawyer shifted forward and adjusted his tie. "Ah, you must be the federal agent we've been waiting for. I'm Adam Sloan. Of course, you know my client." The lawyer extended a hand to me.

I ignored his gesture and jerked the third and final chair out away from the table, my gaze fixed on Hector. "As a matter of fact, I don't. Hector's not your real name, is it?"

"I assure you my client is compliant and registered with BSI."

"You'll understand if I don't take your word for it." I leaned back in the chair and crossed my arms, still never letting my eyes leave Hector's. "So, who are you? What's your story?"

The sleazy lawyer sat back down and turned to Hector. He gave a subtle nod.

"Your records will indicate that my legal name is Timothy Dekker, spelled with two k's and no c's," Hector answered. "However, that name no longer holds any significance for me. I have been reborn."

He said his name in a flat, unattached tone that told me he believed his statement to be true. That was important. Names have a lot of power in the supernatural world, but only when you've got the right one. To do anything with a name, you need to know what a person calls themselves, how they say it. It's why BSI agents adopt new names. Doing so provided an extra layer of protection against some of the more common elements of magick.

I wrote down his legal name anyway in a small notebook I'd carried in with me. "Why'd you change your name, Hector?"

"Just as Simon became Peter when Christ named him a disciple, so too was I changed by the Lord."

"You think of yourself as some kind of thirteenth disciple, Hector?"

Hector smiled and then broke out into laughter.

"He doesn't have to answer that," the lawyer pointed out and then turned to Hector. "You don't have to answer that."

"Technically, I don't have to answer anything," Hector added. "I'm here of my own free will to assist with your investigation. I've come as promised."

"Better late than never," I grumbled.

"And I apologize for the delay. However, there was an incident this morning with a trespassing werewolf that kept my hands tied for some time. We have decided not to press charges."

"How magnanimous of you."

Hector shrugged. "He is only worried about Tamara. I understand they once cared a great deal for each other. As a prospective member of our temple, Tamara has been struggling daily with severing her connections to the outside world, that one most of all. However, I assure you that she is there of her own free will."

Hector gestured to the lawyer, who swung his briefcase up onto the table and began to sort through it. "I have several signed and notarized affidavits that will attest to Ms. Speilman's voluntary participation. You will, of course, understand that any further attempts to contact her may mean legal action, up to and including a restraining order."

The lawyer brought out a handful of papers and slid them across the table to me.

Right about that time, the door to the interrogation room opened again and Espinoza stepped in, a folder tucked under one arm and a coffee in each hand. He all but stumbled forward, only barely managing to hold onto the coffees. "Oh, geez," he muttered and then rushed forward to place both cups in front of me. "Anything else I can get for you Agent Black?"

I raised an eyebrow and nodded to the folder tucked under his arm.

"Oh yeah, right." He placed it on the table beside me.

Hector eyed the folder with a frown but he didn't betray the same nervousness the lawyer did when he tugged on his tie. I put a hand over the folder and slid it in front of me, placing the papers the lawyer had handed me on top.

"Thanks," I said to Espinoza. "You mind hanging out a while?"

Espinoza, God bless him, played his part well and beamed like a shark in a fish tank. "Sure thing," he said and fell back to stand near the door.

The lawyer leaned forward. "What's in the folder?"

"We'll get to that in a minute."

"If you have evidence against my client—"

My eyes snapped up to meet his and he clamped his jaw shut. "I said we'd discuss it in a minute. First, I want to hear about what the Adventists do. What do you guys believe? Are you a peaceful organization?"

The lawyer leaned in to whisper in Hector's ear, but Hector brushed him off. "I have kept my end of the bargain, Agent. I have come here to speak with you. I have not pressed charges against your friend. Yet you treat me as if I am the perpetrator and not the victim. The building that burned down was our property. Now, it is your turn to tell me what you know. And don't tell me you know nothing. If it was nothing, you wouldn't be so adamant to avoid the topic."

I lifted the pen and pressed the point into my finger and tilted my head to the side. "I think you know exactly where this is going and it's not a good place. You're old enough to remember Waco. I don't want that. Neither do you. But if we don't stop talking in circles, things could easily go that way."

Hector narrowed his eyes. "Are you threatening me and my people, Agent?"

"I don't make threats."

He stared at me for a long moment before leaning back in his chair and folding his hands on the tabletop. "This is about the rem."

His lawyer put a hand on Hector's shoulder. "Stop right there, Hector. You don't have to tell them anything."

"If I want them to stop hounding us, I do," Hector snapped back and picked the lawyer's hand off his shoulder. "The source of your complaint is the suspicion that we keep rem on the compound. I assure you that there is no drug abuse among people of our faith. It contradicts everything we believe in. Our doctrine teaches that, to be pure of spirit, you first must be pure of body and mind. That is not possible if people have a strong connection with anything on Earth. That goes for romantic entanglements as well as a love of drugs and alcohol. A love for Christ must always come first."

"So you deny having any rem on your compound?" I asked,

even though I already knew that's what he meant. I needed to have a clear yes or no answer and watch how he said it. Hector was smart, I'd give him that much. But everyone's got a tell.

Hector smiled. He said nothing in his defense and yet his reaction spoke volumes.

"You've got nothing," the lawyer said. "Nothing except threats and wild accusations. What is it you think he knows?"

"I think he knows something about Gideon Reed and the rash of arsons all over the county. What I've got, Sloan, is a non-compliant supernatural who is clearly in violation of several statutes, the least of which is failing to register a status change." I pointed at Hector. "And until I clear up who you are, what you can do, and document every penny in every tax return you ever filed, you're going to sit right here."

"*Habeas corpus* says you can't hold him without arresting him if he wants to leave."

I stood, gathered the papers, piling them all inside the folder. "Common sense tells me Hector doesn't like the idea of being arrested. But the ball's in your court, Hector. I can arrest you, force you to stay until we get all this cleared up, and put you through the system. That could take a while. Days, weeks, months even, depending on how fast the IRS decides to be. Or, you can plant your rear in that chair and tell me all about your little cult, how you're growing rem, and everything you know about Gideon Reed. I know you know something. But if you're really dead set on going to prison and playing the martyr..." I shrugged. "Of course, while you're gone, your people will be on their own."

Hector reached out and wrapped long fingers around the lawyer's arm. "I will stay for now. I'm sure you'll find I'm compliant with all your laws as they apply. However, should this stretch on more than two or three hours, I'll have to excuse myself to lead the afternoon prayer service." He smiled. "After that time, should you find the proper warrants, you're welcome to come and arrest me as your conscience demands."

I tapped the file folder on the tabletop once to straighten the papers inside and then turned. Espinoza, who was still waiting beside the door, straightened. On my way out the door, I slapped the file against his chest and he grabbed it awkwardly. "Keep an eye on him while I go make some phone calls, sergeant."

"Yes, ma'am."

I didn't go back upstairs as promised. That was coming, but I needed to see how the next phase of questioning panned out first.

In the interrogation room, Espinoza walked to the table, shuffling the file under his arm. He pulled out the chair I'd just left empty. "Man, these feds are such a pain in my ass," he muttered. "Let me tell you. You're lucky it was her and not the other one."

The lawyer adjusted his suit jacket and sat down again, leaning toward Espinoza. He still wore a wary face, but it was a good sign. Interrogation is all about body language. People tend to lean toward things they like and, by the subtle change in the lawyer's demeanor, he liked Espinoza a whole lot more than me. Hector didn't seem fazed by any of it. He'd seen Espinoza's performance before. But their interactions had been brief before. Maybe he could cut through Hector's defenses with the buddy act one-on-one.

"Can you believe this? She made me go get these coffees and then didn't even touch them." Espinoza tipped one of the cups up and frowned at the contents.

"I don't blame her," said the lawyer. "Station house coffee is second only to prison coffee as far as disgusting goes."

"Actually, this stuff's not bad. I just got in one of those that brews from the little cups. I keep it in my office. Don't tell anybody, now. I don't want to get swarmed by rookies. This stuff is good. I figured I'd win a few brownie points with the feds by raiding my personal stash but, man. You saw how she was." He cast a longing glance down into the cup again. "What a waste."

The lawyer licked his lips. "I don't suppose I could, uh... I mean, since she didn't want it."

Espinoza pushed the cup at the lawyer. "Hey, man, be my guest. Better than wasting it."

Score. The lawyer was clearly now going to be more open to anything Espinoza put forward. Not only had Espinoza trusted him with a secret, which created an instant bond of trust, but he'd given him a gift. Now, if he could pull the same thing off with Hector.

He offered the other cup to Hector. "You want the other one?"

Hector turned his head aside. "No, thank you."

"Yeah, I'm not much of a coffee guy, either." Espinoza pushed the cup away. "By the way, you mind if I ask you about your little group of people? Off the record, I mean. Out of personal interest. Seems like you guys are actually onto something."

"What would you like to know?"

Espinoza put his forearms on the table and leaned forward. "I was raised Catholic. Maybe you know and maybe you don't, but I got a little magick talent myself. And you can guess how well that went over with my Catholic family when they found out."

Hector turned back to face Espinoza. "The church isn't universally open to the idea that different isn't necessarily evil."

"Right, right. But from what I gather about you Tribulation Adventists, you still consider yourself part of all that, right?"

Hector's jaw flexed and his eyes narrowed as he searched Espinoza's words for the danger in his question.

The lawyer took another sip of the coffee and then placed it on the table in front of him. "Mmm. That is *good* coffee."

Espinoza leaned forward more and dropped his voice to just above a whisper. "Look, man, off the record. Help me understand, one former Catholic to another, what's the difference between you and them?"

"What makes you think I was ever Catholic?"

Espinoza shrugged. "I'm not really allowed to ask that."

"And you don't have to answer," the lawyer reminded Hector and sipped at the coffee.

"I'm interested on a personal level," Espinoza continued. "I don't do the whole God thing anymore, but I know what it's like to have the church turn their back on you like that. I just can't figure out why you'd still be a part of that. I mean, what kind of God lets stuff like the Revelation happen? The riots? All those people?"

I chewed on my lower lip. Hector wasn't buying Espinoza's good cop act, but he didn't have to. Any info we got was more than we had before.

Hector lifted his chin. "For then shall be a great tribulation, such as was not since the beginning of the world to this time, nor shall there ever be again. And, if those days had not been cut short, no one of the flesh would be saved: but for the chosen, those days will be shortened." He flattened his palms on the tabletop. "What you call the Revelation, Sergeant, was the beginning of the end. It was the birth of the Great Tribulation and we few, those who are called into our order, are the elect, destined to be spared the extended suffering of the rest. God allows events like the Revelation to occur because of the fall of mankind. Because of sin. All flesh answers for its sin, Sergeant. All flesh is tainted. Our Earthly bodies are cages and, soon, we will be free of them."

Espinoza frowned. "You're not one of those suicide cults, are you?"

"God alone determines the time and place we will leave our bodies. Suicide is a perversion of God's will. So, no. We are not."

"So, what?" Espinoza pressed. "How does one decide they're one of these chosen?"

"They are called by God."

"And if they decide to be un-called? Can they be un-chosen?"

Hector frowned.

"Like this Mara girl," Espinoza continued. "By all accounts, she was messed up. But you were trying to save her, right? The feds want to call it kidnapping but, let me tell you, you probably helped more than you hurt. This kid—" He opened the file folder and took out a picture of Mara. "—she was homeless. She had nobody. Just because she's a runaway or whatever doesn't mean you ought to turn her out. She was chosen. It was your job to help her, right? I get all of that. You're doing good work, better than most mainstream churches."

He pulled another page from the file, this one with Gideon Reed's picture on it. "But the feds think you know something about this guy. He's hurting people. One of the fed's friends is in the hospital right now and this guy is on the loose. He took a bullet to the chest and just kept on going. They want to know what he is, but they don't want to admit they don't know. Now, I don't know why they think you know something, but they do. Do us all a favor. Give me something, anything, that I can use to get the feds off my back, Hector. I don't like them anymore than you do."

"I don't know what I can give you that I haven't already."

"Access," Espinoza said with a definitive nod. "Let someone into the compound so we can put the feds' fears at ease. That's all they really want, Hector. This fire, it was probably an accident or it's unrelated. Either way, if you give us access to check things out, we can clear you from any wrongdoing. Everybody wins. And I promise, nobody will hurt any of your people. Not you, not Tamara, not Warren..."

At the mention of Warren's name, something flashed through Hector's eyes. It was the wrong thing to say. "I have nothing else to say to you. I've done nothing wrong here and I'd appreciate it if you would let me pass the time I must wait in silence."

"Just one more question, Hector. Your people, are they all

human? I don't see any fangs. Didn't see any last night, either. No vampires allowed in the Tribulation Adventists?"

Hector sneered. "Any creature that subsists by stealing life from another is an evil creature. Vampires are welcome among us, but only if they prove they can deny their baser instincts. So far, not one has proven that. We are a peaceful organization of non-violent believers. Creatures that prey on the flesh and blood of innocents have no place among us."

"Right, right. And what about women? Do you let them lead? You practice equality in your organization, Hector?"

"Women must be subservient to men, just as beasts are to all humans. Those are God's words, not mine. When the world began to place the rights of the lesser above those of God-fearing men, that is when we chose to exclude ourselves from the world. So, no, although I assure you everyone, male or female, who is part of our temple understands and obeys this. I cannot ask someone on the outside such as yourself to understand."

Espinoza stole a quick glance at the window we stood behind before gathering the papers and exiting the room. He came to stand with me in the viewing room.

"You knew in advance their position on vampires and women," I said with a frown.

"Well, yeah. Says right on their website." He shuffled the folder under his other arm and pulled out his cell, showing me the webpage. "But the point isn't that it's a no vamps allowed club. The point is how he said it. Did you hear it in his voice? It's personal. Humans only. That's something, isn't it?"

When it comes to interrogation, the goal is to find the truth. And Hector had lied. I couldn't prove it yet, but make him repeat his story enough times and hopefully he'd slip up somewhere. Suspects are more likely to make a mistake when emotions run high. Making him mad, getting him talking about something he was passionate about, neither of those had worked. The one thing Hector had reacted to was the idea of a woman challenging his position as a leader. Given how much Hector seemed to like to be in control, putting him in a room with someone else, a woman like me who might back him into a corner, I might be able to shake him if I got a little more aggressive. I could use his sexism against him. It was time to see if we could crack him under the pressure.

"I'm going to give him another try," I announced and passed by

Espinoza.

"Can I assume you are finished validating my registration?" Hector asked, crossing his arms as I re-entered the room. "Otherwise, I have nothing else to say to you or anyone else with a badge until I've been read my rights."

I crossed the room and pulled out the chair, bumping against the table as I did. One of the two cups of coffee still sitting there tipped over and landed on its side. Steaming, light brown liquid splashed over the table and into the lawyer's briefcase. The lawyer gave a yelp and jumped up. He grabbed at the pile of napkins Espinoza had left on the corner of the table and spread them over it in a panic.

I restrained a smile. Served him right. "My bad."

"Do you have any idea what..." He continued mumbling as he flipped open the briefcase, but it was incomprehensible. The papers inside were soaked in coffee. "Every last page, darn it. How am I supposed to work with these?" He pulled out the sopping pages and shook them at me.

"Whatever paperwork you need, you'll be able to print it upstairs, free of charge," I said.

The lawyer exchanged glances with Hector. "If they decide to hold you, I'll need some of this paperwork."

Hector pressed his lips together and glared at me. I had taken a huge gamble with that move, spilling the coffee. Hector was probably onto the tactic, but there wasn't anything he could do about it. Since I hadn't yet pulled his paperwork and verified his status, I could still arrest him. Even if I couldn't make the charges stick, it would buy me time. But Hector didn't want to have to go through that process. That's the thing with bad guys. They always think they're going to get away with it.

Hector nodded and the lawyer stepped toward the door, grabbing more napkins along the way. "I'll be back soon. No more questioning until I'm back. And don't talk, Hector. My client's invoking his right to remain silent."

As the lawyer reached the door, I gave Espinoza a motion with my head through the mirror, telling him to go play interference. Anything he could do to stall the lawyer would help. I hoped he caught my meaning.

Meanwhile, I stood and followed the lawyer to the door. As soon as he was gone, I clicked the lock on the door and gave the handle a gentle pull. It came off in my hands. I pitched it at the camera in the corner. Hector twitched as the doorknob smashed into the camera. I'd have to pay for that and probably get an earful from Tindall, but it was worth it if Hector finally talked.

"Are you supposed to be intimidating?" Hector asked, his tone even.

"I am intimidating. It's why I am good at my job, Timothy."

Hector's whole face twitched when I addressed him by his old name.

I placed my hands on the table and spread my fingers as if I were about to play the keys on a piano. "Now, tell me what you know about Gideon Reed. What's he got to do with you? I have an eyewitness that puts you at the scene, fleeing when he showed up."

"I have rights—"

I reached over the table and grabbed him by the shirt. "You don't get it, do you? You still think I'm in here as a cop. Gideon Reed is a friend and if you fucked him up, I swear to God I will do the same to you."

A smile spread over Hector's face, the smile of a madman. He chuckled and then broke down into laughter until I let him go. "Your witness is useless," Hector spat. "He made sure of that himself when he showed back up, trespassing on my property. No jury will buy that. It's clear he's only saying that because he's stalking poor Tamara Speilman."

"You son of a—"

"As for Gideon Reed," Hector interrupted, "You have no evidence tying him to me, and no hope of obtaining it, especially not once BSI secured the scene of that unfortunate ambulance accident."

I flexed my fingers and then pulled them into a fist. *He knows. Abe knows. Everybody but me seems to know something. Is BSI protecting this asshole for some reason? Why do I feel like I'm getting the runaround?*

*Keep it together*, I thought, shaking my head. Hector had already turned the tables and gotten control back over the interrogation, revealing that he did have more information than me. Hector held all the cards and I had nothing to negotiate with.

I leaned forward further on the table. "When I find out what you and your people are up to, Hector, you're going to regret stringing me along like this. I promise you."

"*If* you find out."

I glanced up at the broken camera hanging from the wall by two wires and pushed off the table. "Next time, that'll be your head, and remember what I said about making threats."

I pulled the door open, hooking one finger in the hole the doorknob had left and giving it a firm jerk. It wasn't difficult, especially considering how angry I was. Two days into the investigation and I had no evidence, no leads, nothing but shaky testimony from an unreliable witness. I needed something to break this case wide open, and Hector's testimony wasn't going to do that.

*I hope Ed has more luck with that hard drive than I had in the interrogation room*, I thought and met Espinoza in the viewing room.

He frowned. "No dice?"

I shook my head. "He won't crack. Would you mind giving me a ride home?"

Espinoza grinned. "Just take my car, Judah. We'll trade back tomorrow."

# Chapter Fourteen

I drove back to Paint Rock and pulled into my driveway. Not the driveway to Sal's trailer, but the house next door. I'd called ahead to let Sal know I wouldn't be over until later. There was too much work to do, and I needed quiet to think. I pulled out my laptop, poured myself a drink and got right to it.

I typed Timothy Dekker into the search bar of the BSI database. The picture in the file that came up matched Hector's and Hector Demetrius was listed under known aliases. Damn. Couldn't hold him on that. He'd registered his change of address, change of name, even dotted every I and crossed every T on his marriage and breeding application. Hector Demetrius was as squeaky clean as clean could come. At least until his file history ended abruptly. There was nothing documenting Hector's existence under either name prior to a date in May three years ago.

*I know this date*, I thought and went searching through the old case files I kept on my computer. It took another twenty minutes to find it again and confirm that, yes, I *had* seen that date on another case before. It was the same day Andre LeDuc blew up Doctor Han's lab and stole all that genetic research.

It could be coincidence that Han's genetics lab got blown up the same day Timothy Dekker suddenly existed. Maybe. If I believed in coincidences.

It didn't prove anything, so I moved on.

There was a section on the BSI paperwork for a personal narrative. Normally, everyone gave a detailed history and testament when they completed their compliance paperwork. Only in rare instances could the registrant waive that requirement and BSI was required to document why that part hadn't been filled out. The code used on Hector's paperwork was one I hadn't seen before.

I clicked on the coded reason in Hector's history and testament box. The database jumped over to a new page that demanded log in credentials from someone with a clearance level C or higher. I blinked at the screen. BSI field agents had clearance up to level Q, their supervisors up to level P. Secret service agents were only cleared up to level K and one of them had the unhappy job of collecting presidential turds to keep them out of the hands of terrorists. The point is, the more access you had to the president and his cabinet, the higher your clearance level. The directors of BSI, the FBI and the NSA only went as high as J. There *was* no clearance level C.

My phone rang and I nearly jumped out of my skin. I quickly closed all the windows and disconnected from the internet, just in case, before glancing at the number. I recognized it as Ed's. "Holy shit, Ed. You scared the crap out of me just now."

"Maybe you should be scared," he answered, his tone serious. "Where are you?"

"Home. Why? Any luck with that hard drive?"

"It's heavily encrypted. Lots of files here to crack. Looks like mostly video, audio and photos. I've been working on it all day." The phone creaked as he shifted it. "Look, I really don't want to do this over the phone. Would you mind meeting?"

"Sure, I can drive back over to your house."

"No," Ed snapped suddenly. "I mean, how about out in front of the clinic?"

"The clinic?" That was a strange place to meet. It was out of the way for both of us and oddly out in the open. Maybe that's why he'd picked it. He was being paranoid and wanted to make sure we'd be somewhere cameras were likely to pick us up. I rolled my eyes. "Sure, Ed. Tomorrow morning."

"No, it has to be right now."

I rubbed my forehead. "Ed, I'm working. I have a case to crack."

"Five minutes from now in front of the clinic," he said quickly. "Don't be late."

Ed hung up.

I stared at the blank screen on my phone a minute, frowning. That wasn't like Ed at all. If he said it couldn't wait, I believed him. His words from earlier flashed through my head. Maybe he'd gotten himself into trouble with that hard drive.

"Dammit, Ed," I growled, rising to grab my keys. "I told him not to plug that in anywhere that BSI could trace it."

~

The clinic looked abandoned when I pulled up in front of it. There was no sign of Ed anywhere. I checked the clock. I'd made it there in four minutes, plenty of time to catch Ed. Maybe he was the one who was running late.

I parked the car, running the passenger side tires up onto the sidewalk, and switched off the headlights. The sound of my door closing echoed through the empty street followed by my footsteps. Above, a streetlamp buzzed. Gnats circled in the light, making the shadows dance. I stepped up onto the sidewalk and turned a full circle. "Ed," I called, "are you here?"

"Keep your voice down," Ed hissed. I turned to face the front of the clinic and watched as Ed stepped out of the shadows. "You want to wake the whole town up or just this block?"

"Is this about the hard drive?"

"Not exactly," he answered. His eyes scanned the street from north to south, darting back and forth like he was expecting to be attacked.

"Why are we here then? You know, you could have just had me meet you at your place."

"If he were just meeting you, maybe." Another figure shifted in the shadows. Light flashed in two circles as he reached up to adjust his glasses. A wobbling mass of hair helped me identify the figure as Doc Ramis. "Did you come alone?"

I glanced around. "What do you think?"

A set of keys jingled as Doc pulled them from the pocket of his white coat and inserted one of them into the door. "If anyone asks, you're both here because you forgot something." He threw open the door and held it.

I exchanged a glance with Ed. "You want to tell me what this is all about, Doc?"

"Once we're inside. Please."

I followed Ed and Doc into the dark clinic. Doc passed by the front desk without stopping, the glow of the emergency exit sign casting a watery red tinge on everything. The hallway was lined on either side with numbered double doors. A long time ago, the building used to be a movie theater. When Paint Rock was converted into a reservation, they gutted the seats from each of the three screens. Doc didn't use them for exam rooms, instead retrofitting them as sterile operating rooms, an autopsy theater, and housing for his six zombies when they weren't on the road. We stopped in front of the third theater, the one he used for dissections and autopsies.

Here, Doc spun around with his hands still resting on the

double doors. "Before I show you, I have to make sure you both understand that what you see inside can't get out. You can't tell anyone I showed you or even that we spoke."

I lifted my chin and gestured to the door. "What's in there?"

"Something no one is supposed to see," Doc answered. "I'm only showing you because... Well, when somebody with a gun tells me not to do something, normally I wouldn't do that. I'm a doctor. Do harm to none is my motto and if keeping quiet saves lives, that's what I'm inclined to do. But this... Some secrets don't save lives. They cost them."

Doc's statement created more questions than answers, questions I pondered as he turned to remove a heavy chain and lock from the door. The chain fell away loudly and Doc pushed the door open, charging through. Ed and I followed.

Because the room was an old theater, the floor sloped gently downward before evening out in the front. The front was where the two tables waited. Our footsteps carried all the way down and bounced off the floor before being eaten by the curtains running along the walls. As we came closer, I saw that each of the two tables was occupied by a body. Doc had tossed a white cloth over each body, but I could vaguely make out the outlines of a face, nose, and feet. A rolling table with all manner of hacking and cutting medical tools sat between the tables. Doc walked up to the rolling table and pulled out a cardboard box of gloves, offering them to each of us.

Ed gulped. "I think I'll pass."

I took two and put them on. "Who're the stiffs?"

"Not who," Doc said, snapping on a pair of his own gloves. He went to stand by one of the tables. "What. Now, what you're about to see will probably shock you. I need to remind you that you can't tell anyone what you see here tonight. Your life probably depends on it. All of our lives."

I made a rolling gesture with my hand. "Yeah, yeah. Let's get on with it, Doc."

Doc nodded, sucked in a deep breath and pulled off the first sheet with a flourish.

The body underneath didn't seem remarkable at first. He was a normal, thirty-something male in good shape except for some ash and blackened, burned skin around his face. He was pale, lips and fingertips blue. I noted some bruising on his forehead and knuckles, but nothing to suggest what I was looking at warranted all the secrecy.

Doc took up a scalpel from his tray of instruments and instructed, "Observe." He pressed the scalpel to the man's sternum.

It snapped in two, the sharpened blade flying off and clattering to the floor.

"Damn, Doc. Be more careful with that, will you? You should probably replace some of that second-rate material, huh?"

"That scalpel was surgical grade," Doc replied and picked up something that looked like a battery powered rotary saw. "This is meant for cutting through bone. Its diamond plated, Judah. I've never had to use it before."

The saw buzzed to life as he switched a button on. I plugged my ears as he put the blade to the man's clavicle. After a moment, a small cloud rose from where the tool made contact with the body and the nauseating stench of burning flesh filled the room. My stomach tried to do a somersault. I moved my hands from my ears to cover my mouth and nose.

Doc suddenly shut off the saw and held it up. When it stopped spinning, I couldn't believe my eyes. The blade was completely worn off, leaving only an uneven, spinning disc. The dead man's body was still intact.

"What the hell?" I asked, leaning in. "Who is this guy?"

"That's just the thing." Doc put the broken saw down and grabbed the dead man's hand, flipping it over to show me the palm. I squinted for a better look. In the dim light, it was hard to make out details until Doc switched on a flashlight and handed me a magnifying glass. I held it over the man's hands, searching for whatever it was Doc wanted me to see. "Look at the fingertips," he encouraged. "What do you see?"

I did as instructed, but shook my head. "Nothing."

"Exactly."

I lowered the magnifying glass to give Doc a doubtful look.

"No fingerprints," he explained.

That wasn't possible. I looked again. Sure enough, the lines and contours that decorated a normal person's fingertips were absent, leaving behind completely smooth skin.

"I can't identify them," Doc said. "I wasn't asked to. I was only asked to store them here for pickup overnight. I'm not supposed to have access to them."

"Spill it, Doc," I said, lowering the magnifying glass. "I want to know where these guys came from. Everything you know, I need to know."

"I didn't have any information at all," Doc said and moved to the other body. "At least until I moved onto her."

He pulled the sheet off, revealing a woman of similar age and build to the man. Again, she looked completely unremarkable except that she still had shreds of clothing clinging to her skin. It looked like much of it had melted onto her, as the area around the clothing scraps had turned black with burns.

Doc grabbed a pair of long tweezers and tugged at some of the scorched fabric clinging to her hip. Some of the layers flaked away as he separated them and pulled something from what would have been her pocket. He held it up for a moment before dropping it gently to an empty space on the table. It clanged as if it were made of metal, despite being blackened.

"I found this and knew I had to call you," he said.

I cautiously reached out to pick up the scorched metal. It was small enough to fit in the palm of my hand with chunks of something black stuck all over it. The shape was similar to that of a medieval shield, round on the sides and coming to a point on the bottom. On the top, there was a small, warped point and two swooping lines that kept it from being flat. I ran my thumb over it, scraping bits of the black material away, but I knew what it was even before I could see the picture. It was a badge, not at all unlike the one I had clipped to my belt. The black material was probably scraps of the leather it had been pressed into.

But it wasn't until I scraped away more of the material and saw the engraved picture underneath that I understood why Doc had called me. The words "Federal Agent" decorated the top in a band that would have been blue before the fire. At the bottom, three letters told me everything else I needed to know: BSI.

I met Doc's eyes. "You want to tell me why you've got two dead BSI agents in your autopsy room, Doc?" I glanced over at the man with impenetrable skin. "Two really weird BSI agents?"

"A black van pulled up this afternoon," Doc said, glancing to Ed. "Two military types got out, told me to shut down the clinic for the day. They brought these in as is and placed them on my tables, telling me they'd be gone by morning. I just needed to make sure they stayed secure. I was forced to sign some sort of agreement that I wouldn't disclose any information whatsoever. They implied doing so could be fatal and I believed them." Doc looked back at the man with impenetrable skin. "But professional curiosity got me, Judah. I had to know. My guess is they died of smoke inhalation. Nothing else could've done it. But why the secrecy? Who are these agents?"

I exchanged glances with Ed. "I bet the military types were the same ones we ran into at the blockade earlier."

"I told you there was a cover-up going on," Ed replied.

"What blockade?"

"I'm sure you heard about the fire at Reed's place?"

Doc nodded.

"Well," I said after a sigh, "I shot Gideon Reed in the middle of that and he was supposed to have been taken by squad to the hospital."

Ed jumped in. "Only the squad never made it to the hospital. It crashed out at Four Corners Concho. We went to investigate but, by the time we got there, they weren't letting anyone through. Bunch of military tough guys and Abe Helsinki basically assaulted us and told us to turn around." His eyes widened. "Hey, what if these were the guys in the squad? It'd make sense. The reason they're all burned up is because Reed roasted their asses on his way out. Paramilitary guys show up, remove the bodies and place them here for safe keeping before BSI cleaners can get here."

"BSI doesn't have cleaners," I snapped, though I was suddenly unsure whether or not that was true. "Besides, what reason would they have for trying to take Reed wherever they were trying to take him?"

There was a sudden, loud squeal that made all three of us jump. Doc sucked in a panicked breath and grabbed me by the arm. "That's my door alarm! They're here. You two need to go." He hauled us toward a side exit that would have once been the theater's emergency exit in the front near the screen.

We passed under a heavy curtain and Doc jerked open the emergency door. Bright searchlights flooded over us, behind which I could just barely make out the shape of an armored truck. Doc yelped and pulled the door shut. "Not that way."

"What other way is there?"

Doc turned a full circle in a panic before his eyes settled on the heavy curtains lining the walls. "There!" he shouted and pointed. "Hide. I'll keep them busy."

There was no time to argue. Voices in the hallway told me that whoever had come to collect the bodies was right outside. I grabbed Ed and we pushed aside the curtains, sliding in behind them just in time to hear the doors flap open.

It was dark back there, darker than it had been in the rest of the room, and I couldn't see anything, but I heard the heavy clink of boots and body armor moving down the ramp toward Doc.

"Doctor Ramis," said a soft but familiar voice.

I slid to my right to stand in the tiny space where the curtains met so that I could see a sliver of what was going on outside. Doctor Han stepped onto flat ground, escorted on either side by more of those paramilitary goons. Their guns were pointed at the ground, but they stood ready to snap them up at a moment's notice.

Doc glanced nervously back and forth between the goons. "I don't think we've been formally introduced," he said.

I couldn't see clearly, but Han's voice told me he was smiling. "No, we have not, but you know who I am just the same."

One of Doc's hands closed into a fist. "What's a geneticist want here?"

"Now, now, Doctor. I realize the position you must be in. You feel threatened."

"As well I should, given that you've brought guns into my clinic." He gestured to the goons and then behind him. "And making me sign non-disclosure agreements concerning dead bodies that you've come to collect in the middle of the night. I think I have every right to be worried, and every right to examine what you and your goons are hiding in here."

Han gave a lighthearted chuckle. "One can never be too careful. The world of supernatural medicine is a dangerous place, especially for curious humans."

"I know something's going on here. I won't say anything, not as long as no one gets hurt." Doc straightened and stood taller. "*Primum non nocere*, doctor. First, do no harm. There's no need for violence here."

"Is that so?" Han lifted his head and folded his hands behind his back.

I had to hand it to Doc. He stood his ground, despite the fact that he was probably quivering on the inside. Doc had always been a jumpy guy and Han scared the piss out of me. The fact that Doc didn't immediately yelp at Han's tone of voice spoke to his courage.

After a long moment, Doc stepped aside. "Collect what you came for and go."

Han made a quick motion with his hand and half a dozen paramilitary goons filed forward. They worked like bees, efficiently and without verbal communication, three to a body. Two of them spread black body bags out on the floor while a third lifted the body and placed it inside before zipping the bags up. It was less than ten seconds before both bodies had been bagged and slung over someone's shoulder as they headed for the emergency exits in the front. Four remained behind with Doctor Han.

"I trust you will keep your word, Doctor Ramis," Han said. "We were never here. There were no bodies in your autopsy room today. You saw nothing. You know nothing."

Doc narrowed his eyes. "I understand."

"Good." Han stepped up to Doc, who took a cautious step back. That didn't stop Han from standing toe-to-toe with him. Han grabbed Doc by the shirt, but instead of striking him as I expected, Han unwrinkled Doc's white coat and dusted off some unseen debris. "I'm so glad we could come to an understanding as professionals. However, I am afraid my employer left specific instruction."

He stepped back and made another gesture. The four paramilitary guys closed on Doc while Han turned his back. I jerked out of view of the crack in the curtains as his eyes scanned the wall where Ed and I hid. There was the sickening sound of metal striking flesh and bone and a muffled cry from Doc. Ed shifted next to me until I put a hand on his shoulder, stopping him. His fingers closed into fists and, in the darkness behind the curtain, I watched his eyes turn a frightening shade of yellow as the beating continued.

It went on for a good minute or two before Han called his dogs off. "That's enough," he chirped in a pleased tone. "I think we have made our point."

Heavy footsteps carried away toward the back exit along with the rustle of clothing and armor. The door squealed loudly as it opened and then closed. Ed and I waited until we heard the roar of several engines pulling away before we came out from behind the curtain.

Doc lay curled up on one side, his whole face red. Blood streamed from his nose and mouth while tears flowed from his eyes. Every breath was a pained whimper. By morning, he'd be black and blue from the chest up. I knelt next to him. "Don't move, Doc. How bad is it?"

"I don't think... anything is broken but my pride." I helped him sit up. He turned his head and spat out blood and part of a tooth. "Scratch that. Bastards got a tooth."

"What the hell was all that?" Ed asked, standing over us.

I turned my head and stared at the emergency exit. There were no answers, not yet. Two strange, maybe genetically modified BSI agents had been moved by the paramilitary group from the crime scene Reed disappeared from and into Doc's clinic for holding. A few hours later, Han showed up to collect them. Han, who worked for Marcus.

Not Marcus, I realized. Fitz. That was the only connection I saw between BSI and Han. But what, if anything, did that have to do with Gideon Reed?

I turned back to Ed. "We'd better find out what's on that hard drive, Ed. Pronto."

"What about Doc?"

Doc waved us away. "I'll be fine. And you two had better get gone in case they come back to check on me."

"You sure you'll be fine, Doc?" I asked, helping him to his feet. "I can get someone to watch the place."

He shook his head. "I don't want to be any more trouble than I've already been. Besides, I've played my part. I told you everything I know. This is where I get off the crazy train."

~

Ed and I left the clinic in a hurry. The night outside was once again silent but for the buzzing street light.

I paused out on the sidewalk, looking up and down the street, fearing that they'd be back any minute to tie up loose ends. I was almost sure Han had known we were there. I had nothing but a gut feeling about it, but those had been right often enough I learned to trust my gut. Han was bad news, and if he knew we were there, he and his goons might be waiting anywhere to silence us before we could dig any deeper.

If Han and BSI were working together, and they were willing to kill to keep their secret—whatever it was—as they'd inferred, then there was nothing I could do to stop them. Nowhere was safe, not anymore.

# Chapter Fifteen

The trailer Ed shared with Shauna and Daphne was on the other side of the rez, but it was only a short drive. On the way, we passed the church and I stole a glance over at the burnt-out remains of Reed's house behind the church. In the darkness, the shape of it looked alive, as if the burnt and bent wood were a resting giant, waiting to be woken. I wondered if the cat had gotten out fine and if he'd found a place to sleep for the night. All kinds of things lived on the rez, things that might look at a cat and think of it as food. I swallowed and redirected my attention forward. Best not to think about the cat's fate, then.

I parked the car next to the trailer. None of the lights were on in the house, but the pale blue light dancing across the closest two windows told me his two female roomies were probably watching TV.

"I don't know what my program has recovered off the hard drive so far," Ed said, "but you're welcome to come in and see."

The idea was tempting, even though my mind and body were both exhausted. Even partial information could be better than nothing at all. So far, I had no answers, nothing to go on and no leads to track them down. At best, what I could hope to work through legal angles was to try and pin a drug charge on Hector, but I didn't have enough evidence to go in and perform a search. No judge would sign off on searching a religious compound for drugs, not unless I had some kind of proof that they were manufacturing and distributing them. Collecting that evidence would take weeks, if not months. I needed to find Reed and figure out what was going on now.

I pursed my lips and blew out a breath, resting both hands on the steering wheel and watching the light in the windows. "I can stay a few minutes, I guess."

"Great!" Ed unbuckled his seatbelt, threw open the door and bounded up the stairs, rushing inside before I could even get out of the seatbelt.

I rolled my eyes at his conspiracy theory enthusiasm and got out of the car.

Daphne and Shauna were curled up on the sofa as I suspected. Daphne wore a pink snuggie and stretched out over the sofa, her head resting on Shauna's leg. Shauna was still in her work clothes, the gray jersey tee and sweats that with the weightlifting wolf emblem.

"Hey," Shauna said as I came through the front door. "Beers are on the counter if you want one. Didn't make it to the fridge."

"No thanks," I answered and glanced around the room. My eyes stopped on the salmon colored loveseat on my right and I had to fight not to cringe at the color.

"Never known anyone to want to deal with Ed when he's like this sober, but that's your call." She jerked her chin toward the kitchen, past the salmon loveseat and the darkened hall beyond. "Ed's room is that way. I'd be careful where you sit."

I thanked her again and followed her directions down the short hall to the open door where Ed's bedroom was.

He sat in a worn, leather swivel chair in front of a desk with three monitors set up in a panoramic view. The pale, electric blue light coming from those screens was the only light in the room. It cast shadows over empty bags of chips, overturned cans of energy drinks and soda. Clothes carpeted the floor while anime posters plastered the walls. Something crunched under my shoes when I took my first step inside and I cringed. Ed didn't seem to notice.

"Whoever pulled your hard drive didn't take very good care of it. I was worried it wasn't going to work because of how beat up it was."

"It was in a bit of a firefight," I told Ed, coming to stand behind his chair.

"Uh-huh," he answered absently as his fingers moved over the keyboard at lightning pace. Small, black windows with white text popped up on various different screens as he worked, each new one a layer over a desktop with another anime girl that was half robot.

I don't pretend to know much about computers. I had no idea what the hell he was doing because, from my end, it looked like magick. Heck, maybe it was. I didn't know how deep Ed's skill with technomancy went. As I stood and watched him work, I considered the possibilities of such a talent. He could do a hell of a lot more than track people. With Ed's talents, he could work out a way to use his powers for criminal things like remote hacking, disarming alarms, disabling security of all kinds. I shivered at the idea of Ed becoming some kind of hacker thief. No, not Ed. Ed would only use his powers for good, wouldn't he? Besides, just how much trouble could a werewolf with a gaming and anime obsession get in?

A folder opened and then a subfolder before I could blink. The subfolder contained a list of files named after gibberish. "Looks like there are some spreadsheets and a couple of videos."

"What about the videos? Those seem helpful."

A blue-lined window opened containing a media player I wasn't familiar with, but the window remained black. The computer made a sound and a grey box with a red X popped up center screen containing something technical. I didn't need to understand the jargon to know what the red X meant. Error.

"Looks like some of the data is corrupted." His voice sounded as if he were in physical pain.

I cursed and tightened my fingers on the back of his chair before asking. "Is there anything useful?"

The keyboard keys clicked loudly under Ed's fingers. "Maybe, but that's going to take some time. Let's try another file."

He clicked on another file and a spreadsheet opened. Ed and I both leaned in, squinting at the numbers and letters on the screen. "What am I looking at?" Ed asked.

I pointed to the first column. Every line all the way down the screen in that column was filled with a ten-digit combination of letters and numbers. "This could be an identifying code, sort of like a name. Sometimes, agencies use them in place of names for security reasons. I can call into any precinct or BSI station house in the nation and give them my code to identify myself. This reminds me of that."

"So, each row is a person?" Ed scrolled down through screen after screen, making me dizzy. "There must be a thousand people in this document."

"Stop scrolling a second so I can look." He did and I glanced through the other columns. Most of it meant nothing to me, but it looked like several columns held different weights, measures, and dosages. "This looks like medical information. Scroll over." He did and the text of the document changed colors in the last column, which either contained a bright red D or a blue A. There were notably fewer blue A's.

I filed all the information away in the back of my head, knowing the document had to be important. Until I knew what all that information meant, however, it was useless to me.

"Do you think you can fix the video files, Ed? We need more

information."

Ed sighed and shrugged. "I'll do what I can, but the guy who stole this probably knew more about it. I'd be asking him if he knew what he was looking for. At the very least, maybe he can tell you who wanted it and why."

I pushed away from the chair and rubbed my forehead. "And maybe the crash scene isn't guarded anymore."

"If it was BSI hiding evidence, I doubt they left anything." Ed swiveled the chair around and crossed his skinny arms. "Can they conceal magick stuff or do you think you can find something?"

I stared at the clothes littering his bedroom floor, chewing on my bottom lip. This was BSI, the federal government and my employer. I had no way of knowing everything they had up their sleeve. A good power washing of the site would disturb enough magickal energies that getting a good read on what happened there would be impossible. It would also wash away most of the physical evidence, or at least what little any fires might not have destroyed. Abe could have placed early warning runes there as well, which would notify him if anyone came snooping around. If I went to check it out, there was a good chance I wouldn't be able to do so without him knowing. Since I didn't know whose side Abe was on or what he was doing, I couldn't trust him.

But I was an officer of the law, dammit. It was my job to investigate accidents like that. If Abe wanted to stop me, I'd make him break a sweat doing it.

"I don't know, Ed," I answered after a long pause. "But I'm going to find out."

I went to the door and stopped when Ed called, "Be careful out there, Judah. Two other BSI agents are dead and you don't have impenetrable skin."

"Neither do you," I said, putting my hand on the doorknob and turning around. "At the first sign of trouble, you fry that hard drive, Ed. I've got a feeling it'll be better to destroy it than to get caught with it."

Ed turned his chair around. I waited until I heard his fingers moving across the keys again to leave.

~

I sat at a crossroads. Turning left would take me to Eden and to the hospital to check on Creven. He was a good friend who had gone through hell with me earlier. If it weren't for him, we wouldn't even have the hard drive. It would have been lost in the fire and I'd still be clueless.

To the right lay Four Corners Concho and an unexplored crime scene. Abe and his flunkies might have sterilized the scene and removed any evidence, but they might have missed something. Even the smallest clue might help me pick up Reed's trail again and I needed to find him before he hurt someone else. Going there meant waiting to check in on Creven. It meant putting the case before a friend, but if I went to the hospital first, I'd lose valuable time. Any metaphysical evidence at the crime scene was fading with every passing second and could be gone by the time I made it back.

Either way I turned, I gave something up. It didn't seem like much of a choice, but that's all life really is, a series of choices and consequences. It's living with the consequences that's tough.

Creven wasn't in any danger of dying, and so the visit seemed less urgent. Reed was still out there, still dangerous.

I turned right and rationalized the decision by saying it made more sense in the long term. I was saving lives going right.

The barricade was gone, but I slowed at the spot where the roadblock had been, glancing around. No sign remained other than a little freshly overturned dirt to the side of the road. I could have gotten out of the car there to poke around, but the real interesting stuff would be down the road at the station itself, so I eased on the gas.

A quarter mile down the road from where the roadblock had been sat the dead husk of an old gas station. The pumps had long ago been removed and the building vandalized. Jagged bits of broken glass marked the windows and spray-painted graffiti in both Spanish and English painted the walls. Chipping blue paint and sandstone served as the canvas for the graffiti.

I pulled the car up under the awning and next to where the pumps would have been. The scene was quiet with no signs anyone was still there. There were also no signs an ambulance had crashed there earlier in the day, but I'd need a closer look. I left the car running, headlights on, when I exited. My shoes scraped over bare concrete. Not even rocks or sand remained. I knelt and squinted at a patch of cracked concrete in the headlights. Most of the rest of the parking area was covered in a fine, reddish dust commonly found in the Texas desert. This circular patch, about ten feet in diameter, was a shade of bone white. It gave off the slight burning chemical scent of bleach or something resembling it.

*Dammit*, I thought, leaning back. They'd scrubbed the crime scene. Not only would that remove all the physical evidence, but it would destroy any real link to an impression that might have been left. Still, I had to try. If there was even one drop of blood left at the site, one hair they'd missed, I might be able to tap into the smallest of residual energies and find out something.

I carry a tape measure on my key ring for occasions like that. Magickal energies are stronger in the center of things. I'd need to stand in the center of the gas pumping platform to have any chance of locating that residual energy. Finding the mathematical center meant taking measurements. But I was in a loaner car with loaner keys, meaning I didn't have my tape measurer. I had to wing it.

What looked like the center of the platform placed me between two columns that would have divided the station's two gas pumps. I squeezed in between them and tried to triangulate the distance using my fingers to make sure it was the mathematical center. If it wasn't, it was as close as I was going to get. Then, I closed my eyes, extended my hands and focused.

Reading energies is more difficult in some places than others. Homes, for example, are easy enough to read that I barely have to try. Anyone can do it. Walk into a happy home, and you know it. Stand in the center of a house in turmoil, and you'll feel the broken or violent energies all around. Public places are harder because of the way people come and go. When someone passes through a space, they leave behind a temporary energy like a footprint that fades with time. As days and months pass, though, that energy builds up and a place can take on its own energy based on what passes through.

The Four Corners Concho station had been derelict and abandoned for years. The only people who came out there were people up to no good. Vandals, underage kids with a case of daddy's beer... Anyone who didn't want to have an audience. An energy of secrecy, lies, pain and loneliness lurked like a whisper in a canyon. With no walls to contain it, the energy dissipated out in all directions, making it weak, but there was no mistaking that had become the dominant energy of the place. It appeared to me in dark hues of blue and green fog, drifting lazily around the place.

The weak energy, however, had been overridden by something stronger, two energies at war with one another. No, not war. That wasn't the right word. This didn't have the violent, conquering feel of battle. It felt more like a hunt. The energy of a predator, large, black with jagged edges and the tiniest spark of iron blue hung as a pale shadow near the pole next to me, not far from the bleached area.

I turned and searched for some sign, anything that might tell me more. There was nothing on the pole that I could see. No splash of blood or other fluids that were visible. The only thing I saw was an old plastic bin, the kind that used to hold windshield washer fluid and a squeegee. Dirt and some unidentifiable sticky substance caked the edges of it. It was perhaps the one thing in the area that hadn't been thoroughly scrubbed. Still, I couldn't see anything on the outside. Whatever I was sensing might be on the inside.

My nose wrinkled and my stomach protested at the idea of sticking my hand in there. I had no idea what might be inside.

"The things I do for this job," I muttered and rolled up my sleeve.

It was full of what I hoped was slimy water, though the slight odor of stale beer or old piss—I couldn't tell which—made me think otherwise. I gagged, fought back vomit and felt around in the bin for something solid. My fingers brushed the bottom and something tiny but rock hard. At first, I passed it over thinking it was just a rock, but in the absence of anything else, I pulled it out and held it to the light coming from the headlights.

"A tooth?" I said, turning it over.

More specifically, it was a human incisor. Well, at least it wasn't a vampire incisor, since it didn't look like a fang, though I supposed it didn't *have* to be human. Nevertheless, it was a body part and nothing was better for a basic tracking spell than a piece of the person you want to track. If this was Reed's tooth, I'd hit gold.

Pain lit up my ribs out of nowhere, the momentum of an unseen strike sending me sprawling backward. My only thought as I flew back was that I needed to hold onto that tooth. I closed my hand around it and, when I landed, curled up over it. Lights of pain flashed in my vision and water threatened in the corners of my eyes. Whoever had hit me, got me good.

"You were told to leave it alone, Judah."

I blinked tears away as a tall figure in a hat and long coat stepped between me and the headlights. Abe? What the hell was he doing here and how had he gotten the drop on me?

Abe advanced on where I lay prone and adjusted the hem of his gloves, tugging them tighter. "The moment you showed up, I knew that you would not. Stubbornness is both a strength and a weakness in your case, Judah. It would be to your advantage to learn to know when to quit."

I sat up and scooted back, pocketing the tooth as soon as I got the chance. My ribs screamed in pain as I dragged myself backward. "Why don't you really tell me why you came to Paint Rock, Abe? It wasn't to evaluate my performance and check up on the Vanguard, was it?"

Abe stopped several paces away. "Contrary to what you may believe, I told you to stay out of this for your own protection. Sometimes only having a piece of the puzzle is more dangerous than having the whole thing."

"Spare me the philosophical bullshit." I staggered to my feet, clutching the aching spot in my ribs. "You can't hit me and then pretend to be my friend."

"I am not here to be your friend, Judah. I am not here to be your partner. I have... ulterior motives."

"Kinda guessed that."

His hands flexed. "It is not what you think."

"I know about the BSI agents you guys were hiding in Doc's clinic," I shouted. "I know Han is involved. I know Reed is connected. I know everything!"

"You know nothing. Your ignorance is why they have left you alive. However..." Abe removed his hat and tossed it off to the side like a Frisbee. "Sometimes the only way to teach a stubborn dog to heel is to beat it into submission. If you will not leave this alone, then I have no choice but to incapacitate you to prevent you from throwing your life away."

I tightened my hands into fists. I'd seen Abe fight. As a half-vampire, he was strong. His sucker punch to the ribs earlier had proven he could do the damage. But I could take it. I had magick aplenty and I'd been training with Creven. I had moves he hadn't seen yet. On an even playing field, I was pretty sure I could take Abe.

But we might not be on an even playing field. Vampires got

stronger after dark. I didn't know how much vampire Abe had retained, but I knew even if I walked away from this fight, I'd take a beating that'd slow me down.

I licked my lips and tried to gauge the distance to the car. If I could just get to it, I could get away.

I stepped to the side as if to circle Abe, but he didn't take the bait. He charged me, moving so fast I didn't have time to get my shield up. His left fist came in hard against my ribs, just opposite his earlier strike. The punch pushed air out of my lungs and I gasped as heat and pain flooded my ribcage. My brain went blank as it got to the more important task of processing the pain and preventing more. Instinctually, I curled up, which might have been the worst thing I could do. He brought a fist down to strike the back of my head, which would have brought a quick end to the fight. If I'd stayed put, that is.

I dropped and tackled his legs, taking them from under him.

I'm not particularly strong without magick to back me up, nor am I an expert martial artist or trained brawler. I picked up some stuff in the academy that had seen more use recently fighting Creven, but Abe wasn't like Creven. Abe was like the other guys at the academy: bigger, stronger, taller than me. Take the legs out from under a guy that relies on upper body strength to get the fighting done, and take away the advantage. On the ground, I had knees, elbows, fists and teeth if nothing else, and he'd be forced on the defensive. In theory.

That had been a messy tackle, though, and done in a panic, which meant I threw myself along with him. Hitting the ground jarred us both, but he wasn't suffering from some bruised ribs. Abe kicked at me, a boot making contact with my side below the ribs. I sat up and scrambled to try and put myself over top of him, but there were too many limbs flying at me. I got in one good punch to his nose before the side of his palm struck the side of my head and the world spun. Dizziness and a flash of nausea overtook me, making it easy for Abe to push me off him.

I stumbled to the side and blindly tried to crawl away, fighting the ever-worsening pounding in my head. The headlights blinded me in hazy streaks of white and I suddenly remembered the car. *Get to the car. Escape*. I crawled toward it.

Abe's foot came down on my outstretched hand, the finer bones of my palm crunching under his weight. I screamed in pain, feeling the bones creak and shift.

"I am sorry for this," he said and removed his foot. His long fingers curled around the back of my shirt and he dragged me back away from the car, away from safety.

"Sorry my ass! Why are you doing this?"

"Bruises heal," Abe said and dropped me on the far side of the pumps face-down. He lowered one knee on the center of my back before I could crawl away. No matter how much I squirmed or fought, I couldn't get free. Whatever he'd done to my head ensured I could barely move. "Broken bones mend. Any damage to the body can be repaired, but death... Death is the point of no return. There is no coming back if they kill you. And you must live. Do you understand me, Judah? You. Must. *Live*." Abe grabbed my right arm with both hands, placing one at the elbow and the other on the wrist.

"Who are they, Abe? Who's out there?"

Abe paused, something in his posture changing. I thought maybe he wanted to tell me, but how could that make sense? He'd just spent the last few minutes beating the hell out of me for not backing off. Whoever *they* were, Abe was clearly on their side.

"I am truly sorry," Abe said and twisted. One hand turned forward and the other back, wrenching my arm along with them either way. With all the strength of a vampire behind the movement, both bones in my forearm snapped.

I howled in pain and cursed.

Abe let me go and stood. "Hate me if you want, Judah. I would not blame you. But you must know there are some truths better left uncovered."

I tried to breathe through the sudden pain. Broken bones are no small thing. You don't just shrug them off. When Abe stepped back from me, I blinked through the tears and met his eyes. Rage shook in my voice as I asked, "Why? Why are you doing this to me?"

"Because if I did not stop you, not only do I believe you would uncover the truth, but my loyalty would be in question. I cannot allow that." He raised his head, looking out over the desert before rising. The soles of his boots scraped as he walked to collect his hat, dusted it off and placed it over his head.

Abe walked back to the car I'd left running and climbed in. The engine roared and the tires spun, sending a wave of dry dirt spraying over me before he tore out onto the road, headed back toward Paint Rock.

My right arm throbbed, useless, but my left was still mobile. I used it to reach into my right pocket with shaky hands and draw out the phone Espinoza had tossed to me. Abe had said he'd call me a squad, but I couldn't trust anything he said right now. I'd have to find my own help. It took me three tries to punch in Tindall's number. He picked up on the fourth ring, sounding exhausted. "Sheriff here."

"Tindall?" My voice cracked and my jaw quivered.

There was a momentary pause before Tindall said in a more alert tone, "Where are you?"

"Four Corners."

"How bad is it?"

The pounding in my head suddenly got worse. My stomach turned and I rolled over, retching and expelling everything in my stomach. The move accidentally put weight on my broken arm and I choked.

"Stay where you are," Tindall's voice shouted from the phone I'd dropped. "I'm sending help."

# Chapter Sixteen

I don't know how long I fought not to lose consciousness. Whatever Abe had done to my head had been more of a finishing blow than I realized. The broken bones in my arm throbbed, making the nausea worse. Sitting up made it worse, too, so I lay on my back on the concrete floor of a derelict gas station, staring up at the stars.

There's nowhere on Earth where you can see stars quite like the Texas desert. I was still close enough to Eden that the city lights colored the far edge of the sky, but the deep, palpable blanket of midnight blue still held its dominance over the sky. Tiny sapphires shimmered against light on either side of a dark cut in the sky, an arm of the galaxy millions of lightyears away. Somewhere out there, it made sense that my partner had just beat the shit out of me. It made sense that the one reliable and stable person in Paint Rock had flipped his lid and started trying to kill people. Mara joining a cult, Ed getting arrested, cats and dogs getting along, all of it made sense somewhere out there. How high would I have to climb to get enough perspective to understand? Could I get the full picture from a mountaintop? An airplane? Maybe Mars would be far enough. Where I lay on the ground listening to an owl hoot and an engine rattle in the distance, nothing made sense.

If I could just close my eyes, I could think through it. Maybe a little sleep. I hadn't slept in forever. As late as it was, I should have been curled up in bed next to Sal, listening to him snore gently.

Muffled voices and movement in my arm made open my eyes. I hadn't realized I'd fallen asleep, but I must have blanked. The sky seemed lighter and the throbbing pain in my broken arm had turned into an adrenaline-fueled numbness that spread up to my elbow. Two shapes bent over me, one of them responsible for the sudden return of pain in my forearm.

"I thought you said you were watching her?"

Sal? What was he doing here? Where was Tindall?

"You know how good she's gotten at dodging us. The last time we spoke, you said she was with that half-vampire. She had an escort." The second voice belonged to Bran.

Sal's grip tightened on my arm. I tried to say, "Ouch," but it came out more as a pained grunt.

Sal tightened his grip and forced my arm to straighten out,

resulting in another hiss of pain from me. "Quit trying to move it, Judah. It's a good fracture. How'd you manage it this time? Jesus, you're out in the middle of nowhere with no one around and you still somehow manage to get hurt. Who did this to you?"

My head spun with pain as a faint pulse of magick spread from his hands into my arm. His healing magick felt weaker than normal, maybe because he was still recovering himself.

I wanted to tell him it was Abe, but I was afraid to. More than afraid, maybe. Ashamed. Here I was, someone who had gone up against ice giants, demons, and zombies. I'd faced down my own death and come out on top. But I had let Abe mop the floor with me. I should have fought harder, pushed more. If I hadn't hesitated, if he hadn't hit first, maybe... Whatever I wanted to think was lost in a sea of agony as Sal tightened his grip on my arm even further.

"Perhaps we should let her recover before we drown her in questions, brother."

I cringed and squeezed my eyes shut. Beads of moisture trailed down my cheeks. "Tindall?"

Bran's hand came down gently on my back, steadying me in my seated position. "He's the one who called us. If he'd come himself, it would put him in an awkward position."

Of course. He'd have to call a squad and hospitals asked a lot of questions. There would be an investigation, inquiries. It would go on record that I'd been injured and I'd have to make a report on how it had happened. That'd be bad for me because it would draw BSI's attention. Tindall couldn't have known that, though. He might have guessed something was going on because I had called him instead of an ambulance, but he also might have been called somewhere else. Being sheriff meant constantly being pulled in all directions. Poor guy.

"I don't know that I can fully repair the broken bone." Sweat trailed down the side of Sal's face and neck and his forehead wrinkled in concentration. Setting a broken bone and mending it was normally child's play for him. "I can get it started, but it's still going to hurt like a bitch and be vulnerable."

I flashed a goofy smile. "Patch me up, doc. Send me back out."

Something dark flashed behind his eyes, a memory maybe. He shook his head and the look was gone. "You still need to tell me who did this. I'm not letting that go. Now, hold still. This is really going to hurt."

Setting a broken bone is never fun, but doing it with no medical gear in the middle of nowhere is definitely not ideal. Sal's healing powers could help mend enough bone together that it'd heal the rest of the way on its own in time, but he couldn't do anything for the pain, which meant he hadn't lied. It was going to hurt. A lot.

He had Bran stand behind me, his hands gripping my upper arm tight, tugging it away from my shoulder. Once Sal moved things back in place, that would keep me from jerking away on instinct, which would complicate everything.

Sal grabbed my arm with both hands an inch or so below the break and looked straight at me. "Do it on three?"

I winced at the pain. The fog in my head meant I could barely remember what we were about to do. I tired to focus on it, but I couldn't do that and talk at the same time so I just nodded. The move left me blinking away stars and double vision.

"On three. One, two..."

He did it on two, the bastard.

Sal gave my arm a good pull. Bones shifted. Something snapped inside my arm like a rubber band. I ground my teeth and held in the scream until I was afraid I'd break my teeth. When it finally came out, it was more a roar of anger than pain.

Sal finally released my arm and probed the breaks gently with a finger. It throbbed, the pain threatening to overtake the pounding in my head again. "Move a muscle and we'll have to do it again. Hold. Still."

He placed his palm over the breaks and the other under, as if my arm were sandwich meat and his hands bread. Warmth spread out over my skin under his hands. It wasn't hot like fire, but rather like the sun on a warm summer day. A comforting feeling at war with the pain. Inside my arm, it felt like someone was jackhammering at the bones rather than putting them back together. It lasted a minute, maybe two, before he pulled his hand away and held one out to Bran. Bran slapped a men's magazine into Sal's waiting palm.

I made a face. "You're going to patch me up with porno?"

"They don't exactly keep *Better Homes and Gardens* laying around at the clubhouse, Judah. I grabbed what I could on the way out." Sal positioned the magazine under my arm and folded it up on either side.

I watched what he was doing, but I couldn't make sense of it. The memory of what had happened suddenly felt out of reach. "What happened to my arm?"

Sal exchanged glances with Bran. "Do you know where you are, Judah?"

I glanced around while Bran handed him some masking tape and he used it to make a makeshift splint for my arm. Bran's motorcycle sat off to my left a few feet and Sal's truck had come in behind it. I was out in the middle of nowhere with no clear reason. "Who's with Mia and Hunter?"

"Hunter's got Mia for a few hours." Sal's voice was muffled as he ripped the tape with his teeth. "I was at the clubhouse. Emergency meeting. I didn't have time to call a sitter."

"Where's Hunter?"

Frustration crept into his voice and his hands moved a little faster. "I just told you. God, Judah. You're really messed up."

"Did you say something about the club? Were you there? Why?"

Sal paused what he was doing and looked behind me at Bran, the look on his face telling me he wasn't supposed to talk about it.

Bran came to his rescue. "Help for a friend of the club."

Sal sighed through his nose. Bran handed him the red bandana that he usually wore around his head. Through a series of knots and strategic draping, they fashioned a quick sling for me and eased my arm into it.

I frowned at the awkward silence. "You're not going to tell me, are you?"

Sal shook his head again. "You'll have to clear it with Istaqua or another officer."

Bran cleared his throat.

"You know something?" I tried to scramble to my feet but the dizziness and Bran's hands on my shoulders kept me down.

Bran shrugged. "Istaqua and Phil know something. I only know a little, but I know that what they know could be useful. Of course, they won't be willing to help you for free."

Something buzzed against my ass and I jerked. It took me an extra long time to realize it was just my borrowed cell phone ringing. I'd somehow wound up on top of the dumb thing. Using my uninjured arm, I fished the phone out from under me. Hairline cracks spread over the screen from the center, but the display seemed to have held up. My fingers fumbled to slide over the broken screen to answer the call.

"Judah!" Ed sounded exasperated. "I finally got two of those video files to work and took a peek at one. I didn't get far. You're going to want to see this ASAP."

"Video files?" Sal raised an eyebrow. Damn werewolves and their impeccable hearing.

I shook my head, dismissing Sal's questioning. The less anyone knew, the better. If Abe was willing to beat me up to stop me, I didn't want to think about what he'd do to Sal or Ed. "Ed. Didn't we just talk?"

Ed was silent a beat. "You okay, Judah? You sound kind of funny. Never mind. This is more important than that. It's bigger. Seriously, you need to see this."

Sal's hand closed around the phone in my hand and he jerked it away. "Someone just beat the shit out of her, Ed. Rattled her brain pretty good. I'm taking her to the hospital. Whatever you have can wait."

Hospital? Over my dead body. Sal hated hospitals. "I don't need to go to the hospital."

I tried to pull myself up and winced at the pain. Even though I hadn't moved my arm, gravity acted on it and even the tiniest of shifts hurt. My head spun with the movement. Sudden contractions in my gut forced me to bend over and gag on vomit.

Sal swept me up in his arms. "Bran, an escort?"

"You got it, brother."

Concrete and sand passed under me as I floated to wherever Sal had decided I should go. I was too dazed to do much objecting. Everything felt surreal, as if I were watching it through a monitor instead of experiencing it. The last time I'd felt that lightheaded, I had died for a full four minutes. Icy fear formed a lump in my throat at the memory of my short stint in the afterlife. Was I dying again?

I floated from a prone position to sitting upright. Warm air struck my face and neck along with the distant smell of burning ash. My eyes saw road moving in front of us at seventy miles an hour, maybe faster, but I had no sense that we were actually going anywhere. Every set of headlights that passed made the back of my eyes feel raw. Every blast of sound ached. When I tried to move my arm to cover my eyes or ears, the nerve endings lit on fire. Pain felt like my only anchor, the only thing keeping me awake and alive.

~

I don't recall my initial exam in the emergency room. I remember the doctor coming in briefly and speaking to Sal and not to me. Even when I tried to direct his attention to me instead of to Sal, he barely gave me the time of day, the jerk. Not that I would have understood anything he had to say. His voice sounded like it was underwater.

It wasn't until I was lying on my back, listening to the rhythmic pounding of the MRI that I had any sense of just how serious my injury was. The fog cleared a little, but didn't lift entirely. I blinked and thought, *I'm in a hospital. Sal brought me here when he wouldn't even bring Mia for her check up. He must have been really worried about me.*

Slowly, things came back to me.

Espinoza was going to be pissed when he found out Abe took his car. I hoped he'd stash it somewhere easy to find at least. Maybe I could report it stolen. It wouldn't be too much trouble for Abe to get that sorted out, but if I could inconvenience him in the slightest, I wanted to try. I sure as hell wasn't going to try fisticuffs with him again anytime soon. I'd have to get back at him some other way, at least until I was better.

I stared into the mirror inside the plastic helmet encasing my head. What then? Was I supposed to just go back to work, be his partner and pretend like he hadn't just beat me up? I couldn't report him to our superiors, not until I knew for sure about those BSI agents Doc had been hiding. People higher up the chain could be involved and, if I tipped them off that I was poking around...

*Judah, you idiot!* If I hadn't been crammed inside a plastic tube and suffering from a concussion, I would've smacked myself in the head. *That's exactly why he tried to stop you!*

Abe's intervention proved that Ed's theory was right. BSI was trying to cover something up, something to do with Reed. Abe didn't want me to find out. In his own weird way, he thought that busting me up bad enough would put me down for the count. I'd have to spend time recovering. Every moment I was down and out, he got closer to succeeding with his cover-up. I needed to get out of the hospital and fast, before he destroyed everything.

It suddenly dawned on me that I'd stripped out of my clothes at some point and put on the oh-so-flattering hospital gown for the MRI. The tooth I'd found at the scene was still in my pocket. I really hoped they hadn't tossed it out or that it hadn't fallen out in all the excitement.

An intercom buzzed and a pleasant female voice filtered through it and into my head. "Make sure you stay nice and still now. We don't want to have to do this again."

"How much longer?"

"Twenty to forty minutes, hon. Just try and relax. It'll be over soon."

I squared my jaw and stared into the mirror above my head. My eyes crossed, but at least I could see and process information again. Maybe Sal's healing had given my brain a little recovery boost as well. Whatever time I had left in that machine, I had to use it to try and figure things out. I had to connect Reed to Hector and BSI, whatever the cost. Abe hadn't deterred me. All he'd done was make me even more determined.

# Chapter Seventeen

After an eternity in a freezing, sterile room with little to no privacy, the doctor decided I could go home. There was no internal bleeding or visible damage. All the scans had come out fine and there was nothing wrong with me that rest wouldn't fix. I was to go home, rest, report back to the ER if symptoms continued longer than two days or got worse. Sal was supposed to monitor me. Doctor's orders.

To say I was unhappy about it was an understatement. I sat with my arms crossed, staring out the side window, and refusing to look at Sal all the way home. The night had faded, replaced now by the endless blue Texas sky. I watched buzzards circle in the distance while Kenny Rogers sang *The Gambler* on the radio.

Sal didn't seem to take the hint that I didn't want to talk. All during my time in the hospital, he'd barely said two words to me. I knew a scolding was coming, I'd just hoped we'd make it home before he started.

He reached over and turned down the radio. "So, what is this? You trying to kill yourself?"

I shifted in my seat. If I could have turned my back to him, I would have.

"I don't know what all is going on, Judah, but I know you shouldn't be out in the middle of the desert, alone, in the middle of the night. And this thing you've got Ed looking into... It's one thing for you to go off and get hurt, but for you to drag Ed into it—"

"Ed involved himself."

Sal gave me a look, one he often shot Mia when she was about to do something that'd get her into trouble. The kind of look that made every kid stop what they were doing. The dad look. What right did he have to be throwing that look at me?

I shot back. "You saw him at the first fire. You know he's been involved since the beginning. And you know how stuck on Mara he is, Sal. He's not going to back off just because someone tells him to. Would you if it were me?"

"That'd be different. Ed and Mara aren't like you and me."

"Aren't they?"

The cab of the truck was silent but for the radio. Kenny Roger's upbeat tune had ended and Johnny Cash had come on with his rendition of *Hurt*.

Sal reached over and turned the radio off. “You know, when Ed and Daphne came here, everything was falling apart. Zoe and me were at the height of our fighting, facing down the split that was to come. Silvia’s death was still fresh for Chanter and Valentino and Nina’s breeding permit had just been turned down. It felt like the whole world had gone to shit. Daphne was quiet, reserved. She smiled a lot, and that helped, but it was Ed who really put us back together. He brought an energy with him so that you just couldn’t help but laugh. It’s hard to explain, but that energy really changed us. He’s always been the heart of the pack. Ever since Mara, things have changed. He’s different.”

“Growing pains.” I smiled and closed my eyes. “He’s not a kid anymore. Hard to watch him grow up, to not think of him as someone that needs protected, but someone who can handle himself.”

After a long moment of silence, Sal nodded. “Yeah. Maybe. It’s my job to protect people, to keep my pack safe and happy. But everybody keeps telling me they don’t need me to do that anymore. What good am I to anyone if I can’t stop them from getting hurt?”

I suddenly felt even worse about being short with Sal. I’d been dodging his protective detail for months and frustrating the hell out of him. If I’d known it meant that much to him, I might not have tried so hard.

From a parent’s perspective, I understood. Here I was, watching Hunter grow up and not need me. It stung to be told to drop him off a block from school, to hear him tell me to butt out. I missed being close enough to share secrets.

Sal was in that same position with Ed. Ed was the baby of the pack in a lot of ways. Both Sal and Valentino had looked at him like a younger brother. While Valentino had been pushing Ed to be more like him, Sal had always done everything he could to preserve Ed’s innocence. He’d tried and failed. It was inevitable, really. No matter how hard you try to shield those you love from pain, you know deep down it’s impossible. Facing that hurt down when it came, that change in status from an innocent to be protected to a peer, can destroy a relationship if it’s mishandled. There had to be a balance between giving someone their space, letting them fail, and being a guiding hand there to pick them up when they fell.

Not only was Sal going through that with Ed, but with Mia and me, too.

I sighed through my nose and winced at the dull throbbing in my head. "You know I can't promise you I'm going to give up and rest easy."

"It's just not in you. Sometimes, your tenacity is what I love about you. Other times, I'm so damn worried that's what's going to get you killed."

He flipped on the turn signal and the truck slowed. Off to our left, the massive concrete wall of the reservation loomed. Black shapes patrolled the towers, the border patrol. It seemed like there were more agents up there today than normal, but maybe that was just because I so rarely paid attention. The border patrol agents lifted the barrier and we drove right through without being stopped.

As we pulled into the reservation, Sal tapped his fingers on the steering wheel, deep in thought. "I know you won't promise me that you're going to rest and get better, but will you at least promise me you won't go anywhere alone? At least not for a few days until you've had your follow up appointment with Doc. No more walking around in the middle of nowhere late at night."

"If you promise to trust me enough to choose who goes with me, sure."

Sal nodded. "I trust your judgement. I just want to know you're safe."

"I think I can do that, then." I offered Sal a tired smile. More than anything, I wanted to curl up in bed next to him and sleep for days, but I couldn't afford it. If I was lucky, I'd get a nap. Time off was a luxury I just couldn't afford, broken arm and concussion or not.

We pulled into the driveway and parked. Sal didn't come and open the door for me, but waited for me, a hand out if I needed it. I took it to climb down from the truck and we went hand-in-hand to the front door.

Hunter and Mia were still in their pajamas watching cartoons on the TV. Rather, Mia was watching her cartoons while Hunter had his feet up on the coffee table, texting away. Hunter looked up as we came in, his face changing as he took in the splinted arm, the bruises and scrapes. Gold flashed through his eyes as he rose to his feet. "Tell me you got the asshole that did that to you."

Sal held up a hand. "There won't be any getting anybody for at least a few hours. Your mom needs to rest, kid. Our job is to make sure she gets it."

Mia toddled over. She had a half-eaten cookie in her hand that she held out to me with a smile. "No thanks, kiddo. You enjoy your cookie."

When I didn't take her cookie, she latched onto my leg in a tight hug that sent a prickling sensation through me. I wouldn't be able to pick her up, not until my arm fully healed. Without picking her up, how was I supposed to change her? Put her in her high chair? In her car seat? I'd barely been home a minute and already I felt even more helpless. Tears welled in my eyes as I bent down to return the hug. It hurt and made the dull throb in the front of my head even worse, but I'd been through worse. I'd go through worse any day of the week, so long as it meant I got to come home. Sal was right. I needed to be more careful. I had a family waiting for me.

"Alright, bratling, that's enough." Hunter came by and scooped Mia up. "It's about time for Sesame Street."

"Elmo!"

"Yeah, and that freaky red monster puppet you like so much." Hunter nodded to me, the message clear. *Don't worry, mom. I got this.*

I was relieved, but felt a pang of loss at the same time. When had my boy grown up so much?

Sal took me to the bedroom and tucked me in, drawing the blankets up to my chin. "What about you? How the cut on your side doing?"

He shrugged. "Healing. Slowly. As I have the energy, I'll try to do what I can for your arm, but the concussion is serious. Healing that is delicate work and I just don't have the strength for it. Chanter was good at that kind of thing. I'm more the kind of healer that can get you good enough to go back at it." He wagged a finger at me. "But if you keep getting hurt, there's going to be a point I can't help."

"I know, doc." I yawned, stretched and turned over. "Thanks for the pep talk."

Sal grunted, probably in approval, and closed the door behind him on the way out.

~

Heavy shadows darkened the room when next I opened my eyes. The curtain moved in a slight breeze coming through the cracked window. Sweat rolled down my upper arm and settled inside the cast, making it itch. Red digital numbers on the alarm clock next to the bed told me I'd slept through the day. It was already going on eight thirty in the evening.

I sat up with a groan. The pounding in my head had faded slightly, but the dizziness was still there. It would probably linger for another week or so, the doctor had said. I hoped the nausea would fade before then, though.

Something hard had dug into my thigh through the jeans I'd fallen asleep in. A little pinprick of pain prompted me to reach into my pocket and pull out... a tooth? Memory of what I'd found at Four Corners came back. I hadn't yet had time to figure out whose tooth it was or even if it would be useful to my investigation.

I lifted the tooth into a tiny beam of light, turning it. "Well, I've got all the time in the world now."

Science could have identified the owner of the tooth if I wanted to wait six weeks and bag it as evidence. Or, I could do a little magickal heavy lifting and get an answer.

I tossed aside all the blankets and piled the pillows behind me before pulling my feet in to sit cross-legged. It's not necessary to do magick in any particular position, but I find it easier to focus on an object if I'm comfortable. Some spells require specific ingredients, mathematical equations, special times of days, or can only be performed on a certain day of the year. The one I wanted only required a biological sample, intense concentration, and a physical or mental connection. I didn't have a physical connection to Gideon Reed, but we were friends and allies. What I knew would have to be good enough.

As I sat, I cleared my mind, blocking out pain and distraction. The overbearing warmth in the room was the most difficult thing to ignore, but I worked past it in time. Once I'd cleared my mind, I focused my attention on the tooth resting between my thumb and forefinger, giving it a little pulse of will. In my mind's eye, I worked at reconstructing Gideon Reed.

I made him slightly taller than the average man, with broad

shoulders and short, perfectly trimmed auburn hair. A well-proportioned nose, attractive face, piercing eyes and hands worn by work in a low-moisture environment. But people are more than just what they look like on the outside, so I threw in a dash of kindness, represented by a sparkle in the eyes, and a firm belief in justice, represented by the sword he gripped firmly in both hands. Finally, the last and most important ingredient went into forming a complete picture of Gideon Reed in my mind: his unshakable faith in his God. I placed it on him in the form of a plain, silver crucifix, one I had seen him carry on several occasions. It shone in imagined light, the reflection of it filling in the missing contours of his face and body. This image of Gideon Reed was as complete as any I could make.

Once I had that, I sent another stream of my will down into the tooth in my hand. If the tooth belonged to Reed, the magick should have resonated in the image I created. That was, if I had created a complete enough picture, and if the tooth was still fresh enough evidence. After all I'd been through, the psychic connection between Reed and the tooth could have been broken because I'd waited too long.

Reed's image shimmered in a wave beginning in the center of the image and moving outward like ripples.

I'd been right all along. It *was* his tooth. Now, I just had to muster enough energy and the right ingredients for a tracking spell and we could use the tooth to track him down.

A buzz on the nightstand caught my attention. I turned to see the burner phone Espinoza had given me dancing and glowing, Ed's number displayed on the screen. I grabbed for it and answered, hoping Sal hadn't heard it buzzing in the next room. "Ed, did you get those video files decoded?"

"It's called decrypting, Judah, and I told you hours ago that I did."

"Sorry. I hit my head. Memory's fuzzy."

"Why are we whispering?"

I cast a long glance at the door. No one had come through it and the TV was still on. That didn't mean they couldn't hear me. Werewolves have an uncanny sense of hearing. "Because if Sal hears me planning to go out, I'm sure he'll stop me. He doesn't want you involved either, Ed."

"This line might not be secure, so the shorter a conversation we have, the better. You need to see what I've seen, even if that means bringing an escort. In fact, you might not want to come alone. This is bigger than we thought."

I sighed and rubbed the back of my aching head. "Alright, Ed. I'll see what I can do."

"Don't take too long." Ed hung up.

He didn't have to tell me why. Eventually, Abe would figure out I knew something. They might find the laptop in the wreckage of the fire. Even if it was damaged, they'd probably notice the missing hard drive. Abe knew who I'd go to for help with that. Dammit, I had to see what was on it that and then destroy it for Ed's sake.

Walking across the room wasn't as difficult as I thought it would be. I was still dizzy, but once I managed to get my feet under me, it was just a matter of putting one foot in front of the other.

Outside of the bedroom, all the lights were off and the curtains drawn. Only the blue light of the television was available to cast shadows. Hunter and Sal sat on the sofa, both of them turning around when I came out of the room. I tried to catch a glimpse of what they were watching, but my eyes were too sensitive to the light and I had to look away.

I used dodging into the bathroom as an excuse not to talk to them just yet. While I was in there, they turned whatever they were watching off. Sal stood outside the door when I opened it, leaning against the washing machine. He had his arms crossed, an eyebrow raised, waiting for me to give him some kind of report. Best cut to the chase then.

"I need to go over to Ed's." I felt like a teenager asking to borrow the car.

Sal eyed me with heavy scrutiny. "You want me to take you?"

"Unless Hunter suddenly learned to drive."

Hunter, who had remained on the sofa, turned around, his proverbial ears perked at the prospect of driving.

I held a finger out at him. "Don't even think about bringing that up until you're sixteen."

He turned around, grumbling. "I can get a learner's permit at fifteen and a half."

"I'll take you over to Ed's. I need to talk to him anyway. Get your coat."

"My coat?" I scrunched up my nose. "It's got to be eighty

outside."

"Storm coming in." Sal went and grabbed my coat from the back of a chair, tossing it to me. "I figure once you see what Ed has to say, you'll go running off to save the day. I can't stop you, but I can at least make sure you stay dry while you're out there."

I caught the coat and then stood on my tiptoes to plant a kiss on his chin. "Thanks for looking out for me."

"Yeah, yeah." He winked at me. "Now move it, Kimosabe. Tanto's got shit of his own to do."

# Chapter Eighteen

Shauna and Daphne weren't home when we got there. Ed threw open the door as soon as I reached the porch, my hand raised to press the buzzer. His mouth hung open, halfway through saying something, but the words halted when he saw Sal standing behind me.

Ed blinked once, straightened and swallowed. "Alpha. I didn't expect… I mean… Good to see you?"

Sal tilted his head to the side. "You've been dodging my calls."

There was no hint of malice or anger in Sal's voice that I could hear, but Ed shrank. "Uh, yeah, sorry about that. I've been busy."

"That's fine. This time. In the future, you're not going to be too busy to answer my calls again, are you, Ed?"

Ed cleared his throat. "No, no. Once I get all this figured out, I'll be golden." He pulled the door open wider. "Come in, both of you. Judah, is he up to speed?"

"Not really." I stepped through the door and steadied myself on the other side by holding onto the arm of a chair.

"How much does he know?"

I held onto the chair as I turned to gauge Sal's reaction to Ed's question. I knew Sal wasn't happy about Ed keeping secrets from him. He was also perplexed by it. Ed shouldn't have been able to lie to Sal without Sal detecting it. Keeping secrets from his alpha should have been even more difficult. Werewolves in a pack instinctually shared information with each other. Sal was supposed to be his guidance, his mentor, like an older brother or a parent.

Sal put his hands in his pockets as the screen door bounced closed behind him. "Let's just say I know enough and leave it at that, huh?"

"Uh-huh." Ed gestured back toward his bedroom. "This way."

Ed rushed on ahead and, by the time Sal and I made it to his room, he'd picked up most of the clothes on his floor and tossed them into a growing mountain in the far corner. With a quick sweep of his arm, he pushed half the trash on his desk into a trash can on one side before sinking down into his chair.

"Now, there were five video files on the computer and I managed to get three totally decrypted. The fourth and fifth ones are corrupted beyond repair. Let's start at the beginning."

He moved his cursor to the first file and double-clicked it. Just like last time, the video player opened, but no error came on the screen. Instead, the video displayed the image of a young woman on a bed in a minimally furnished room. She wore a pale blue hospital gown with a dizzying Greek key pattern on it, open in the back. Her back was to the camera, which also sat several feet above her head. The woman stood and paced several feet from the camera before turning and glaring up at it. The look on her face, it was raw hatred.

A familiar voice started up over the video footage. Doctor Han's. "Subject Thirty-Six upon entering week three of the program. All tests confirm that she entered the program in good health, optimal mental function, alert and responsive to all stimuli. After the initial batch of tests and exposure to serums one through twenty, tests indicate no change in anything other than her mood. Of course, that could be due to hormonal changes. Female subjects were less than ideal on that front because of such a variable, but for phase two of the program, we will need both viable male and female subjects. Tomorrow, Thirty-Six will be the first female subject exposed to Doctor LeDuc's twenty-first serum. He may have discarded the effects initially, but as time has proven, he was far less interested in the program than in his own side project. Nevertheless, his work will fuel the future for both man and supernatural kind. I must admit, I wish he were here to see it."

All through the video, the woman just stood, staring at the camera, rage in her eyes. The more I stared at that gaunt face, the more I noticed. Bruises of varying sizes and ages colored her cheeks, neck and arms. A cut on her forehead looked like it had been stitched closed.

I swallowed growing tightness in my throat. "Anyone else recognize that voice?"

"Doctor Han," Sal growled next to me. "Marcus' personal physician and the asshole who helped keep Mia from me."

"If you don't like him now, just wait until you've seen all the videos." Ed snorted and opened another video file.

The same woman appeared on the screen in the middle of a different room, this one without any furnishings. She stood, surrounded by men in guard uniforms, her fists balled and raised. The men held batons. It didn't take much imagination to see what was about to happen.

The woman, Subject Thirty-Six, leapt forward first with a roar and drove her fist into the stomach of one of the guards. It was all for nothing, as the guard must have been wearing some type of armor. She cried out and drew her fist back. Then, the beating started. They beat her down without mercy or regard for her life. Again and again, the clubs came down and lifted away bloody. All the while, Han's voice droned on excitedly in the background.

"There was a breakthrough with one of the other subjects yesterday. When final preparations for his liquidation began, the subject was able to conjure fire in the palm of his hand! We subdued the subject and proceeded with liquidation, but the event sparked an epiphany. Some organisms develop defense mechanisms under extreme duress."

Here, Han's commentary paused while a bright flash covered the screen. I flinched away, squinting in the darkness. When I turned back, Subject Thirty-Six stood, bloodied and with her fists clenched, in the center of a massacre. Body parts had been scattered all over the room. Blood spatter painted the wall. One of the poor guards was still alive and used his one remaining stub of an arm to try and crawl away from her. Thirty-Six marched over, grabbed him by the head, and twisted. The guard fell limp.

"We've done it," Han whispered into the microphone. "Forced evolution, manifesting the powers of magic in mundane humans. If it can be done with human DNA, then we are only a breath away from taking the healing powers of the werewolves, the speed of the vampire, and combining them to make something entirely new."

Ed paused the video with less than two seconds remaining.

Silence fell on the room. Blood rushed in my ears and my palm ached from where I had dug my fingernails into the meat of it. "Human experimentation. Doctor Han is doing this? What did he mean by liquidation?"

Sal crossed his arms next to me. "When the government uses words like liquidation, assets, and casualty, it usually means some politician is getting rich while someone else is getting dead."

Ed shook his head. "But Han doesn't work for the government. He works for Marcus Kelley."

I dug my fingernails in harder. "Yeah, Marcus Kelley who owns Fitz Pharmaceuticals, which has the largest medical government contract in history. Not only does Fitz get federal funding to develop and manufacture supernatural testing and medical supplies, but they get one hell of a block research grant."

Ed's eyes widened. "Shit, you're right. Do you think Marcus knows?"

"If he doesn't, he's about to hear about it from me." I took a deep breath and let it out. That was another problem, a big one, but a distraction from the issue at hand. "What does any of this have to do with Hector and Reed?"

Ed turned his chair back to the computer. "All answered in video number three."

He queued the next video up. It was security footage from somewhere else, maybe another building entirely. The image was a grainy black and white sequence taken from the corner of a small room, showing a group of men standing in front of a large wall. They all had their backs to the camera, making it impossible to know who they were.

"We had an inspection today," Han's voice announced. "Those damned Sicarii showed up again to inspect the facility with a group from the BSI board of directors. As much as I would have liked to turn them all away to focus on the research, that's impossible, considering they're funding it." He sighed. "I owe too much to the Sicarii. Without the rem, all my efforts would be fruitless. It really is the key to forcing the mutation, while extreme stress seems to be what causes the expression of the genetic mutation. It may be brutal to drug the subjects and then beat them, boil them, or freeze them until they show their true colors, but all scientific advancement comes at a cost. Today, thousands of lives are saved thanks to the advancements the Nazis made. Yet Hitler is remembered as a monster. He wasn't. He was a man. Misguided perhaps, but a man of true vision. These Sicarii are much like him. They have a vision for how they wish to shape this world, but their execution is lacking. No matter. So long as I am free to learn, it is of no consequence to me."

At the end of his speech, three of the men in the security footage turned, their faces captured by the camera.

"Pause it!"

Ed jammed his thumb down on the space bar and the image held, the tops and bottoms of the screen blurred by tracking marks.

"Is that...?" Sal leaned forward.

I raised a shaky finger to point at the screen, first pointing to the man on the right. "Hector Demetrius." My finger moved to the man on the left. "And that's Gideon Reed."

"And the man in the center is Senator Robert Grahm," Ed finished, pointing to the man in the center. "He's the Ohio state senator who's credited for thinking up this whole reservation in some committee somewhere."

I frowned. "I remember him. Dealt with him once in Ohio. My very last case. I'd hoped to never see him again."

"Outspoken anti-supernaturalist, pro-humanist and suspected member of the Vanguards of Humanity," Ed continued.

"I don't get it." Sal leaned back away from Ed. "What's Reed doing with guys like that? He's a nobody sitting on the ruling council of the reservation. A priest of some barely-attended church in the middle of nowhere. What's he doing with a senator and...whatever the hell Hector Demetrius is?"

"I think the better question has to do with these Sicarii," I said. "Han said they have a vision for the world. What does that mean?"

Ed spun his chair around and flashed his hands in the air. "Illuminati confirmed!" When I glared at him, he added, "What? That's exactly what they sound like. Look, if you're interested, I did do a quick Google search. The Sicarii were supposed to have been a group of assassins living in Ancient Rome. They opposed the Roman occupation of the province of Judea. Apparently killed a lot of Romans in crowds and were branded terrorists and enemies of the state. Judas Iscariot might have been one of these guys, but the last time they were mentioned in history was in like 70 A.D. There's nothing else anywhere about them since then. They just kind of disappeared."

I raised a finger in the air. "So, the million-dollar question is what do a bigot senator, a magick-using cult leader, a small-town priest, and a secret government experiment have in common?"

"To find that answer, you'll have to talk to one of them," Sal said.

Ed nodded. "And, unfortunately, Hector's not talking and Reed is missing."

"The senator isn't going to talk to me." I folded my arms over my chest. "But, armed with this information, Hector just might."

That meant keeping the footage to use as leverage, something that would put Ed in danger. I turned to look at Sal, who had probably concluded the same thing.

He stared hard at Ed. "How secure is this information? Any

chance someone else is going to figure out we know what we know?"

"It's always a possibility." Ed shrugged. "But there are things I can do to reduce the likelihood of that happening. I'll disconnect from the internet and pop the hard drive, store it in a safe place. Unless you want me to destroy it?"

Sal looked at me. "Your call."

I chewed on my bottom lip a minute, imagining those paramilitary goons busting down Ed's door and hauling him away. If that happened, there'd be nothing I could do to get him back. He'd be as good as dead.

I sighed and closed my eyes. "Not yet. Give me until tomorrow morning to think about it. Do what you can to protect the information. If you haven't heard from me by tomorrow night, get rid of it. No one else knows about this, understand, Ed? Not Daphne, not Mara. This has to be a secret."

Ed nodded once. "Got it. You stay safe, Judah."

"You too, Ed," I said and showed myself out.

~

I walked outside and stood under the cloud-covered sky, watching the silver crescent moon rise. It seemed peaceful, more peaceful than the world had any right to be. Everything felt like chaos.

All this time, I had been defending BSI. I knew they weren't perfect—no branch of the government is—but it had always seemed better than the alternative. Without BSI, people would live in fear. The whole country might have risen up and killed the supernaturals soon after the Revelation, just like what had happened to Alex. Back then, BSI put a stop to it. Maybe they'd gotten too strict and let fear cloud their judgement, but the bare bones of the idea were still there. With the right people and enough time and effort, I had believed it could all be fixed from the inside.

I sank down to sit on the first stair outside of Ed's house. Look where that belief got you, Judah. Sent out to Paint Rock, to what was supposed to be the end of your career. Beaten up by your partner. Case after case lands on your desk with no end in sight. No help. You're too busy to make a difference, they've seen to that.

If BSI was experimenting on humans, torturing people and

drugging them to try and force some perceived next evolutionary stage, then what could I do about it?

I put my head in my hands. LeDuc had known. All those years ago, when he boasted that I needed him to help stop what was coming, what if that wasn't a lie? What if I had killed our only chance of destroying and exposing a corrupt government? What if innocent people had died because of me?

The front door swung open and Sal's footsteps stopped behind me. His lighter clicked and I listened to the small whoosh of flame, the sizzle and burn of tar, tobacco and paper as he lit another cigarette. "Ed said he was able to pull dates from those files. The first one was from about six months after LeDuc would have blown up Han's lab, long before you ever got here, babe."

I clenched my fists against my eyes. "That doesn't absolve me of some of the responsibility. I've spent all this time working for them, Sal. More than a decade. I've been part of the problem."

He grunted and sat down next to me on the step, the cigarette hanging loosely in his fingers. "You can't blame yourself for wanting everyone to be as good as you think they are. World's an ugly place. That's hard to come go grips with. People like me, we signed up to see that firsthand. War is the worst mankind has to offer. Once you've seen that, you learn to recognize a battle when it's coming. The air changes, feels charged, like right before a lightning strike. The world feels unusually calm. It's all wrong because you know, you just know, something's not right. It's like the world doesn't know, though. Like it doesn't give one goddamn."

Sal put the cigarette to his lips and took a deep drag, lifting his face to the sky. Dark shadows passed over his sharp features and he squinted at the moon as it broke through the clouds. "You walked into Paint Rock on the eve of a battle, babe. It's going to be a while before the sun comes up, but when it does, and the smoke clears, nobody's hands are going to be clean."

I nodded.

Sal stood and offered me a hand. "But if you're willing to work with a criminal and an outlaw, I think I might be able to help you on this case. Think you can ride?"

I shifted the shoulder of the broken arm, wincing. It'd be a pain, but I could hold onto his back with one arm. If he wanted to ride, though, that could mean only one thing. We were going to see the Kings. "If you keep it low speed, then probably."

I put my good hand in his and he pulled me up. "Where are we going?"

"Chanter's," Sal said without missing a beat. "To meet a friend."

~

I had been out to Chanter's house only a handful of times since he passed away the previous November. The pack still held their monthly full-moon hunts out there, but I found it easier not to go most of the time. Going meant staying behind in the house with a dead man's things and that was still unsettling to me. It was as if I could still feel his presence. Every clink of dishes, the scoot of a chair across the floor, the low murmur of the television, the faded odor of old cigarette smoke absorbed by the walls, it all reminded me of how he had sacrificed himself to save me and my son.

The house itself wasn't much. It was a three-bedroom with low ceilings and narrow hallways. Outside, there was a shed and a small patio where the pack kept a grill chained to the porch so no one stole it.

But the most important thing about Chanter's property was that there were no fences, no barriers, and no walls. I was reminded of that as we came down the long driveway. Blue hills rose in the distance into sharp edges layered one on another. Stubby bushes and trees marched across the landscape in an uneven parade of brown and green. An old, rusty metal pole marked the property boundary a long way off, but that was the only unnatural thing I could see on the horizon between Chanter's house and the hills. The desert was his back yard.

His driveway, however, was full of motorcycles and a single truck that I'd come to recognize as Bran's. He drove it sometimes, but kept his bike chained down in the back in case he needed it.

Sal parked behind them and waited for me to hop off before he did the same. He removed his goggles and hung them on the handlebar, running a hand over his hair to smooth it out from the ride.

"So, what are a bunch of Kings doing at Chanter's place?" I tried to keep my voice down. Some of the Kings were werewolves and could probably still hear me. The ones that weren't were all shifters of some kind. Who knew how good their hearing was?

"Remember, Chanter was an officer in the Kings. He was the vice president, Judah. The club probably spent as much time out here while he was alive as the pack did. Chanter wouldn't begrudge us the use of the space, even if you do."

I sighed and rolled my eyes, settling on a patch of grass in the backyard near the shed. A few months ago, Sal had shot two men there. They were members of the Vanguards of Humanity, and two of the three men who had gunned down Chanter. Even then, the kill hadn't felt justified, but that was their code. A life for a life. I'd turned a blind eye to it because I'd been ordered to do so. Marcus and Istaqua both had made it clear doing anything else would be bad for my health. I wondered if I would have given them the same lenience if Sal and I hadn't been sleeping together. The idea made me feel sick to my stomach. Was I really so different from the corrupt people I wanted so badly to stop?

Sal jogged to the porch where he stopped and gestured for me to follow. I sucked in a deep breath and did as he bid. He put his hand on the doorknob, but it opened before he could turn it.

Bran's huge form blocked our entry. He raised an eyebrow at me, then looked at Sal and said, "What has happened? Why is she here?"

"Because she needs to be," Sal answered firmly. "It's time to bring her in."

Bran's expression hardened as he scrutinized me. "Are you sure?"

Sal answered with a firm, singular nod of his head.

Bran opened the door wider and stepped aside. "Istaqua is not going to be happy."

"Istaqua can kiss my—" Sal broke off whatever it was he was about to say when he saw Istaqua sitting in the blue corduroy armchair in the center of the living room. Chanter's armchair.

I studied Sal's face carefully, trying to gauge how he felt seeing Istaqua claim the chair. It had always been empty every time I had come over. Not even Sal dared to sit in Chanter's chair.

Istaqua's fingers gripped the arm rests. "Don't stop on my account. By all means, bring a cop in here and insult me to impress her. Or were you planning on making that a proper proposition, *brother*?"

Sal let out a low growl. "I'm not here to fight with you, not today."

"Good." Istaqua pushed himself out of the chair and strode forward several paces, focusing on me. "Because if she's here, we have bigger problems."

"If you're tempted to distrust me just because I work for BSI, don't." I pushed past Sal to stand in front of Istaqua. "They might sign my paychecks, but I owe them no loyalty, especially after what I've just seen. If they're involved in that..." I trailed off and shook my head. How was I going to continue to work for them if it turned out they were involved?

Istaqua laid a heavy hand on my shoulder. "It's not me you have to convince." His hand trailed down to my back as he turned and ushered me down the hall to Chanter's spare bedroom. "If you seek the truth, it comes at a price. Be sure you're willing to pay the toll."

I hesitated, then drew in another deep breath, nodding. "Show me."

Istaqua ushered me down the hall and paused in front of the door to the spare bedroom. He said nothing before he opened it.

The room was almost exactly as I remembered it. Wire shelves lined one wall laden with books and artifacts, some of which I could never hope to identify. The headboard of a twin-sized bed butted against the outer wall of the house under a squat window with a blue curtain.

Lying on that bed was the beaten, battered, and burned body of Gideon Reed.

# Chapter Nineteen

I stiffened at the sight of him and took a step back, expecting him to sit up and charge at me. Every time I'd seen Reed over the last few days, he'd attacked me. There was nowhere further back to go, since Istaqua blocked my path.

Reed's eyes opened and he lifted his head. "Judah? Is that—" He broke off whatever he was about to say to clutch at his side and wince.

I wanted to go to his side, to check him over and make sure his wounds weren't fatal, but I also didn't want to die. "Are you yourself or are you going to attack me?"

A dark chuckle escaped his lips. "Even if I wanted to, I couldn't get up out of this bed right now. I think you're safe."

"What are you doing here?" I turned to Istaqua looking for an explanation but found no answers there, so I turned back to Reed. "And what the hell's been going on the last few days?"

Reed closed his eyes and drew in a shallow, wheezing breath, the breath of a dying man. My feet carried me forward of their own accord until his eyes snapped back open again. "Mind the circle."

I paused and looked down. A line of ash arced over the floor right in front of my feet. It traveled to the wall on either side of the bed, circling underneath to encompass the bed.

In magick, circles create small areas of power, or small areas where a person on the inside is cut off from the energy on the outside. In short, it's a metaphysical barrier that can either exponentially increase power on the inside, or cut the inside off from any power on the outside. It all depended on how it was crafted. This was a simple circle without any advanced runes, carvings, or symbols. A circle didn't need all of those to be powerful. Sometimes, simple is best. A circle made of ash could mean anything, depending on what the ash was made of. One thing was for sure; breaking that circle would be bad.

I stepped over the circle, careful not to disturb it, and knelt next to the bed. "I saw the files on your laptop. Please, Reed, I need some answers. How did all this happen? Hell, how are you even still alive? Why does BSI want you?"

"Always so many questions." Reed smiled. "But I do owe you an explanation, don't I?" He was quiet a moment before he took another wheezing breath. "To really answer that, I suppose I should start at the beginning with the Sicarii."

I shifted my weight, getting comfortable. "Ed says they were dissidents in Ancient Rome protesting the Roman occupation of Judea."

"That was only a small group of a much larger machine. Our history goes back further, much further." Reed closed his eyes again and said, "Since the beginning of time, the Sicarii have influenced the balance of power all over the world. From the fall of Rome to the collapse of the Soviet Union to the ongoing conflicts in the Middle East, the Sicarii have been involved in all of it in one form or another. Whenever and wherever the Sicarii form a presence, bad things happen. The balance of power shifts. The world changes."

I frowned. "I'm not sure I understand. Who are they? What are they?"

"We've had many names over the years. To some, we were gods. We were the heroes of myth, the immortal men who both guided and shielded the world, molding and bending progress to our will. True immortals."

Gideon Reed didn't look like an immortal. He bled like any other man. He slept and ate and lived just as any other human would. Then again, I'd seen a wendigo rip out one of his organs and Reed seemed no worse for wear afterward. He'd gotten up from injuries that would have killed normal men, but that didn't make him immortal.

"You have doubts."

I met Reed's eyes and sighed. "I might be a BSI officer who's seen some weird things over the years, but asking me to believe in immortal beings is a stretch. Especially considering right now. You look like you're on death's door."

Reed spread his lip into a smile-like grimace. "Immortal is a poor word. It's a failure of language. We can die. Cut off our heads, force us to lose enough blood quickly enough and we are as mortal as the next man. But we do not age or decay. We heal faster, move faster, become stronger. Most of us live among humans undetected for twenty, thirty years before we disappear and get new identities from the Sicarii. A select few are chosen each generation to be a part of the ruling council. That's the group that decides the fate of the world."

He shifted one hand to his chest and fixed his eyes on the ceiling. "During the Revelation, I served along with Hector and several others. We guided the creation of BSI. I did my best to put safeguards in place to prevent what's happening now. It was never supposed to be like this. Everything changed. They saw it as their opportunity to control the other supernaturals, the one wildcard that we had never been able to fully influence. They just wanted more power." His hand formed a fist. "When I saw the others weren't going to listen, I left. I chose to disappear. I ran like a coward instead of fighting for what I knew was right."

I reached out and gripped Reed's hand. "Is Doctor Han one of these... immortals too?"

He shook his head. "No, he's something else. But he knows about us. Of that I'm sure. Judah—" He squeezed my hand. "—something is wrong. The ruling group of Sicarii have been in power too long, longer than they should be. Hector shouldn't be here. When I found out he was, I went to confront him.

"He lured me into the compound where I learned he was manufacturing rem from plants brought from the fae. This rem became a key ingredient in research being conducted by Han, who had a blank check from the government, at the Sicarii's urging, to synthesize a formula that would give normal humans supernatural powers. BSI has been testing this for years, Judah. Their goal is to develop agents for the field who are capable of unprecedented destruction. Disposable super-soldiers, humans able to stand against legions of werewolves, vampires, fae, and magick practitioners."

"Holy hell," I breathed, my voice barely above a whisper. "What the hell do they need an army of anti-supernatural soldiers for?"

Reed met my eyes, his gaze level. "You know what for, Judah."

"Extermination."

I turned my head to regard Istaqua standing in the doorway, his arms crossed.

He took a step into the room. "Why do you think they've corralled so many of us into the reservation? There's talks of opening more and making residency mandatory. Once every supernatural has been herded into a reservation, how much do you think it will take for them to turn their guns on us?"

"People won't let that happen," I said, shaking my head. "There are too many agents inside BSI who are practitioners like me that would stand against it."

"Agents that are to be replaced with the super-soldiers they are developing." Reed hissed and clutched his side. "The research has to be shut down. Han, Hector, all of them must be stopped. Those videos, they were sent to me from another source. They were supposed to be delivered to Marcus Kelley as proof of Han's involvement. You must get them to him."

That explained a lot, but not everything. I still needed answers.

"None of that explains why you've been attacking everyone and why you're suddenly back to your old self inside this circle." I gestured to the circle of ash.

"It's Hector's doing. He is gifted with psychomancy. He cast a powerful spell over me, Judah. I've got no control over my actions if I leave this circle. If not for the Kings apprehending me and bringing me here, I would be back in the hands of BSI, spirited away to be executed." He winced again. "Of course, that came at a price. They had to severely injure me to get me here and, well, inside this circle, I don't seem to be healing at my normal rate."

The pieces were coming together. Hector must have spelled Reed to get him out of the way. Reed would be the one person who could put everything together and bring in Marcus to shut everything down. If Han was fired from Fitz, he'd lose access to all his research and, as a controlling investor, Marcus could shut down the whole project. The Sicarii would be set back a long way. They'd be dealt a huge blow, but not defeated. It might buy us time to shut them down completely, though.

*Am I crazy? If what Reed is saying is true, these Sicarii are immortal. They've been around for thousands of years and have more knowledge, strength, and power than I can ever hope to have. I'm just one federal agent living in a small town. What can I do against that?*

I looked back at Istaqua. The Kings must have felt the same at one time, but they didn't just stand by and do nothing. That's why they were moving people out of BSI reach, to safety. They didn't have to save the world; they just had to save one person at a time.

*That's all I have to do, take down one of them at a time.*

I turned back to Reed. "If we shut down the rem production, will it make any difference at all?"

Reed thought a moment and then nodded. "But you need to get those videos to Marcus, too. Hector probably isn't the only one producing rem, but shutting him and his operation down will make it harder for Han to get it, especially once he's removed from the Fitz team."

I stood and moved to go, but Reed grabbed my arm, forcing me to turn back.

"Hector is smart," Reed said. "His followers are likely all addicted to the rem. He's used it and his psychomancy to bring them all under his control. They'll defend him and the facility with their lives."

"What about Mara?"

Reed licked his lips. "If she's there, she's likely under his control to some degree. The night we were at the barn, it was to be her initiation into the group. With everything going on, they may have postponed that. If you hurry, you may be able to stop him from solidifying his influence over her."

I closed my eyes and took in a deep breath. There was just one more thing I needed to ask Reed, and I wasn't sure how to say it. Honesty is probably best. I've never been one to dance around it, so I might as well just come out and say it.

"There's just one more thing I need to ask you, and I'm going to need an honest answer."

When I opened my eyes, Reed had wrinkled his forehead looking at me. "I'll do my best."

"The sword you carry, is it known as the sword of light?"

The room was quiet for a long time, the only sounds Gideon Reed's rough breathing.

He answered in a voice barely above a whisper. "Who told you that?"

"Seamus."

"That sword must not fall into his hands, Judah. It must be protected. You have no idea what he can do with something that powerful."

"I have an idea," I mumbled. "I know it would be bad."

"Don't worry," Istaqua chimed in. "Even Finvarra couldn't pass through this circle, priest. You're safe for now. This business with the sword can be settled at a later date. You have bigger problems."

"Thank you." I nodded to Reed. "You stay inside this circle and get better. I'm going to go stop all of this."

"Be careful," Reed called after me as I walked to the door. "Don't underestimate Hector's power. He overcame me with ease. I know of no way to defend against his psychomancy, Judah. He is powerful, and one of the Sicarii. If you kill him, you will draw their attention and that is not a good thing."

I stopped in the doorway next to Istaqua and turned back, a smile on my face. "Come on, Reed. This is me you're talking to. When have I ever not been careful?"

Istaqua's hand came down on my shoulder. "We've got her back. Don't you worry, priest."

I slid by Istaqua and made my way back out to the front room where the rest of the Kings waited in silence. Sal looked up from his place at the kitchen counter and put down the beer in his hands. The room smelled of barbeque and there was a spread of food on the bar where Chanter used to keep his medicines and car keys. Someone else sat in Chanter's chair, someone I didn't know and someone that didn't deserve it. I caught the whiff of cigarette smoke in the air.

My broken arm ached and my head felt heavy. The light was suddenly too much, and it made my temper flare. I shifted my arm and growled, "What the hell are you guys looking at?" When no one answered, I spun on my heels and stormed back to Chanter's bedroom, slamming the door shut so I could finally get some peace.

But peace wasn't what I found.

On the other side of the door, I sank to the floor fighting tears. It was stupid, how upset I'd gotten over so many little things. It felt wrong, seeing the place without Chanter. Even after so long, I still expected to see him every time I rounded a corner, every time I smelled smoke or heard deep laughter. I still felt like I had failed him somehow, like there was more I needed to say. Even though I'd gotten more of a goodbye than most, it never felt like enough.

A gentle rap sounded on the door. "Judah?" came Sal's muffled voice.

I stared at the door and debated telling him to go away, but that would change nothing. It was selfish of me to want to keep all of Chanter's memory to myself.

He opened the door when I moved away from it and quickly closed it behind him, cocking his head to the side. "What is it?"

"Everything and nothing." I choked on a sob and pushed tears away with my palm. "It's just... Chanter would know what to do. He always knew. Not having him here to ask, it's been so hard. And seeing Istaqua sit in his chair, seeing anyone there... I just miss him, Sal. I miss everyone."

Sal stepped forward to wrap his arms around me, careful not to squeeze the broken arm. "I know. Trust me, I know."

"Did he know? About all of this?"

Sal kissed the top of my head and then shook his head. "I don't know how much he knew."

"This isn't just some monster, Sal. This is the government. This is BSI. This is my boss, the people who know everything about me, things even you don't know." I raised my head and fought the tightness in my throat. "How am I supposed to fight that? Shutting things down here will have consequences. This isn't going to end when Marcus fires Han. This goes all the way to the top of the government. How do we stop that?"

Sal squeezed me tighter. It made my arm ache even more, but I didn't care. I wouldn't have traded that hug for anything in the world. "You don't do it by yourself, that's how. You've got friends, allies. I know it's hard for you to trust us because we've been on the wrong side of the law, but Marcus, Istaqua, the Kings, and others... We're fighting a war against that already."

"But how am I supposed to fight for what I know is right without endangering Hunter? If I quit, BSI will come for me."

"Then don't quit." Sal leaned back to look at me. "You keep doing your job, Judah, and doing the best that you can."

I swallowed. "And what about when orders come down from above? Eventually, they'll figure me out. I might have to run."

"We'll worry about that as it comes." Sal nodded. "Today, we shut down Hector's operation and get Han out of the way. Then, we worry about tomorrow."

I sniffled and wiped the rest of the tears from my face. Somehow, talking to Sal always made me feel better. "Sal, there can't be a we this time. I might have a way to defend myself against the spell that hit Reed, but I can't extend that to other people. If one of you werewolves gets hit by it, that could be even more disastrous. We can't risk that."

Sal's face hardened. "Well, I'm not letting you go in alone."

I looked down at my hands. The skin was red and splotchy. My face probably was, too. It'd be a while before I could go out and face people without looking like a mess. "Espinoza," I mumbled. "I can bring Espinoza. He works for the local cops, so he's not connected to BSI, and he's got some low-level psychomancy of his own. He might be able to protect himself. Yeah, if anyone can, he can."

"What about you? What are you going to do to keep him out of your head?"

"It's not going to be easy." I shrugged. "But I can do it. I was trained in the academy to keep things out. If it works on demons and ghosts, it should work on Hector too."

Sal didn't look convinced, so I leaned forward and kissed him. "Don't worry so much, Sal. This is my job. This is what I do. I wouldn't have gotten this far if I wasn't at least a little good at it."

He offered a weak smile in response. "Fine, but one of us drives you out there so I know you got that far safely."

I grinned back. "Deal."

# Chapter Twenty

When Sal said he would let me call in whoever I wanted for back up, I don't think he thought I'd call Ed. He didn't seem pleased when I got off the phone, asking Ed to drive out to Chanter's and pick me up, but he didn't voice an objection either.

I leaned against the counter, staring at the lock screen of the burner cell phone, wondering if I should bother to call Espinoza in. Hector wasn't likely to go that easily. He'd probably resist any arrest, but that was the only way we were going to get any real answers. If BSI figured out that the jig was up, they'd silence him. Permanently. Hector's only chance of survival was to place himself in police custody. We'd wind up protecting that asshole. Believe me when I say I wished it wasn't that way, but that was the only way I could see going forward.

I dialed Espinoza's number and raised the phone to my ear. He answered on the third ring. "Espinoza."

"Hey, Espinoza. It's Agent Black."

"Judah, how are you? I heard you got pretty busted up."

My eye twitched at the memory of Abe snapping my arm. "It takes more than a broken arm to keep me down. Listen, I need a favor, and it might be a dangerous one. I can't even tell you everything."

"This is one of those need-to-know basis things, huh?"

"Pretty much. You're just going to have to trust me, because you're not going to like what we're about to do."

I gave him the short version, leaving out most of the evidence that incriminated BSI, the government, and the Sicarii. I also didn't tell him I knew where Reed was or about the Kings' involvement. Which, I suppose, means I didn't tell him anything other than that we needed to place Hector in protective custody.

He sighed. "I'm going to trust you have a good reason for that, Judah. You know how slimy that guy is."

"Yeah, but the only way I get done what I need done is to make sure he survives, and we don't have enough evidence yet to arrest him. I'm sorry. I wish I could tell you more, but the more you know, the more danger you could be in."

"I'm a big boy," Espinoza purred. "I can take care of myself. But I'll trust you. I'm your back-up. You tell me where you need me and

I'm there."

I glanced up at the clock on the wall. "I can meet you down the road from the compound in say, an hour?"

Espinoza agreed and I hung up just as loud, feminine laughter belted out from the other side of the room. I turned my head. There hadn't been any women in the main part of the house when I first arrived. Maybe one of them had come in while I was in the back and I'd missed it.

She stood with her back to the wall, peering over Bran's shoulder while Bran played cards with Sal, nursing a beer. Dark makeup and a punk-rocker look set her apart from the other girls that hung around the Kings. She wore her hair in an elegantly feathered mohawk, the sides of her head shaved. She was also the only woman I'd ever seen wearing a leather vest with a Kings patch, though the one on her chest said "property of" above the Kings label.

Figuring she'd be better conversation than the guys, I wandered over closer to the table to watch the poker game. When I got to the table, two guys threw their cards down and bowed out of the hand, leaving Sal and Bran to win a pot made of a handful of tens and fives plus some quarters. I put a hand on Sal's shoulder to let him know I was there.

"It's all over now," Sal said and pushed a few more quarters into the middle. "My good luck charm just got here."

I frowned and leaned in to look at his cards. "I don't know. Good luck can only do so much for a hand like that."

Sal sighed. Bran chuckled and met Sal's bet, adding, "Angel, have you met Judah Black before?" Bran asked and gestured to the woman behind him.

The woman, Angel, took a long pull from her beer and then gave me a sultry smirk. "I don't think I've had the pleasure."

I held my hand out to her for a friendly handshake, but she bypassed it and stepped way into my personal space. When she sniffed at me, I jerked back. She laughed. "Oh, sweetheart. You don't have to play that game with me. I could eat you alive and you'd love every minute of it." Angel snapped her teeth at me and I flinched again. Her laugh vibrated through the room and several people looked up. "I'll get you a refill, babe," she said and walked off.

I frowned after her. "What's her problem?"

"She likes you," Sal said as if he barely noticed the exchange.

"She's got a funny way of showing it."

"Angel takes a little warming up to, but she's worth getting to know."

"Careful," Bran said in a warning tone and lowered his cards to give Sal a slight smile. "That's my wife you're talking about there, brother."

"Relax, brother, I know. Haven't thought of Angel like that in a long time."

Angel returned with two handfuls of beer bottles and leaned into Sal, purring next to his ear. "You can think of me like that anytime." When she saw me scowling at her, she stood and threw an arm around me. "You too, sweetheart. I don't mind a bit. It's only fair. I think you're worth remembering." She kissed my cheek and walked away laughing to pass beers to everyone at the table.

Sal threw down his cards. "Well, now that Angel's seen my hand, seems I'd better show you mine before she tells you to up the ante."

"Three of a kind," Bran said nodding. "Not bad."

"Unless you've got a full house over there like I think you do."

Bran lowered his hand, revealing two eights and three twos with a big grin. "Still got a good nose, don't you?"

"I can smell your bullshit a mile away, Bran." Sal looked up at me while Bran collected his winnings.

I hadn't stopped glaring at Angel and, the more I looked at her, the more irritated I got. I'd never considered myself a jealous woman. Then again, I'd never had much of an opportunity to be jealous. The night I'd spotted Sal and the other Kings in Aisling, Kandie had been all over him. I'd broken her nose as much for that as getting in my face and telling me to step off. That was the one and only time I could think of where I let my feelings for someone turn me to violence and even then Kandie had provoked me. Angel hadn't really done anything to me, but inside I was simmering. *Haven't thought of her like that in a long time*, Sal had said. They'd had a thing and that bothered me.

"It was a long time ago," Sal said quietly.

"Well, not that long," Angel added. "After that Zoe bitch hung you out to dry. That was shit. Nobody here would deny that." She put her bottle on the corner of the table and crossed her arms and tilted her head to the side. "You smoke?"

"No."

"Course you don't. Well, I'm going to step out front under the awning for a smoke in case you want to chat." Angel bent down and gave Bran an open-mouthed kiss with plenty of tongue and then she walked past me toward the front door.

I moved to follow her. She hadn't said it outright, but I was sure she either wanted to fight me or talk. Either way, I was game.

Sal caught my arm before I could step away. "Play nice," he said and motioned to Bran with his head.

I looked back at Bran, who frowned and stared down at his hands as he shuffled the cards. "If she picks a fight, that's not my fault," I said and pulled away from Sal.

As I was walking away, I heard Sal mutter, "Women. God."

"Deadliest in any species," Bran replied.

I yanked open the front door. The rain was coming down gently while thunder rumbled and rolled over the open desert. Angel leaned against the porch wall, sucking on a cigarette. She glanced over at me, her face expressionless. "For a minute, I thought you wouldn't come. Takes guts for a human to come out here like that."

"You're not human?" I pushed the door closed behind me.

"Werewolf." She plucked the cigarette from her mouth. "My husband turns into a bear, too, if you didn't know."

"I didn't." I put my hands in my pockets, musing, *Werebears. What next?* A long silence passed and I fumbled to make small talk while she smoked. "How long have you and Bran been married?"

"A little over four years."

More silence. I did the math in my head. Sal had only been divorced from Zoe about three years. I turned my head to study her.

She blew out a mouthful of smoke and smirked at me. "Did the math, huh?"

"You cheated on Bran?" I hissed, quietly. Not that it was a secret. Bran seemed to know and Sal hadn't acted like it was a big deal.

Angel laughed. "It wasn't like that, hon. It's not cheating if they're both in on it."

I sighed. The last thing I needed to hear was her bragging about her past sexual conquests, especially when they involved Sal. "You clearly wanted me to come out here. Why? What do you want?"

"To clear the air, first of all." She smirked. "I'll be the first to admit, I'm a terrible flirt, but I do it 'cause it's fun to watch the boys squirm. Me and Sal had our fun, but that's all it was, just a one-time thing. I ain't interested in your man, Judah. Truth is, I was a hangaround for a while, which basically means I've fucked just about every one of the guys in there, your boyfriend included."

"Why are you telling me this?" I said, folding my arms.

"Well, partly because you still like to think your boyfriend's some kind of white knight. That just isn't the case. You're not doing him any favors, thinking like that. And also..." Angel plucked her cigarette from her mouth and stomped it out before she pointed to the patch on her chest that said "property of." "See this? There's a reason I wear it and none of those other bitches in there do. They can't patch me in because I don't have a dick, but I've got bigger balls than half of them. I know better than to shit where I eat. I don't have no beef with you and I don't want you to have one with me."

"And?"

"And," Angel repeated, "as someone who's been where you are, I don't want you to have no illusions that you're safe. Sal's a good guy, better than most of them, and he won't pass you around like Istaqua does to his women, but this life ain't for everyone. You can't be half in or half out. People die half in."

I smiled and shook my head. "What? You think I should ditch my car for a bike and dress in leather?"

Angel threw her head back and laughed. "You ever want to go that route, you give me a call. You can pull off the look. But no, that ain't what I'm saying." She bent over, picked up the cigarette and flicked it out into the desert. "Men are stupid. They think too much with their dicks and not enough with their heads when it comes to us. Sal's got a long history of falling hard for women and letting that get him into trouble. Situations like what happened to you earlier are only going to get more frequent. With as much as Sal cares about you, Istaqua can back him into a corner. You know what I'm talking about."

I did. Memories of another rainy day at Chanter's home flashed through my mind. The last time Istaqua had manipulated Sal into killing two people. The men Sal killed deserved it for killing Chanter, but watching Sal pull the trigger and murder two men execution style still gave me nightmares.

Angel kicked off the wall and stood in front of me. "Right now, you've got nothing, no status here. You might be sleeping with him, but in Istaqua's eyes, you're just another hangaround. You want to change that and fast because Istaqua doesn't like you."

"Sal wouldn't let him touch me. *I* wouldn't let him touch me."

"There's a lot worse things that can happen to you here than getting raped, Judah. You got a boy to think about. Don't give him the chance to push you." Angel put a hand on my shoulder. "First chance you get, you need to establish your place here and you'll have to do more than break Kandie's nose with a quick pop she never saw coming."

I smiled to myself at the memory. She'd been all over Sal in Aisling and I'd let my temper get the best of me. There were no regrets there. "How do I do that?"

"I'm sure you'll get your chance." She took her hand away and smiled. "So, are we good?"

I nodded. "We're good."

"You ever need back-up, don't be afraid to give me a call, especially if the assholes in the club give you trouble."

I didn't know what to say to that. I'd come out there expecting her to pick a fight with me and, instead, she seemed to be mostly on my side. "Thanks, I think."

"Hey, anyone who beats the shit out of Kandie is a friend to me. I hate that Barbie doll wannabe. Us badass bitches got to stick together. I got your back." She gave my shoulder what she must have perceived to be a gentle punch, but it actually hurt quite a bit. Then, she pulled open the door and stepped back inside.

I stayed outside, watching the rain fall, considering my life. I wondered if BSI counted on my meeting the Kings and helping them. Probably not, I decided. They seemed good at keeping what they did secret and staying under the radar. With Marcus Kelley backing them, it must have been easier.

That must have put him in a difficult position. Han worked in his lab, heading his research department at the hospital. It didn't seem like Marcus knew about Han's little experiment for BSI, which I hoped meant Marcus would fire him once we got the evidence to him. I'd asked Ed to bring the hard drive when he came, which I planned on handing off to Istaqua with the understanding that he'd take it directly to Marcus. At least that would be one less thing for me to do. Marcus would take care of Han while I arrested Hector and got a full confession. Once I had that, we could go public, expose what BSI was up to and maybe even stop them.

Or maybe exposing this would get me and everyone I loved killed.

Is this my future? I wondered. Constantly second guessing every choice I make, wondering who I can and can't trust because any one of them might be a spy for the government? I can't live this way. I wish I'd never seen that recording. Maybe the illusion of choice is better than knowing you really have no choice at all.

The door opened and Sal stepped out onto the porch with me. He lit up a cigarette and pocketed his lighter. "You and Angel work things out?"

"You still should have told me."

Sal shook his head. "You want a list of every girl I ever spent the night with I can draft you one, but it won't make you feel better."

"Just warn me whenever I've got to be in the same room with one of them." I turned my head and looked up at him.

He sighed. "Guess that's fair. To be honest, I didn't even think about it."

I closed my eyes and tried not to imagine the two of them together. It was harder than I thought it would be. "I might be out a little later. You think you can handle the kids by yourself? I think I'll sleep a week once this is all over."

"Yeah, no problem. Hunter's got Mia tonight and I asked Shauna to look in on them. Actually, I was thinking about crashing here tonight so I could clean up in the morning. I've probably had enough to drink, I shouldn't drive anyway." He turned and gave me a serious look. "I don't want you to think there's anything between me and Angel or anybody else. That was a long time ago and I was really messed up after Zoe. You going to hold it against me? I told you, I was fucked up."

I was surprised how hard it was to keep from smiling at the way he shifted uncomfortably. In truth, I wasn't mad. I wasn't even upset. Hard to blame him for something that happened before I even knew him, but there was a part of me that enjoyed the apology in a sadistic sort of way. Watching him stutter through an uncomfortable conversation was a welcome change from the cool confidence he normally displayed.

"I don't know if that apology's good enough." I let myself smile and offered a wink. "I think maybe you can apologize better tomorrow night."

Tires crunching on gravel and wipers squeaking against the windshield of a powder blue Prius drew our attention to the driveway as Ed pulled in behind all the bikes.

Sal let out another frustrated sigh as he turned back to me. "You confuse the shit out of me, you know that?" He leaned in and kissed me. "Get you and Ed home safe and then we'll see about another apology."

"Get a room," said Ed after he'd run up the stairs to stand under the relative dryness of the awning.

Sal gave Ed a gentle shove back into the rain, where Ed unceremoniously flailed and tried to stay upright. Ed caught has balance, but only after getting wet. He yelped at the cold rain and scampered back under the awning against our laughter.

"You ready to hit the road, Ed?" I said once we'd calmed down. "We're meeting Espinoza outside the compound. Remember, you're just my ride tonight. This is police business."

"Uh, yeah. I can hang back as long as you promise not to get into any trouble." Ed pulled off his glasses and tried to clean the rain off them.

Sal said and leaned down to kiss me again. "Be safe. I love you."

I flashed him back a smile. "I know."

Ed and I jogged into the rain to his car and scrambled inside, soaking wet.

"So, what's your plan if Hector doesn't come quietly?" Ed asked, breathless from the run.

"I won't give him a reason to resist. Once the rem plants are gone and he knows we know the truth, he'll have no choice. BSI will do anything to cover this up, up to and including killing Hector."

"I thought you said he was immortal?" Ed huffed as he pulled off his glasses, this time to clean the fog from his lenses.

"They can still die if you cut off their heads, bleed them dry, or burn them up. Not immortal, but they don't age and they're hard to kill."

Ed started the car and bobbed his head in agreement. "Like in *Highlander*."

"What?" I turned my head to scrutinize him.

He slid his glasses back on and belted out in song, "We're the princes of the universe!"

I struck my face with the palm of my hand so hard it made my head pound. Only Ed could reduce our current situation to lyrics from a Queen song.

# Chapter Twenty-One

About a mile and a half from the compound, red and blue police lights lit up the rear-view mirror. Ed cursed, checked his speedometer, and pulled over. "Seriously?"

I smirked as the car pulled up behind us and Espinoza got out of the driver's side. He was in uniform with a black bullet proof vest and dark sunglasses. Somehow, the functionality of his attire didn't detract from the attractiveness.

He walked to the passenger side and rapped two knuckles on my window. When I rolled it down, he tipped the sunglasses down. "Looks like you don't need a ticket, girl. You've got fine written all over you."

I rolled my eyes and swatted away his hand when he put it on the door. "You can do better."

He took a half step back to flex his arms. "Careful, ma'am. These guns are loaded."

Ed put a hand over his mouth to stifle a chuckle.

Espinoza lifted his cap and brushed a hand through his hair. "So, I don't suppose we're going in with a warrant or any kind of legal documentation? Or are we just planning to stomp all over this asshole's constitutional rights?"

"In the interest of national security, I can act without regard to that. I'd call this a matter of national security."

Espinoza pursed his lips and nodded. "Patriot Act it is, then. Well, just remember my ass is on the line. I don't get a free pass like you feds. You're absolutely sure you can get a confession out of this guy? That didn't go so well before."

"Before, I didn't know who and what I was dealing with." I turned my gaze forward, watching as a pair of headlights slid over the horizon and passed us by. "Espinoza, if we don't get this guy, I'm pretty sure BSI is going to kill him. He has some damning testimony, but he's going to be reluctant to sell out his employer. We might have to resort to less conventional methods to get that confession. If you're not okay with that, now's the time to make that known."

He thought a long moment, placing his hands on his hips. "I'm game so long as we understand that there are some lines I'm not willing to cross. We're still the good guys."

I nodded. "Alright then. Let's go get him."

~

Espinoza's squad car switched on the sirens and lights as soon as we turned down the driveway and swerved into the grass to speed on past us. Ed kept up his leisurely pace and we pulled in behind the squad car, which had blocked off the driveway and parked. The front door opened and Hector Demetrius stepped out in a plain, gray button-down and jeans, too well dressed for this late.

"Stay here," I said to Ed. "And at the first sign of trouble, you back up and get out. Promise me."

Ed frowned at me. "Are you sure?"

"Promise me, Ed. Swear it."

He let out a loud huff. "Fine. I promise."

I grabbed the bag of gear Ed had brought for me and stepped out to scan the property, stopping when the door to one of the greenhouses opened and Mara stepped out. A cautious glance back at Ed told me he'd seen her to. His fingers tightened around the steering wheel and he lowered his head.

Instead of going forward to address Hector, I turned and walked up to Mara. She bristled and raised her chin as I approached.

"Step aside, Mara. Please."

Her eyebrows scrunched together. "You don't know what you're doing. This isn't what you think it is."

"I know that's rem in there and I know Hector's not human. I don't want to hurt you, but I will remove you from my path if you don't step aside."

She narrowed her eyes at me. For a long moment, I thought she'd engage me. In a straight-out fight, I was pretty sure I could take Mara, especially since I'd been training with Creven. I still didn't want to have to test that theory. She may have hated my guts, but I still didn't want to hurt her.

When I pushed forward, though, Mara moved aside at the last second. I pushed open the door and stepped through.

The greenhouse was warm and humid. Bright lights hung from the ceiling, mimicking sunlight over long troughs of dark soil. Small drains ran down from each trough, directing a trickle of water into slanted drains on the floor. There were a dozen troughs lined up end to end, each one home to five fern-like plants. But these were no ordinary plants. Their leaves were a rainbow of colors from deep indigo to fiery red and snowy white. Each one let off a soft, humming glow.

I stepped forward and reached out to touch one of the leaves. It abruptly changed from a pleasant blue color to a deep shade of crimson. When I touched the fleshy leaf, ripples of neon blue pulsed out from underneath my fingertips.

"What are you doing? You can't be in here!"

Hector barged through the door behind me with Espinoza on his heels.

One of the worst things anyone can do is surprise an officer at a potential crime scene, especially when that officer is suffering from a concussion. At the sound of Hector's voice, I pulled my nine millimeter from its holster and pointed it at him. "Stay where you are."

Espinoza's arm twitched, but he didn't draw a gun.

Hector's face hardened. "Excuse me?"

Behind him, Espinoza whistled. "It's beautiful." He wandered forward to touch another plant, this one giving off pulsating ripples of violet at his touch.

"It's rem," I said and kept my gun pointed at Hector's head.

He sneered at me. "This is an illegal search."

"No, Hector." I lowered the bag slung over my shoulder and rummaged around in it before pulling out a container of lighter fluid. "This is a crime scene."

Hector moved to stop me, but Espinoza stopped him, drawing his gun and resting it against Hector's back. "I wouldn't."

Someone else burst into the greenhouse, prompting all of us to turn our heads. It was the boy from before, the one who had been with Mara. He took in the scene, eyes dancing back and forth in panic, and then charged forward. He stopped only when Hector shouted, "Warren, don't!"

"You can't do this!" Warren stammered as I walked to the nearest line of plants.

I upended the container and squeezed, walking down the line of plants. The acrid smell of lighter fluid made the lining of my nose burn.

"This is more than just sacred ground you're defiling," the

young man continued. "This is our *home*. These are our lives. You have no idea what you're doing!"

"I know exactly what I'm doing." I walked to the next line of plants and started down it.

"Since you won't listen to reason..." Something in Warren's voice changed, turned darker, rougher. Whatever it was, it made me turn around instead of finishing the work.

Espinoza's eyes widened and his hand shook. Slowly, the gun shifted away from the back of Hector's head. Espinoza's breath came out quick and panicked as the gun traveled to rest against his temple. His eyes met mine, filled with terror.

I opened my mouth and started to step forward, but quickly found my body refusing to obey commands from my brain. Through no effort of will on my part, my fingers tightened around the bottle of lighter fluid in my hand. My arm jerked out, then up, allowing the flammable liquid to pour over my head. When that was done, the unseen power controlling my body forced me to discard the container and draw out the lighter I'd borrowed from Sal. My jaw shook and my breathing became as ragged as Espinoza's as my thumb rolled across the tiny metal wheel, striking the flame.

"What are you doing?" Hector snapped. "Warren, this isn't the way."

"Shut up! I'm so sick of listening to your lies!" Warren swept out a hand, pointing two fingers at Hector.

Hector's hand went to his throat and he fell to his knees, making a choking sound.

*Holy Hell,* I realized as thoughts raced through my brain. *This is Warren. But how? Why?*

Warren marched the few paces to tower over his father, who looked up at his son, eyes wide. "All this time, I've had to sit by while you took the credit for everything I've done, for the world I'm building."

"War...ren..." Hector choked his name out as his face changed from beet red to blue.

"Your God is nothing but a fairy tale. We are the real gods. We should be worshipped. *I* should be worshipped! If you weren't so pathetic, you'd see that. But you're not worthy. All you've ever cared about is lining your pockets with the government's blood money." Warren placed a bare foot on his father's chest and kicked him over.

Hector fell with his face toward me, eyes locked on mine. His body jerked and twitched. He clawed desperately at his throat, arcing his back in a desperate attempt to be free of Warren's magick, but it did no good. Just a few seconds after Warren kicked him over, Hector lay still, his eyes glassy.

"Don't worry. He's not dead. Takes more than that to kill one of us. But he will wake up with one hell of a headache." Warren turned to me, a dark smirk on his face. "I bet you're really confused right now, aren't you?"

I gritted my teeth, tasting the burn of lighter fluid on my lips. "Just a little, yeah. I didn't expect a little punk like you."

Warren threw his head back and laughed. "No one ever does, do they? Gideon Reed certainly didn't. That spell that made him go berserk? My doing. Father may be gifted, but not like me. You see, I'm what you get if you took my father's paltry abilities and dialed them to eleven. Not only can I not die, but with mere thought, I can have anything I want. Women." He held his hand out to Mara, who stood in the doorway. She stepped in to take his hand, smiling. "Drugs." He gestured to the rem. "And I can have your life if I demand it."

He sneered down at Hector's still form. "My father wasted his gift making deals with your government that would make him rich. What's the point? If I want money, all I have to do is walk into the nearest bank and they'll fill my pockets with a smile. All I have to do is ask."

"Are you one of them?" I ground out. "One of these so-called immortals?"

"I'm better than an immortal!" He placed a hand proudly on his chest. "I was *made* to be better."

"Made?"

Warren grinned. "That's right. Your government made me what I am."

Holy shit. I was looking at the living, breathing incarnation of Han's research. Warren had to be the result. Yes, now that I was looking, I could see it. His aura was impressively bright, a blinding shade of glittering gold, but it wasn't right. Barbed wire grew in and out of his skin at seemingly random intervals through bleeding wounds that would never heal. It circled his body from the soles of his feet to end in a crown of barbs pressing into his forehead. Dark tentacles made of shadow wriggled from the bleeding wounds, caressing his skin. The amount of metaphysical pain Warren had to be in was staggering. Someone had infected him with this darkness and then subjected him to unbearable pain to get results.

If I hadn't been paralyzed, I would have been sick.

"Was it all you?" I asked, fighting for breath. The fumes were making me gag.

Warren laughed again, clutching Mara tighter to him. He turned her head so that he could look into her eyes. "It was easy. Father had a deal with a lord of Faerie to import these plants, which he sold at a huge profit to your government. The night your priest friend came to confront him was a very bad night for my father. You see, I was already there. I had lured him out to that abandoned house with the intent of killing him. I was to take over here. Do you know how many months I spent molding the minds of these people to my will? The rem wasn't enough. Even addicted, some of them wanted to leave. I fixed all of that. When father found out, he wanted to undo it. I couldn't have that. When Gideon Reed showed up, he should have made my work easier. That is, until that werewolf messed everything up." His hand tightened around Mara's throat and she let out a small cry.

"Let her go." Espinoza's voice was hoarse and wavered, but he was still firm.

"Why? I saved her." He loosened his fingers from around her throat and Mara gasped for air. "She's mine to do with what I will. She's not the problem here. The question is, what am I going to do with you two?"

Warren discarded Mara, shoving her aside so that he could stand in front of Espinoza. "I could have you shoot yourself. The stress of the job does get to you, doesn't it?"

Espinoza spat in Warren's face.

Warren wiped it away and shook his hand, a disgusted look on his face. "Then again, that wouldn't be any fun." He turned to address me, his eyes sparkling. "Is it true that you can summon shadow fire?"

I glanced at the little fire in my hand. One wrong move and I'd go up in flames along with the whole greenhouse. "You want to talk? I'll be much more inclined if I'm not fighting for my life here."

"You think so?" Warren cocked his head to the side. "I think there's a part of you that's like me. Pain changes you, you know. It makes you powerful. With a little work, I think you could be worthy of serving me."

"No thanks. I'm good."

His thin lips spread into a wicked smile. "I didn't say I was giving you a choice."

He gestured to Mara, who picked up a shovel in the corner. With sluggish movements, she came to stand behind me. "Mara, you don't have to do this. Fight him. Fight him with everything you've got."

"You want to know the funny thing?" Warren strode up to me, his hands folded behind his back. The little bastard leaned in and whispered, "She didn't fight me at all."

The shovel struck me in the back of the head. My head jerked forward and the world spun. Everything fell into a jumbled mess of light and sound as I fell.

# Chapter Twenty-Two

I didn't quite lose consciousness after Mara hit me, but my memory of the next hour is very fuzzy. I remember the sensation of being lifted and placed on something hard. Magick washed over me and I thought I would be sick at the sensation of it. That lasted a while. The only thing I remember seeing were the shadows of the men along with Warren, each one surrounded by a halo of light. I thought maybe Mara hitting me had done something to my brain, probably worsened the concussion that was already there, but I didn't have enough medical knowledge to be sure.

After the nausea faded, the world spun as they lowered me to the ground somewhere else. The floor beneath my hands was flat and cool to the touch, smooth like linoleum. There was a bright light above, and looking at it hurt my eyes, so I closed them tight.

My arms and legs were left unbound, but I wasn't coordinated enough to move them after being struck in the head. It took everything I had to fight the grogginess. When they lowered me to the floor, though, they decided it was time to change that. Someone jerked my arms above my head. I screamed at the pain of having my broken arm moved before I doubled over and threw up. My captors didn't care. They fixed something metal with sharp edges around my wrists. Whatever they used had sharp teeth on the inside that dug into my flesh enough that I felt the trickle of blood. As soon as those teeth pierced my skin and tasted blood, a new feeling settled over me. It felt like I'd suddenly stood up too fast and all the blood rushed to the wrong place. Dizziness followed by the sensation that the bottom dropped out from under me. That lasted only a moment before an absolute and utter emptiness settled into my chest in the place I normally felt my magick. I reached for it and found nothing. It didn't slip away from my grasp, wasn't there just out of reach. There weren't traces of it I could call on. It was just gone.

I panicked and opened my eyes, fighting for breath. I tried to wiggle my arms out of the restraints, but the metal teeth just bit in harder.

"Don't fight. You'll only make it worse." Warren grabbed a handful of my shirt and ripped it away. I screamed and fought, finding that I could scoot back and curl up against the wall if I really worked on it. Even curled up, I couldn't stop them from ripping, cutting and tearing away my clothes to leave me naked, helpless, and alone in the tiny room with the bright light.

Once he'd stripped me, Warren let me curl up against the wall again, sobbing, and he stepped back, the painful light forming a halo behind his head. "Over the next few hours, days, months, years...however long it takes to break you, you're going to lie to yourself, Judah Black. You're going to tell yourself that someone is coming for you. You'll convince yourself that someone out there is coming to your rescue. They aren't. The shackles you are wearing, this place, all of it has been designed to cut you off from everyone and everything. As far as the outside world is concerned, you no longer exist. Killed in the line of duty, your body never recovered. No one is looking for you."

"Why are you doing this?" I shouted. "I'm not the only one who knows. There are others. They'll stop you. Even if I die, it changes nothing!"

Warren laughed. It was a cold, bitter laugh. "You have no idea what you are, do you? What you can do?"

His footsteps echoed through the room as he came closer. Warm hands touched my face and held it, even when I flinched away. "You're like me. I can see it in your mind. There's a part of you that's been sealed away, a part they don't want you to find, the part that makes you strong. I'm going to help you open the doorway to that part of you, Judah. I'm going to break your mind, take everything away from you, hurt you until there is nothing left but raw, unfiltered power. And then, when I am done, I'm going to use you. You will be my champion in this new world."

"You won't break me," I shouted, glaring at him. "Better men than you have tried and failed."

Warren just smiled. "We'll see about that, won't we?"

He turned his back on me, gestured to the ceiling and folded his hands behind his back. The bright light finally died and I relaxed a little as Warren's footsteps echoed away from me. His figure hung in the door a long moment before stepping out and closing it behind him, leaving me in complete darkness.

For a long time, I sat in silence, listening, trying to learn what I could about the room I was in. Then, when I could hear nothing but the sound of my own breathing against the darkness, I started to think about what Warren had said. It wasn't true. Ed knew where I was. He must have seen everything.

Espinoza, was he alive or dead? Maybe they'd found Ed, too and held him captive. My heart jumped into my throat at the thought. *No*, I reasoned. *Ed is smart*. Maybe he'd done the smart thing and turned to run away. If so, he could tell Sal and the others where I was. He would tell them everything. The pack and my few friends in the Kings would come and tear the compound apart looking for me. But even with all that manpower, could any of them stand against Warren's powers?

My heart sank as I realized I was on my own, helpless against whatever Warren planned to do to me.

I thought of Mara and how I had failed her again. I should have taken her out of there the first night I saw her. Warren had her completely under his control. Inside, she was probably screaming for help and I had walked away, leaving her behind enemy lines all alone.

Hunter and Mia, what would they do when I didn't come back? I shed my first tears in that place, imagining their reaction to the news that I was missing and presumed dead. Tindall would go with Abe personally to deliver the news. Over and over in my mind, I watched as Tindall tried to be delicate, as Sal lost his temper and Mia burst into tears. Hunter stood by, angry and numb.

My shoulders shook with cold and sobs. I tried to tell myself that I'd been in worse situations, but I couldn't think of anything. At least when I'd been down in the pit when LeDuc held me captive, I had Ed. I had help. He'd left me my arms and legs and the glimmer of hope that someone might find me. I could die alone in that room and no one but Warren and his people would ever know.

At some point, the crying turned into screaming. I stood back up and set myself to trying to pull my arms free. I'd cut my own hands and feet off before I let that bastard get his satisfaction. The metal teeth cut in deeper with searing pain until my arms and chest were wet with blood. I shivered even harder from the blood loss, but I didn't give up, not until I was too weak to keep going.

Defeated, I slumped and fought the quiver of my jaw. I couldn't cry, not again. I didn't have the fluids to waste. Exhaustion threatened to force my eyes closed and, if it hadn't been hoovering near freezing in that room, I might have fallen asleep. But it was just cold enough that getting comfortable was impossible. Instead, I hung there, fighting fatigue, waiting for something, anything to happen to me.

~

Light flooded the room after what felt like many hours. It was as blinding and painful as fire. I flinched away from it, my head down between my knees, suddenly torn from my groggy state. I shifted my arms up over my head and curled into a tiny ball as best I could, pressing myself against the wall to make myself as small as possible. Every inch of me hurt. My brain wanted to associate the strange, new pain with the light, but I knew better. Light doesn't hurt.

Heavy footsteps came into the center of the room followed by a clang and something very wet sounding. "Supper time," said a harsh woman's voice. "Eat up."

"I'd rather die than eat whatever poison you've brought me," I spat.

The woman reached out and grabbed me by the hair, jerking my head up. "Leave her," called another woman from the doorway. "She'll eat. They always do." I finally recognized Amanda's voice. Hector's wife.

"I won't," I said, fighting the chattering in my teeth.

"Maybe not today or tomorrow, but by the end of the week, you'll eat. Come now, Pam. We have more to do."

The second woman let me go and turned to join Amanda at the door.

"Wait!" I screamed after them and strained against my restraints, drawing more blood. "Espinoza. Ed! Tell me if they're still alive!" They started to shut the door and I pounded against the wall with my foot. "Hey, I'm talking to you, bitch! Where are my friends? Tell me. *Tell me*!"

I screamed at her long after they shut the door and left me in darkness, until my throat was dry and painful.

I didn't bother with whatever gruel they were feeding their prisoners. It had to be low in calories and nutrients. They meant to wear me down, keep me weak so I'd be easier to manipulate. I had no idea what they wanted from me but I also had no intention of waiting around to find out. I still had some strength left and, over time, that was going to wear down. If I was going to make an escape, it would have to be sooner rather than later. I didn't have the luxury of being able to wait for an opportune moment.

Without access to my magick, though, that was going to be a

difficult task to accomplish on my own. I still had no idea how they were keeping me from accessing it. There had to be wards in every stone of the place or some kind of anti-magick circle around the whole building for it to work. Just leaving the room wouldn't be enough to get me my power back. And I had to save Espinoza, Mara and Ed. I couldn't leave without them. That wasn't even an option, not after everything.

If they were bringing food, that would have to be my chance. I had to convince them to free my arms or legs. Maybe if I hurt myself bad enough that I was in danger of bleeding to death, they'd pull me down. It was dangerous. I'd have to take myself to the brink and do it at exactly the right time. That meant right before I expected them to show up and open the door. Without a clock or any sense of time, I didn't know how I would do that other than to hope my ears worked well in the dark. So, with no other plan, I curled up as tight as I could to keep warm and waited, listening.

# Chapter Twenty-Three

## Ed

The air was alive with smells. It was always that way after a rain in the desert. Rain pulled down the cold scent from the upper atmosphere and churned it with the dry dust. Back in Colorado, I could always smell snow on the rain. Texas rain smelled different than Colorado rain. It smelled of electric ozone, like the scent of exposed wiring. I'd never gotten used to it.

That's why I doubted it at first, that weird, cold but spicy scent of magick Judah always leaves behind. The blood on the ground had to be hers.

I circled the spot where it had fallen, wolf nose to the ground, deciding what I should do. I could shift back and drive the car away in search of help, but shifting would leave me weak and vulnerable inside enemy territory. The wolf in me didn't like that idea.

A flash of light from one of the second-story windows made me perk my head and ears up. Muffled voices on the wind, male, and something that made my nose itch. I sneezed. Someone was in trouble, someone who wasn't quite pack. If it was one of the pack, I would have felt the gentle tug of them in my head. This was different, too distant to be one of them. *Judah.*

I lifted one paw, intent on throwing myself at the front door. Maybe I could knock it down? On second thought, who was I kidding? Even as a werewolf, I only weigh in at a hundred and thirty pounds or so. I'd break my shoulder trying that stunt. I lowered my paw into the squishy mud and panted, deciding. Judah might not be pack in the strictest sense, but Alpha loved her. I couldn't let anything happen to her, not on my watch.

So, I did the only thing I thought might help. I threw my head back and let out a loud howl with a small yip at the end. "I am here!" I shouted from the back of my wolfy throat, hoping Judah and Espinoza would hear me and know I hadn't left them.

I trotted forward to a patch of grass that smelled faintly of car exhaust and motor oil. Someone had parked there recently, close to the door. "I'm still here!" I tried to howl, but it came out as a sort of whining howl.

A shuffling sound filtered through the door and out into the night. I moved directly in front of the door and crouched a little, pulling my ears back and making my teeth visible. When the door opened, it was a man in dark jeans and a white t-shirt. He walked out on the porch and down the steps before he stopped. The man didn't have a gun, but I could smell the silver on him from where I stood. I recoiled when the scent of it stung my nose and snarled at him.

Adrenaline bled out over the wet Earth and ozone smell of Texas rain, carrying with it undertones of fear. Prey scent.

I crouched low, ready to spring at him when he attacked. Instead, he did the absolute worst thing prey can do in the presence of a predator. He let out a frightened whimper, turned and ran.

I don't like to chase and kill things, but I can do it. Valentino made sure of that. Where most werewolves see fleeing prey and charge to take it down with the intense urge to *kill* and *devour*, the only thought that I usually entertain is *chase*. But, when this man turned, I caught a whiff of something else, something that crowded out the instinct to *chase* and *catch*, replacing it with *pain*.

Judah's pain.

I felt it for an instant, the fluttering of fear in her chest, strange hands on her wrists. She fought, was fighting, cursing, hurting. It was a flash and then it was gone, replaced with something new that made me pull back and cower. Alpha's rage. He must have felt it, too.

The shock of it stayed with me. What did that mean? Judah and Sal weren't bonded, not the way pack is, so that should have been impossible. Chanter had always said werewolves and humans cannot bond. Was Chanter wrong?

I shook the thought from my head. Something else was coming through the pack bonds now, a call down through the ranks, one I had to answer.

A low, feral growl echoed through the night, shaking my bones. I was charging across the yard and up the stairs after the man before I even realized that it was me who'd made that sound. The terrified man scrambled behind the safety of his threshold and into his den, swinging the door closed behind him. I reached the door just before it caught and wedged a foot into the narrow space. I snapped at him through the gap, saliva dripping, my heart pounding. The thoughts in my head weren't my own. They were the alpha's and I was little more than an instrument of his will.

Behind the door, the man screamed and kicked at my paw with his steel-toed boots. He slammed the door harder and put all his weight against it, crushing my paw. It was too much. I had to pull my paw back or risk them cutting it off. I pulled it free. The door closed. I stepped backward and charged into it first, and then tried the window beside it.

That's when I saw the guns.

There were two men at the bottom of a set of stairs, each one with an assault rifle pressed to their shoulders and aimed at me. Something about staring down the barrel of a gun snapped me out of my mindless rage and I put my paws down halfway through my run at the window, causing me to slide across the porch. Lightning flashed and gunfire popped. Glass shattered and I slammed into the side of the house between the window and the door. I let out a loud yelp when a sharp pain hit my hindquarters and scampered to move away and crawl down the stairs.

The gunfire let up and I knew they were about to come out and get me. I couldn't run, not at full speed, but I could still outrun a human. I booked it the hell away from that house as fast as I could, trying not to put much pressure on where my back leg had been shot. I ran through the field, across the road, until I was so far away there was no way they could catch me. Then I kept on running.

When I finally stopped, it was because the adrenaline had finally worn off and my back leg hurt even worse. The burning pain spread up the leg, into my butt and tail, making it all but impossible to move once I went down. Eden was still a good ten miles away, and Paint Rock closer to twenty. I wasn't going to make it if I shifted. Only my wolf could cross that distance, and the bullet in my hindquarters meant I couldn't even do that.

I lay on my side in tall grass for a minute, panting and whining to myself, cursing. Now what? Judah could be dead, Espinoza too, and it was all my fault. Judah and Espinoza had trusted me and I let them down. I had to get them back, but I couldn't do it alone, and I couldn't do it lying in an open field in the desert.

I tried to get up and fell back down. Nope. Not going anywhere. At least, not like that.

The sound of tires crunching over rocks vibrated through the ground. I lifted my head and let my tongue fall over the side of my mouth, breathing fast to cool myself. Headlights danced through the tall, dry grass. A car rolled by and shook the pebbles near my snout. Another drove by after I waited a few minutes. The road, whichever it was, seemed to be well-traveled. I could shift back and maybe catch a ride, but I didn't think anyone would stop for a naked man standing in the middle of the highway. They would stop for a dog. At least, I hoped they would.

With a mighty huff, I forced myself back on shaky legs. It was a risk, pulling the old injured dog maneuver. I was as likely to get hit as I was to actually get a ride, and I had to bank on not being driven pronto to the nearest emergency vet clinic in San Angelo. I needed to go the other way.

I limped up to the last bit of grass near the highway and crouched down, waiting. The trick was in the timing...and hoping the guy at the wheel wasn't drunk or asleep. Oh, and avoiding trucks. I might survive being hit by a car, but a truck not so much.

A car appeared in the distance on my side of the road. I hunched down and waited, counting and holding my breath. When it was close enough that I could read the license plate, I leapt out and stopped, turning my head to face the car. The hood dipped as the driver applied the brakes. Tires squealed. I braced for an impact that didn't come. When I was sure it wasn't going to hit, I cracked open one eye. The grill was right in front of my face.

The car door opened and I hurried into position, lying splayed across the road with my injured rear leg displayed. I whined when the figure leaned over the hood to get a better look. "Ed?"

I cracked open an eye, cut off my whine halfway through, and looked up into Bran's face.

The passenger side door opened and Angel got out. "What is it, babe? Is it dead?"

Now, it was one thing for Bran to see me lying there, playing the injured dog card to try and snag a ride. He wasn't a werewolf and so I didn't have to worry about making an appearance for me. However, it was another for Angel, his wife and a wolf outside my pack, to see me like that. I rolled as soon as I heard her coming but paused when I had to move my injured leg. I turned for a better look and saw my whole leg was red and sticky with blood. As soon as I saw it the fur started to itch so I leaned over to give it a good cleaning with my tongue. Maybe that'd ease the pain.

"Edward Petersen. One of Sal's wolves," Bran said.

Angel squatted down next to me and tilted her head to the

side. "Is that a bullet wound?"

I tried to scoot away from her, to hide the wound in some way. Angel may have been a werewolf, but she wasn't in my pack, and that meant she was potentially dangerous. Being injured in front of an outsider made me prey, something I didn't want to be.

"Looks like," Bran said and slid one arm under me.

The last thing I wanted was for Bran to pick me up. I squirmed, but that just wound up making things awkward. And it hurt a lot, too.

"Calm down," he said and hauled me up as if I weighed nothing. "We'll take you back to the pack. You can shift in the back seat. Angel can help."

If it'd been anyone other than Bran, I might have bit him for how he manhandled me, especially in front of a werewolf who wasn't pack. But Bran and Sal were practically brothers. The only reason Angel wasn't pack was because she had a record. Chanter didn't let anyone who had done time into the pack. Arrested was one thing, time inside was another.

Angel climbed into the back of the car on one side while Bran opened the door on the other. He deposited me on the seat so that my head had to lay on her lap if I wanted to keep my legs up on the seat. Then, Bran got back in front, did a U-turn and headed back toward Eden.

I didn't get much time to think about where we were going or how I was getting there. Angel placed her hand firmly under my chin and made me raise my head to look her in the eyes. I jerked away, trying to avoid it, but she held me, so I just growled.

"Don't give me that macho bullshit," she snapped at me. "I know you're about as likely to bite me as you are to fuck me so don't even try. I'm not going to hurt you. Well, much anyway." Her dark lips turned up in a smile and her grip on my jaw tightened. "Now, that bullet's probably silver. Shifting's going to be a bitch, but you've got to do it unless you want to get stuck like that, you hear? I'm going to help you, like it or not. Now, look me in the eyes, dammit."

I kept my gaze averted. A lot of humans think that werewolves don't look each other in the eye because it's a dominance thing. It's way more complicated than that, especially for someone at the bottom of a pack like me. Locking gazes like that is overwhelming, especially if the other party is stronger than me or has more status.

It's like being hypnotized but by something ugly and horrible. I can see the monster inside, the ugliest, darkest side of their wolf and it scares the piss out of me, sometimes literally. Seeing that activates the fight or flight parts of the brain and can have other effects other than feeling queasy. Someone at the top like Sal or Valentino could force me to shift or keep me from shifting with nothing more than an intense glare.

That's what Angel was going to do. She wanted to force me to change, and I didn't want to change. With the bullet inside, it could tear more, bury it deeper. There could be more serious damage, especially considering all the other injuries to my legs when they were broken before. What if it hit an artery during the shift? Sal had always said—

Angel dipped her head into my vision and caught my eye. She had beautiful eyes, the kind that were hard to look away from. They were blue with lines of green and a ring of brown that danced around the center. The pattern in the color made it look like someone had cracked a precious gem and let another one grow inside. But they were also sad eyes. Painful eyes.

Then I saw the beast. She was small and black with wild eyes. Blood and saliva coated her teeth and lips as she snarled. The fury that burned inside those eyes was raw and pure, threatening to boil over at any minute. Just one wrong move and that beast would rip someone's throat out.

The image of the beast faded, replaced by a curious reflection of a face I knew all too well. Dark, curly hair sat in a mess, eyes bruised and saggy from lack of sleep, a head too big for that scrawny neck. My own reflection stared back at me.

And that's when I knew the beast I had seen wasn't Angel, but me.

I drew in a deep breath and felt a sharp, stabbing pain in my left ass cheek. At the same time, I was suddenly aware of how cold I was. I looked down and saw that, without realizing it, I'd shifted back into my human self. Five fingers on each hand, every mole in its place. "What was that?" I asked Angel, my voice strained from the sudden change. "I've never..."

*Again*, I heard the wolf inside demand. *Look at her again.*

I wanted to. I wanted to see myself in Angel's eyes all over again. I needed to so I could understand what she'd done. No, that wasn't quite right. I just *needed* to. There was no good explanation why.

She pulled a wool blanket up from the floorboards of the car and wrapped it around me without meeting my eyes again. "Quiet, now," she said. "And try not to bleed on the upholstery too bad." She sat down, crossed her arms and legs and fixed her gaze forward.

Between wherever we were and Paint Rock, I tried to strike up a conversation twice. Angel made it clear she didn't want to talk and Bran reiterated the fact by telling me to shut my damn mouth.

"Don't you want to know what happened or how I got shot?" I gestured to the window. "Look, Judah and that cop need help. I can take you to them. I know where they are."

"Sal would be very angry if we went with you without speaking to him first." Bran shot me an angry look in the rear view and then adjusted it so he didn't have to look at me. "Rushing in without a plan is not a good idea, Ed. We must speak with the pack."

"You're not listening to me!" I shouted. "They could be hurt or dead. We have to go back!"

"We will speak with your alpha," Bran said, calm and firm as always.

No matter what I said, he wasn't going to budge. The guy did what he always did and treated me like I was still a kid. I was almost twenty-two, hardly a kid by anybody's standards. Bran wasn't the boss of me.

But Sal was, and when he found out I'd let Judah be taken, he was going to lose his shit on me. I'd be one werewolf sans a head. "He's going to kill me," I muttered and sank further into the blanket.

"No one on our side dies tonight." Angel sounded sleepy. Her eyes were closed, too.

"We have to go back and get them," I said, leaning toward her.

"The pack has no responsibility to retrieve those humans," Angel said, turning her gaze out the window. "And if they were any other humans, they probably wouldn't."

I worked my fingers into fists. "What do you know about pack life, huh? Outsider."

I meant it as an insult, but Angel took it in stride. She turned back to me, a bored expression playing on her face. "One day, pup, but not today."

We didn't say much else to each other until we pulled into Chanter's driveway. All the lights were still on. The door opened when we pulled up and Sal stepped outside.

When he saw it was me and not Judah, the pain was evident on his face. Sal tore down the stairs to meet me, turned me around and sniffed the air before pushing me back to stand at arm's length. "Where is she?" he demanded, his temper waking the wolf inside to peer through his eyes.

I shrank away. "I'm sorry," I managed before I stepped wrong. Pain shot up into my lower back. All the blood rushed to my head along with memories of being trapped in the cave pit with Judah two years ago when my legs were broken. The next and last thing I remember thinking was, *Wow, the ground is really close.*

~

I woke up on my back, naked, surrounded by faces staring down at me. My vision spun, but I recognized them by smell.

"He goin' to make it?" Istaqua asked and then bit into a cracker.

"If you're going to take a bullet, the best place is in the ass," Bran said. "Plenty of padding."

"If Ed had an ass, maybe," Sal added. I couldn't see where he was, but I had the weirdest pressure in my left hip, going down my left leg. "He should be ready now. Roll him."

"Wait," I croaked, but nobody listened. Istaqua grabbed my feet and Bran my shoulders. On a three count, they flipped me like a pancake face down onto the sofa.

"All right, hold his arms."

"Thought you said he'd be numb?" Istaqua said as Bran grabbed my wrists and pinned them to the pillow.

"I said ready. I don't have any of the good stuff left. Best I can do is dull it. Digging out bullets hurts like a son of a bitch either way. Hold him good, Bran."

I turned my head sideways and choked out a panicked "Wait."

Sal didn't listen.

On a pain scale from one to ten, getting shot rates somewhere around a ten. Digging out the bullet with decade-old army medic tools while lying face down on a sofa is probably at least a sixteen. I think I ate half the pillow and had started in on the cushion before it was over. While he was digging, I could barely breathe, so talking was out of the question. When it was over, I didn't want to talk. My throat was scratchy from all the screaming and whining. But I didn't have a choice.

"They've got Judah," I moaned as soon as Sal started bandaging.

His hands paused in their work. "I know."

I told him everything I knew, down to the last detail. I wasn't sure if they needed every detail, but I also didn't know what would help. It was always best to overshare than not say enough in my experience, at least when it came to werewolves. Sal would know if I lied or left something out and, with Istaqua and Bran sitting right there, I didn't want to give them any excuse to not like me. That could be bad for my health.

When I'd finished telling everyone everything, the room fell silent. Istaqua was the first to speak. He crossed his arms, tilted his head up and said, "Judah Black is a human and not bound to the pack. I see no reason that pack should risk their life to rescue her. She chose her path. There are consequences for going in alone. No more blood needs to be shed over this."

A loud growl echoed through the room. I pushed up but didn't dare flip over onto my back. My ass was still way too sore.

"That's my mother you're talking about," Hunter growled. "Maybe you're too much of a coward to go after her, but I'm not."

The front door opened.

"Hunter, wait," Sal called. He stepped into my field of vision to glare at Istaqua. "We're going for her. You going to stop us?"

Istaqua narrowed his eyes and crossed his arms. "You should let the humans see to humans, Saloso. You are overextending your reach. How many times have you run to save her?"

"Fewer times than she's saved the rest of us. We owe her, but this isn't about that. Life isn't a scale to be balanced." Sal raised a finger and pointed in Istaqua's face. "It's not about exploiting people to get something back that helps you. That's not how we do things here in Paint Rock. Here, we look after our own. That means pack and the family and friends of pack and anyone else I feel like taking care of. This is my territory. My people. And I'm going after her, me and anyone else who wants to come."

"Hell yeah," said Angel. "Count me in."

Bran nodded his head. "I'm with you."

I winced as I pushed up off the couch to stand and stumbled.

Bran helped me stay on my feet. "Me too."

"No, friend," Bran said, shaking his head. "You're already injured."

I narrowed my eyes at him. "If you don't take me with you, I'm just going to go anyway. I don't need your permission."

"And if I forbid it?"

I turned to face Sal, unable to read his face. The scent coming from him was a mix of worry and fear, but also anger. "My alpha is about to walk into hostile territory with a bear shifter and a packless werewolf and leave the heart of his pack behind?" I raised my head. "After he took a bullet for the alpha's girlfriend?"

Sal grabbed his leather Kings jacket from the back of a chair and shrugged it on. "Ed took a bullet and got back up. I'd say he's proven himself. If he wants to come, I won't turn him away."

"I'm coming, too."

Every head in the room turned to the hallway where Gideon Reed stood, hand gripping his side. He was pale and sweaty, but I still jumped back at the sight of him. Last time I saw him, he was trying to kill me, after all.

Sal pushed toward him. "You need to get back inside that ash circle right now."

Reed lifted his clenched hand, letting a small trail of ash fall from his fist to the floor. "Cedar, sage, tobacco, and rose."

"You forgot the redwood." Sal crossed his arms. "What of it?"

"For the last day, it's protected me against that spell. It may work to keep the rest of you from falling under it if it can be applied. Right now, I have some tucked in my pocket and some in my hand here. It's weakening the effect, even if I can still feel it pulling at me." Reed held his hand out, the silvery ash resting in his palm. "Without it, you've got no chance of resisting him."

Sal sighed. "I have more and I can apply it, but that still doesn't mean you should come. Look at you. You're half-dead. These people have already done a number on you."

Reed pushed off the wall with a shoulder. "These *people* are making a mockery of my beliefs, hiding behind their church and using God as their excuse to do evil. And if I had stopped them a decade ago, they wouldn't have been able to do what they are doing. They are here because of me and that gives me more right than anyone to fight."

"If you want to come, I won't stop you," Sal said, nodding.

Reed nodded back in thanks.

"What about Mom's new partner? That half-vampire guy?" Hunter asked.

The room went quiet and everyone exchanged glances.

"Hunter," Bran said after a long pause. "I don't think that's a good idea."

"Tell him the truth, Bran." Sal gripped the back of a chair. "The night Judah got the shit beat out of her, his scent was all over her."

"Are you saying Abe broke her arm?" I shook my head. "Why?"

"I don't know, but I don't trust him."

I sighed and looked down at my hands. Without some kind of focus, I wasn't going to be much use to Sal in a fight. My teeth and claws were mostly for looks. Still, I'd be damned if I was going to sit this one out. Judah needed me. I needed to be there for Mara, too.

Sal sighed. "Ed, you go with Bran and Angel. Reed, you're with me. I'll drop Hunter and Mia off with Nina."

Hunter huffed. "I can fight."

"Not if I say you can't!" Every wolf in the room, Angel aside, lowered their heads when Sal barked in his alpha voice. "And you're going to stay with Nina and stay safe. Now, go and get your sister and her diaper bag. We're going." Sal turned the collar on his jacket up and grabbed his keys off the counter before turning to face Istaqua. "You need to get gone before I come back." He jerked open the front door.

"Careful, Sal, that you don't let a human dictate your decision-making again," Istaqua called after him. "You know how that turned out last time." The old coyote spun his keys on his finger, took to whistling a tune, and swaggered out of the house.

Angel frowned at me as I stumbled forward to grab the wall. "You sure you want to go? You don't look like you're in the best shape, Ed."

"I just need something to lean on," I answered her. "Now that the silver's out, I'll heal pretty fast." Angel came to my side and an idea hit me, the best idea I'd had all day. "You guys mind if we swing by my place to pick up something? I've got an idea."

# Chapter Twenty-Four

Time loses meaning in the dark. Eventually, exhaustion won out and I found a way to balance myself to minimize the pain in my wrists and ankles to sleep lightly. That just made keeping track of time even more hopeless. When noise woke me, I was too groggy to remember my plan. My throat hurt and my head swam in pain and congestion. The blood that had flowed down my arms and over my chest was dry and itchy, but I couldn't scratch it.

The noise that roused me turned out to be the lock turning on the door. Light flooded the room and I jerked back as before, shielding my eyes. Judging by the size and shape of the shadow, it was Warren, but he wasn't alone.

Slumped over, motionless in his arms was a body. Because of the painful light and long shadows, I couldn't make out who it was, but my heart thundered and my head raced with possibilities. He took two steps into the room and dropped the body with a dull thud, letting it roll forward to stop just out of reach.

I squinted against the light to glance at the body he'd tossed at me. "Mara?" She, too, had been stripped down. Her body was bruised and battered, blood crusted over her nose and mouth. Mara's entire chest was purple.

She cracked open a blood-crusted eye. "Heya, teach." She winced.

"Don't talk, Mara. Please."

"Shut up, you two. This isn't a social call." Warren strode into the room, stopping behind Mara. "I've been told BSI officers are conditioned to resist physical torture. Is that true?"

I shifted my weight, wincing when the metal bit further into my wrists and ankles. "Why bother? If you're going to kill me, just kill me."

A white smile flashed in the darkness. "Oh, you know better than that. You're no good to me dead."

"That's right. You think I'm one of Han's fucked-up experiments."

"Wrong again." Warren's foot shot out of the darkness and stomped down hard on the side of Mara's knee. Mara screamed in pain, trying to writhe and twist away, but Warren held her by applying more pressure. "I believe you're a success like me, like those two bodies you saw in that little clinic of yours. Only, nobody knew. Maybe your abilities didn't manifest right away. Maybe someone covered it all up. Who knows? But you *are* like me."

"I'm nothing like you," I spat at him through clenched teeth.

"Then how do you explain that shadow fire, hmm?" He kicked Mara aside and closed the distance to stand in front of me. His cool, thin fingers wrapped around my jaw and squeezed. "Seamus told me all about what you can do."

I grimaced. Seamus, that son of a bitch!

"Did you think it was coincidence that led to you developing that ability? Chance? Fate?" With each question, his fingers tightened until I saw stars. "You may not be immortal like me, but you're not entirely human, either. There's a part of you that wants power, to be worshipped and feared, and I am going to draw that part of you out." He released me and chuckled to himself before pacing away.

I stared down at the light reflecting off the slick floor, remembering the last time I had called up that shadow flame. It had felt sentient, like it had a life of its own. The overwhelming need to devour and destroy had nearly taken over. Whatever that power was, it was dark and frightening enough that I never wanted to use it again.

"What's your connection to Seamus?"

Warren shrugged. "My father and he had a deal having to do with those plants. But father was short-sighted. Seamus is a lord of the fae and soon he'll be High King. Seems wasteful to treat transactions with him as simple business when you can win favor and power instead."

"Oh, yeah?" I raised my eyes to Warren's shadow. "How do you plan on doing that?"

He flicked his hand out and something metallic clattered to the floor next to Mara. "Take that. Get up."

In Mara's condition, I didn't think she could stand, especially after what Warren had done to her leg. It shouldn't have been possible, but Warren's magick was strong enough that Mara had no choice but to obey. She growled and grunted in pain, hissing and breathing hard, but she eventually rose, placing most of her weight on the uninjured leg.

Warren turned sideways so that the light illuminated him in profile as he stared at me. "Place the point of the blade against your stomach, about an inch above the navel."

Mara's whole body shook as she fought Warren's control.

I strained against my restraints. "What the hell are you doing?"

"Illustrating a point. Get it? A point?" He laughed at his own joke, even though no one laughed with him. "If you want to save her, you'll call your power forth. Go ahead. Use it to strike me down."

"If you're so damn powerful, why don't you just make me?"

Warren glared at me before sneering and gesturing to Mara with two fingers.

Mara lifted the dagger away from her skin and then promptly plunged it back in. Mara doubled over, the knife still in her stomach.

"No! Stop this!"

Warren rotated his fingers and the knife in Mara moved with them.

"You son of a bitch! You'll kill her!"

"A small sacrifice to pave the way to future glory." Warren went to stand behind Mara, putting his hands on her shoulders. "She's utterly insignificant, just like everyone else. Completely replaceable. If she dies, I'll just bring your cop friend in here next. Then, maybe I'll have my people grab that little girl I saw you with outside the clinic the other day. How old is she, by the way? Very cute."

I ground my teeth. "You lay a hand on Mia and the pack will tear you apart."

"So you keep saying. But for big, bad wolves who supposedly protect their own, the one you had with you abandoned you rather quickly."

My eyes widened and my heart skipped a beat. Ed! He was alive. He'd gotten away!

"Don't worry, though, he didn't get far, not after that silver round we put in him. I can always bring him in next, if you prefer."

Rage welled up inside me until it felt like my chest was about to burst. It erupted in a scream as I tried fruitlessly to tear my way out of the restraints.

"You should be more concerned with your own well-being. Do you even know where you are? This Way is one of the few that naturally occurs in this part of the county. Time here passes at a different rate. What seems like days may well be years out there or it could go the other way. It tends to be rather unpredictable. The more time you waste resisting, the more time you could be losing on the outside."

I screamed and fought the chains, letting the teeth dig deeper. "You'd be nothing without that rem, you pathetic coward. That's why you're so powerful. Even after those experiments fucked you up, you still couldn't live up to daddy's expectations. This is nothing but an ego trip. You're no god. You're a teenage boy with low self-esteem and daddy issues."

Warren jumped forward with a scream and placed the palm of his hand over my face. I tried to struggle away, but I was weak and he had me in a death grip, palm pressed against my mouth and nose so that I couldn't breathe.

Suffocating wasn't the worst of it. When his hand made contact with my skin, fingertips digging into my temple, the dark cell and all the pain associated with it faded away and I was treated to a horrific vision.

I stood in the center of a dusty wasteland, blood and bodies all around me. My whole body ached head to toe as I limped along a filthy road on a foggy morning. My right arm hung limply. The left was caked in dried blood while I held an assault rifle in the left. Every breath hurt. With my next step, I stumbled and fell, pain shooting through me on impact. Tears burned in my eyes and an agonizing scream caught in my throat. I blinked back the tears, opening my eyes to see what I had tripped on.

The dead, glassy eyes of my son stared back at me. His body was dirty. A string of congealed blood stuck his face to the ground and a massive concrete block had crushed everything from the neck down.

I screamed in a panic at the sight. Magick surged into my muscles. Bone and tendon snapped as I gripped the block and pried it away. There were bloodstains on the other side. A twisted line of barbed wire marked the block of cement as belonging to the walls of the reservation.

The more I dug through the rubble, the more bodies I found. Sal had been ripped apart, his insides strewn over the rocks. I fell to my knees, sobbing. My hands shook as I pushed tears away and left bloodstains behind. As I looked up, something else caught my eye. A tiny toddler hand protruded from the rubble a short distance away, the arm of one of Mia's favorite dolls dangling from its still grip.

Warren's fingers left my face and I fell forward, gasping for air, still trying to cope with the scene he'd shown me. He staggered back a step and shook out his hand. "Stupid bitch. How are you fighting me? You should be cut off from most of your magick. That's impossible."

"Maybe," I gasped and spat, "you just can't get it up without some rem."

"I am the *Divine*," he hissed in response. "How dare you speak to me that way! I hold your life in my hands, Judah Black. Were I you, I would be more careful with my words."

"Can you even hear yourself?" I forced a bitter laugh. "Someone left the Heaven's Gate tapes on repeat one too many times."

"You'll be singing a very different tune shortly," he promised me.

I strained against my restraints to raise both middle fingers. "Kiss my scrawny white ass, you wannabe Jim Jones."

He sighed, unimpressed. "Then you leave me no choice. Do it."

My attention snapped to Mara, who was somehow still standing. She jerked and made a choking sound as she shifted the knife, and then drew it out before plunging it back in. I screamed and begged for her to stop, but my cries went unanswered. Mara stabbed herself maybe a dozen times before she was too weak to continue and fell over, bleeding everywhere.

My mind went numb. I went limp against my restraints and quit fighting the tears. My whole body shook with grief.

"This is your fault!" Warren screamed and stomped a foot. "You can't blame me. You made me do this, Judah. You drove me to it! You have no one to blame but yourself!"

He was right. It was my fault. I should have saved her. I should have helped her. If I hadn't been so weak, she might still be alive. The realization only hurt more. I exploded with a scream of rage, suddenly somehow finding the strength to fight. I hauled myself up and struggled to get to Warren, growling and spitting like an animal. "You monster! You'll pay for this!"

He backhanded me across the mouth, hard. "My hands are clean!" he insisted. "Now you hang there and think about what you've done. When I come back, you'd better be ready to do more than just hang there and insult me!"

Warren growled in frustration and went out the door. All the light and warmth went with him. If I hadn't been so horribly dehydrated, I would have allowed myself to continue crying. *This place is going to kill me,* I realized and then I corrected myself, remembering my cellmate. *No, Judah. There are things far worse than death.*

~

Someone came to collect Mara shortly after. I should say Mara's body. After she fell, I didn't see her move or hear her make a sound. With all those stab wounds, her chances of survival were slim.

I was left alone in that dark place, cold and wet, with nothing but my thoughts to occupy me. At first, all I could think about was what they might be doing to Ed after Warren said they caught him. I tried to listen for cries or screams of pain but I heard nothing through the stone. The silence was more frightening than the sounds of torture might have been.

*Come on, Judah,* I told myself eventually. *What is it accomplishing, sitting here feeling sorry for yourself?*

"What else can I do?" I muttered aloud. "Even if I wasn't tired, cold and hungry, which I am, I've got no chance of getting out of here. What hope do I have? I've got nothing."

*Then don't think about escape. Think about something else.*

"But what?"

*What about Seamus?*

I sighed. Seamus telling Warren about me had started all of this. He might not have known Warren planned on keeping me prisoner and torturing me, but he probably knew the kid wasn't mentally stable. He had to have planted some seeds in Warren's mind of what to do. This was what I got for not helping him get Reed's sword.

But I couldn't blame Seamus for everything. Warren might have been a fanatic, maybe even insane, but that didn't excuse him. His little fit earlier tipped me off that he knew what he was doing was wrong. The minute he saw Mara fall over, he'd panicked and tried to shift the blame to me. People who genuinely believe they're innocent don't bother doing that. He'd had his first taste of guilt. If I had my way, I'd give him a whole lot more than that.

The door opened again and another figure, this one larger and more masculine, stood against the light in the room beyond. He took two steps into the room. A chain jingled around his ankle as light from above flooded the room. I scampered away from it, shielding my face. Whoever the man was, he stood, waiting in silence while my eyes adjusted. Once they had, I blinked away the pain and turned back.

"Espinoza?"

Espinoza's stare was blank and distant. I'd seen that look before when I helped Tindall haul an overdose to the hospital one time. He looked high out of his mind.

He stepped forward, lowering his eyes to the wooden tray in his hands. It held a bowl with some kind of grainy, white gruel inside, and a bottle of water. "You need to eat," he said and stepped up to me. He placed the tray on the ground, took up the spoon, filling it with the gruel and held it out to me.

I shook my head, fighting back tears. "They've already gotten to you, haven't they?"

He didn't answer. He just held the spoon out to me more insistently.

"Warren's done something to you, hasn't he? You're under his control." I strained to the end of my chains suddenly, but he didn't even flinch back. "You have to fight it. Whatever hold he's got on you, you can fight it!"

"I am here of my own free will," Espinoza said in a robotic tone. "I like it here. You need to eat."

"Espinoza, please—" He interrupted me by shoving the spoon in my mouth. The gruel tasted as bad as it looked. I spat it out. "He's *using* you!"

"I'm here of my own free will," he repeated and shoved the spoon at me. "I am happy."

When he shifted closer, I strained against my restraints to knock the bowl from his hands. It clattered loudly to the floor, the contents overturned. He stared down at the smear of chunky white on the floor. He blinked, but the blank stare in his eyes didn't lift.

"Please, if you're in there, if you can hear me, fight him. I know you're strong, stronger than him. Whatever drugs he's given you, you have got to think through them. Please, if there's even a shred of the man I knew left in there—"

"There isn't." My head jerked up and I saw Warren standing in the doorway flanked by Hector and Amanda. They looked as passive as Espinoza. He probably had them under his control now, too. "This one was very weak-minded. He wasn't very hard to break. All it took was a little rem, a little toying with the mind. I wanted you to see for yourself. All that pain he was carrying is gone. It can be gone for you, too. He's happy. Can't you see?" He walked up and put a hand on Espinoza's shoulder. He didn't even react.

"If this is what you call happy, I think you need your head examined."

He turned his eyes downward to the bloodstain on the floor. "Or, you can resist like Mara and Espinoza can die, too. You'll have no one to blame but yourself."

He turned back to Espinoza and patted him on the shoulder. "I honestly don't know why you're fighting so hard. You're all in such pain. Take this one, for example. All those jokes, it's all a mask, a band aid over a gaping wound. But it doesn't have to be. All his pain is gone now, replaced with a calling of the highest order: to serve his betters."

"You're not his better. You're a slimy asshole using power and religion to manipulate the broken. I see through your mask, Warren. You're disgusting and you're going to get what you deserve in the end."

"Won't we all?" he said with a smile and turned his attention back to me. "This is the last time I will offer you an escape before I take more drastic measures."

I shook my head and said in my best Luke Skywalker impression, "I'll never join you!"

Warren wasn't impressed. Either he didn't get the reference or didn't care. His response was a frustrated hiss through his teeth.

"Now is the part where you lament that I don't know the power of the dark side."

"Do you think you're funny?" He smirked. "You know, I'm starting to think that maybe I should break you exactly as I did Mara. She fought me, too." Warren leaned in close to whisper next to my ear. "In the end, she liked it. She begged me to put my hands on her."

I snapped at him with my teeth and he jerked back. "Do to others what you would have them do to you," I muttered.

"What?"

I didn't answer him.

He growled to the men behind him, "Take her to the cross. I

want her broken by dawn."

Hector and Amanda came forward and reached for where my chains were bolted to the wall to undo them.

*Now's my chance*, I thought. I can fight them. *Even if I don't overpower them, at least I'll go down fighting.* I watched them fight to pry the chains from the wall, waiting for my opportunity to strike.

It never came. Something hard slammed into my neck and sent a stunning bolt of electricity flowing down into my body. My brain stopped. My heart jumped. Everything stopped, everything except for the icy, electric fingers of pain. Only after I fell over, groaning and completely unable to move did they finally get the chains free from the wall.

Strong, calloused hands wrapped around either of my arms. I remained slumped over, groaning and fighting for breath as they dragged me forward. As soon as I could breathe steady again, I fought to shout at Warren as they dragged me past him. They didn't let me go but it caused a small pause in our procession, long enough for me to turn and squint at Warren. "It's called the Golden Rule, asshole, and it's going to come back and bite you in the ass."

There was no sunlight in the hall, but there was the comforting hum of fluorescent lights. Beyond that and the buzzing feeling in my limbs and the pounding in my chest, I was barely aware of anything until they summarily dumped me on a slanted tile floor. I lifted my head weakly for a look around and found no sign of an actual cross. Instead, there was a big post in the middle of the room, just before the floor began its slant toward a metal grate. Ominous stains populated the floor in spatters and pools. Tables lined one side of the room where a man in one of those black ski masks stood decked out in camo gear. His tables were lined with silver pins, scalpels and other various instruments crafted to maim and cause pain.

Torture it was, then. Great.

I lowered my head and tried to think about the best way to get through this. Their goal was to break down my mind, which they must have thought they could do by first breaking my body. I wasn't in any state where I could physically protect myself, as the room was still warded against magick, but I could protect my mind.

There's a method for steeling oneself against even the most brutal acts called compartmentalization. It involves mentally creating a safe place, be that a room, a chest or wherever you might feel safe, and then going there, closing and locking a door behind you. Compartmentalization is a common technique used by children who are frequently abused, rape victims, and it's also taught to Special Forces soldiers to guard against torture. It's why in movies they're always spouting their name, rank and serial numbers, because that's the mantra that somehow takes them to their happy place.

I hadn't had such training. I'd only read about it. Creating a safe place was going to be mentally taxing and take time, time that perhaps I didn't have.

My captors came again and picked me up. Hector and Amanda did something that connected the shackles on my wrists together like handcuffs and then repeated the process with my ankles. Then, they lifted me and tied me—not to the post as I'd expected—but to a cold, metal bench. Still naked against the cold, I shivered at the contact and then again when I realized I wasn't to be the object of their torture today.

Espinoza went to stand before the post in the center of the room and unbuttoned his shirt.

I looked to Warren with panic choking me. "Stop, please! Leave him alone. If you want me then torture me and not him."

Warren laughed as if we were having tea instead of witnessing torture. "Because torture won't break you. You'd shoulder it, use it as fuel to make you stronger. The key to breaking you is breaking those you care about. We'll start with him and move on to the others next."

I fought to think of something, anything I could do to stop this, but I was out of options. I wasn't going to sit there and watch them torture an innocent man.

As they worked to affix Espinoza to the post, I lowered my head and dug in deep, searching for the pit of anger and darkness at my core. It wasn't hard to find, not after everything I'd just gone through. The power felt like it was on the other side of a brick wall, however, just out of reach. Warren might have cut me off from most of my magick, but not all. I was sure that if I concentrated hard enough, I could break through.

I closed off my mind, pushing out the chill in my bones, the hard bench underneath me, the sound of ropes tightening around Espinoza's wrists as he went willingly to be beaten. It all came out in a breath, leaving behind nothing but a silent buzzing in my mind and the deep thrum of power just beyond my reach.

Warren's backhand caught me off-guard. It struck with supernatural force, sending me tumbling to the side, my vision spinning. "Open your eyes and pay attention!"

I spat blood and forced myself to sit up, even though my head spun. The wall in my chest cracked as I glared at him and the tiniest bit of power leaked through. "You want to see what I can do so badly?"

Black fire danced in my hands behind my back and raced up my arms, ready to devour anything it touched. With a word, I could have sent it after Warren. I could have torn his aura apart and left him a drooling mess. It was no less than he deserved.

Before I could send the fire, however, I remembered what I had seen before, the barbed wire weaving in and out of Warren's skin. He was being tortured, too, every day of his life. Maybe I could save him. Maybe nobody had to die.

"Stop!" Warren screeched and his voice cracked. He hit me again, this time hard enough to knock me off the bench.

The hold I had on my power slipped away as I crashed to the floor, all the wind knocked out of me, and struggled to draw a breath into my burning lungs. I turned my head and spat blood. "Not so fun when the power's directed at you, huh?"

Warren leapt over the bench and grabbed a handful of my hair, hauling me up. "So you can do it," he hissed at me through clenched teeth. "Now that I know for certain, I don't need you to show me. You're going to serve me, Judah, whether you like it or not. And you're going to wish you'd kept that smart mouth of yours shut."

I swallowed and fought the urge cry. Me and my big mouth.

# Chapter Twenty-Five

## Ed

"Nunchucks?" Angel arched an eyebrow. "As in Bruce Lee *Enter the Dragon* nunchucks?"

Why is it that whenever you bring up nunchucks, that's the movie everyone goes to? I rolled my eyes and sighed at the window. The house sat empty. Sal must have called Shauna and Daphne already. Otherwise, I would have called one of them to bring me what I needed. Angel and Bran might have been badass, but they had no clue when it came to gaming.

"No, not that kind of nunchuck. It's like..." I tried to think of how to describe it and came up empty. "Look, have you never seen a Wii before? Seriously?"

Angel wrinkled her nose. "I don't have time for games, kid. Tell me what you need and I'll find it."

"It may be better for him to go and get it," Bran said. "Is your behind healed?"

I frowned and rubbed the left cheek through my borrowed pair of sweats. It wasn't completely healed, but it did feel a little better. I could walk on it, I'd just be stiff and slow going. And I didn't know exactly where my nunchucks were. It could take a while to find them. Dammit, I should've listened to Daphne and cleaned my room last month. "Yeah, I think I can manage. Just don't go anywhere without me, okay?"

"I think I'd better go with him just in case," Angel volunteered. "I don't like the idea of letting an injured werewolf buddy of mine walk into an unguarded house at night with predators around."

"Buddy?"

She reached in front of me and opened the door before pushing me toward it. "Don't get hung up on it. Let's go."

I stumbled out of the car and winced at the pain of putting weight on my left leg. It hurt, but it was bearable. Angel went up the stairs and propped open the storm door while I fumbled with the false rock that hid the spare key. I popped it open and found it empty inside. "The hell?"

"What is it?"

"Spare key's gone." I showed her the empty plastic rock.

Angel cursed and grabbed for the door, turning the knob. It went without protest and opened.

"That shouldn't be open. Daphne always locks the door. She chews my ass if I don't." I bit my lower lip.

"I'll go first," Angel whispered. "You stay behind me."

I huffed, but obeyed. I still hadn't figured Angel out. Granted, she wasn't in my pack so I didn't exactly have to bow to her commands, but she wasn't a normal werewolf. She acted like Shauna or Sal, someone way up a hierarchy, but not quite. And what she'd done with her eyes, reflecting that back on me... I'd never seen anything quite like it. She acted protective like an alpha, but didn't seem to get all worked up when other people challenged her position in a group. Maybe it was because she wasn't in a pack. Hell if I know. I just like to chase rabbits and fetch balls under the full moon.

Inside the house, it was dark. Everything seemed in order. The living room smelled faintly of Daphne's favorite powdered deodorizer and the tofu she'd probably made for dinner. I paused and sniffed. There was something else, a new, metallic smell with strong undertones of earthy decay, rust and... Was that Axe body spray?

"Smell that?" Angel whispered as she pawed at her nose.

I sneezed and nodded. "Can't smell hardly anything through it. Yuck."

"Probably the point. It's what I'd spray to cover my scent from werewolves." She stepped into the center of the living room and let out a loud snarl. "Whoever the hell is in here, show yourself right now and I promise I'll rip your head all the way off instead of leaving it dangle."

A shotgun pumped right next to my head, forcing my heart to jump into my throat. "I could have killed you three times before you even knew I was here."

Angel spun with a growl, but was suddenly blinding by the beam of a flashlight as it swept over us. "Who the hell are you?"

I squinted against the flashlight. "Abe?" It sounded like him and looked like him. At least, whoever it was had the big, floppy hat and long coat. Without my sense of smell, I couldn't tell for sure.

"Abraham," he corrected, sounding annoyed. "And you two should be more alert."

It hit me suddenly that he'd broken into my home and deliberately tried to mask that he was there. My heart stopped beating in my throat and fell into my stomach. Shit. He had to be there for the hard drive. I clenched my fists and turned my head to glare at the half-vampire behind me. "If you're here for the hard drive, it's gone."

Abe shifted the flashlight and arched an eyebrow. "Ah, so you are the one who had it, as I suspected. Have you seen what was on that hard drive?"

I swallowed and nodded slowly. "Are you going to kill me?"

"Not on my watch!" Angel growled.

Abe shifted the barrel of the gun to her, holding it there for a long moment before lifting it away. "Contrary to what you might believe, I am on your side."

I stumbled out of reach as quick as I could and turned on him. Having my back to another predator made me uneasy. "Then explain why you beat the shit out of Judah and why you were with those unmarked military guys."

Abe frowned. "That is a complicated answer, too complicated for the time we have, so I will give you a simple, yet incomplete answer. Despite appearances, BSI is not one cohesive group. There are opposing factions within the organization. There are those of us who disagree with many of the policies in place, but doing so is dangerous. What I do is even more so. I work in intelligence."

I blinked. "You're a spy?"

Abe's whole chest heaved with a sigh and he rolled his eyes. "Of sorts. That hard drive is important evidence. I must reclaim it."

"How do we know you're not lying?" Angel muscled forward to stand between Abe and me, arms crossed.

"You do not. However, if I do not get this hard drive tonight, things will get much more difficult for everyone. Those military guys—" Abe moved his fingers in the air, making quotes. "—are a suicide squad. In less than two hours, they will storm the Tribulation Adventists compound and neutralize everyone inside before setting the place on fire, erasing all evidence."

My mouth suddenly felt dry. I exchanged a glance with Angel. "Judah is there right now."

"What?" Abe reached out and grabbed me by the shirt and tugged me closer.

I may or may not have let out a surprised, very unmanly

sounding yelp.

"What do you mean Judah is there? She should be incapacitated! I made certain—"

Abe stopped, his eyes widening with realization. He let go of my shirt, muttering something profane in Russian. "That woman's stubbornness knows no bounds."

"Well, she's not there of her own free will, you know." I tugged on the hem of my shirt, straightening it. "And it's not Hector that's the problem from what I saw. It was the kid. He's got her and Espinoza hostage."

"Explain," Abe demanded.

"In a minute. First, I need my nunchuck," I said and pushed past him.

My room was on the other side of the kitchen at the end of a short hallway. I flipped on the light and took in the mess of candy wrappers, chip bags, and empty Red Bull cans. It's a wonder we don't have mice, Daphne would say. But I didn't think mice would frequent a home where three werewolves lived. Not smart mice, anyway.

The last time I'd seen my Wii remote was when Daphne was thinking about having a yard sale. She wanted me to sell them because I didn't use them enough and put them in a shoe box with all my other old controllers. Daphne was like that, a clean freak, environmentally conscious, a goody two-shoes. I love my sister, but man she can get on my nerves.

Anyway, most of my shoe boxes went under my bed when I got my new chair a few months ago, so I got down on my knees, pushed aside the trash and started digging. Video game controllers weren't the only thing I kept under there. I had to move whole stacks of old games, cheat codes, manga and a couple of old game guides to get to the boxes.

Angel sighed from the doorway. "You know, most single guys your age keep porn under their beds and not..." She bent over and picked up an old binder and flipped it open before spinning around to show it to me. "Pokémon cards?"

I snatched the binder away from her. "Magic: The Gathering!"

"Whatever."

"And I'm not single. Bad guys got my girlfriend."

"Uh-huh," said Angel, crossing her arms.

"Contrary to popular belief, not all nerds are socially awkward, live in our parents' basements, and live to troll people on the internet who can't spell."

"How is your sister's spare bedroom different from your mom's basement?"

I ignored her comment, mostly because I found the shoebox I was looking for and placed it on the bed. The box was full of cables, batteries and other odds and ends, with the Wii remote and nunchuck buried at the bottom. I grabbed both and hooked them up, waving them at Angel with a triumphant smile on my face.

"Video game controllers?" She rolled her eyes. "You made us stop for that?"

I turned and dug around in the plastic bin beside my bed where I'd collected all the things Mara had left in my room. Lipstick, nail polish, a bobble head... My fingers caught something metal. *There it is!*

I pulled out the pair of brass knuckles and tossed them to Angel, who caught them and whistled. "Now that's more up my alley."

"Don't mess them up. They're my girlfriend's." When Angel gave me a curious look, I added, "She used to have a dangerous job." I didn't tell her Mara used to be a stripper and had nearly been killed by a stalker because Angel would have just poked more fun at me.

She tucked the brass knuckles away. "You have everything you need?"

"Yeah, let's go."

I stood. Angel turned and we both paused when we saw Abe waiting in the doorway with his arms crossed. "She went back to the compound," he said, referring to Judah.

"Pretty sure Hector and his goons have them," I answered. "We're going to go and get them back. You feel like helping?"

Abe's lips rolled back, revealing vampire fangs. "Judah is my partner, and my employer would not be happy if something were to happen to her. I also happen to like her a great deal."

Angel and I exchanged glances. "Is that a yes?"

"That is, as you would say, a hell yes."

~

Bran got out of the car when he saw us coming back with Abe. "Look who we found," Angel reported.

"He's with us," I clarified. "And our little rescue just got a lot more complicated. We need to get Sal and the others up to speed."

We piled into the car while Abe waited outside. His truck was parked down the street, he said, and he'd follow us as soon as everyone was on the same page. Bran dialed Sal on his phone. I told him what Abe had said. After a moment of silence, Sal answered, "That doesn't change anything. It just adds a layer of urgency. You guys need to meet us here yesterday."

"Wait," I called before Sal hung up. Everyone froze and looked at me. "Shouldn't we come up with a plan or something?"

"I think the plan is..." Bran started.

Angel made a fist and hit the palm of her hand. "Tear the place apart board by board if we have to and get our people the hell out."

"And if they're hostages? What then? They might shoot Judah, Espinoza and Mara as soon as they see us."

"We will meet with Sal and the others at the rendezvous point and discuss strategy," Bran agreed. "We have to be prepared for a hostage situation."

"We have to be prepared for anything," Abe agreed and tipped his hat.

~

The first rendezvous point was outside of the rez on the side of the road. Sal had pulled over there. Shauna, Daphne, Hunter and Reed sat in the bed of the truck with Reed huddled near the cab. Sal leaned against the tailgate, smoking. Three cigarette butts sat, crushed on the side of the road at his feet. Bran pulled up behind Sal and Abe stopped behind us.

Sal pushed away from the truck when he saw Abe get out and snarled, showing gold eyes and teeth. "What the hell is he doing here?"

"I am here for Judah, not you." Abe adjusted the collar of his coat. "Besides, what protection do the rest of you have against the spell that reduced Gideon Reed to little more than an attack dog?"

Sal walked back to the cab where he grabbed a Tupperware bowl. He opened it when he came closer, revealing a thick, gray paste.

Abe recoiled and coughed. "Really? That crude magick is the best you could come up with?"

"These are sacred herbs, used for hundreds of years to—"

Abe cut Sal off with the wave of a hand. "I'm well aware, but we don't have time for war paint and chanting."

Sal narrowed his eyes.

Abe turned, grabbed me by the wrist and yanked my arm forward. I yelped as something cold slapped against the inside of my arm, just above the elbow, and slid across it. It didn't hurt so much as it surprised me. The stinging scent of sharpie made me wrinkle my nose, but another scent hung underneath it. The itchy, cinnamon spice scent of magick. When Abe leaned back and took his hands away, I saw he'd drawn something there in hurried lines and curves. "What the hell is that?"

"A symbol by itself has no meaning unless imbibed with power from an expert in protective runes. I happen to be such an expert." Abe turned and held up his sharpie. "Anyone else?"

Sal stuck his fingers into the gray goop and drew a line with it across his forehead. "You've got your protection and I've got mine."

Abe sighed as Sal turned and swiped more of the ash paste over Daphne and Shauna's forehead. One by one, everyone—including Bran and Angel went to Sal, accepting his method over Abe's.

I swallowed. It felt weird to be the only one who didn't have the same gray mark over my forehead, and I didn't want Sal to think I trusted a stranger over him, so I stepped up last. "Better safe than sorry, right?"

Sal grinned and marked me with the ash paste.

"What about you?" I asked of Abe.

Abe pulled off his hat and flipped it over before waving a hand over it. The inside lit up with dozens of silver-blue runes, just like the one he'd drawn on me.

I nodded. "Functional fashion. I like it."

"Do we know where in the house they are keeping them?" Abe re-affixed his hat.

"I saw a bright light in one of the upper windows," I said. "It was definitely magick."

"They may have opened a Way." Abe drew his lips into a thin line. "It makes sense. That's where he would be safest."

"That leaves just one problem." Sal put the lid back on his

container and set it in the bed of the truck. "Getting inside. Way I see it, there's two ways in. Either we fight our way in, or sneak in. I think everyone knows which one I'd choose." He cracked his knuckles.

I shook my head. "If we go in guns blazing and this is a hostage situation, though, there's going to be bodies on both sides."

"Bodies I will have to explain away," Abe said and rubbed his chin.

I turned to Abe. "Can you open the Way if you know where it is?"

Abe shrugged. "I cannot open Ways, but I could tell you where one was should I be looking for it."

"A Way, you say, lad?"

I jumped half a foot at the sound of a new voice. Pretty sure everyone else did to except for Angel and Sal, who turned to growl at the elf who'd appeared out of nowhere. He leaned on an ugly, twisted piece of wood and smiled at us.

"Creven," Sal growled. "What are you doing here? I thought you were in the hospital."

"I got better." The elf frowned and leaned back from the stick. "The rest of you only know half of what's going on. You're walking blind into a trap."

"Hector's expecting us?" I asked.

"Someone is, aye, but not him. Seamus has a hand in this. He wants the sword the priest carries." Creven's eyes slid to Gideon Reed, who clutched his sword tighter. "I expect he'll be making his move soon. He may even be using this situation to his advantage if he's made any deals with Hector."

Sal's upper lip twitched. "He'd trade her for the sword."

"Aye." Creven nodded. "Might be best if the priest hangs back."

"I won't," Reed said, pulling himself up slightly. "Especially not on a hunch. I can help. There is more than one immortal in that compound and they aren't easy to kill. Even your claws and teeth may be ineffective, but I know this sword can do it."

"I believe you." Sal rubbed his injured side. I could still smell the blood on it. He wasn't fully healed. "And we need all the help we can get. If Seamus makes his move, we'll deal with it then."

Abe narrowed his eyes at the elf. "You are privy to a lot of information on both sides, elf. How is it you know about Seamus' deal?"

"Because I know Seamus better than anyone. I know how he operates and I might just be the only one of you who can stand up to him in a fair fight. So," he said, lifting his staff and planting it again in the ground, "if ya need a Way opened, if you need to get in and out of anywhere unseen, I'm your elf. But I don't think I can take all of ya. Even my powers have their limits."

"How many can you manage?" Abe asked.

Creven rubbed his chin and surveyed the crowd. "Myself and two others. I might be able to do more, but I figure Sal here wants to go after his woman and, no offense, but your magick and mine will be oil and water. Cutting through that means extra work."

Sal nodded. "You'll take me and Abe into the house and through the Way."

Angel crossed her arms and leaned back with her bottom lip out. "What about the rest of us? You expect us to just sit while you boys get to have all the fun."

"No," Sal said. "Your job is to have all the fun you want as loud as you want. Draw everyone away from our position so that we've got a clear path. Think you can do that?"

Angel smirked and looked at me. I nodded. "We can do that."

"Good." Sal struck the side of his truck and stepped back. "Let's load up." He turned as if to go back to the cab.

"It would be best," Abe said, "if you and I traveled together with the elf, I think."

Sal tossed his keys to Shauna. "Take care of her."

Shauna caught them and hopped over the tailgate to go to the cab.

The rest of us piled into our respective rides and our caravan took off with Abe's truck bringing up the rear. After a few minutes of cruising down the road in silence, I turned around to check on the truck behind us. It had disappeared.

"Fucking elves," Angel muttered.

"Fucking fae," Bran added and sped up.

Angel fidgeted, trying her fingers in the brass knuckles a minute. I plugged the nunchuck into the Wii remote and closed my eyes to concentrate. "What's with the controller?"

"It's my magick wand." I cracked open an eye to see her stifling a laugh.

I couldn't help myself. I've been laughed at and underestimated my whole life. People see me and think they push me around. Even well-meaning people like Angel couldn't help but not take me seriously. Well, I was done with that.

I pulled the nunchuck and the remote apart, stretching the cord between them, and concentrated really hard to send a burst of magickal energy down into the nunchuck. *Please work this time.*

A blue bolt of lightning shot out of the transmitting end of the remote. The head rest of the front passenger seat exploded into a mess of foam padding and torn fabric. Smoke filled the cabin and we all started coughing. Bran swerved a little but kept us on the road, partially thanks to Angel's quick thinking when she rolled down the window.

When the smoke cleared, the head rest was nothing more than two bits of metal sticking up out of the rest of the seat.

"Umm," I said and looked down at my nunchuck and remote. "I'll pay for that."

"Holy shit, kid," Angel said, still coughing. She waved a hand in front of her face to clear more of the smoke. "Glad I didn't sit up front. That would have been my head!" She raised an eyebrow at me and slowly smiled. "You're more dangerous than you look, aren't you?"

Bran frowned into the rear view. "Point that thing somewhere you can't do any damage until we get to where we're going, okay kid?"

I lowered both the remote and the nunchuck, pointing them to the floor. "Yeah, okay."

~

We turned down the long driveway leading back to the compound at what might have been a hundred miles an hour. The back end of the hatchback fishtailed out. Angel and I were tossed around in the back but got righted pretty quickly. Bran slammed his foot on the accelerator and swerved to the side of the driveway, carving out a spot right next to Sal's truck.

The huge, three-story house loomed ahead. We were close enough that I could make out the ugly floral pattern on the curtains.

"Um..." I started.

"Brace for impact!" Bran shouted.

I fell back and fumbled to get the seatbelt buckled. I had just enough time to secure it before the front of the car swerved and slammed into one of the greenhouses with a deafening crunch. A white marshmallow exploded in the front as the airbags deployed. The impact sent me straining against my seatbelt. The remotes went sailing in front of my vision and, for some reason, all I could think about was grabbing them and making sure I didn't lose them.

I don't think I blacked out, but memory gets a little fuzzy directly after an impact like that. Next thing I knew, the car was sideways in a pile of metal and plastic and Angel was pulling me from inside, screaming at Bran, "He said be loud, not kill us!"

"Nobody is dead," Bran countered from a few paces away. He grabbed his shirt and ripped it off, tossing it in a wad to the ground beside him. "But they are aware that we are here. Hurry. I can smell the others. They are already around back."

I hopped down from the side of the overturned hatchback, still clutching my remotes, and looked around. Shauna had been a little gentler with Sal's truck, opting instead to pull up against the house sideways and lay on the horn. She stood on top of the hood of the truck now, halfway through her shift into wolf form.

The house came to life. Lights flipped on. Curtains shifted aside and curious faces peered out. We had only seconds before they'd be out on the porch with guns aimed at us, guns with silver bullets. I spotted movement in the front of the house near the windows, exactly where they'd gathered to shoot at me last time. Everyone else was still climbing out of the back of the truck, getting ready. Shauna and Daphne were in the middle of shifting and wouldn't be done in time. I had to do something to keep whoever was coming through that door busy to protect my pack.

I walked to the center of the yard and stood in front of the porch. The door opened and three men poured out onto the porch, pausing when they saw me standing off from the others.

*Keep calm, Ed. Keep calm and kick ass. You got this.* I let out a heavy huff. "I have come here to chew bubblegum and kick ass." I threaded the cord that ran between the nunchuck and the remote through my fingers and lifted the remote high. "And I'm all out of bubblegum!"

I pointed it in the general direction of the three men and powered it up.

An arc of blue lightning shot out of the end of the remote and struck the front of the house next to one of them. It erupted into a big puff of sparks and smoke, not quite the explosion I'd gotten in the car. Maybe the spell had a better effect at close range. Either way, it didn't have exactly the intended effect. The other two sneered and raised their rifles to fire.

And that's when they were blindsided by a grizzly in blue jeans.

Well, torn up bits of blue jeans, anyway. Bran, who was now a seven-foot grizzly with teeth and claws, jumped over the porch railing and knocked over both gunmen. I'm pretty sure that, when he roared in their faces, both of them wet themselves. Bran didn't kill them. Not that the guy had any qualms about killing. I knew the katana he kept on his motorcycle wasn't for show. But he suddenly had bigger fish to fry. A whole new group of people stumbled into the front room with more guns.

When they realized there was a grizzly in the way, some of them must have turned and decided to come out the back because, a minute later, they were pouring from either side of the house.

"Keep them coming out front!" Reed yelled and hopped off the truck. There was a glint of moonlight on metal as he did and, a second later, he had driven his sword into someone's chest. Fire raced down the blade, setting the man alight. Reed kicked him off the sword and swung it at another.

I am not a fighter. Even when I play RPGs, I prefer to hang back and assess the field before acting. In a real fight, I didn't have time to think like that. There was no pause button. It was chaos and I couldn't think.

I froze up.

The crack of gunfire echoed through the front yard and something whizzed past my face, close enough I could smell the air cook. One of the men who'd come out of the house ran up closer to me, pointing the gun straight at me. I knew what I should do, but I didn't want to. My brain was still in a fog of confusion, stuck between the desire to survive and the commandment against killing.

Before I could get myself straightened out, Angel flew by in a blur and socked the guy with a mean right hook. Blood went flying out of his mouth and he fell over, jaw broken, dazed, but not dead. She wrenched the gun from his hands and tossed it aside.

"You okay, little buddy?" Angel asked, standing up straight.

I swallowed and nodded.

"Then stay close. I've got your back."

I smiled and took a step closer to her when a flash of light from the center second-story window lit up the yard. I shielded my eyes against it. Was that Abe, Sal and Creven going in or Warren coming out? No way to tell from where I stood. And no time.

More and more people were pouring out of the house. Only some of them engaged us. Others took off running through the fields beside and behind the house. Shauna turned as if to go after some of the fleeing people. I got off a shot of blue magick that hit the ground right in front of her and she turned to snarl at me. "We're not here to kill everyone!" I shouted. "Let them go."

Daphne fell into step beside me after she was done shaking a gun from someone's hand. My sister stopped in front of Shauna and growled, showing her teeth. I felt a twinge of pride, knowing my big sister had my back, too.

Shauna huffed and sat down, panting.

"It looks like most of the riff-raff is taken care of," Angel commented and pointed to the porch.

Bran the bear sat down and yawned.

I glanced through the crowd, looking for the people on my side to make sure they were all standing. I counted everyone except for one. "Hey, has anybody seen Reed? Where's Gideon Reed?"

Angel scanned the faces next to me and Bran stood up on his hind legs for a look.

Just then an unfamiliar engine roared to life. Bright headlights blinded us. Rocks crunched as tires spun and then squealed. The car lurched forward, plowing straight for us. If Angel hadn't reached over to jerk me out of the way, I would have ended the night as a hood ornament. As the car cruised by, I caught sight of Warren in the driver's seat. I fought free of Angel and chased after them, but they were too fast. They were gone.

I stood glaring down the empty lane, grinding my teeth and considering shifting to chase after them. Then, all of a sudden, the lane wasn't empty anymore. A pair of headlights shone through the darkness, followed by another. Then, another. As they came closer, I could make out the shape of armored trucks.

"Shit!" Angel shouted and grabbed me by the back of the shirt. "We're out of time! BSI is here!"

Everybody scrambled. I tried to turn and run, but with Angel gripping my shirt, it was all but impossible. Even running, we weren't as fast as the trucks coming down the lane. We made it just a few yards further toward the house before the first shots rang out. A few of the Adventists who hadn't run off fell to my right. Another, an unarmed woman Adventist, took off running for the woods. A shot hit her in the back of the head and she fell, eerily still.

Shocked and panicked, I stopped running, pulling Angel to a stop with me. "What are you doing?" she screamed. "Run!"

But there was no time. Little red dots danced all over us. Spotlights clicked to life, scanning the yard as men with guns checked the fallen, placing bullets in every Adventist just to make sure.

Against the light, a figure in a long coat emerged. I squinted to try and get a better look at him, but it was no use with the spotlights. His scent was masked heavily by cigarette ash and an undertone of rot. Whoever this man was, he was dying.

"Mister Petersen," said the man.

I flinched as he flicked on a lighter. Long fingers with thin skin lifted a delicate looking cigarette to his mouth. The flame illuminated only the lower half of his face when he held it to the cigarette, revealing he was probably a middle-aged white guy in an expensive looking suit.

The man sucked on the cigarette a moment before flipping the lighter closed. "I think it's time we had a chat."

# Chapter Twenty-Six

Warren's goons tied me to the cross, good and tight. They had to unhook my cuffs from each other to do it and, when they did, I tried to take a swing at one of them. It landed but, with as weak as I was and without access to my magick, he barely noticed it.

Even my best struggling was wasted and so I resigned myself to focusing on compartmentalizing my mind, creating a safe space that not even Warren could touch. I was ready to withstand whatever physical torture they were about to throw at me.

Too bad that wasn't what he had in mind.

Once I was strung up, a rope tied around each arm and my ankles, my chains locked securely to the back of the wooden crossbeam, Warren stepped up to me, rolling his sleeves back. "Last time, you still had a little fight in you. I doubt it's still there. You're hungry, alone. No one is coming for you." He readied his pointer and middle fingers, stretching each out toward me.

I jerked my head back. There was nowhere to go.

"Now, I will break you, just as I did your friend."

My breathing was fast, my body stiff, and Warren was right. I was hungry and alone. But I was still me, dammit, and if some basket case was going to turn my brain to mush, I was going to make damn sure he remembered me for the rest of his life. When his fingers got close, I snapped at him with my teeth, managing to get one of his pointer fingers. The bone crunched when I closed on it. Warren tried to jerk away and the coppery taste of blood filled my mouth. Something hard struck me in the stomach and I had to let him go so I could breathe.

"Bitch!" Warren cradled his hand as blood streamed from his finger.

I smiled and his blood dripped down my chin.

Rather than make a hasty retreat to see to his bleeding finger, Warren rushed forward and gripped my head, digging his fingers into my temples.

Images flooded my brain, pictures of death, rot, disease and suffering from all over the world and all through history. I saw pits and trenches full of bodies burning, tanks and napalm and swords and fists when men had no other weapons. I saw war.

War brought famine. People wandering in desolate wastelands

with the distended bellies of starvation, bodies left to rot by the side of the road during some migration to only God knew where. Mothers wept dry tears, holding the emaciated bodies of children.

But that wasn't the end of it. Armies marched on the unarmed. It was slaughter, bloody, bloody slaughter until the world was left dead and bare. And I had to watch every single one of them die, helpless to do anything about it.

If I had only seen it, maybe I could have endured, but Warren's illusion was too strong. I didn't just see death and the end of all things. I felt it, felt knives go in and twist, felt it when a child was snatched from my arms to have his head dashed against the rocks. I knew the pangs of hunger, the dry and bloody sandpaper tongue, the empty, indescribable feeling of loss.

Hopelessness. That is what Warren showed me while I hung on his cross.

~

I don't recall it being over. I don't know when he stopped or how I was taken down. The images didn't stop for a very long time.

The next thing I was aware of, I was lying back in my cell, curled into the fetal position, sobbing dry tears. My fingers were bloody and nails torn down to the cuticle. Scratch marks lined the floor. I must have tried to claw my way away from the horrible sights, sounds, and feelings. Seeing death once was enough to drive most people to insanity. With what I had just gone through, I had no idea how bad the damage was.

I lay there, numb to everything for a long time. The cell was still dark. I was still hungry, still cold, still trapped. All my fight had been for nothing. What was the point of fighting? Warren had already won. Any resistance at this point was just a waste of my energy. Whatever he wanted from me, it would be easier on everyone if I'd just let him have it.

*No*, said a small, distant voice in my head. *We have to keep fighting.*

*There's no point*, I answered and shook my head before muttering aloud, "There's no point."

*You want Hunter to find out you just gave up? What kind of example is that to set for your kid, Judah?*

I shook my head again and pressed my nose against the cool floor. "It doesn't matter. Warren won. He can tell any story he likes. The truth doesn't matter anymore. I can't take another session like that, not again. I'm lucky I'm not drooling on myself and screaming in the corner after the first one."

*But if you give up—*

"Nothing. Nothing happens if I give up. Nothing different than if I don't. I just don't have to fight anymore."

I slumped over and pressed my forehead to my hands. The movement felt oddly uncomfortable, like I strained something doing it. And then I realized why. Before, I hadn't been able to touch the floor. I jerked my head up and moved my hands to my wrists, feeling for the metal teeth that had been biting into my wrists. They were gone.

"I don't understand," I whispered into the dark. "Why? Why aren't I bound?"

I turned my head toward where the tiniest sliver of light usually crept under the door. The light was gone, too. The room beyond was dark. *They left me,* I thought. *They locked me up here and left me to die. Then it really is over.*

I curled up on the floor facing where I thought the door was and drew my knees up to my chest, waiting to die.

Just as I gave up hope, I heard a sound. It was a new sound and, at first, I didn't think it was real. Then I heard it again. My head perked up as footsteps echoed into my little room. They stopped in front of my door. Warren was back. I shrank against the wall, too tired and defeated to think about fighting back. The door opened and I threw my arms over my head, screaming, "No! No, leave me alone! I'm done! I've had enough!"

Hands came down on my head, on my shoulders, warm, calloused hands. "Judah?"

I pushed them away, frantic. "I won't fight you anymore! I won't fight! Just don't...don't make me see it, not again. Please."

"Judah, it's me."

"Please, I'll do anything! Just don't..."

Hands tightened my shoulders firmly and shook me before one of them moved to my chin and tilted it up. "Judah, it's me. It's Sal. You're safe."

I stared at the shadow in front of me. It couldn't be. This was a trick, another one of Warren's games. "No."

"It's me. You're safe."

He tried to pull me against him and I did my best to fight back, but I was so weak and he was so warm. Who cared if he was real? Wouldn't I rather die with a warm illusion than in cold reality? Wouldn't I rather go with his arms around me, wrapped in his scent with the promise of false safety, than alone in filth?

He pushed dirty, grimy hair out of my face. Dim light flooded the room and I flinched away from it, afraid it would get too bright. It didn't. For once, it was light I could bear to look at, soft, warm and yellow. It hovered at the end of a long piece of wood in front of another familiar face. "Oh, lass," he said with pity in his voice.

"Creven?"

"Collect her." Abe stepped into the light and handed his shotgun to Creven so that he could strip off his coat. He held it out to Sal who knelt in front of me. "Put this on her, but we must go. The squad will be arriving at the compound any moment."

"When I find the bastard that did this..." Sal's growl shook every bone in my body.

"We must see to Judah's safety first," Abe reminded him.

My jaw quivered. It was all too much. Too much. This couldn't be real, could it? It had to be a trick. Even if Creven, Abe and Sal had come for me, he was probably waiting to kill us all. There had to be a spell that would activate as soon as I walked out the door and it would kill us all.

Sal began to lower Abe's coat over me.

"No," I said, my voice slurred and dreamy sounding. "You don't understand. I can't go. I can't go!" Sal hesitated when I screamed in his face, "No!" He looked like I had stabbed him in the heart.

"She is not in her right mind," Abe said. "Collect her so that we can get her medical care, despite what she says."

Sal wrapped the coat around me and reached down to pick me up. Rather than fight, I went limp the moment the coat was around me. It was warm and comfortable, but more than that, it felt *safe*. If that's what it felt like all the time, no wonder Abe wore it everywhere he went. Sal adjusted me in his arms and turned around. "You're safe," he promised as we made for the door.

I took a deep breath and closed my eyes, burying my head in the leather of Abe's coat. "Safe," I repeated. It was the first time I fully understood the meaning of that word.

A scraping, shuffling sound made me look up. The blood in my veins went icy when I saw Hector standing in the doorway, armed with a sword. "I can't allow her to leave."

Abe flashed a set of fangs. "You don't have a choice."

Creven readied his staff.

Sal clutched me tighter to him.

Hector raised the sword stiffly. It was a broadsword, not dissimilar to Reed's, but with a more intricate design.

Abe charged at him.

I tried to scream out a warning. Hector wasn't a mere human and it would take more than claws and fangs to take him down. Well, maybe Abe would have a chance if he could bite him, but I didn't know what effect that would have on Abe.

It didn't matter. Abe didn't get close.

Hector swung the sword, forcing Abe to dodge. When Abe shifted to the side, Hector pulled a dagger from his belt and threw it with practiced efficiency. It caught Abe in the chest, right where his heart would be. Abe looked down at the blade sticking out of him. His hand drifted toward it, but it was too late. "Blood," he cursed and fell back, stiff as a dead man.

Creven sprang into action, throwing up a blue barrier around us. Hector hacked at it, a determined grimace on his face.

"I'm not sure how long I can hold it," Creven said, wincing.

I closed a fist around Sal's shirt. "He's an immortal. You have to cut off his head or bleed him dry. You'll never get close enough."

"I'm not going to stand here and let him kill us!" Sal ground the words out through clenched teeth and moved to put me down.

"Hector Demetrius!" A voice rang out clear and strong through the chaos.

Hector immediately stopped and shifted his focus away from our barrier to the figure standing in the doorway. When the figure raised his sword and fire spread down the blade, there was no question in my mind. It was Gideon Reed.

"What the hell's he doing here?" Sal growled.

"He must've opened his own Way." Creven turned back. "I can't extend the barrier far enough to cover him. Afraid he'll be on his own unless you want me to put this down."

Sal looked down at me and then turned away. "No. Reed's on his own."

Reed didn't seem to mind. He charged at Hector, their two swords crossing. They pressed in against each other, each one grappling for control over the other, until Hector swung a knee into Reed's side. Reed might have been immortal, but he was still hurt. He doubled over and Hector seized the opportunity, bringing the sword down at the back of Reed's head.

Reed tumbled forward in a roll, allowing Hector's blade to hit the ground instead. Hector drew the sword back again and took another swipe at Reed, who had rolled over onto his back. Instead of slicing across, however, Hector changed tactics at the last second and drove the blade straight down into Reed's chest.

I flinched as it went in and almost turned my head away from watching Reed squirm. He opened his mouth in a cry of pain, but choked on blood. Hector scowled and twisted the blade, prolonging Reed's suffering.

It was the last thing he'd ever do. With a battle cry, Reed used the last of his effort to swing his sword. It slid through Hector's neck as if his whole body was made of butter. Hector's head shifted down and then detached completely. His body went limp and fell to the side, blood flowing everywhere.

Everything else happened in slow motion.

I screamed.

Creven waved away the barrier and moved to pull the knife from Abe's chest, unstaking him.

Sal put me down and raced to Reed's side.

I sat for a long moment, shaking, still trying to process everything. Then, I rose on trembling legs and dragged myself to Sal's side. Reed was an immortal, too, I told myself. I'd seen him recover from far worse. He'd pull through this too. But, when I reached his side, he didn't look like he was recovering. Sal had pressure around the wound, but had left the sword in.

"Why isn't he getting better?" My voice was small and distant, still not my own.

"Shit, shit, shit!" Sal was in panic mode, working to wipe away something gray on Reed's forehead.

Reed smiled, showing bloody teeth. "Don't. It won't matter."

"You're not healing because of that damn ash!"

Reed's arm rose weakly to grip Sal's. "I'm still under Warren's spell. If you remove it, I won't be myself."

"But you'll live."

"I will kill you. I can't fight it, not without the ash." Reed shook his head and then pressed his chin to his chest to look at the sword.

"I would rather die like this than harm another innocent."

I put my hand to my mouth and sank to my knees next to him, not caring that I knelt in a pool of blood. "Reed..."

"It's alright. I'm not afraid. I know where I'm going." He tried to shift his sword but he was so weak, he could barely move his arm.

Sal put his blood-stained hand over Reed's and helped him move the hilt of the sword to Reed's chest.

"Thank you," Reed said, his voice strained. "Judah, the sword."

I swallowed the growing tightness in my throat and blinked away tears. "I won't let Seamus have it. You have my word."

Reed closed his eyes and moved his hand until it was over mine. "Father, watch over her. Protect her where I could not. For our struggle is not against flesh and blood, but against the rulers, against the authorities, against the powers of this dark world and against the spiritual forces of evil. In...Your name...Amen."

The air left his lungs in a deep, rattling wheeze. His head rolled to the side and Gideon Reed stayed still.

I slumped forward, but Sal caught me.

Abe removed his hat. "We still have to find Espinoza."

"We can't leave him here," I insisted, shaking my head.

"We must worry about the living before seeing to the dead. Get her up. Let us go before the suicide squad gets here."

Sal picked me up against my will. I was too weak to fight.

We left Reed's body where he had fallen, but I made Creven take the sword. There was no way I was breaking my word to a dead man, especially not after everything he'd done for me.

The light in the hallway was blinding and felt heavy on my skin. I tucked my head into the coat against Sal's arm to block it out. The first time I'd been out there with Warren, I hadn't had time to look around and I wasn't sure I wanted to do it this time, either, but when I heard Abe mention splitting up, I had to open my eyes. I didn't want him to leave my sight. I didn't want *any* of them to go. They might not come back. Losing Abe might be worse than losing anyone else because it would be my fault. I had his coat, his protection. I tried to say something about it, but the words wouldn't come.

Abe gave me a heavy look. "Stay out here with her, wolf. If we find Espinoza, we will bring him back."

Sal's hand tightened its grip on my shoulder. "And if you run into Warren? Then what?"

"I'm fuming enough that we should've no problems dealing with that fecking gobshite," Creven said and tapped his staff on the floor. "If t'wern't for him, none of us'd be in this mess."

Creven's speech was what finally convinced me beyond the shadow of a doubt that I wasn't in one of Warren's illusions. Warren might be good, but Creven's odd manner of speaking wasn't something anyone could duplicate, especially when he got mad enough to mash three and four words together at such a quick pace.

While Abe and Creven hurried down the hall in search of Espinoza, Sal lowered me toward the floor. I knew I couldn't stand, and I couldn't bear to be put down just yet, either. It was silly, but I was still deathly afraid something would happen and freedom would slip away. I closed my fingers around his arm with a death grip.

"Just a minute," he said. "It's just for a minute, Judah."

He lowered me to the floor. I reached out and kept a hand on his shoe, just in case.

Sal stripped off his shirt and put the collar over my head. It took longer than normal for me to remember how to get my arms through the arm holes. My head still felt fuzzy and every time I focused too hard on anything, it hurt. I tugged his shirt over my knees and stared at a big, red smear on it. Breath caught in my throat as the barrage of images struck me again.

Blood. Death. Famine. War. Pain. Suffering. I was buried underneath the weight of it all, suffocating as each image piled, one atop the others, and threatened to crush my heart.

And then, the weight lessened. As if each painful, horrible thing were an item of clothing on a laundry line, someone wheeled them backward, tugging some of the weight away.

I gasped as the image faded and flailed forward, looking for someone, anyone to hold onto. But Sal's hands were already in mine and his eyes were wet. "Jesus, the damage is...What did they do to you?" His jaw shook and then set, his eyes darkening. "When I find that fucker, I'm going to peel the skin off his bones and make him watch."

"Oi, Sal," Creven called, standing in another doorway further down. "You'd better come quick. It's Espinoza."

Sal stood, took a half step away, then paused. He was going to pick me up and carry me again. As much as I wanted that, I didn't want to restrict him in any way. He'd need the use of his hands and arms to help anyone, and I needed to find my own feet. I grabbed for the fabric of his jeans to pull myself up, but he caught my hand and pulled me to my feet. Once I was upright, he put an arm around my shoulders and we limped down the hall together.

Espinoza's cell was identical to mine. Linoleum floor. Rocky, unfinished wall. Drain in the middle. Espinoza himself was splayed, naked, over Abe's lap. He looked like someone had dipped him into a vat of red that painted up to his shoulders. There was so much blood everywhere and he was so pale, I was sure he was dead.

"Life signs are faint," Abe reported in a small voice. "I am told you can help?"

Sal left me standing alone in the doorway and went to kneel on the other side of Espinoza. He took a pulse, checked his pupils, looked over wounds, nodded. "I can try."

Sal was a healer, the most powerful healer I'd ever met. Still, there was a limit to his power. He could only heal as much damage as he could take. Thanks to the accelerated healing of werewolves, he could take more damage than most, but there was still a hard limit to what he could do, especially since he was still healing from Reed's first attack. If he took too much, he could die himself. I had never seen him heal someone as far gone as Espinoza, but Sal had also served as a medic in the army in Iraq. If anyone could save Espinoza, it was him.

Sal pressed one hand to a wound in Espinoza's side and placed the other on his forehead. A beat of silence passed before Abe licked his lips and said, "Is it working? Nothing seems to be happening."

"It's this place." Sal sighed, removing his hands. "I'm cut off from magick here. You need to take him out of this Way right now and call EMS to the scene if you want to save him, Abe."

"But if we move him—"

"You don't have a choice," Sal barked and stood. "Get him out of here."

Normally, Abe would have glared at Sal and they would have gotten into an argument about who could tell who what to do, but Abe was too worried to argue. He scooped Espinoza up in his arms, much the same way Sal had done with me and sprinted toward the door with supernaturally fast speed.

He stopped suddenly in the doorway and took a step back, revealing a dozen tiny, red dots dancing on his head and chest. Through interlocked fangs, he announced, “Blood, we were too slow.”

A squad of men in black, unmarked body armor filtered into the room, visored helmets obscuring their faces. They swept their weapons right and left, gauging the threat as they progressed, before eventually deciding to split their attention evenly between Sal, Abe, and Creven, surrounding us. The last two stopped next to the door and knelt down.

A moment passed before someone else strode into the room. He was of average height, middle-aged with salt and pepper hair. The beginnings of wrinkles marked the corners of his eyes and mouth. Whoever he was, he hadn’t even bothered with a bullet proof vest. He just wore a long coat over an impeccable suit. Gray eyes peered out from underneath a wrinkled brow. Polished two-tone shoes shone in the dim light as he stopped in the doorway to adjust his gray suit jacket.

“Good morning, gentlemen, and to the lady in the room.” He bobbed his head in my direction.

“Who the hell are you?” Sal snarled.

Abe lifted his chin and shifted Espinoza in his arms. “Deputy Director Rich Richardson.”

Richardson smiled and lifted a cigarette to his mouth. “Call me Dick.”

# Chapter Twenty-Seven

## Ed

For wanting to chat, mystery guy wasn't too chatty. Shortly after we were all blinded by the spotlights, the armed guards grabbed me, twisted my arm behind my back and forced me forward. I didn't dig my heels in, worried they'd shoot me if I resisted.

Angel fought. It got her the butt of a rifle to the back of the head.

Bran's roar was so loud it threatened to explode my eardrums. Still in bear form, he charged down off the porch and swatted at one of the officers, batting him aside. A series of quick shots rang out, the bark of a machine gun pointed at the bear. Bran rose up on his rear legs and let out another loud roar that chilled my blood. When he came down, it was to swat the rifle away. The soldier's arm went with it, twisting too far. The crack of bone was unmistakable.

Angel's head shot up. "No, Bran!" she shouted firmly. "Stop! I'm okay! I'm okay."

Bran paused with one arm raised, teeth bared. It was all the time the soldiers needed to fire nets at him. The nets came down and, like the trained professionals they probably were, the soldiers closed. The dancing lights on Bran changed from red to blue and different shots rang out, these were more air-filled, softer. Tranquilizers.

Hands shifted my arm further and forced me forward. My head slammed against the side of the armored transport. I fought to swing my head around and searched wildly for my sister. She was half-changed. When they shot her with the tranquilizers, I felt it in my bones. A new, protective rage stirred up and I tried to twist free only to have my head slammed against the side of the vehicle again, this time harder. "Resist and you'll get some, too, werewolf." The soldier's voice filtered through his helmet, sounding almost computerized.

They lined us up like that, facing the side of the trucks, slipping silver handcuffs on each of us. My heart was in my throat the whole time. *This is it. This is how I die, handcuffed and shot in the back of the head. Dammit. Mara, I'm sorry.*

Angel shifted next to me, coming closer. Somehow, even though we were both handcuffed, she managed to link one of her fingers in mine. "It's gonna be okay, little buddy. No matter what they do to you, don't let the bastards break your spirit, okay?"

"Quiet!"

There was a wet crack and Angel made a loud grunting sound, sliding away.

"And keep your hands to yourself."

Angel growled. "If you're going to kill me, just fucking do it already, you dickless coward."

The guard drew his rifle back to strike her again, but stopped cold when the remains of the front door opened. The whole yard fell silent as, one by one, heads turned. I lifted my head from the side of the car and careened my neck to see what they were all gawking at.

The man in the long coat had come back out of the house, leading a procession of armed guards and injured people. My people.

The first one I saw was Officer Espinoza in Abe's arms. He looked dead. God, what had they done to them? It hadn't been more than a few hours.

Then, I saw Sal. He carried Judah out with Abe's coat draped over her. I breathed a sigh of relief when I saw her moving. She was alive then. We'd come in time.

My heart sank when the next two came out, each hauling a body. Well, the first guy had part of a body, Hector's to be exact. I assumed the head was in the plastic bag the soldier had slung over his arm. The rest of him had been wrapped in some plastic and tossed over the soldier's shoulder as if he were just a stack of wood.

Behind Hector came Reed's body. There was no doubt in my mind that the priest had died, not with the way his arms hung limp and his head bobbed like dead weight. There was too much blood all over him. God, I hoped he went down fighting. He must have. He'd taken Hector with him. At least there was that.

The sight of the last one out made my breath catch in my chest. The body in his arms was limp, just like Reed. He carried her like a child, one arm under her knees and the other holding up her upper body. Her head hung upside down, lips blue and skin the wrong shade of pale. A numbness spread from the top of my head all the way down as my heart pounded through the realization. The voice that came out of me was small, broken like when I was thirteen. "Mara?"

It didn't matter that there were dozens of guns pointed at me or that I was being held in place by someone stronger than me. Not even the cuffs on my wrists would hold me. In a fit of rage, I pulled and twisted. The metal groaned loudly and then snapped, freeing my hands. I pushed away from the vehicle and shoved my captors aside, dashing across the yard, jumping over bodies and screaming her name. "Mara!"

Guns raised, pointed at me. I didn't care.

The man in the long coat raised his hand. No one shot me. They should have. If she was... if they had...

"Get away from her!" I screamed as I came up to the man holding her. "Get away!"

He lowered her limp body to the ground in the middle of a drying bloodstain. I hit the ground on my knees next to her with enough force that it sent a shockwave of pain through me. My hand shot out, preventing her head from striking the ground.

I choked on something. It felt like my throat was swelling shut and that my chest was about to explode. My limbs were numb and my head pounding. Tears spilled over. I didn't even try to hold it back.

There was blood everywhere, all over her, and her dress was ripped. I touched her face, finding it cold. The skin didn't feel real. Nothing did.

"No, no, no." I just kept saying over and over. What else was there to say? "It's my fault. I didn't come back soon enough. It's my fault!"

"Ed?"

I couldn't see through the tears, but I could feel Sal's presence across from me, kneeling on the other side of Mara. "Help her. Please. Do something!"

Sal sighed. "She's gone, Ed. I can't. I'm sorry."

My hands balled into fists. "It's not fair." I struck the ground. "It's not fucking fair! It's my fault. This is my fault..."

Sal reached out to grip my shoulder and pull me into a tight hug. He didn't say anything because there was nothing anyone could say or do. Mara was dead. Words are for the living.

Inside, it felt like I was dying too, like the very idea of her not being there was ripping my insides apart. There was a black hole in the center of my chest and it was swallowing the rest of me whole. If I didn't let it out somehow, I was going to wither away and die with her. For a long moment, I thought I would. I couldn't go on alone. Mara was the whole reason I'd learned to be stronger, to stand up for myself. I owed her everything. What was the point in going on all alone?

A feeling cut through the pain, trickling down through the pack bonds and growing stronger. Something hard to explain. It felt like hands, a half dozen pairs, linked together around me forming a protective barrier. At the same time, they somehow reached for me, resting unseen on my back as I wept, just letting me know they were there. I drew strength from the pack, strength enough to lift my head and let out a low, mournful howl.

After a long moment, Sal pulled me up, his hands still tight on my shuddering shoulders. "Ed, we have to go. Espinoza needs medical attention and so does Judah. I promise you, we're going to take care of Mara's body. I'm going to make sure you get the chance to mourn her properly, but right now we have to see to the living."

I nodded slowly.

"I need you to do everything these men tell you to do, okay?"

My head bobbed, even if my heart wasn't in it. My heart was still with her, still as hers.

Sal patted my shoulder. "Good man. Now, go with them."

"Come with us, sir." Their robotic voices prompted me to dry my eyes. The soldiers stood on either side of me. One waved with his rifle.

I took in a deep breath and turned my back to Mara to march to the waiting trucks. I may have turned away, but I left part of my heart with her.

# Chapter Twenty-Eight

Lacerations. Contusions. Dehydration, fractures and blood loss. Whatever doctors Dick had look at me had a list of my ailments a mile long and that didn't even scratch the surface of what was really wrong with me. No amount of fluids, rest or x-rays was going to make me feel better.

We had arrived at some underground bunker not so far from the Adventists' compound by armored car. To prevent us from being able to guess the location, our hosts had made us wear black hoods. The werewolves, whose senses were good enough they might have been able to sniff out our location, wore bags laced with some kind of deodorant spray that had them gagging and sneezing all the way. Well, Sal did. Ed went in a different truck with Angel and Bran.

Espinoza and I went in the largest of the trucks, which was loaded with medical equipment. The back was a makeshift ambulance, and space was tight, but Sal wasn't leaving me alone, not with them. He convinced them to let him come on the basis that he was a trained field medic and healer. It took a lot of convincing before they let him squeeze in and keep his hand on my forehead.

It was comforting enough that I eventually drifted off to sleep, only to wake in a white, sterile room. I'd been changed out of Sal's bloody shirt and into a hospital gown. My open wounds were closed, my arm back in a cast. An IV in my left arm delivered fluids while a series of monitors to my right silently tracked my progress.

I stared at the pulse monitor racing up and down like cars on a hilly road. I knew where I was, some underground, off-the-grid BSI facility. Any other time, I would have been freaking out, screaming, plotting to fight my way out. But I barely had the energy to stay awake.

After a long while, the door on the far side of the room slid open with a loud hiss. A nurse in pink scrubs shuffled into the room with a cart. She stood beside me in silence, not even acknowledging me, prepping an injection. Maybe she was there to kill me. Silence me. Get me out of the way. My mind was so numb, I didn't care. I watched her with disinterest as she gripped the port in the IV and brought the needle to it.

"That won't be necessary."

Another figure appeared in the doorway of medium height, wide shoulders and a strong, chiseled jaw. Shoulder-length auburn hair styled back behind his head, green eyes and a flawless, expensive suit marked him as Eden Memorial Hospital's CEO and largest donor, Marcus Kelley. The fangs in his smile told everyone he was a vampire and proud of it.

Marcus strode into the room and placed a hand on the nurse's shoulder. "She's been out long enough. Now that she's back with us, you should inform Deputy Director Richardson."

The nurse's cheeks flushed and she smiled. The slight buzz of the vampire's power rippled through the air and incensed me enough that I snapped out of my funk to growl, "Leave her alone."

Marcus took his hand away, grinning. The nurse's complexion paled a little. "Nurse, please, don't let us keep you. I'm sure you have other patients to attend to. I'll see to Ms. Black personally for the time being."

"Yes, sir," said the nurse. She gave Marcus a warning glare before exiting the room.

"I didn't realize you had your M.D., Marcus." I sat back and crossed my arms, ignoring how the corners of the room blurred. It was the effect of whatever drugs in my system as they wore off.

"I hold advanced degrees in sociology and business administration, but I haven't pursued medicine yet. An interesting thought." His wide smile tightened to a thin, amused smirk. "But you do pick up a few things when you're the CEO of a pharmaceutical company and a major donor to a research hospital."

"Like that your head research scientist is involved in some really sick human experimentation?"

Marcus' smile faded. "Doctor Han's employment at Fitz has always been something of a double-edged sword. Much like my agreements with BSI." He sat down on the edge of my bed, resting his hands in his lap. For a long beat, he stared down at his fingers, the expression on his face hoovering between pain and worry. "My people are being persecuted. For a long time, everyone believed that the dust would settle and we'd all hold hands and stand as one. That was always the dream. But people like the Stryx, like Andre LeDuc, share a different belief. They believe supernaturals are superior and that a war of subjugation must be waged against humankind. On the opposite side, you have the Vanguards of

Humanity and the various other human rights groups who have taken up their cause. The middle ground grows emptier with every passing day."

"So you make a deal with the devil." My voice came out scratchy and thin. "You ally yourself with both sides and straddle the middle?"

"The system is broken. Hatred on both sides is driving us toward a conflict that neither can win." Marcus sighed and rubbed his forehead. "The split is so deep, even BSI is divided. You have stumbled into that divide headfirst and without a flashlight. And yet, beaten and bloodied as you are, you still lie in a hospital bed and find the strength to lecture a vampire."

His shoulders shook. I didn't realize he was laughing until he burst out into loud, gasping guffaws.

"I don't see what's funny about it, Marcus."

"You! No matter how much we've all tried to keep you out of this, you keep insisting on thrusting yourself into it. If I don't laugh, I may be tempted to do as I was told and kill you." He wiped away a tear.

"Kill me?"

Marcus stood and paced to the end of my bed, hands behind his back. "Yes. When you came to Paint Rock, it was with a bounty on your head, a rather sizable one. You'd made quite a name for yourself in Cleveland, arresting that senator's son. The spotlight on you was still too bright and public opinion was very much on your side, so BSI couldn't act openly to silence you. They determined your existence was too much of a threat to allow you to continue." He turned around and tilted his head to the side. "You'd be very dead if Dick hadn't taken such an interest in you. He and I worked together to remedy that, but that was not without its risks."

I winced as I fought to sit up. Whoever this Dick guy was, he had to be pretty high up the BSI chain. I'd never heard of him, but then I didn't normally concern myself with the higher-ups. I knew none of them liked me. If they did, why would I wind up in one of the most despised posts in the whole country?

"You're trying to tell me that this Dick guy saved my life?"

"No, Judah. Not just once. Have you never questioned why you get away with the things you do? Why your son has never been detected?"

I stared down at my shaking hands. God, he was right. I'd

suspected someone up the chain had been looking out for me, someone sympathetic or maybe just a good Samaritan who thought the same way I did, that BSI needed to be changed from the inside. I'd never suspected someone that high. It made sense, even if I didn't want it to.

I slowly raised my head to stare at the wall beside Marcus' head. "What's going to happen to me now?"

"That's not for me to decide, but I suspect you'll be released to continue with some added layers of warning. Or Dick may decide you're no longer worth the investment and kill you. Personally, I'd much prefer the former. He'd put that Upyri half-blood upstart forward as a replacement and I can't trust him. You might be a nosy bitch, Judah, but you're a known quantity and I think you've more than earned your position. Besides, the werewolves like you and they don't like anybody." He smiled. "For now, I'm going to go see if I can find you some clothes and if the nurses can get you a bath. Two days in recovery has done nothing for your smell."

He nodded his head to me and started for the door.

"Marcus, what about Espinoza? Mara? Ed?"

The vampire stopped and turned his head so that I could see his face in profile. "You don't remember?"

I rubbed my pounding temples. "Everything is a blur. Warren gave me visions and it's all mixing in with reality. I don't know what's real and what he put in there."

"Ed Petersen is alive and well. He suffered only very minor injuries. Espinoza's injuries were quite severe. He's currently in the room next to yours on life support. The doctors have placed his survivability incredibly low."

I leaned forward. "And Mara? What about Mara?"

I remembered watching Warren force her to stab herself to death, but it didn't feel real. Part of me held out, hoping it had all been part of his torturous mind control.

"Tamara Speilman died of multiple self-inflicted stab wounds, Judah. I'm sorry. Genuinely, I am."

Tears raced down the side of my face. I shut my eyes against them. I'd failed her again. My fingers closed into fists around the hem of the blanket. Dammit, why couldn't I do anything right? Everyone I cared about got hurt. Ed, Mara, Sal, Hunter... how long would it be before someone else got killed because of me?

I was suddenly aware of the gentle weight of Marcus' hand on my shoulder. "There is one more thing to discuss. If you're up for it, of course."

I tried to still the shaking my shoulders and the tears streaming down my face, pushing them away with a fist. "What?"

"Espinoza. Given the situation, I'm unable to reach out to next of kin and we are faced with a difficult choice. He may die, but he doesn't have to."

My head shot up and I glared at the vampire, suddenly understanding his intent. "You mean to turn him?"

Marcus shrugged, withdrawing his hand. "The option is on the table. Of course, a turned vampire has its own drawbacks. He may not survive the turning. Even if he does, he will never be the same. It's a risk to me as well, especially considering the torture he has been through."

"You can't, Marcus."

"I can. The question is, will I? You see, I'm approached all the time by loved ones in this line of work. The grieving will do anything if it offers even the faintest glimmer of hope to save their loved ones. I have always turned them down. Death is part of the cycle of human life and, most of the time, my interference would make little to no difference. The dying are too aged, too young, too crippled, maimed, their mind's broken. There are many reasons why I don't turn patients, even if the next of kin begs me to. But most of all, I don't do it because it's involving." He relaxed and crossed one leg over the other. "You're a parent. On some level, surely you understand the importance of such a decision. If I turn Espinoza, I am responsible for his well-being. More than that, I would have to give up a significant amount of my already valuable time, something I have no desire to do."

I sighed, partly out of relief. "Sounds like you don't want to. Then why are you here asking about him?"

"Because if there is one thing I've learned from you, it's that not wanting to do something is not a good enough reason not to do it." He steepled his fingers. "Your partner, the Upyri half-blood, seems rather fond of Espinoza. It was him that came to me, which is unusual in itself given the current state of my relationship with the Upyri."

Abe and Espinoza? That was the most unexpected thing he could have told me. The two of them were as different as night and day. They barely even knew each other. Or maybe they did. Hell, I hadn't had time to keep tabs on my partner's social life. They could have moved in together and I'd never have known, not with everything else going on.

Marcus continued. "I won't bore you with the details, but the political climate puts me in a delicate position."

"He's basically Upyri royalty and you're just some clanless American upstart. You turn his boyfriend, it saves Espinoza's life in a manner of speaking, but it also means that he's yours and not part of the Upyri. Have I got that about right?"

Marcus smiled. "Your understanding of our world is always impressive. It is unusual for him to petition me for such an action. I thought at first it was a political move, but I can think of no reason why a human officer would be politically important to the Upyri."

"It's my world, too. It's everyone's world now."

Marcus inclined his head. "Indeed. The matter at hand is less political and more philosophical. I cannot come to a firm decision either way and Abraham is clearly biased. I thought perhaps you could offer some insight. Were you in my position, what would you do?"

I looked down at my hands, suddenly even more aware of the oxygen monitor wrapped around my middle finger. The little red light lit up dark capillaries under my skin and nail. Marcus was basically asking me to decide for him. If I said no, I wouldn't do it, he'd leave Espinoza to his fate. A good cop, one of the best, would likely die on an operating table, barely remembered for his service.

If I said yes, save him, I might be subjecting Espinoza to a life he resented. Maybe he didn't want to be a vampire, least of all one that belonged to Marcus Kelley. Or maybe he did. I didn't know how he felt about it because I'd never asked.

I could go back and forth in my head all day, speculating maybe this or maybe that. It wouldn't help Espinoza. Marcus said he'd already been going back and forth himself. He was a smart guy. He already knew the pros and cons, probably better than I did. Marcus didn't come to me to have that explained all over again. He came to me so that I could make a tough call.

Did I want Espinoza to die or didn't I?

I wanted Espinoza to have the choice himself, and he couldn't do that if he died.

"Espinoza's a good man," I said, nodding. "I'd do everything in my power to keep him around as long as he felt like staying around."

I met Marcus' eyes and held them. Generally, that's a bad idea with vampires. They can enthrall people with their gaze and make them do whatever they wanted. Marcus and I had already established what would happen to him if he tried that with me, though, and I knew him well enough to believe he wouldn't try in this case.

"I'd turn him," I said.

Marcus stood, smoothed his hands over his suit jacket and buttoned it. "That's what I thought you would say. I wish you a speedy recovery, Agent Black."

He stepped toward the door. "Get some rest. Deputy Director Richardson will want to speak to you as soon as you're well enough to walk."

~

It was the better part of the night and a good chunk of morning before the nurse thought I was well enough to try and walk. I made it only a few steps across the cold, linoleum floor before the dizziness hit me and I bent over, blind and nauseous.

"That's it," said the nurse, coming to my side. "You can't be up. It's too soon."

"Haven't you heard?" I grunted as I hauled myself along toward the door. "You can't keep a good gal down."

She pressed the pager she wore around her neck. "Gonna need some help in here. Bring the sedative."

"You give me any more drugs and I swear, I'll be the worst patient you've ever had. I want to see Deputy Director Richardson *now*."

The nurse narrowed her eyes and pressed her lips together. I was sure she was gearing up for a fight, but she surprised me when she opened negotiations. "How about we get you a wheelchair?"

Eventually, we came to a compromise. She would bring me my clothes if I could make it to the wall and back without falling over. I made that nurse eat her words, of course, but the stingy nurse still made me go in a wheelchair part of the way, and she made me go under guard. Once I explained to her that I didn't want the director to see me as unfit for duty, even though I clearly was, she rolled her eyes and stopped the chair down the hall from where I was to meet the director. "Go on. Kill yourself if you want. I'm sure not going to stop you."

"If an alpha werewolf and a vampire CEO couldn't stop me, you shouldn't feel bad." I pushed myself out of the chair using my one good arm and stood on wobbly feet. I was still weak after everything, but I could draw on my magick to keep me going.

The armed guards escorted me to an unmarked set of double doors and held the door open for me. A conference table waited on the other side, lined with comfortable looking leather chairs. Familiar faces occupied the chairs. Sal, Daphne, Shauna, Ed, Angel, Bran and Creven all turned their heads as I hobbled in.

Sal jumped up from his seat and moved toward me. "Judah! God, you have no idea how good it is to see you." He came to put his arms around me. The weight nearly made me fall over. "They wouldn't tell us anything."

I patted his back and then gripped his shirt, choking on whatever words I was trying to say. My eyes were fixed on Ed just beyond as he stared blankly at the tabletop. "Ed?" Sal moved aside to support me as I hobbled over to stand next to Ed. "Ed, I'm sorry."

"I'd rather not talk about it." His voice was strained and raw like he'd been crying recently. His shoulders tightened and the hands resting on his knees turned into trembling fists. "Because the minute I know where that coward is hiding, I'm going to go and rip his throat out."

A chill ran through me. I'd never heard Ed talk like that. Sal and Valentino, sure, but never Ed. He'd always been the one to crack a joke or make light of a tough situation. Even when things looked their worst, I could count on Ed to lift my spirits. There was no hint of that person when he spoke, and when he looked at me, his eyes were completely gold.

Sal pulled me away from Ed. "It's best you don't talk to him right now."

"I'd like to know why we're all here." Shauna crossed her arms. She, like everyone else in the room, including me, was dressed in gray sweats and a black t-shirt with a pocket on the chest.

"Mostly, you are here because you have all decided to involve yourselves, despite my warnings not to."

I turned my head.

Sal growled.

Abe stood in the doorway decked out in his hat and coat. He strode in and placed his hat on the table in front of an empty seat. "Either out of stupidity, stubbornness, or sheer luck, you seven have stumbled into a mess that many with top-level government clearance do not even know about."

Abe shed his coat and tossed it over the back of the chair before gesturing to another set of empty chairs near him. "Please, sit. Deputy Director Richardson will be with us shortly."

I remained standing, but leaned on the table with my good arm. "You owe me an explanation."

Abe didn't look up from where he was situating several stacks of papers he'd brought with him into piles. "I owe you nothing."

"You broke my arm!"

"For your own good!"

"And you gave me a concussion." I pointed to my head.

"That was..." Abe huffed. "Excessive, I admit." He finally looked up at me, but only after sitting down. "Had I not severely injured you, you would have continued on with your investigation and continued to involve yourself in matters that you were not prepared for. However, it seems that not even a broken limb will keep you out of trouble. I should have known better. I apologize for underestimating your..."

"Stubbornness?" Sal crossed his arms.

"Obstinacy?" Shauna said, mimicking his position.

"General orneriness?" Creven raised his eyebrows.

"I was going to say persistence." Abe shrugged. "But all of those fit as well."

I tugged out the chair across from him and sat. "I prefer tenacious."

Sal sat down in the empty chair next to me. "We've been here for two days under guard. It's time someone told us what the hell is going on."

Abe leaned back in his chair and surveyed the faces in the room. "During the Revelation Riots, the government sought to form a new branch, what you now know as BSI. With the nation in chaos and funding limited, your government had no choice but to seek outside help."

"They found that help in an organization known as the Sicarii," I finished. "An organization of people who call themselves immortals and dedicated their lives to directing and controlling the flow of history. Hector Demetrius and Gideon Reed were members of their ranks. How am I doing so far?"

Ed leaned forward and placed his hands on the table. "Like the Illuminati." His eyes were still gold, but his posture had relaxed.

"An immature understanding of a complex matter." Abe waved a dismissive hand. "Conspiracy theorists would have you believe that such an organization works in secret to conceal information toward a nefarious purpose. The Sicarii are an organization of balance. One immortal, one human, one vampire, one fae, and one to represent the shifter races form a council of five to promote understanding, prevent war, and further common goals. They are not world leaders or people who have political ties. This is supposed to be a prerequisite for securing a position. But something changed during the Revelation. An impasse was reached." Abe lowered his head and tapped a finger on the bill of his hat. "The fae retreated. The vampires waged an internal war and forced their representative into hiding. As a result, the Stryx gained a significant amount of power and have been able to influence far more than they should. In turn, two immortals rose and sought to increase their influence. They went to the government and offered the funds and the means to help create what you now know as BSI."

"Hector Demetrius and Gideon Reed." I closed my eyes, my heart dropping into my stomach.

"Two sides of an opposing coin," Abe agreed. "Hector represented a conservative group within the Sicarii, one that gained much support during the Revelation. Their answer to the supernatural threat was to control it and, if necessary, eliminate the rising influence of the vampires and shifters, drive all the fae back into Faerie, and seal this realm from theirs. Doing so would give the Sicarii complete dominion over humans, which they believed was the only way to maintain peace.

"On the other side, Reed spoke for the smaller, more liberal group of Sicarii that believed peace could be achieved not through overwhelming force and iron will, but love, compassion, and a strong push for universal rights for all sentient beings to live as they saw fit."

Shauna showed her teeth. "You're telling me all this is over politics?"

"Aye." Creven nodded. "But isn't it always?"

"Truer words have never been spoken."

All heads turned to the doorway where Dick stood with his hands folded in front of him. He'd shed the long gray coat and changed into a charcoal suit.

Abe rose when he saw the deputy director standing there.

Dick wrinkled his nose and waved a hand at Abe. "Sit down, Helsinki. Nobody likes a suck-up."

Abe sank slowly back into his chair.

"So, politics." Dick clapped his hands together and then rubbed them as he strode into the room. "As you can see, there have always been opposing sides at work. The divide between them has grown. Even when Gideon Reed stepped aside, he left behind those of us who have made it our life's work to pursue that dream of equality."

"You've got a funny way of showing it." Ed's voice came out as a near-inhuman growl. "Shooting down those Adventists as they fled. Every single one of them was under Warren's control. They were innocent."

Dick opened his suit jacket, pulled out a pack of cigarettes and tapped them against his palm until one cigarette dislodged. He plucked it out and tucked the pack away. "Do you know why you're able to sit in that chair with clean hands and judge me, Mr. Petersen?" Before he answered his own question, he lit the cigarette and blew out a long trail of smoke. Dick waved the cigarette, gesticulating. "My dirty hands bought you that right. I shoulder the weight of hundreds of innocent deaths so that thousands can live a life of relative peace. Unless you've worn the mantle of leadership, you have no idea how many difficult decisions you'll have to make. You'll never know how many lives you'll have to take so that others can enjoy a life of mundanity. Isn't that right, Mr. Silvermoon?"

Sal's low, rumbling growl rattled my chest.

"Not that I don't approve. The Vanguard are one of the biggest threats to our continued existence." Dick nodded to Abe. "As Helsinki informed you, BSI itself is divided along the same lines as the Sicarii. Director West, my superior, is in the far-right camp. As we speak, he and his pet, Senator Grahm, are pushing Congress to approve a second, larger reservation in Alaska. With the conservative majority in Congress, that measure stands to pass with little resistance."

"What's so bad about another reservation?" Daphne asked.

"Because the facility in Alaska will be very unlike the Paint Rock project." Dick took a long drag on his cigarette. "They're putting it out in the middle of nowhere, accessible only by government helicopter. Far from prying eyes. I also happen to know Doctor Han has been tapped to be the physician on staff. Now, you tell me why that sounds like a bad idea?"

"Jaysus, Peter, Paul and Mary." Creven rose from his seat. "It's not a reservation. It's a bloody internment camp to feed Han and BSI's research."

"A breeding ground for their army," Bran added.

Angel looked left and right before adding, "It's fucked up, is what it is."

"It means shutting things down here won't make any difference." I made a fist and struck the table. "Not one damn difference."

"On the contrary," said Dick, gesturing to me with his cigarette, "you've made your opening moves. A little prematurely, yes, but you dealt a strong blow against their side. You'll deal an even stronger blow by killing Warren before they can extract him."

"They're going to use that fucker?" Ed jumped from his seat, toppling the chair.

"They'll kill him, more like." Dick shrugged. "Which is what you'll have to do. Before you think it doesn't matter who deals the killing blow, consider this. You have no legitimate means of investigation at the moment. All your evidence, every lead you had in the arson case, has been destroyed. The compound went down in a fire and the residents all committed ritual suicide. Or, at least that's the story the public will be told." He grinned.

"When in reality, you've destroyed my case, killed the witnesses, and burned my evidence?" I frowned at him. "So much for justice. You're as manipulative as everyone else."

"I never claimed not to be, only to be doing it for the right reason." His smile faded, the wrinkles in his forehead growing deeper. "Agent Black, do you play chess?"

"Not well," I mumbled. "And I don't see what that has to do with anything."

"I'm not surprised. Grahm and I have been playing for some time. The country has been our board. So far, all we've managed to move in the game are pawns. What you did by so graciously butting in is bring a gun to a chess game. Now, you can't very well wave a gun around without using it and still be taken seriously, can you?" He dropped his cigarette to the floor and stomped on it. "Find

Warren. Make sure he doesn't leave Concho County alive. I'll make sure that opens up an avenue for a legitimate investigation into Senator Grahm."

"And if we don't?" I matched his gaze and held it.

"Grahm has his queen and I have mine, but don't think for a moment I won't sacrifice a queen. I've already traded a bishop and have yet to take a pawn. Either you fall in line, or I'll see to it that all your friends gathered around this table answer for their crimes. And there are several murderers sitting at this table. That's a capital crime in Texas."

I shifted my hand to place it over Sal's, knowing that's who he was referring to. If I didn't do as I was told, he'd see to it that Sal was put on Death Row for murdering those two Vanguard. My back was to the wall. I might not have been happy about the way Dick forced my hand, but it didn't mean Warren didn't deserve what was coming.

"You need to let us bury our dead first," I said, turning back to Dick.

"Any time you waste is your own. The risk is yours, as is the reward."

"Reward?" Sal's hand closed around mine. "What reward? From my end, it looks like we're all getting screwed."

"I'll give you the one thing in the whole universe that can kill a Lord of Faerie."

"Claíomh Solais," Creven said through gritted teeth. "The Sword of Light. That's why he wants it so bad. He'd remove the one thing that can kill him from play."

"It's why he told Warren about me." I stared at my hands. My mouth felt dry. I could feel the images lurking just on the other side of my awareness. If I closed my eyes, even for a second, that's what I would see. It was always there. I had to keep my mind on something else or they would take over. "I wouldn't bring it to him."

"The sword is in my possession," Dick said. "And if you want it, you'll follow orders."

Not only was this my chance to stop Warren and strike a major blow to the oppressive forces inside BSI, but if I did as I was told, Dick was going to give me the means to win my fight with Seamus? It felt too good to be true. Of course, it wouldn't be easy. Warren was powerful, even if he was alone. But we had a means of overcoming his power. Abe and the others had done it somehow.

"I know you're also responsible for the shadow fire that I have."

He raised his eyebrows. "Oh?"

"Why me? Have you been protecting me all this time just for this?"

Dick fiddled with the buttons on his jacket. "I haven't been protecting you for this. I'm using you to win. There's a difference. Don't forget it." Once he'd buttoned his jacket, he stood straighter. "You'll be escorted from this building, blindfolded just like when you came in. Shortly after your release, you'll be given the tools necessary to locate Warren. The bodies of your fallen friends will be returned to you and Officer Espinoza will be released into Master Kelley's care. This is, of course, with the understanding that you were never here, you've received no orders or information, and I don't exist. I will have extra eyes and ears inside the reservation to make sure we all hold to our ends of the deal. Do we all understand one another?"

Heads reluctantly bobbed around the table.

Dick smiled. "Good. Have a nice afternoon." He turned on his heel and marched confidently out of the room.

# Chapter Twenty-Nine

"I can't believe she's gone." Ed clenched his hands into fists as they rested on his knees.

Dick had kept his word. We'd been loaded up into the armored cars, dark hoods over our faces, and dropped off inside the reservation. Somehow, they'd gathered all our trucks, cars, and motorcycles into one place and parked them on the street in front of Doc's clinic. Well, the cars that remained. Apparently, Angel's car had been smashed up when they came to rescue me.

That night, nobody felt like being alone so they all decided to pow-wow at Sal's place to try and grasp the situation.

Nobody but me, of course. All I wanted was to fall in bed and cry until I fell asleep. Inside, I felt broken, violated in ways I hadn't thought possible. Even free, I felt helpless.

Everyone else gathered around the sofa, pulling chairs from the kitchen to make up for the minimal seating. Nina, Valentino and Leo, who had sat out the raid on the compound took over cleaning, cooking, and helping with Mia. Hunter stood, positioned in front of me protectively, arms crossed while Sal had an arm around me from the other side. The faint buzz of healing magick vibrated around where his hand made contact with my back.

Nobody could look at Ed. He was still mostly beside himself with grief.

Ed took a deep breath. "I don't even know who to contact. I don't think she had family."

"She didn't." I looked at my hands and swallowed the tightness in my throat. "And as far as I know, neither did Reed."

I jumped when Angel slammed her fist into her palm. "You idiots. *You're* their family. There's no reason to sit around lamenting what's been done. Ed, I know how you feel. I lost someone I loved once, too."

Bran, who stood behind Angel, squeezed her shoulder.

She put her hand on top of his before continuing. "We all have. It doesn't stop hurting. You just get better at hiding the pain. I didn't know either of them real well, but I know you guys. We're all hurting. We need to heal before we can move on. That's what a funeral is for. Saying your goodbyes, punctuating the sentence of your past relationship and looking forward to the next. The details don't matter. Hell, we've got everyone who cares right in this room. There's no reason to get caught up in details. Let's go to the church. Invite the whole town. Come together for once instead of tearing each other apart, especially in light of all that's happened."

"Do you really think it's that simple?" Ed shook his head.

"No, I don't. Nothing ever is. The healing and coping takes time, but in that time we will find something to focus our energy on, like finding and killing the one responsible for all this."

Sal withdrew his hand. "Judah's still hurt. Half of us are. I don't know that anyone is in any shape to be going after this guy. He's still at full power."

I stood and felt all eyes on me. "No choice, not if I want to beat Seamus in three months."

"Judah, you've got three months," Sal said. "There's still time."

I looked to Creven, who sat cross-legged on the floor, his staff across his knees. "Creven?"

The elf huffed out a sigh. "While she's improved a lot over the last few months, it isn't enough. I've fought Seamus and lost in my time, and there are other Lords of Faerie who would cower at the very idea of crossing Finvarra. The old legends made him a god for a reason. Remember that he can raise legions of the dead to fight at his side. Without the Sword of Light, no one stands a chance at beating him."

"Besides, did you miss the part where Dick threatened all of us if we didn't do it?" I gestured wide. "I want to grieve for our fallen, too, but every moment we aren't actively hunting and fighting Warren is a moment he has to plan his escape." I drew in a deep breath to calm the shaking in my legs. "I'll handle everything."

"Mom, you don't have to shoulder this alone." Hunter put a hand on my shoulder. "You write down who I need to call to make arrangements and I'll do it."

"I can make and print programs." Ed rubbed his eyes. They were red and swollen. "Maybe find a few songs I know Mara liked."

"I can go up the chain, see who in the church would want to come down and conduct something for Reed," Valentino volunteered.

Several people turned to look at him. He shrugged. "What? I might not be a good Catholic, but I'm still Catholic."

"The pack will help with expenses," Sal offered.

"No, they won't." Creven crossed his arms. "Marcus has money to spare. I say tap that resource. I'll get him to pay for whatever you need."

Daphne stood from her folding chair next to Shauna. "And in the meantime, if anyone wants someone to talk to, come and find me." She looked directly at me and offered a sympathetic smile.

"And if you need something to punch, I've got the gym." Shauna nodded in my direction. "There's more than one way to get therapy."

My eyes watered. Even after all they'd been through on my behalf, they were all still willing to give more when I needed it. I pushed away the tears. "We'll schedule everything for tomorrow. Make sure the whole town knows. Then, we go and get Warren."

Everyone murmured their agreement and then, without many more words, they rose and began to file out.

I sank back to the sofa, wincing when the move jarred my arm. Dammit, I needed to get better by tomorrow. How was that even going to be possible? My head was a jumbled mess. I was an emotional wreck, barely holding it together, and my arm still hadn't healed.

"Judah?"

I opened my eyes as both Sal and Hunter stepped in front of me, growling at Abe as he approached. He'd been allowed to come into our home only because I insisted. Sal was not happy with him for breaking my arm.

He removed his hat and turned it in his hands, a sheepish look on his face. It didn't look good on him. "A moment of your time? In private?"

"No way in hell I'm letting her—"

I cleared my throat loudly and Sal stopped. "I can decide for myself, Sal."

He dropped the pointed finger he had in Abe's face and lowered his head in submission.

"Anything you can say to me, you can say in front of Sal and Hunter, Abe."

Abe glanced from Sal to Hunter. "Not this. This is for your ears only."

I frowned. The way he said it, I knew it was a message from Dick. There weren't many private places in a house full of werewolves, not with their hearing as good as it was, but there was one place I could go.

I stood and pushed past Abe, motioning for him to follow. We went down the hall to Hunter's room. The sour smell of teenage boy and old socks wafted out when I opened the door. Abe wrinkled his nose.

"You want to talk, this is the only place we'll get any privacy," I said.

Abe sighed and stepped in.

I followed and shut the door behind me. Once inside, I turned to the shelf behind the door and switched on Hunter's stereo system, turning it up.

Abe's hands went to his ears. "What is that?"

"I believe it's what kids call music these days. Now, lower your voice. Read my lips if you have to. It's the only way to make sure they don't hear."

He lowered his hands and shifted his coat. "First, I am to extend an offer to you on behalf of Marcus. He has offered the use of an experimental treatment to accelerate the healing in your arm. The effects are temporary, however, but it can buy you a few hours of time at your full potential."

I glanced down at my arm. It sounded too good to be true, especially the part about it being an experimental treatment. It'd probably come out of Han and LeDuc's research, the same research that had created Warren. But it might be my only chance at winning a fight against him.

"What's the catch?" I narrowed my eyes at Abe, scrutinizing his every move.

"The offer is only good until dawn."

"Dammit!" At the volume I shouted, there was no way they hadn't heard me. "What happened to Dick's promise that we could bury the dead, rest and recover?"

"Would you have them join you in your hunt?" Abe shrugged. "An injured alpha werewolf and his inexperienced pack, the packless wolf and the bear shifter who are nursing injuries of their own? Or were you counting on your son as back up?"

"What about Ed? He deserves to be in on this."

Abe shook his head. "You must leave all the werewolves out. Claws and teeth on the body will only draw attention to the pack, exactly where you do not want it to go. For the cover story in place to work, it must be you who kills him, Judah. Ed will not understand this. The wolf in him wants vengeance. If you take him, if you let him kill Warren, we cannot protect him."

"I'm not sure I can take him on my own, Abe. Look at what happened last time. He made a mess of me." I placed the palm of my hand against my aching head.

Abe gripped both of my shoulders firmly. "You will not go alone. You will have me and the elf. The others cannot know." He took a folded slip of paper from the inside pocket of his coat and held it out to me between his second and third fingers. "Come here at the time listed. A car will pick you up." He walked past me.

"Abe?" I turned to find him standing with his hand on the doorknob, one eyebrow arched. "Thanks for trying to save me, even if you did break my arm."

His lips turned up in a smile that showed his fangs. "It is good to know how much you can get back up from. However, I think next time I will have to break *both* your arms and maybe a leg if I want to stop you."

I turned off the stereo as soon as Abe was gone and unfolded the paper. The address he'd listed wasn't far, just far enough that Sal wouldn't hear the car door. So long as I managed to get out of the house without being detected, it'd be easy.

The paper was suddenly warm in my hand, and then outright hot. I dropped it, flinching when the paper burst into flame. It hung in the air a moment before the bright, intense fire turned it to ash that fell to the floor.

Sal and Hunter were waiting for me when I came out, arms crossed, chins raised. Hunter might have been a smaller, paler carbon copy of Sal. It was almost cute.

"Well?" Hunter demanded. "What did he have to say?"

I knew better than to try and lie to two werewolves, so I skirted the truth. "He had a message from Dick, a work-related message. Sorry, but I can't tell you. Don't worry so much, guys. The worst thing that could possibly happen has already happened."

I mumbled the last line as I walked over to where Mia sat with her coloring books. Crayons were strewn all around her in a rainbow of repetitive patterns. She gripped a purple crayon with her whole fist and scribbled away at the page, tongue out, pigtails waving. "Hey, kid. Long time no see."

She didn't look up.

"Mind if I color with you?"

She put down the purple crayon in front of me and took up a

blue one. I fumbled to grab the purple crayon and put it to the page.

That's as far as I got before the next barrage of images hit me. For a long moment, I was back in the dark cell, shaking and bleeding. Alone. All alone.

A new pressure introduced itself on the back of my hand and I snapped back to the present with a gasp. Mia was staring at me, her brilliant brown eyes shining with a hint of gold. Her face was full of concern that was beyond her years for a moment, reminding me too much of her father's worry-laden features. Then, she tilted her head to the side and smiled. "C is for crayon."

I couldn't help but smile back and pat her on the head. "You're right, Mia. It most certainly is."

# Chapter Thirty

All through the rest of the day, I alternated between periods of intense business and restless napping.

Once I gave Hunter and Sal a list of all the places they needed to call to begin funeral arrangements for Reed and Mara, I shut the bedroom door and went digging through the closet. I searched through shoeboxes and suitcases, wincing whenever something struck my broken arm. It still hurt through the cast. That was one thing I'd be glad for, anyway. Having a broken arm sucks.

I'd reached the back of the closet without finding what I was looking for and was about to give up when the bedroom door opened and Sal walked in, closing it behind him. "Looking for these?" He held up three white envelopes with names written on them. They were the letters I'd written to him, Hunter, and Mia the last time I thought I wasn't coming back from a battle.

My shoulders slumped. "How did you know?"

"Because I know you," he said, lowering the envelopes. "And I know how people like Dick Richardson work. He wants to frame someone for this, someone who isn't a werewolf. That means you have to go in without us."

I pushed a box back into the closet. "Are you going to try and stop me?"

"You know better than that." He sat down on the floor across from me and reached out to hold my hand. I turned and tried to catch his eyes, but they were fixed on the floor. "Everyone I've tried to protect just gets hurt."

I squeezed his hand. "Maybe you're trying just a little too hard to protect us, Sal. We all need room to breathe."

"Chanter was the only lead I've ever followed. When I took over, I thought I would fix things, do all the things he was too tired, sick or busy to do. Now, I'm tired and busy too, and people I love are hurt because of it. Because I'm not strong enough."

I touched his cheek and tugged his head up so that I could look him in the eyes. There was a time when doing that would have been dangerous, when he might have seen it as a challenge and I would have been too afraid. Now, it was different.

There's something special about looking into the eyes of someone you love and someone who, in return, loves you back.

There's both a deep, searing pain in your chest and an icy chill. Your heart skips a beat and floats into your throat. When it comes back down, it's with the pace of a runner's pulse.

But it's more than something physical. The Ancient Roman orator Cicero once wrote that the eyes were a window into the soul and people have been quoting it ever since because it's true. When you look someone in the eyes, everything else melts away, leaving behind the person they truly are underneath. Underneath everything, Sal was just a man fighting to leave his mark on the world and protect those he loved.

I smiled. "None of us are strong enough alone. That's why there's family."

"You just make sure you come back to yours."

"Of course I will, Sal."

"Then you won't be needing these." He lifted the envelopes and ripped them in half before stacking the halves and ripping them into fourths. When he was done, he scattered the ripped paper in the air like confetti before gripping me by the chin and pulling my lips to his, holding me until I couldn't breathe.

Had my arm not been broken, my head aching, and the floor littered with bags and boxes, it might have been more than a kiss, but there are times when a kiss is all you need.

For a long time after that, I sat in his arms in silence, listening to him breathe and his heart beat. I thought a lot about what I should say, if anything, before I left. My mind was still broken from Warren's assault, my heart still aching over Mara and Reed's loss. I could cry, but that felt like wasted energy. I had already shed too many tears.

Maybe I owed him an apology. I'd made bad decisions and I had to own that. He'd warned me about getting Ed involved, and I'd ignored those warnings. Because of that, he was hurt more than he might have been. If I hadn't been so hard on Mara all those months ago, she might still be alive, too.

All those could haves and might haves pounded away at the inside of my head for hours before I remembered something Chanter had once said to me.

"You can't help everyone," his voice rang in my head.

If I closed my eyes, I could almost see him standing in his kitchen, scolding me when I came to him with some mundane problem. He wore a brown apron, a white tank top and blue jeans.

While he spoke, his hands worked to chop the celery and carrots on his glass cutting board. The room smelled like roasting meat and old smoke.

Chanter lifted the knife and pointed it at me to emphasize his words. "There are people in this world who don't want to be saved, girl. Some of us are doomed from the day when we first draw breath to end in tragedy. You are not one of those people."

I crossed my arms and leaned forward on the bar. "What makes you so sure, old man?"

"I could say it's because I'm an Indian and we know these things." Chanter smirked. "But you wouldn't believe me." He turned back to chopping his vegetables, a somber look now on his face. "But one day, something bad is going to happen to you. Bad things happen to all of us. We can't always choose to avoid tragedy. What we can do is decide how to respond. Do we play the victim and wallow in our own self-pity, asking again and again, 'what if I had done things differently?'" Chanter lifted the cutting board and dumped the vegetables into the stock pot, taking his time to continue, as he always did.

"Or?" I pressed, impatient as always.

He waited until he had put the cutting board back down and cleaned his hands on his apron to turn and lean on the counter himself. "Or you pick yourself up, you acknowledge what happened, and you learn from it. That is the difference between someone who cannot be saved and someone who saves themselves." He leaned back and sighed. "You should wake up or you're going to be late."

I blinked. "What?"

"Wake up!"

~

I woke from the dream with a start. The room was dark with long shadows. My right foot was asleep and my arm itched like crazy. It had been late evening when he came in. What time was it now?

Sal drew in a deep breath and cleared his throat. "What time are you supposed to be wherever it is you're going?"

"Four thirty." I grunted and hauled myself up, which was more of a task than normal given the pins and needles in my foot. The alarm clock on the other side of the bed announced it was four fifteen. "Shit, I need to go."

"Need a ride?"

I shook my head. "It's not far. Listen, Sal, you weren't supposed to know. If you let on that you did—"

He interrupted me with a dismissive snort. "I used to work for the government, too, Judah. You don't have to tell me what happens when people don't play by their rules. Go. I'll be waiting for you when you get back. Just do me one favor."

I stopped limping around, trying to get the blood going to my foot again. "What?"

"You make sure that bastard can't hurt anyone else again the way he hurt you."

"I will," I promised and opened the door.

Hunter was standing on the other side with a very sleepy Mia holding his hand.

I sighed. "Not you, too?"

Hunter grinned. "If you think I'm going to let you run off without giving me the password to your Netflix account, you've got another thing coming."

He didn't hug me, but he did let me hug him.

"God, Mom," he said and sounded like he rolled his eyes. "No need to make a scene. This isn't the first time you've gone off to certain death and it won't be the last."

I kissed him on the cheek and he cringed.

Sudden pressure on my leg alerted me that Mia was clinging to me. I bent over and kissed her, too. She giggled. "Be good for your daddy, okay?"

"Love you, bye," she said, as if I were just leaving for any old day at the office. I wondered how much of all this she understood. Would she even notice if I didn't come back? One look at her smile and all thoughts that she wouldn't vanished. Mia might not have been related to me by blood, but she was still as much my child as she was Sal's.

I paused in the doorway to look back at Hunter, Mia, and Sal one last time. No, to look back at my family. I might have been a mess, but I wasn't going to go through life being a victim, not when I had people I needed to protect. I knew what Warren could do now, and I knew how to fight him. When I got my hands around his neck, he was going to wish he'd finished me in that Way.

~

I'd recognize Marcus' Range Rover a mile away. He had other cars, most of them flashier, but that was for his public persona. The vampire underneath, the one hardly anybody got to know was ruthlessly efficient with an ego the size of the whole Lonestar State.

Also, a few months ago, I'd slapped a bumper sticker on the back end that said, "I'd rather be in Transylvania." The sticker was faded and peeling from where he'd tried to scrape and wash it off, but I'd special ordered one of those high-grade, permanent stickers. A girl's got to get her revenge somehow.

The Rover pulled up at the meeting spot and the back door opened. I hesitated when I saw it was Doc who had had opened it. His afro bobbed in the light wind as he leaned out and gestured for me to get in. "Come on, Judah. I'll explain on the way."

What choice did I have?

I got in, sliding in next to Doc. Creven waved from the seat across from me. The back seats in Marcus' Rover aren't the standard back seats. They faced each other, which made the back of the SUV kind of surreal to sit in.

Marcus adjusted his mirror. "Good to see you."

"Did you fire Han?" I asked.

Marcus turned his attention forward and gripped the steering wheel tighter. "No. He didn't report for work today. I expect BSI has whisked him away to safety already. It would be pointless to eliminate his position now, especially when I can just as easily fill it."

I turned to Doc and raised an eyebrow.

He waved his hands frantically. "Don't look at me. I don't work in R and D. I don't even have a license to practice outside the reservation. The state took that away after they found out I kept zombies."

"Rightfully so." Abe twisted in the front seat to frown back at us. "They're dangerous creatures."

"They're misunderstood!" Doc shot back as the car slid out onto the road.

I cleared my throat. "So why *are* you here, Doc?"

"To administer the...uh...treatment." He pushed his glasses up his nose with a finger. "I haven't had a lot of time to study it, but the research he gave me seems to suggest it'll do what he claims. Not only will it heal you, but it will accelerate your healing for a short while. But, you know, full disclosure. This hasn't been tested on humans yet."

"Although it performed admirably in the chimpanzee trials," Marcus said, turning his head. "Nine out of ten were able to recover from significant injuries."

"And the tenth one?" I asked.

"Died in a lot of pain," Marcus answered and waved a hand, dismissing my concerns. "But that won't happen to you. You should see what the Viagra trials were like and the FDA approved that. You'll be fine."

"So, what is this treatment?" I turned to study Doc.

He fidgeted until Creven tapped him on the knee with his staff and nodded below the seat. "Oh, right."

Doc threw himself forward and hauled out a metal briefcase that he placed on his lap and opened. The inside was lined with foam except for a cutaway area where a series of no less than five hypodermic needles and syringes sat. A few alcohol wipes and a pair of rubber gloves had been shoved into the lid.

He pulled one of the needles out. "Ideally, we would be in a laboratory setting and I would use monitors to keep an eye on your oxygen saturation, heart rate, maybe an EKG every few hours—"

"There is no time for that," Abe growled from the front seat. "We know where Warren is now and he is unlikely to remain there once the sun rises."

"Well, you'll at least have to pull over." Doc sounded firm, but his chin quivered. He was, after all, just a doctor in a car with a bunch of supernatural creatures. "I'm not injecting anything into a patient's spine in a moving vehicle!"

I cringed. "That goes where now?"

Marcus pulled the car over to the side of the road just short of the exit from the reservation.

Doc turned to me, one of the needles in hand. "Five injections into the dura. You've been through childbirth. They did an epidural, right? Same idea, except this isn't going to make you numb. It stimulates the autonomic nervous system directly. It's quite astounding. Breakthrough research." He gestured for me to turn around.

I started to lift my shirt.

"Oh, there's no need. These go in the cervical lumbar."

"Huh?" I turned my head and made a confused face.

Doc rolled his eyes. "Base of your neck. Now please turn back around, Judah."

I shivered as he wiped the base of my neck with an alcohol wipe. "Hold absolutely still, Judah. If you move, the needle could paralyze you or have other unintended consequences."

I don't like needles. I especially don't like needles when I can't see them. Having five of them jabbed into my neck between two vertebrae in short order was so horrible sounding, even my nightmares hadn't thought it up.

It wasn't as bad as I expected. A little cold pressure, a strange rush followed by a wave of nausea, and it was all over. The first one was, anyway. I sat through it four more times before Doc wiped the area one final time and applied a band aid. "You'll probably be sore for a while."

I looked down at my arm in the cast. It didn't feel any different. "How long until it starts working?"

As if on cue, there was a sudden, burning pain in my arm. I could feel exactly where the break was, where the jagged edges of bone butted against one another. It felt like someone had taken a soldering gun to the bones, forcing them to fuse back together.

"It's working!" Doc grinned ear to ear and then pulled out a scary-looking tool with a circular blade attached. "Let's cut the cast off and you'll be good to go!"

I was still in doubt. There had to be a drawback to this magic cure, even if I wasn't seeing it. But hey, I was fit to fight. Now wasn't the time to look a gift horse in the mouth.

I extended my hand to Doc and turned away, cringing at the sound of him cutting into the cast. "So," I said, trying to raise my voice over the sound, "where's Warren? Where are we going?"

Marcus smirked and pulled out onto the road. "We're going to church."

# Chapter Thirty-One

Saint Phillip's Mission was an old Spanish mission of adobe and faded, red tiles. Surrounded by sagebrush and dry, cracked earth, the church stood a forgotten relic down an overgrown path several miles off the highway. It was just shy of dawn when we arrived. Streaks of red and orange colored the sky. Clouds wove through the painted color like mountains in the sky.

An old Oldsmobile was parked conspicuously against the side of the church. My fingers curled against my leg at the sight of it. I raked my teeth against my bottom lip, biting hard until it hurt so bad I couldn't think. That seemed to keep the images at bay. There, so close to him, I feared they'd come back. I couldn't afford to be reduced to a quivering mess. That meant I had to keep Warren's hands off of me at any cost.

Abe turned in his seat and held a Tupperware container out to me. "I took the liberty of securing this from your boyfriend's truck," he said. "Smear it on your head and it will lessen his ability to affect you. You may still feel his pull, but you should be able to resist."

I took the Tupperware and opened it, recoiling at the smell. The mixture felt thick and grainy on my fingers. "This won't keep me from healing like it did Reed?"

"No," Marcus reported. "Unlike Gideon Reed, you aren't relying on magick to heal your body, but science."

I smeared the strange mixture on my forehead. If Abe had taken it from Sal, that meant it worked. I trusted Sal enough to believe that. I offered the Tupperware to Creven who mimicked my movements. Abe refused, saying he had protections of his own in place. I decided it was best to just leave it at that.

"Alright," I said once everyone who was going was protected, "I'm ready to go."

"There is one more thing," Abe said. "A gesture of good will from Deputy Director Richardson that he feels will be useful in your fight."

He pointed under my seat.

"This is beginning to feel like I'm on an Oprah episode." I reached down and my hand fell on something cool and metallic. When I closed my fingers around it, there was no doubt in my mind what it was.

I pulled the Sword of Light from under my seat and held it in front of me. There was no mistaking the faint buzz of magick as I held it, but there was something more. Most magick has a feel to it. Magick can be dark and greasy like the ghost I'd fought, or light and crisp like Creven's magick felt. This magick felt like standing on a tall building to watch the sun rise. Hope. I held hope and light in my hands. There was no way handing that over to Seamus would be a good thing.

Doubt settled in where the hope had been a moment ago. "I don't know how to use a sword, Abe."

"We have had this conversation before and you did fine then."

"The Sword of Light is no ordinary blade," Creven said, regarding it with sparkling eyes. "The legends my people tell of it would have you believe a child could pick it up and slay a dragon. It is the sword of heroes." He smiled at me. "Something tells me you'll do fine."

"Once you three are out, I'll take the doctor to safety." Marcus unlocked the doors. "Agent Helsinki, you know how to contact me. If I haven't heard from you in a few hours, I'll assume you failed and that you're dead. I, of course, will deny any involvement."

"Encouraging."

"And if Warren gets away like last time?" Creven asked.

My grip tightened around the sword and I felt the rush of magick flow out of me and down into it. "Warren is mine. I'm not letting him get away. I'll drag him to Hell with me if I have to. He doesn't get to walk away, not this time."

I pulled the door handle and climbed out of the SUV, walking around to stand in front of the church. There wasn't much of a path leading up to it, but there was a place where no plants grew. The dust was heavier going in a narrow line up to the door. There was a loud thump as Creven and Abe closed their respective doors, coming to stand beside me.

Abe checked the shotgun he carried to make sure it was loaded.

Creven paused, dusted himself off and shifted his grip on his staff. "Lass, I feel there's something you should know before we walk in there together."

"Save it," I said and took my first step forward. "There'll be time after."

We walked up to the door. It was an old, rotten slab of wood, broken down by time and the elements. Heavy, iron chains that once served to secure the building now hung in pieces, fine red desert dust half burying them. The door creaked loudly as I pushed it open.

The sanctuary had no ceiling. Dust danced in the pillars of late afternoon light that filtered through the holes in the walls. Broken half round shapes cast strange shadows over ancient pews that no longer sat in a line. They'd been moved against the walls or placed about haphazardly. The way they were arranged reminded me of barricades. Some of them were broken, some burned. Others held the carved initials of lovers forgotten by time. The adobe walls had been the victim of spray paint and decay, the artwork ranging from swastikas to poetry.

The raised platform at the front of the church stood empty but for several dozen lit candles. Their tiny flames danced at the feet of Christ on the cross. His face was missing, chipped away by vandals. The cross was huge, taking up almost the whole wall. With the marred life-sized iron sculpture of Christ on it, it must've weighed several hundred pounds.

Creven, Abe, and I stepped into the empty church, letting the doors swing closed behind us. "Warren!" I called, stepping further in and avoiding a hole in the floor. "Show yourself! We know you're here!"

Another door on the far side of the front stage, to the right of the cross, opened and Warren strode out. He'd had a change of clothes since I'd last seen him, changing out his cassock for a black suit and polished shoes. His collar was pristine white. A silver cross hung from around his neck on a thick chain. His green eyes danced back and forth at a rapid pace. Just our luck. Warren was on rem.

"I was wondering who they would send," he said, pacing to stand in front of the cross. "I'm not surprised they'd send you, only that you're well enough to stand. You've made a rather swift recovery, Judah Black."

I shifted the sword. "I had help."

"So did I before your help gunned them down in cold blood." Warren stepped down off the dais. "You're no hero. You're a murderer just like me."

I stopped halfway to the front of the church. There was no room to cross here except over two rickety-looking boards. It wasn't a far fall into the church's foundation, but it'd be a good way to break my ankle if I wasn't careful.

"You've come to kill me." He spread his arms wide. "It's poetic, isn't it? They created me, both of us. They put this thing in my head, gave me these powers." He looked down at his hands. "What was I supposed to do with them? Grow plants? Raise followers to protect those plants?" He swept an arm wide. "I was meant for more than life as a simple farmer! I am a god among men, and they have sent an ant to silence me."

Creven stopped behind me and planted his staff. "We can make it painless and quick, but only if you don't fight."

Warren raised an eyebrow. "Oh? You would be so generous?"

"He would," Abe said, "but I will not. You do not get to go easy after causing so much pain and suffering."

"My hands are clean," Warren sneered. "It was Hector who killed your friend, the priest. If the priest hadn't interfered, he would still live. And the girl... Mira, she was *your* fault, Judah. You forced my hand!"

My hands tightened around the sword. "Mara. Her name was Mara!"

Warren smiled, clearly unmoved. "I have no intention of dying today." His eyes shifted to something behind me. "Kill them."

I turned, swinging the sword as I did, but I was too clumsy with it. It was a good thing, too, because it was Ed who was behind me.

Ed.

Warren had gotten to Ed.

Panic rose in my throat as he dodged my swing with ease before grabbing my arm and twisting it until I dropped the sword. I reached for my magick, pumping it into my muscles when I drew back to punch him in the face.

Abe had drawn his hand back like claws and readied a killing blow.

"No," I choked out. "He's controlling him!"

Abe paused and, in that moment Amanda, Hector's wife and Warren's mother, appeared behind him, a bat in her hand. She swung it and it struck him in the head with a resounding crack.

Creven moved, swinging his staff to strike at Amanda, but something in the air changed. It thickened and, suddenly, it felt like we were all struggling underwater. The smell of wet earth and the crack of magick tore through the room as a loud voice boomed,

"Enough!"

My arm froze where it was, unable to move. The same magick that held me, kept Creven, Amanda, Abe, and Hector where they were. I shook with the need to move, fighting the magick, but it was too strong. I couldn't even blink.

Footsteps stomped across the raised dais. The narrow boards over the open floor creaked. In the corner of my eye, I saw a figure bend over and take up the sword. My anger flared when I recognized that polished silver armor. Seamus.

He held the sword upright, staring at his reflection in the polished blade before he lowered it and snarled, "Let them go. The bargain is complete."

The spell released me and I almost tumbled forward. I used the momentum to fall to my knees beside Abe and check him. He swatted me away but put a hand to his bleeding head.

"Bargain?" Warren snarled up on the dais. "The bargain was I get you the sword and you get me out of here!"

Seamus turned on Warren, a bored expression on his face. "I believe the exact words of our agreement were that I would provide you with an escape." Seamus turned and smiled a wicked smile at me. "There it is. You need only put them down and walk through the door to your freedom."

Warren looked at me, then back at Seamus, licking his lips. I knew that look. He was deciding whether Seamus had cheated him or not and if it was worth the confrontation.

"I see how it is," I said, stumbling forward. "You used us, all of us, to get that stupid sword. Warren takes the fall for all of it and your hands are clean."

"It could have been different," Seamus said, shrugging. "You turned down my offer. I warned you there would be consequences."

I turned my attention to Warren. "No matter where you run, they'll find you. You know that. What kind of god lives his life on the run from a government?"

Warren slowly turned his head to glare at Seamus.

Seamus sighed and shifted the sword. "Think this over, Warren. Think about who I am. Do you really want to fight me?"

"Yes!" Warren screamed and dove forward. He latched onto the side of Seamus' head, just as he'd done to me and... nothing.

Nothing happened.

The sword moved so fast I didn't see it. One minute, Warren's fingers were digging into Seamus' temples. The next, his arm was on the floor and he was bleeding everywhere. Warren screamed and stumbled back, desperately holding the stump of his arm.

"I did try to warn him," Seamus said.

An enraged scream cut through the room. All eyes turned to Amanda who stood, breathing heavy, staring at her hands. She raised her wild eyes and focused on Seamus.

Amanda screamed again and took off running. She jumped on Seamus' back, throwing him off-balance. When she wrapped her hands around his throat from behind, he was faced with the choice to either drop the sword or let her strangle him. Even Faerie Kings need to breathe.

I seized the opportunity and rushed forward to take the sword back up again, but Warren kicked it out of reach when he stumbled on it. He fell, slamming his back into the wall.

Seamus finally ripped Amanda off him and tossed her against the wall next to Warren. The impact was hard enough it rattled the cross that hung there. Amanda's head slumped forward and she lay still.

Seamus stumbled forward and fell, his arm outstretched, reaching for the sword which waited just out of reach.

I got there first.

I picked up the sword and stomped on his hand. He cried out as the bones cracked, but I ground my shoe in harder. He shook as he raised his head to look at me. "You're going to regret that," he spat at me.

Creven's staff came down hard on the back of Seamus' head, followed by a baseball bat that flew across the room. I turned and saw Abe struggling with Ed, doing his best to keep the werewolf off of him without hurting him. Ed had his claws in Abe's gut, his eyes glowing brilliant gold, but Abe had still managed to throw the bat. Abe swung a fist and made contact with the side of Ed's face, freeing himself.

I turned back to Seamus. The double tap put him down, but not out. Seamus groaned and rolled his head back and forth.

"Quick," Creven urged. "Finish this while he's out."

I raised the sword, ready to put it through Warren, but hesitated as he cried out to his God. His head fell forward and his shoulders shook as he began to weep. "God, why? Why have you turned your back on me?"

"It's you who turned your back on Him, Warren. You can't claim to be God and then ask for him to save you!"

Warren's shoulders stopped shaking. He lifted his head. "Do you think... after all I've done...?" His chin shook and then he set his jaw to stop it. "No, I don't want forgiveness. I want to live!"

Warren made a grab for the sword.

I reacted out of instinct, throwing a magick-laced punch that struck Warren in the face. He flew back, slamming into the wall hard enough to send a crack racing up the rotten wood behind him.

This time, the heavy cross came loose from the rotten wall. It tumbled down and landed on both Warren and Amanda. Hard. The wood and iron fell on them with a loud crunch of bone and a wet smack. Warren's limbs twitched, but he made no further movement. Blood poured out from where his head would have been under the weight of the cross.

Amanda let out a loud and desperate cry of pain. It had fallen over her middle, just below the rib cage. Creven and I ran to the cross and tried to move it, but the iron was too much for Creven. He hissed and pulled his hands away, steaming. "I'm of no use here, lass."

"Abe!" I shouted. He sat opposite Ed on the floor, both with their hands loosely around each other's necks, a dazed look on their faces.

I grunted with effort, trying to lift it, but the cross was too heavy. I couldn't budge it. "A little help!"

Creven nodded. "I'll get them." He started to move toward the doors, but scrambled to a stop when Seamus loomed in front of him.

Seamus glared down at Creven, gold eyes firm and uncaring. Blood raced down from a cut on Seamus' forehead. "I'll have the sword. Now."

"You'll back away *now*," Creven said in response, readying his staff.

Seamus' mouth turned up in a smirk. "You of all people should know better than to challenge me, Creven."

Amanda coughed up blood and her fingers tightened on mine. "Please, I don't want to die. Not with him."

"I need help now!" I shouted. "She's dying!"

"She's of no consequence to me," said Seamus with a shrug. "I am here for the sword and make no mistake, I am taking it with me."

"Even if she were t'give it to ya, I'd still stand in yer way." Creven lowered his head.

I put all my effort and magick into moving the cross, but still it wouldn't budge. Even with all my power, I couldn't lift something that heavy. "*Claíomh Solais* will never be yours," Creven said. "I'll die before I let it go with you."

Seamus let out a deep laugh. "I dare you to stop me."

Creven shifted his staff half an inch, maybe only a quarter. Seamus lifted a single finger and Creven, the strongest and most skilled practitioner I knew, went flying back, helpless. He slammed into the wall and then through it into the tiny graveyard behind the church. Creven rolled to a stop and struck the back of his head against a headstone. He groaned once before his head fell forward, limp.

Seamus smiled, made a satisfied noise and turned to me, hand outstretched. "Now, the sword if you please."

# Chapter Thirty-Two

The sanctuary stilled. Even the dust floating in the dying light seemed to freeze. I held my breath. There was no way I was giving Seamus the Sword of Light. I'd promised Reed I'd keep it safe, and I don't break my word.

I lifted my chin. "You can't hurt me. Not for three more months. You'd be violating your word."

Seamus' hand drifted back to his side. His eyes gleamed a brighter gold, but maybe that was just the dying sunset reflecting through the window. "I don't have to hurt you to get what I want."

His head snapped to the side and he threw a hand out toward Ed. Ed's body jerked forward and he bent over with an agonizing sound.

"He came to avenge his lost love," Seamus said as he lifted Ed with unseen power. "A noble cause. He even had some of that marvelous dust with him that should have protected him against Warren's power. But Warren found him first. Sad, isn't it?"

Ed's cheeks puffed outward a moment before blood exploded out of his mouth. Seamus dropped him and he went to his knees and clutched his stomach, crying out in pain.

Seamus made a fist and Ed bent over again, vomiting more blood.

"Let him go!" I shouted and rushed forward. Green flame raced down the blade. I swung it at Seamus' unprotected head with a loud grunt.

Seamus put a hand up and caught the blade with his bare hand. I threw all my weight behind it, but the sword wouldn't cut through. All I managed was to slice into his skin. Seamus grimaced and his eyes gleamed even brighter as his blood dripped down the blade. "You got lucky before. Don't expect to strike me again. You should know better than to use a fae blade against a Lord of Faerie!"

In the front of the church, a shotgun clicked and fired. Seamus extended his other hand toward Abe and the buckshot froze in the air, trembling a moment before falling harmlessly to the floor. Abe lowered his gun, eyes wide and jaw slack.

Seamus' fingers tightened around the blade. I thought he was trying to pull it away from me, so I pulled back. Instead, he used the momentum and his magick to redirect the sword. It flew out of my hands at the speed of a fired bullet and straight for Abe.

I blinked and, the next thing I knew, Abe had been skewered through the lower abdomen with the sword, a sword now covered in poisonous fae blood. A sword that inflicted injuries Abe couldn't heal.

Abe looked down at the blade sticking out of his stomach, reached to pull it out and then crumbled to the ground.

Unarmed, I was still far from helpless. I drew my hands into fists and threw a hard, magick-backed right hook at Seamus. He ducked it, but only barely. When he bobbed up, he swept a foot against my ankle and sent me falling forward. I caught myself and turned, expecting him to attack again, but he didn't. Seamus just stood there while Abe died of poison, Creven lay unconscious, and Ed continually vomited blood.

"My patience is growing thin and you are running out of friends," Seamus said in a calm voice. "Give the sword to me."

I pushed off the ground to stand. "If you want it so bad, why don't you just take it?"

"Because it won't obey me!" Seamus hissed. "The sword only heeds its master's call. Give it to me and surrender your ownership." He pointed a finger at Ed, who screamed and convulsed. "Once I run out of people here, Judah, I'll have to go to your home. I'd hate to harm your children, but if I must, I will."

I turned my head and focused on the sword still sticking out of Abe. Seamus would do it. I knew he would. He'd kill everyone in Paint Rock if he had to. Keeping the sword away from him wasn't worth that. Whatever he did with it, at least I would still have the people I loved. Wasn't that what was important?

"Don't do it, lass." I turned and saw Creven standing, bloodied, with one foot on the hole in the wall. "You've no idea what kind of damage he can do with that."

Seamus smirked at Creven. "Yes, but that damage will be in Faerie, not here. What does a human care?"

"Judah cares. She won't let a monster like you have it."

My hands shook and I felt panic rising in my throat. All the images Hector had shown me flashed in front of my eyes again. I re-lived holding my dead son in my arms, watching Sal die, watching Mia scream and reach for me, begging to be saved as the life was torn out of her. A tear raced down the side of my nose and I wiped it away. "I can't, Creven," I said in a shaky voice. He turned his head toward me slowly. "It's my family. I can't."

Creven's eyes dimmed. He closed them and turned away a moment before recovering to glare at Seamus. "Then I will." Magick crackled in the air and Creven hurled his staff at Seamus.

Seamus put an arm up. The staff exploded in midair. A particularly large chunk hurled forward and sliced into Seamus' face. The fae necromancer stumbled forward, turning back with a growl. "That is the last time you'll strike me, *son*."

"That's the last time you'll call me yer son!" Creven shouted and swept his arm in a wide arc. Blue fire erupted in the air. Seamus put up a shield of spinning black magick.

I turned to assess the situation. Ed's body was pale and still. He lay on the floor in a fetal position, surrounded by blood.

I took a step toward Abe. He wasn't moving, either, and the pool of blood around him had stopped growing. Was he dead already? How many more would have to die before it was too many?

Blood rushed in my ears. My limbs all felt numb as I marched toward Abe, the battle between Creven and Seamus raging behind me.

Abe's eyes opened when I stopped beside him. "Judah," he said weakly, "take it. Leave. Run. Hide the sword. Do not give it to him."

I swallowed the lump in my throat. Behind me, there was a loud crack. I turned and watched as Creven stumbled back, bloodied now from head to toe. He fell to one knee as Seamus closed in on him for the kill.

"I'm sorry," I said to Abe. "I'm not running. Not this time."

He grunted when I pulled the sword out of his stomach. It was more effort than I thought it would be and had to leverage myself by putting a foot on Abe's chest. It came free with a wet sucking sound.

"Seamus!" I screamed.

He halted his advance on Creven and turned toward me, expectant.

I screamed and swung the sword, striking the ground. Black fire sped from the blade at lightning speed across the floor. Powered by me and filtered through the sword, I couldn't predict the effects, but I hoped I was right. It slammed into Seamus. He fell back, roaring in pain and swatting at the fire. I was right. It wasn't just the sword that could hurt him, but any magick that came through it. I might not have known how to handle a sword, but I did know about magick.

I swung the sword again, visions of a world on fire flashing through my mind.

And again.

I was blind to where I was swinging, letting the shadow fire guide me. It latched onto my anger at being helpless, the pain at being tortured, the loss. It wasn't just Seamus who deserved to die. The whole world could burn. What good was it to live in a world with so much pain and suffering? All that waited for me was death.

I squeezed my eyes shut and saw Mia staring up at me, big eyes gold and innocent.

Something in my heart seized.

Mia.

Family.

Hope.

*That* was worth living for.

I opened my eyes and focused on regaining control over my hands. They shook as the magick raced through me and into the weapon. Flame curled up all around me, searing my skin. Tears raced down my face and then evaporated in the heat. With a loud scream, I pulled my hands away from the sword.

It clattered lifeless to the floor and I sank down next to it.

"Lass!" Creven coughed and tugged on me, but I didn't have the energy to get up. "Get up, lass!"

*Get up!* The memory of Chanter's voice in my head cut through the exhaustion and I somehow found the will to stand, leaning on Creven.

As I rose, I caught sight of a shadow in the fire. The flame cleared a moment to reveal Seamus glaring at me with an arm protectively in front of his face. Part of his silver armor had melted and some of his unprotected hand was black from where he'd been burned. If hatred were a living, breathing thing, Seamus was its embodiment.

The fire surged and hid him from view. When the flame danced away, all that remained was the swirling green vortex of a Way.

Creven knelt and grabbed the sword. "Let's go!" He pushed me toward the door.

"What about Abe and Ed?"

"Have to come back for them," Creven huffed.

We burst through the crumbling doorway and Creven shoved me forward. "Go!" he shouted before turning and walking back into the fire.

I staggered back from the burning church, jaw dropping. What had I done?

What was left of the roof caved and my heart jumped. My friends were still inside. I'd be damned if I was going to let them burn alive because of me. I closed my eyes and concentrated, calling up the tiny, magick shield. Then, I charged into the fire after Creven, Ed, and Abe.

The heat took my breath away. I felt it biting at me, burning me. My shirt and pants caught fire and burned, taking my skin with it. Still, I pressed forward.

I found Abe and knelt next to him, shielding him as best I could from the fire.

"You stupid, stubborn woman," he said. "I am dead anyway. Why come back for me?"

I turned my head away from the heat to draw in a breath. "That's what partners do!" I shouted over the roar of the flame. "You came back for me."

A shape moved nearby and I thought I heard someone call my name. I squinted in the direction of the noise and watched as the flame parted in front of Creven. He broke through the ashes, Ed slung over his shoulder and stopped to tug Abe up. Together, we managed to lift Abe and hold him between us.

"Keep that shield up, lass. I'm no pyromancer, but I'll do my best to move the worst of the fire away from us! Now, let's go!"

We must have looked the sight when we stumbled out the broken door of the church, all holding each other up. Once we were a safe distance from the fire, the four of us collapsed, gasping and patting flames.

"Is he breathing?" I asked Creven of Ed.

"Aye. And yours?"

I turned and gave Abe a weak punch in the arm.

"Let me die in peace," he growled.

"Still kicking," I reported and leaned my head back to stare at the smoke rising against a bright, blue sky.

Sirens sang in the distance.

I smiled. "Looks like you're going to make it after all, Abe."

Abe's answer was a pained moan.

# Chapter Thirty-Three

The trip I took in the ambulance was is a blur. I remember feeling light, as if I would float away if they removed the straps from over me. There were words, numbers, frantic calculations and measurements tossed back and forth as monitors went on and off. I was tired, so tired, but with all the noise, I couldn't sleep. All I wanted was for the noise to stop.

We went over a bump and my hand flopped free of its own accord. Strong hands closed around mine. Sal's face loomed in my vision. At least I wouldn't be alone. "Don't close your eyes," he said.

I tried to tell him how tired I was, but no sound would come out. He'd understand. I just needed a little nap. I closed my eyes.

The next time I opened them, it was against more beeping. My eyelids fluttered open just a slit to look through the blinds on a third- or fourth-story window out into a gray afternoon. Rain tapped lightly against the window. Sal stood with his back to me, facing out the window with his arms crossed. His body language looked stressed. I couldn't understand why.

"Sal?" My voice was dry and cracked.

Sal turned around. "Judah?" he rushed to my side and called, "She's awake in here! Judah, try not to move. You were burned really bad." He put his hands on my shoulders, trying to force me back into bed.

"Burned?" Memories of the fire came back to me. Warren was dead. I'd kept Seamus from getting the Sword of Light. We'd won, and I was still alive. But the others... My eyes widened and I grabbed Sal's shirt. "Ed? Abe?"

"Both alive." He put his hand over mine. "Abe was touch-and-go for a while. It's not often the doctors around here get to patch up a vampire. They normally heal on their own."

I relaxed in the bed and stared up at the ceiling. "What day is it?"

"You went to the church yesterday." Sal brushed some hair out of my face. "When you came in, they thought they were going to lose you. No one can explain your miracle recovery. You're hardly hurt at all now."

I smiled to myself. Marcus' little miracle drug was responsible for that.

"You might also be interested to know that the local leaders of the Vanguards of Humanity have been arrested and charged with three counts of arson and a whole lot of murders each."

"So, that's who Dick decided to frame." I closed my eyes.

"I suspect they'll find at least one of them was connected to Senator Grahm, however remotely. That's been his plan all along, framing the senator."

I nodded. Framing the Vanguard would likely make things worse in the short run. The few that were in hiding might come out and cause problems, especially for the Kings.

"So what now?" I said. "Where does everything go from here?"

"Well, first of all, you finish healing. Whatever crap Marcus gave you to help you heal faster seems to have worn off. I'm almost back to normal, so I can help." He leaned over and kissed me on the forehead. "Second, with everything that happened, I thought it best to delay the funerals. I thought you might want to speak. It's supposed to be tomorrow. I think, with a little help from me, we can have you on your feet by then."

I nodded. "Has anyone heard anything from Seamus?"

Sal shook his head. "But he gave you his word. He'll be back."

My fingers closed around the blanket, pulling it closer. Yeah, he'd be back, and this time I knew how to hurt him. For the first time in nine months, I had a shot in the dark of taking that asshole down.

"Hey, Sal? What happened to Espinoza? Did he make it?" I studied Sal's face as he considered his answer.

"As far as I know, he's alive...somewhere. No one's seen him. My guess? Marcus has him somewhere. Maybe he's got him to keep Abe in line. You know how vampires are." He shrugged. "Then again, maybe it's just because he's a new vampire and not very good at controlling himself. Either way, Tindall says he's holding Espinoza's post open until he knows one way or the other."

I raised an eyebrow. "A vampire cop?"

"Come on, Judah," Sal said with a chuckle. "The guy is already a walking cliché. Why the hell not?" Sal slipped his hand in mine. "Now, how about we get you fixed up and take you home?"

~

The little white church in Paint Rock could only hold about a hundred people in the sanctuary, so the crowd spilled outside. Ed hadn't recovered enough to climb up any ladders, so that left the rest of the pack to try and figure out how to wire speakers into the place so the people outside could hear.

It was a sunny day, perfect weather for everyone but the vampires, but even they showed up in force. I had a feeling that, even if it had rained, there would have been a hell of a turnout.

I twisted in my seat in the front row, glancing back at all the faces. It wasn't just the people of Paint Rock who had come. Everyone was there. Marcus slid in to sit in the back in a deep, black suit. Patsy slid in beside him and she hadn't stopped talking since. Marcus' attention was fixed on his daughter, Kim, and Robbie who had managed to find something that wasn't gaudy to wear for once. Yes, Robbie was actually in a suit, and he looked miserable in it.

The Kings sat together in one of the middle rows. They were easy to spot since all of them had worn their patched jackets with the Kings' logo on it.

And, of course the pack was there. Everyone but Ed sat in the third row, crammed together to be there for Ed.

The last of the viewing line neared the two coffins at the front of the church. Mara was in the one to the right. Ed had insisted she be buried in an old shirt of hers he'd kept, a long-sleeved black hoodie. Looking down at her, it had been hard to believe it was Mara. She looked so small, so frail. She wasn't the girl I'd known. Mara was tough and strong. She'd died fighting in her own way and that's how I would choose to remember her.

Reed, of course, had to be buried in his cassock with his rosary in his hands. There was a part of me that wanted to leave the sword with him, too. It felt wrong to see him unarmed. In the end, I'd decided to arm him with the old, leather Bible he kept in his study. His Faith had always been his strongest weapon, after all.

Sal put a hand on my leg. "You sure you're up for this? You don't have to go up there. Everyone will understand."

"I have to do it for them," I said and patted his hand. "They did this for me. I can say a few words, even if what I have to say will never be thanks enough."

Once everyone had taken their seats, the bishop came out and began his part of the service. Valentino had gone to a lot of trouble to get someone important to come down, insisting that this was not just another church in the middle of nowhere. We were somebody, Reed was somebody, and he was going to have the best damn send-off we could manage.

When the bishop finished his short sermon, he opened the pulpit to anyone who wanted to speak. Ed rose from the front pew on the other side of the sanctuary, leaning heavily on a four-legged cane. He winced as he climbed the few stars to stand in front of the pulpit. The microphone squealed when he pulled it down to his height.

His hands shook as he unfolded a crumpled sheet of paper. "Mara was a lot of things," he began, "but she never thought of herself as a good person. She didn't think she was ever smart enough, strong enough, pretty enough... good enough." Ed paused to swallow. "They say everyone's got an inner battle. You never know what someone is going through. Those inner battles we fight every day made her feel weak, but she wasn't. Mara was the strongest person I knew. She was strong because she kept going, even fighting those battles. Even when she was alone in her fight. She kept me going. She was...She was enough. I always used to say it wasn't her that wasn't good enough for the world, but that the rest of the world wasn't good enough for her."

He broke down, sobbing with a hand over his face.

Sal's arm left its place around my back and he rose, trotting up the stairs to stand with Ed. He put a hand on Ed's shoulder and squeezed. Pews creaked as more of the pack rose in tandem and made their way up to stand with Ed, placing their hands on him. When there wasn't room, they formed a line, each placing their hands on the one in front of them. Even Mia squirmed out of my lap to go up with Hunter. By the end of it, Ed wasn't the only one trying to overcome tears in the room.

Ed raised his head and wiped away tears. "Mara's journey doesn't end here. As Gandalf said, 'Death is just another path, one we all must take. The gray rain curtain of the world rolls back, and all turns to silver glass. Then you see it: white shores and, beyond, a green country under a swift sunrise.' So, I guess she's finally found a place that's good enough."

Daphne lifted her hand from Ed's back and threw her arms around her little brother. He cried in her arms a minute while the others came to take their seats. Then, the two of them walked off the dais together.

The bishop came back out and asked if anyone else would like to say anything.

I stood. There were dozens of people who had wanted to speak when the funerals were being organized. Few of them knew how to articulate, and had come to me with their stories and notes. It had been somehow decided that I would be the *de facto* speaker for everyone in Paint Rock, having known both Reed and Mara.

The stairs creaked under me as I walked up. An expectant hush fell over the crowd when I took my place in front of the pulpit. I looked down at all the faces of the hurting, the lost. Was this what Reed saw when he stood up here to give his sermons?

I cleared my throat. "If you've ever been to one of Father Reed's sermons, you probably know the sanctuary was never this full on Sunday afternoon. But it never needed to be full. If even one person was here, and sometimes when it was empty, he still led prayers and song, just in case someone would wander in. If I had to choose one word to describe him, it would be dedication. Rare is the one among us who can live as he asks others to live, pure of heart, unwavering in his faith, and devoted to the service of others, always before himself.

"Reed and I didn't always see eye-to-eye, but we agreed on one thing. Love your neighbor. Whether that person is a vampire, a werewolf, an addict, or even a killer, everyone is deserving of love, even when you can't condone their actions. He taught everyone who would listen that love and faith are the only important powers, and that forgiveness, especially forgiveness of yourself, is its own power."

I closed my eyes and took a deep breath before looking down at where Mara lay. "I'm still learning that last part. I've made mistakes. A lot of them. I can't change that, but what I can do is go through every day as Reed would have, as Mara would have wanted, and choose to do a little better every day I'm alive. Nobody's perfect, but we can all learn to be a little more perfect every day.

"It might be a little cliché to say they're gone but not forgotten, but every time you help a friend, you honor their memory. Every time you stand against oppression, inequality, and racism and instead choose acceptance and love, you remember what it cost, the price they paid, fighting for those very things."

I stopped and shuffled the papers I'd brought up with me. I'd reached the end of what I'd written, but it didn't feel like I'd said enough. There was one more thing I wanted to say.

I swallowed the tightness in my throat, but my voice still came out shaky. "I'm not big on religion, but you don't have to believe to have faith. Faith is supposed to be what you hope for, something you believe in without seeing it. I have faith that the world Mara wanted so desperately, the world Reed worked so hard to create, it can exist. But we're going to have to fight for it, tooth and nail if we have to. That's what they would have wanted. Thank you."

I left my papers on the podium and wandered back down to my seat. Sal put his arm around me and squeezed. Hunter leaned into my shoulder and Mia grabbed my arm.

Lennon's "Imagine" and "Turn, Turn, Turn" by The Byrds played and then the bishop gave some closing remarks.

I didn't listen much. I kept replaying it all in my head, trying to find a rhyme or reason for why things had turned out this way. It didn't feel fair that I got to sit there with my family while a young life had been cut short and a good man had died. Sometimes, life just isn't fair. There isn't always a reason. It's human nature to look for patterns, to look for that cause-and-effect relationship. No matter how hard I looked, I couldn't find what I was looking for.

Gideon Reed and Tamara Speilman were buried in the small graveyard behind the old, white church under a sunny sky.

We spent the next few weeks trying to find some way to get back to normal. Doctor's appointments, meetings, and work took up my time again during the day. At night, nightmares plagued me. More often than not, I woke up screaming, barely remembering the dream that had driven me into that state. I added counseling once a week with Daphne. I had to work through everything with Warren somehow.

It was almost a month after the funeral that I went back. I parked my car in front of the building and looked up at the towering steeple. The church had sat empty since that day. As far as I knew, the local diocese was still looking for someone to fill the post.

I got out of the car and walked to the little iron gate surrounding the cemetery, only to pause when I realized I wasn't alone. Ed stood in front of Mara's headstone, head bowed. It was the first time I'd seen him since the funeral. Sal said he was checking in on him, so I tried not to worry, but life didn't feel the same without Ed in it, causing trouble.

I walked slowly up behind him, making sure I made enough noise that he knew I was there. “Hey, Ed.”

He turned his head. “Hey.”

I strode up beside him and nodded to him. “I see you’re walking on your own again.”

“Yeah.” He turned his attention forward.

I followed his gaze to Mara’s headstone. Resting against it was a carved and polished stick of wood painted purple, twisted into a spiral at the end with a notch about halfway down. I turned my head and saw that Ed carried an exact replica of the same stick, except his was gray. “What’s that?”

“Our wands came a few days ago. I just couldn’t make it out to give Mara hers.” Ed swallowed and then turned to face me. “Judah, I’m going away from Paint Rock for a little while. So much has happened. I feel like I need to clear my head, see the world a little, you know?”

I nodded. “I understand, Ed. Does Sal know?”

“Yeah, he thought it was a good idea.”

He turned back to Mara’s grave and we stood in companionable silence for a while before I asked, “Where will you go?”

“I’ve always wanted to see Alaska, or maybe the Yukon. There’s a lot of open space up there to run. Who knows? Maybe I’ll get good at hunting.” He cleared his throat. “I need you to do something for me while I’m gone, Judah.”

“Anything, Ed.”

“I don’t want to leave her wand out here where something will carry it off and the weather will ruin it.” He turned his head to smile at me. “Will you take it for me? Keep it safe? Maybe bring it out every once in a while so that maybe...we can kind of be together. I know it’s silly, but it means something to me.”

I smiled and put a hand on Ed’s shoulder. “Of course I will, Ed.”

Ed offered me his hand and I took it, trading grips with him.

“Paint Rock is going to miss you,” I said.

Ed looked around the graveyard and then up at the sky. “Eh, it’s not goodbye. I’ll be back. My pack is here.” He knelt and picked up a long box from the ground, handing it to me. “See you, Judah. Try not to let Seamus kill you in a few months.”

“Have a little faith.”

Ed gave a weak smile. "I've always had faith in you, ever since that night you threw the ball in Chanter's back yard."

Ed walked out of the cemetery, head high and shoulders set. He looked a lot better than he had in a long time, even if he'd had to go through Hell to get there.

We'd all been through Hell. Maybe that's what it meant to be family, to be a pack. When someone you love walks into fire, you don't let them go alone.

I knelt in front of Mara's grave to pick the wand up and a shadow fell over me. I thought at first that Ed had forgotten something and turned around, only to find Dick standing over me. He wore an exact replica of the suit he'd been wearing before, complete with the long, black coat, despite the heat. That black coat, though, was covered in little white hairs from the cat he held in his arms. Reed's cat.

Dick smiled. "Hello, Judah."

Except he didn't call me Judah. He called me by my real name, the name I had before I joined BSI.

I narrowed my eyes at him and withdrew my hand from the wand before I stood. "What do you want, Dick?"

He drew a soft-looking hand over the cat's back. "Just checking in on my investment."

"Investment?"

The smile he wore faded and his cheeks sagged a little. "I'm sure you have questions still, but I can't answer everything. Had circumstances not dictated otherwise, I would have preferred to delay your involvement."

I put my hands in my pockets in an effort to keep them from shaking. Truth was, I was terrified of Dick. He had all the information, knew all the answers, held all the cards. I was a pawn in his larger game and had been for quite some time. If not for the fire that night out near Eola, I might never have known about Deputy Director Dick Richardson at all. Chance hadn't brought us together; it had only revealed one card in his hand a round sooner than expected. The idea that he was using me made me feel sick.

"Is it true what Warren said? Am I like him?"

"No." Dick raised his chin. "And yes. You're far from immortal, and yet you're more than just some young woman gifted with magick. You were made for this. Born for it. Bred for it."

"Bred?" I frowned. So, it was true, or at least Dick wanted me to think it was. Someone somewhere had meddled in my DNA to make me what I was today. Just how far that went was still up in the air. The way he phrased it made me think that the changes were fundamental, instituted at the time of my conception.

It wasn't impossible. I'd been raised by a single mother who was deeply religious. I'd asked about my father only once and my mother was so distraught she couldn't answer me. Or maybe she was overwhelmed. How do you tell your little girl that she's some kind of government-engineered freak?

"Why me?" I asked as a heavy wind swept through the cemetery. "Why here and why now? If you were going to make a mutant weapon, why drop her in the middle of nowhere without resources? And why did it take so long for me to realize I had this...this shadow fire?"

"Shadow fire, is it?" Dick raised his eyebrows. "I suppose that's an appropriate name."

"Just answer the damn question."

Dick shifted the cat in his arms. "Paint Rock may be in the middle of nowhere, Judah, but that doesn't mean no one is watching. The whole world is watching. What happens here will decide the future of this country, maybe even the world. You are here because here is where you're needed."

"And what about the other question? Why didn't I know about the shadow fire before?"

"Some abilities only surface in situations of extreme stress." He shrugged. "Perhaps you experienced the push you needed at just the right time. After all, it couldn't have been easy moving across the country, fighting giants and wendigos and ghosts."

"So Warren was right."

"Warren was a madman, the son of a madman. A failed experiment in a long line of failed experiments needed to perfect the next step in a very long process."

"What process?"

Dick smiled and peeled the cat from against his coat, leaving behind streaks of white fur. He held the cat out to me.

Not knowing what else to do, and not wanting to leave Reed's treasured pet in the care of someone like Dick, I took the cat. "Is it me?" I asked, shifting the cat's weight as he struggled against me.

"No. Warren came after, just like LeDuc's experiments, just like Han's. You're asking the wrong questions. What you should be asking is what exactly Doctor Han has been trying to make in his laboratory for the last ten years?"

Dick reached out to pet the cat, which took a swipe at him, claws out. Dick jerked his hand away. "Goodbye, Judah. Take care of that cat." He turned his back and started out of the cemetery.

"Hey!" I called after him and tried to follow, but stopped at the entrance to the cemetery when I saw him get into an armored car.

Mara's wand lay behind me against her headstone. I'd promised Ed I'd take care of that too and my promise to him was more important than playing a game of riddles with Dick. I turned around and walked back to the headstone where I bent over and picked up the wand. It was lighter than I expected, and balanced oddly, but there was no mistaking the faint hum of magick in the wood. I smiled to myself when I opened the box and found an inscription on the inside of the lid. "Always. Love, Ed."

I put the wand safely inside and closed the box.

THE END

* * * * *

Judah's story in Paint Rock is just getting started. There are more mysteries to solve and newer, more dangerous enemies.

Book 5 in the series will be announced soon!
Join my mailing list for the most up to date announcements and cover reveals. You'll get a free book just for signing up.

# ALSO BY E.A. COPEN:

**Judah Black Novels:**
Book 1: Guilty by Association
Book 1.5: Perfect Storm (FREE to e-mail subscribers)
Book 2: Blood Debt
Book 3: Chasing Ghosts
Book 4: Playing with Fire

The Judah Black Omnibus: Contains books 1, 2, & 3

**The Fairchild Chronicles**
Book 1: Kiss of Vengeance

**Beasts of Babylon**
Book 1: Beasts of Babylon

**Broken Empire: A Space Opera**
Aftermath (Coming December 5th, 2017)

# ABOUT THE AUTHOR

E.A. Copen is the author of the Judah Black novels and the forthcoming space opera, Broken Empire. She's an avid reader of science fiction, fantasy and other genre fiction. When she's not chained to her keyboard, she may be found time traveling on the weekends with her SCA friends. She lives in beautiful southeast Ohio with her husband and two kids, at least until she saves up enough to leave the shire and become a Jedi.

55599257R00166

Made in the USA
Middletown, DE
11 December 2017